His P-
Bride

He will claim her — and her child!

**Three exciting, glamorous romances from
three bestselling Mills & Boon authors!**

*In June 2009 Mills & Boon bring you
two classic collections, each
featuring three favourite romances
by our bestselling authors…*

HIS PREGNANT BRIDE

Pregnant by the Greek Tycoon
by Kim Lawrence

His Pregnant Princess
by Robyn Donald

Pregnant: Father Needed
by Barbara McMahon

A SPANISH PASSION

A Spanish Marriage
by Diana Hamilton

A Spanish Engagement
by Kathryn Ross

Spanish Doctor, Pregnant Nurse
by Carol Marinelli

His Pregnant Bride

PREGNANT BY THE GREEK TYCOON
by
Kim Lawrence

HIS PREGNANT PRINCESS
by
Robyn Donald

PREGNANT: FATHER NEEDED
by
Barbara McMahon

MILLS & BOON®
Pure reading pleasure™

*Harlequin Mills & Boon Limited,
Eton House, 18-24 Paradise Road, Richmond, Surrey TW9 1SR*

HIS PREGNANT BRIDE
© by Harlequin Enterprises II B.V./S.à.r.l 2009

Pregnant by the Greek Tycoon, His Pregnant Princess and *Pregnant:
Father Needed* were first published in Great Britain by Harlequin
Mills & Boon Limited in separate, single volumes.

Pregnant by the Greek Tycoon © Kim Lawrence 2005
His Pregnant Princess © Robyn Donald 2004
Pregnant: Father Needed © Barbara McMahon 2005

ISBN: 978 0 263 87133 3

05-0609

*Printed and bound in Spain
by Litografia Rosés S.A., Barcelona*

PREGNANT BY THE GREEK TYCOON

by

Kim Lawrence

Kim Lawrence lives on a farm in rural Anglesey. She runs two miles daily and finds this an excellent opportunity to unwind and seek inspiration for her writing! It also helps her keep up with her husband, two active sons, and the various stray animals which have adopted them. Always a fanatical consumer of fiction, she is now equally enthusiastic about writing. She loves a happy ending!

CHAPTER ONE

'OF COURSE I knew it would never last.'

The words brought Georgie to an abrupt halt as she was dragged back four years in time without warning.

For most people it had been the summer of the heatwave, when cold, damp Britain had basked in tropical temperatures. For Georgie it had been the summer her life had changed.

She had been just twenty-one then, a fairly typical student enjoying the summer break before returning to college for her final year. Her only plans had revolved around the teaching career she'd wanted and the car she'd been saving up to buy.

The previous term she had been stopped in the street by a clipboard-wielding woman doing a survey for a television programme.

'Do you believe in marriage?'

'I don't *disbelieve* in it.'

'So you would get married?' the interviewer pressed.

'Me...? Oh, I'm far too young to be even thinking about it.' Georgie laughed. 'I want to have some fun before I settle down.'

Barely three months later she had been exchanging vows with a man she had known less than a month.

And yes, her grandmother *had* told her it would never last, but this had hardly put her in an exclusive category! It would have been hard to find someone who *had* thought the marriage was a good idea!

Georgie, floating several feet off the ground, had smiled serenely through the lectures and totally ignored the predictions of disaster. If anything the opposition had stiffened her resolve, made it seem somehow more romantic to her.

Her lips twisted in a self-derisive grimace as she recalled the idyllic future she had seen stretching ahead of her.

'Mummy…!'

Georgie pushed aside the memories crowding in on her and turned to the little boy who was holding up some treasure in his chubby hand for her to admire. Long, curling lashes as black as the glossy curls that covered his head lifted from his rosy cheeks as he raised his cherubic, smiling face to hers.

Not everything that had come from her ill-judged marriage had been negative. She had Nicky; she had her baby. Not that he was such a baby any longer, she thought ruefully as she made the appropriate admiring noises.

As Nicky went back to his game—he really was an extraordinarily contented, sunny child—Georgie banged the sandals she was carrying loudly against the wrought-iron table set on the patio.

It didn't have the desired effect. Too engrossed in their conversation, the women inside remained oblivious to her presence.

This is just what I need! A front-row seat to the dissection of the marriage from hell. Georgie could have saved them the bother; *bad idea* about summed it up.

'Were they together long?' Georgie recognised the distinctive Yorkshire accent of Ruth Simmons, a retired headmistress and keen bird-watcher who had rented the cottage next door to theirs for the summer.

'Six months.'

The way her grandmother said it made it sound like a jail sentence.

'Do you think there's any possibility of reconciliation?' the other woman probed. 'Perhaps if they had given it more time…tried a little harder…?'

'Tried harder…what would be the point?'

Georgie leaned her forehead against the frame of the door and absently rubbed a flake of peeling paint with her thumb.

She was rarely in tune with her grandmother, but on this occasion she agreed totally with the older woman's reading of the situation. She could have spent half her life trying to be what Angolos wanted and she wouldn't have succeeded.

In the end, however, the choice to call it quits had not been hers.

Angolos had ended it. He had done so with brutal efficiency, but then, she reflected, Angolos didn't like to leave loose ends, and he was not sentimental.

'They could,' she heard her grandmother, Ann, reveal authoritatively, 'have tried until doomsday and the result would have been the same.'

'But *six months*…poor Georgie…'

The genuine sadness in the other woman's voice brought a lump of emotion to Georgie's throat. There hadn't been much sympathy going begging when she had swallowed her pride and turned up on her dad's doorstep. Plenty of, 'I told you so,' and a truck-load of, 'You've made your own bed,' but sympathy had been thin on the ground.

'With those two, it was never a matter of *if*, just *when* they would split up. *When* he got bored or *when* she woke up to the fact they came from different worlds. Far better that they cut their losses. He was only ever playing.'

It had felt pretty real to her at the time, but maybe Gran was right. *Were you playing, Angolos?* Sometimes she just wished she could have him in the same room for five minutes so that she could make him tell her *why*. Why had he done what he did?

'By all accounts his first wife led him quite a dance… beautiful, spirited, fiery…*apparently* she could have had a successful career as a concert pianist if she had dedicated as much energy to that as she did partying.

'In *my* opinion after the divorce he was looking for a new wife who could give him a quiet life…unfortunately he picked

Georgie. Inevitably the novelty wore off when he got bored with quiet and biddable.'

It was not an ego-enhancing experience to hear yourself described as what was basically a doormat. Sadly Georgie couldn't dispute the analysis. She had been pathetically eager to please, and it was awfully hard to relax and be yourself around someone you worshipped, and she had worshipped Angolos.

'I think you're doing Georgie an injustice,' Ruth protested. 'She's a bright, intelligent girl.'

Georgie leaned her shoulders against the wall, smiling to herself. Thank you, Ruth.

'Of course she is, but…look, let me show you this.'

Georgie could hear the sound of rustling and knew immediately what her grandmother was doing.

'This was in last week's Sunday supplement. *That* is Angolos Constantine.'

Georgie knew what the other woman was being shown; she had seen the magazine before her grandmother had hidden it under the cushions on the sofa. A double-page glossy picture showing Angolos stepping out of a chauffeur-driven car onto the red carpet of a film première. At his side was Sonia, his glamorous ex-wife. Were they back together…? Good luck to them, Georgie thought viciously. They deserved one another.

'Oh, my…!' she heard the older woman gasp. 'He really is quite…yes, *very*…! They do say opposites attract…' she tacked on weakly.

Nice try, Ruth, thought Georgie.

'There are opposites, and then there is Angolos Constantine and my granddaughter.'

Georgie's lips curved in a wry smile. You could always rely on her grandmother to introduce a touch of realism.

'It was always an absurd idea. She was never going to fit into his world, and they had nothing in common whatsoever except possibly…' Ann Kemp lowered her voice to a confidential whisper. It had a carrying quality that only someone who was a leading light of amateur dramatics could achieve.

'*Sex!* Or *love*, as my granddaughter preferred to call it. Personally I blame it all on those romances she read in her teens,' she confided.

'I'm partial to a good romance myself,' the other woman inserted mildly.

'Yes, but you're not a foolish, impressionable young girl who expects a knight in shining armour to come riding to the rescue.'

'Young, no, but I haven't totally given up hope.'

Georgie missed the dry retort.

A distracted expression stole over her soft features as she rubbed her bare upper arms, which, despite the heat, had broken out in a rash of goose bumps. Low in her pelvis the muscles tightened. She blinked hard to banish the image that had flashed into her head, but like the man it involved it didn't respond to her wishes, or even, she thought, her soft mouth hardening, her entreaties.

In the end, bewildered and scared, she had lost all dignity and begged him to reconsider. He *couldn't* want her to go away. They were happy; they were going to have a baby. 'Tell me what's wrong,' she had pleaded.

Angolos had not said anything, he'd just looked down at her, his midnight eyes as hard as diamonds.

Strange how one decision could alter the course of your life.

In her case, if she hadn't caved in to her stepbrother's nagging and taken him down to the beach, when she had actually planned to curl up in an armchair and finish the last chapter in her book, she would never have met Angolos. Not that there was any point speculating about what might have been.

You just had to live with what was, and Georgie thought in all modesty that she wasn't making such a bad job of it. She had good career, rented her own flat, a gorgeous son. A single friend had remarked recently that she didn't know how Georgie managed to cope being a single parent with a young child and a full-time, demanding job.

'I couldn't imagine my life without Nicky; he's the reason I do cope,' Georgie explained. It was true—not that her friend had believed a word of it.

The fact there was no man in her life was a matter of choice. Not that she had ruled out the possibility of meeting someone; she just couldn't imagine it.

Sometimes she tried to. She tried to imagine another man touching her the way Angolos had. She did now, and it was a mistake. Her nerve endings started to ache as she thought of his long, cool fingers on her skin.

Angolos had made her ache a lot.

When she wasn't thinking about Angolos's ability to make her ache, she occasionally wondered what sort of person she might have been if she had never met him. Would she still be as naïve and trusting as she had been that summer?

Such speculation was pointless, because she *had* met him, and every detail of that fateful occasion, the moment she had laid eyes on Angolos Constantine, the moment her life had changed for ever, was burnt into her brain.

She had been sitting on a blanket, one eye on the paperback she had been trying to finish and the other on her stepbrother, who had been playing with a group of boys farther down the beach. His shoes had been the first thing she had seen, shiny, hand-tooled leather, and then the exquisitely tailored legs of his dark trousers, expensive, tasteful, and *wildly* inappropriate for a beach.

She'd just had to see who would be stupid enough to venture onto the beach in a get-up like that! Georgie had lifted a hand to shade her eyes, squinting against the sun as her glance had travelled upwards.

Oh, my goodness…!

The owner of the shoes had had long legs, very long legs;

the rest of him had been a lot better than OK too. In fact, if you went for lean and hard—and what woman wouldn't, given half the chance?—he was as close to perfect as damn it.

By the time she had reached his face the last shreds of amused mockery had vanished from her amber eyes—*the eyes he had professed to love*—and she had been smitten and had stayed that way until the day he had told her he wanted her to go away.

'Go away…?' Uneasy, but sure this was all a silly mistake, she had asked, 'How long for?'

'For ever,' he had replied and walked away.

But on that first summer's afternoon there had been no hint of the casual cruelty he was capable of. She had been totally overwhelmed and too inexperienced to hide it as she'd stared back into those dark eyes shaded by preposterously long lashes that had thrown a shadow across the prominent angle of his chiselled cheekbones.

Those seductive, velvety depths had held a cynical world-weariness that her impressionable self had found fascinating, but then she'd found everything about him fascinating, she reflected grimly, from his sable-smooth hair to the mobile curve of his sensual lips.

Tall and lean, darkly arresting, his olive-skinned face an arrangement of strong angles and fascinating bone structure, he was the essence of male beauty.

'Hello,' he said, flashing her a seriously gorgeous smile. Like his appearance his voice with its faint accent marked this most rampantly *male* of males out as fascinatingly different.

She was hot, her face was sticky, her skin was glossed with a film of sweat and the salty dampness had gathered in the valley between her breasts. The jacket casually slung over one shoulder was the only concession this stranger made to the heat, which appeared not to affect him.

She lifted a self-conscious hand to her hair and discovered

it was full of salt from an earlier dip in the sea. She wanted desperately to be cool and say something intelligent but all she could manage was a breathless, 'Hello.' Her heart was beating so fast she could barely hear her own voice.

She knew she was staring, but she couldn't help it. She simply couldn't tear her eyes off this incredible man. Men like this did not walk down the beach of an old-fashioned family resort... She hadn't actually believed they existed outside the pages of popular fiction!

Did wondering what a total stranger looked like naked make her depraved? This had never happened to her before; maybe it was the weather? Hadn't she read somewhere that heat had an effect on the libido? But her libido had never given her any problems; in fact she had occasionally wondered if it wasn't a little underdeveloped.

'I'm not familiar with the area.'

'I know...'

One darkly defined brow lifted and she rushed on in hot-faced explanation.

'This is a small place and strangers...well, they stand out.' In the most fashionable and glamorous watering holes on the planet he would have stood out! She couldn't imagine what it would feel like to walk into a room and have heads turn and conversations stop. *What would he feel like?*

She lowered her gaze. Stop this, Georgie!

'Then you live here?'

He's talking to me. This incredible man is actually talking *to me*. What did he say...?

'Sorry?'

'Do you live locally?'

'Yes...no.'

The creases around his stupendous eyes deepened. 'Which?'

Oh, no, he was going to go back to whatever planet he came from—clearly he was too gorgeous to be earthbound—

and laugh about the mentally challenged locals. She made a supreme effort to act as though her IQ reached double figures.

'We spend the summer holidays here. My…' Her eyelashes lowered, as she repressed the embarrassing impulse to give him her life story. Even if that life could be summed up in a paragraph, his stupendous eyes would have glazed over with boredom before she got to the end.

One noteworthy thing had happened in her life and she didn't even remember it! She had been a baby when her mother had run away with a Greek waiter. Since then her deserted father had refused to travel abroad, hence the house here where she had spent every summer she could remember, firstly with just her father and grandmother, latterly with her stepmother and stepbrother.

'But you know the area well? You know all the places to go?'

'Places to go…?' Her puzzled expression cleared. 'I suppose I do.' She was delighted to be able to be of use to this most amazing man. 'Well, actually, it depends,' she told him seriously.

'On what?'

'If you have a head for heights.'

'I do.'

'Not me,' she admitted regretfully. 'The headland walk along the nature reserve is apparently marvellous, but if you prefer something a little gentler the trail across the marsh is very well marked and there are hides where you can… Are you interested in birds?' The area drew a lot of people who were; they arrived with their binoculars in their droves. 'It's not the breeding season, but there are still some—'

'I am not a bird-watcher; I prefer more…active pursuits.'

Now that he said it she had no problem seeing him fitting into the mould of those tough, reckless individuals who indulged in extreme sports… Extreme as in those *extremely* likely to result in injury or worse!

The thought of him breaking his beautiful neck made her unthinkingly blurt out, 'You should be careful.'

'At the moment I'm under strict instructions to relax.' A slow smile that made her tummy flip spread across his lean features. 'And suddenly,' he confided in a husky drawl that made Georgie's skin prickle, 'that doesn't seem such a bad idea.'

Was he flirting with her…? Georgie dismissed the thought even before it was fully formed.

'I was actually wondering about the night-life…?' he went on.

'Night-life?' she parroted. The distracting shadow of dark body hair visible through the fine fabric of his shirt was making it hard for her to concentrate on what he was saying.

'As in nightclubs.'

'Nightclubs?' she echoed as though he were talking a foreign language. 'Here?'

His beautifully moulded lips quirked. 'No nightclubs.' She shook her head. 'Restaurants…?'

Georgie's eyes had got even wider. 'I think you might have got the wrong place. There's the teashop next to the post office—they do a great cream tea—and the fish and chip shop, but… Are you laughing at me?'

'You're delightful.'

Even though she realised he probably meant delightful in a cutesie, cuddly, clumsy puppy sort of way, she couldn't stop smiling.

'And this feels like the first time I've laughed in a very long time.'

Georgie was pondering this enigmatic statement when a football landed in her lap, spraying sand all over her. There was the sound of laughter as she sprawled inelegantly backwards onto the sand.

'Jack Kemp!' she yelled, spitting out a mouthful of sand

as her stepbrother approached. She struggled into an upright position and glared at the guilty figure.

'What's got into you?' asked the freckle-faced twelve-year-old. 'It wasn't hard,' he added scornfully.

Clicking her tongue, she threw the ball back, with an admonition to be careful. 'And five minutes only,' she cautioned, glancing at her watch. 'I promised I'd get dinner tonight,' she reminded him.

'Sure…sure, Georgie,' Jack called back before loping off down the sand.

'Georgie…?'

'Georgette,' she said with a grimace. 'My family call me Georgie. That's my stepbrother,' she explained, nodding to the skinny running figure.

She turned as she spoke and found he wasn't looking at the distant figure of the fair-headed boy, but at her. There was a sensual quality in his dark-eyed scrutiny that sent a secret shiver through her body; the condition of her nipples was less a secret as they pressed against the stretchy fabric of her bikini top.

She looked around red-cheeked and mortified for the shirt she had discarded. She found it in a crumpled heap under the sun cream; hastily she fought her way into it.

'I will call you Georgette,' he pronounced.

She was never going to see him again, but as far as Georgie was concerned this man could call her anything.

CHAPTER TWO

'How old are you, Georgette?'

Georgie flirted briefly with the notion of coming back with a cool, *Old enough,* but she knew she'd never carry it off. Besides, how mortifying would it be if he laughed?

'Twenty-one,' she responded more conventionally.

'Will you come to dinner with me?' he asked without skipping a beat.

Her eyes, round with astonishment, flew to his. *'Me... you...?'*

'That was the general idea.'

Georgie swallowed before running her tongue over her dry lips—they tasted salty—and she looked at him suspiciously. 'You're not serious.' She tried to laugh but her vocal muscles didn't co-operate.

'Why would I not be?' She shook her head, flushing as his gaze became ironic. 'You are the most attractive woman on the beach.'

'I'm the only one under sixty without a husband and children,' she rebutted huskily, 'so I'll try not to get carried away with the compliment.'

Who was she kidding? Her entire life she had thought of herself as an average sort of girl—hidden depths, sure, but was anybody ever going to bother looking? Now totally out of left field there came this incredible man who was looking at her as though she were a desirable woman.

Carried away...? She was quite frankly blown away!

She tried to adopt an amused expression and failed miserably as the screen of ebony lashes swept up from his cheekbones. *Combustible* best described his smoky-eyed stare.

16

'I don't even know your name,' she protested weakly.

His smile had been confident, tinged with the arrogance that came naturally to someone like him. And why shouldn't it be? she mused, four years down the line. Angolos Constantine was used to getting what he wanted; a little bit of complacence was understandable when women had been falling at his feet since the day he'd hit puberty!

'Not an insuperable barrier and I already know yours, *Georgette*.' The way he said her name had a tactile quality. It made the hairs on her nape stand on end and intensified the unspecified ache low in her belly.

She stared back at him dreamily.

It was just dinner.

'It's just dinner,' he said as if he could read her thoughts.

What was she doing, hesitating? All the girls she knew wouldn't have needed coaxing. They saw what they wanted and went for it. Georgie applauded them, but privately wondered if in secret they weren't just as insecure as she was.

When she opened her mouth she intended to say yes, but her dad hadn't raised a reckless child. Caution had been drilled into her from her infancy, and at the last second her conditioning kicked in.

'Thank you, but I couldn't.' He was a total, a *total* stranger who could, for all she knew, be a psycho or even a *married* psycho. She shook her head; she was out of her depth and she knew it. 'Thank you, but I'm afraid I can't. My boyfriend wouldn't like it.'

Under other circumstances the look of baffled frustration on his lean face would have been laughable.

Georgie didn't feel like laughing; she didn't even feel like smiling. She was actually pretty ambivalent about the entire 'done the right thing' situation.

His dark brows lifted. 'Are you saying no?'

She could hear the astonishment in his voice and she realised that being knocked back had never crossed his mind. *No* was obviously not a word this man was used to hearing.

She nodded.

This time there was a hint of annoyance in his appraisal. 'As you wish.'

His irritation made her feel slightly better. Her normal nature, the one she had when she wasn't turned into a brainless bimbo by the sexual aura this man radiated, briefly reasserted itself. Why should he assume she was a sure thing? She might have been a bit *obvious*, but a girl could look without necessarily wanting to touch…

She flashed a quick semi-apologetic smile in his general direction. She wasn't trying to strike a blow for female equality here—better and braver women had already done that— she just wanted to get the hell out of there without making herself look any more a fool than she already had!

Aware that his disturbing eyes were following her actions as she crammed her possessions in her canvas bag made her clumsy.

'Jack!' she bellowed, zipping up the bag with a sigh of relief.

'You forgot this.'

She half turned and saw he was holding out a tube of sunblock.

She extended her hand. 'Thank you.' The fingertip contact lasted barely a heartbeat but it was enough to send an electrical tingle through her body. Her wide, startled eyes lifted momentarily to his and she knew without him saying a word that he knew exactly what she was feeling.

Well, at least someone did!

Without waiting to see if her aggravating stepbrother was following her, Georgie stumbled and ran across the sand to the pebbly foreshore, all the time fighting an insane impulse to turn back.

A childish shout jolted Georgie back to the present. She

made admiring noises as her son proudly showed her a small pile of stones he had placed on the patio.

She could remember doing the same thing as a child herself; continuity was important. Her own childhood had been a long way from deprived, but there was a gap—questions that remained unanswered because her mother hadn't been there to answer them. Now Nicky had an absent father… Continuity strikes again!

Her jaw firmed. Rejection wasn't hereditary, it was bad luck, and if she had anything to do with it Nicky was going to be a better judge of character than his mother.

It was strange—she had changed beyond recognition from that girl running away that day on the beach, but the beach house and the town hadn't. It was as if the place were in some sort of time warp.

The town remained defiantly unfashionable. There were no trendy seafood restaurants and no big waves to attract the surfing fraternity, but despite everything Georgie had a soft spot for this place. She rubbed her sandy palms on the seat of her shorts and accepted the seashell Nicky gravely handed her.

This was the first time she'd been back here since that fateful summer. Partly she had come to lay the ghosts of the past and more practically there was no way she could afford a holiday for Nicky any other way.

The jury was still out on whether she had succeeded on the former!

She inhaled, enjoying the salty tang in the air. Memories sort of crept up on you, she reflected. The most unexpected things could trigger them: a smell…texture. As earlier, one second she had been trying to get the sand off her feet before putting on her sandals, the next—*zap!*

It had been incredibly vivid.

Her foot had been in Angolos's lap, his dark head down-bent, gleaming blue-black in the sun as he'd brushed the sand from between her toes. The touch of his fingers had sent delicious little thrills of sensation through her body. He had felt her shiver and his head had lifted. Still holding her eyes, he'd lifted her foot to his mouth and sucked one toe.

Her hand had pressed into the sand as her body had arched. 'You can't do that!' she gasped. Snatching her foot from his grasp, she lifted her knees to her chin.

Angolos's expressive mouth quirked. 'Why?'

'Because you're killing me,' she confessed brokenly.

The way he looked at her, the hungry, predatory gleam in his glittering eyes, made her insides melt. 'You won't have long to wait, *yineka mou*,' he reminded her. 'Tomorrow we will be man and wife.'

Back in the present, Georgie opened her clenched fists. Her palms were damp and inscribed with small half-moons where her neatly trimmed fingernails had dug into the flesh. She sighed and rubbed her palms against the seat of her shorts. Would she ever be able to think about her husband without having a panic attack?

'They could hardly keep their hands off one another.'

The salacious details… This I can *really* do without.

'I'm no prude,' the older woman continued, 'but really…she couldn't keep her hands off him…'

Mortifying though her grandmother's comment was, Georgie, not a person given to self-delusion, had to admit that it was essentially true.

Always a little scornful of her contemporaries' messy and, it seemed to her, painful love affairs, she had been totally unprepared for the primal emotions Angolos had awoken in her. She had been totally mesmerised by him.

'My son and I disagree on most things, but on that occasion we were of one mind. Robert said to her, "Sleep with the man if you must, *live* with him even, but *marry* him…! *Insanity.*"'

'But one we have all experienced, Ann,' came the rueful response.

To imagine the two elderly women experiencing the insanity of blind lust that she had felt with Angolos made Georgie blink.

'The girl has reaped the consequences of her stupidity.'

The scorn in her grandmother's voice brought a flush of mortified colour to Georgie's sun-warmed cheeks. She had made a big mistake and she was willing to own up to it, but she sometimes thought that if her family had their way she would still be eating humble pie when she was eighty!

'She was very young.'

'Young and she thought she knew it all.'

'The young always do. He…the man in the magazine…he looked older?'

'Thirty-two or something like that, I believe, at the time. You have to understand that Georgie was very young for her age…very naïve in many ways, and he had been around the block several times. Oh, a handsome devil, of course. I'm not surprised she fell for him.'

The admission amazed Georgie; to her face her grandmother had never offered any understanding.

'You think he took advantage…?'

'Well, what do you think? A man with one failed marriage to his credit already and Greek.'

From her grandmother's tone it was hard to tell which fault she found harder to forgive in the man: the fact he had been married or the fact he was Greek.

'I knew the moment I saw him he couldn't be trusted. I told her, we *all* told her, but would she listen? No, she *loved* him.'

'Still, you must be proud of the way she has rebuilt her life, and she has a lovely child.'

'A child who has never even seen his father.'

'*Never?* Surely not…?'

'Refused point-blank. Angolos Constantine made it clear that he wanted nothing whatever to do with the child. And neither he or any member of his precious family have ever been near…a blessing, if you ask me.'

It was foolish, but even after this time the truth still had the power to hurt. The knot of pain and anger in Georgie's chest tightened as her glance turned towards the small figure who was crossing the patchy lawn towards her.

His small, sweet face was a mask of concentration as he carried his bucket of pebbles. Her fond gaze followed him as he placed his burden carefully down on the ground and, falling to his chubby knees, began to dig in the soft ground.

The love she felt for her child—the love she had felt for him from the first moment they had laid his warm, slippery little body in her arms—contracted in her chest. She had imagined that magic moment would be shared with Angolos.

How wrong she had been!

She had given birth alone. There had been no husband to hold her hand or breathe through the pain with her, and no one to share the magical moment of birth with.

So Angolos had fallen out of love with her…or more likely he had never been in love with her at all…?

Just why was the question mark attached to that thought, Georgie? A man could not treat anyone he had had any feelings for the way Angolos had treated her.

She had accepted that.

Sure you have!

But how could he reject this child they had produced together? Nicky was perfect… How could anyone not want him? How could any parent *not* love their own child?

'It's just as well that her family were here to pick up the pieces.'

Her grandmother's observation was clearly audible, but Georgie had to strain to hear the other woman's reply. That was the thing about eavesdropping—once you started it was hard to stop.

'That's so sad. How can a man not want to see his child?'

'You tell me. All I know is he hasn't given her a penny and Georgie is too stubborn to ask for what is hers by rights. I told her she should file for divorce and take him for every penny she can. There was no pre-nuptial agreement. I'm afraid Georgie is just like her mother that way—not a practical bone in her body.'

What would Gran say, Georgie wondered, if she knew about the account that Angolos topped up with money every month? Whatever she said she'd say it loudly, especially if she knew that not a penny of the money had been touched!

By now there was a lot of money in that account.

'Mummy…' The tired treble awakened Georgie to the danger of Nicky hearing the conversation taking place in the cottage.

'I'm thirsty.' The small figure, bucket and spade in hand, tugged her shorts.

With a smile, Georgie dropped down to child-level and swept a dark glossy curl from the flushed face of her son. She would never be able to forget what Angolos looked like; she saw his face, or a miniature, childish version of it, every day.

'So am I, darling,' she said, raising her voice to a level that the two elderly women inside could not fail to hear. 'Let's go and see if Granny would like a lemonade too, shall we?'

CHAPTER THREE

ROYALTY was attending the charity performance and the media were out in force to record the event. On the red carpet the star of a soap was denying for the benefit of the TV cameras rumours that she was about to marry her co-star.

The foyer was thronged with other famous faces all wearing their best smiles and designer outfits. Despite the fact all the men present were for the most part similarly dressed in dark, formal suits, Paul had no problem locating the person he had come looking for.

Angolos Constantine stood out in a crowd. It wasn't just his height and looks; it was that rare commodity—*presence*.

'Angolos…?' he called out in relief.

The tall figure, accompanied by an elegant brunette who was dripping with jewels, turned at the sound of his name. A smile spread across his lean face when he identified the speaker.

'Paul!' he exclaimed, detaching his partner from his arm and moving forward, his hand outstretched. 'I didn't know you were an opera buff…'

'I'm not…and even if I was it wouldn't have got me in here,' the shorter man admitted frankly. 'I only got this far by telling them I was your personal physician.'

The groove above Angolos's strong patrician nose deepened. 'That was resourceful of you.' His head whipped slowly from side to side as he searched the crowd. 'And where is the lovely Miranda?'

Paul Radcliff shook his head and scanned the olive-skinned face of the friend he had known since their university days. 'Mirrie's not here.'

'I thought you two were joined at the hip.'

'Her blood pressure was up a little…nothing serious,' Paul hastened to assure the other man.

Angolos clapped his hand to his forehead. 'I forgot!' he admitted with a grimace of self-reproach. 'When is my god-child due?'

'Last week.'

Angolos's brows lifted. 'The plot deepens.'

'You're looking well, Angolos.'

It struck him that this was something of an understatement. Nobody looking at the lean, vital figure would have believed that a few years earlier his life had hung in the balance… Paul was one of the few people who did know, and he scarcely believed it himself!

One dark brow slanted sardonically. 'Always the doctor, Paul?' came the soft taunt.

'And friend, I hope.' It was friendship that, after a lot of heart-searching, had brought him here—that and his wife's nagging.

'The man has a right to know, Paul,' she had insisted.

He had still been inclined to leave well alone, but very pregnant wives required humouring. She had insisted that he speak to Angolos without delay and, as she had pointed out, it wasn't the sort of thing you could hit a man with on the phone.

So here he was and he wished he weren't.

The hard features of the darker man softened into a smile of devastating charm. 'And friend,' he agreed quietly. 'So what's wrong, Paul?'

'Nothing's *wrong*, exactly,' Paul returned uncomfortably.

Angolos didn't bother hiding his scepticism. 'Don't give me that. It would take something pretty serious to make you leave Miranda alone just now. It follows that this is serious.'

That was Angolos, logical to his fingertips, except when it

came to his wife. Where Georgie was concerned he got very Greek and unpredictable, reflected the Englishman.

'She…Mirrie, that is, made me come,' Paul admitted.

Angolos nodded. 'And I'm glad she did. I would be insulted if you hadn't come to me with your problem. Just hold on a sec and I'll be with you.'

'My…prob…? But I haven't got…' Paul stopped and watched with an expression of comical dismay as his friend exchanged words with the brunette, who looked far from happy with what he said. Seconds later Angolos had returned to his side.

'Let's get out of here,' Angolos suggested. 'There's a bar around the corner. We can talk.'

The first thing Paul said when they had ordered their drinks was— 'Let's get one thing straight. I'm not here to touch you for a loan, Angolos.'

'I'm well aware that not all problems can be solved by throwing money at them, Paul.' The level dark-eyed gaze made the other man shift uncomfortably. 'But if yours ever can be I will throw money at them whether you like it or not.' The hauteur in his strong-boned face was replaced by a warm smile as he added, 'My friend, if it wasn't for you I wouldn't be here at all.'

'Nonsense.'

The other man's patent discomfort made Angolos grin, his teeth flashing white in the darkness of his face. 'Your British self-deprecation borders on the ludicrous, Paul,' he observed wryly. He set his elbows on the table and leant forward, his expression attentive. 'Now what's the problem?'

'I wouldn't call it a problem… It's just that Dr Monroe retired and his patients have been relocated to us…' In response to Angolos's frown Paul breathed in deeply and went on quickly. 'Yesterday my partner was called out on an emergency and I saw some of the new patients.' He swallowed. 'Georgie…your Georgie was one of them.'

Angolos's expression didn't change, but his actions as he picked up his untouched drink and lifted it to his lips were strangely deliberate. A moment later, having replaced the glass on the table, he lifted his eyes to those of the other man.

'Is she ill?'

'No, no!'

Almost imperceptibly Angolos's shoulders relaxed.

He privately acknowledged that it was slightly perverse, considering he had cursed his faithless wife with all the inventive and vindictive power at his disposal three and a half years earlier, that the possibility of her being ill now should have awoken such primitive protective instincts.

'Actually she looked fantastic…a bit thin, perhaps,' Paul conceded half to himself. 'She always had great bones.'

'I have not the faintest interest in how she looks.' Angolos's jaw tightened as the other man turned an overtly sceptical gaze on his face. 'And I don't remember you mentioning her great bones when you told me I would be making the greatest mistake of my life if I married her…'

'Ah, well, I was afraid that you were…'

'Out of my mind?' Angolos suggested when his friend stumbled. 'You were right on both counts, as it happened.' Elbows set on the table, he leaned forward slightly. 'Did she ask you to intercede on my behalf? I thought you had more sense than to be taken in by—'

The doctor looked indignant. 'Actually, mate, I got the distinct impression you're the last person she wants to contact,' he revealed frankly.

'Indeed!'

'She was pretty shocked when she saw me. In fact,' he admitted, 'I thought she was going to run out of the office. And when I said your name she looked…' He stopped; there were no words that could accurately describe the bleak ex-

pression that had filled the young mother's eyes. 'Not happy,'
Paul finished lamely.

Angolos leaned back in his seat and, loosening a button on
his jacket, folded his arms across his chest. 'Yet you are here.'

'I am.' Paul ran a hand across his jaw. 'This is hard. Mirrie
does this sort of thing so much better than I do.'

At this point, if he had been having this conversation with
anyone else Angolos would have told them to get on with it,
but this was Paul, so he controlled his impatience and made
suitably encouraging noises.

'The thing is, Angolos, she brought the boy.' The expression on his friend's face as he looked at him from beneath
knitted brows was less than encouraging, but Paul persisted.
'Have you ever seen…?'

'No, I have never seen the child,' Angolos responded gla-
cially.

'He's a fine little lad and not spoilt either. Georgie's done
a fine job, though I got the impression reading between the
lines that money's tight.'

Angolos's lip curled contemptuously. 'So this is what this
is about—she's been playing the poverty card. I deposit a
more than adequate amount of money in a bank account for
the child's needs. If Georgette has got greedy, if she has some
deluded hope of extracting a more substantial amount from
me, she can forget it. She's taken me for a fool once…'

'She honestly didn't mention money, Angolos, but if she
wanted to bleed you… Did you see how much that rock star
who denied paternity got taken for when the girl took him to
court? DNA testing can—'

'DNA testing,' Angolos cut in, 'has robbed her of the opportunity of passing the child off as mine. If she's that desperate she could always sell her story to some tabloid.' His
nostrils flared as he drummed his long fingers on the tabletop.
'That would be her style.'

''Wouldn't she have done that before now if she was going

to? And if she wanted money I imagine the divorce settlement would be pretty generous.'

'Over my dead body.'

'I get the feeling you mean that literally.'

'I was hoping it wouldn't come to that,' Angolos returned smoothly. 'Are we drifting here, Paul?'

'Yes, well, actually, it's…the DNA thing…'

'The DNA thing?' Angolos said blankly.

'Are you totally sure a test would come up *negative*?'

'Sure…?' Angolos looked at his friend incredulously. 'You of all people can ask me that? The chemo saved my life but there was a price to pay—it rendered me sterile. My only chance of having a child is stored in a deep-freeze somewhere.'

'It was tough luck,' Paul, very conscious of his own impending fatherhood, admitted.

'*Tough luck?*' Angolos's expressive mouth dropped at one corner. 'Yes, I suppose it was tough luck. However, considering that without the treatment and, more importantly, your early diagnosis I would not be here at all, I consider myself lucky.'

'But it's not an easy thing to come to terms with.'

'Actually, *intellectually* I have no problem with the situation, but somehow, no matter how many times I tell myself there's more to a man's masculinity than his sperm count, I still feel…' His mouth twisted in a self-derisive smile, he met Paul's eyes. 'Maybe Georgette was right about that, at least— perhaps at heart I am an unreconstructed chauvinist…'

'Was there ever any doubt?'

This retort drew a rueful smile from Angolos.

'Is that why you never told her about the chemo and the cancer? Were you afraid she'd…?' Paul gave an embarrassed grimace. 'Sorry, I shouldn't…'

'Was I afraid she'd think me any less a man, you mean? What do you think, Paul?'

'I think if I knew what went on in your head I'd be the only one,' his friend returned frankly. 'You know, when it comes to answering questions you'd give the slipperiest politician a run for his money. If you want my opinion, you were wrong. I know Georgie was young, but she always struck me as pretty mature...'

'Mature enough to cheat on me and try to pass off the product of her amorous adventures as mine.'

Paul winced. 'Ah, about that, Angolos...'

'You want to discuss my wife's infidelity?'

'Of course not.'

'If you've discovered who her lover was...' Right up to the end she had refused to admit her guilt or provide the name of her lover. Though he knew who he was. 'I'm really no longer interested.'

'Maybe there was no lover?'

Angolos's dark brows knitted as he gave a contemptuous smile. 'Was no lover...? What are you suggesting—immaculate conception?'

Paul held up his hand. 'Angolos, hear me out. I know that the sort of chemotherapy you had normally results in infertility, but there are exceptions...you didn't have any tests post—'

'No, or the counselling, which apparently would have made me content to be less than a man.'

'Yes, you made your opinion of counselling quite plain at the time.'

'One cannot alter what has happened; one must just accept.'

'Terribly fatalistic and fine.'

'We Greeks are fatalists.'

'You're the least fatalistic person I've ever met. And sometimes it helps to talk...but I didn't come here to discuss the benefits of counselling.'

'Are you likely to tell me what you did come for any time this side of Christmas?'

'The boy is yours.'

A spasm of anger passed across Angolos's face. Paul watched with some trepidation as his friend took several deep breaths. There was a white line etched around his lips as he said in a low, carefully controlled voice, 'Anyone but you…Paul…'

'You'd knock my block off, I know, but I still have to say it. The boy, Angolos, he's the living spit of you. Oh, I don't mean a little bit like—I mean a miniature version. There's absolutely no doubt about it in my mind—Nicky is your son.'

'Is this some sort of joke, Paul?'

'I've got a warped sense of humour, Angolos, but I'm not cruel. If you don't believe me I suggest you go look for yourself.'

'I'm not buying into this fantasy.'

'They're staying at the beach place.'

'I have absolutely no intention of going anywhere near that woman.'

'Well, that's up to you, but if it was me—'

Angolos's eyes flashed. 'It is not you. You have a wife waiting for you at home; you will hold your newly born child in your arms…' He saw the shock on the other man's face and, worse, the dawning sympathy. 'The truth is, Paul,' Angolos added in a more moderate tone, 'I envy you. Never take what you have for granted.'

CHAPTER FOUR

PEOPLE sitting in the hotel sun lounge opposite, munching their cream teas, watched as the tall, dark-haired figure emerged from the Mercedes convertible and adjusted his designer shades. A buzz of speculation passed through the room.

Who was the stranger? There was a general consensus that he looked as though he was *somebody*.

It was exactly as he remembered it, Angolos decided as he scanned the beach. Progress and the twenty-first century had still to reach this backwater.

Despite the fact the sun had retreated behind some sinister-looking dark clouds, there was still a sprinkling of hardy, inadequately clad individuals on the sands. Some were even in the water, which, if his memory served him correctly, was cold enough to freeze a man, especially one accustomed to the warmth of the Aegean, to the core.

Angolos had no specific plan of action. He knew that Paul was wrong; he had made this journey simply to extinguish any lingering doubts. After all, the unformed features of one dark-eyed, dark-haired child looked very much like another.

Saying the resemblance was striking was hardly proof positive. Frankly the unscientific approach from someone who really ought to know better surprised him.

Paul had to be wrong.

Then why are you here?

Because, he admitted to the dry voice in his head, if I don't see this child for myself I'll never know for sure. A niggling doubt—or was it hope?—would always be there. Irrational, of course; if he had a son he would *know*. It was simply not possible.

The part of the sea front he had reached was newly pedestrianised. There were signs excluding litter, dogs, and skateboards...and it had worked; he had the stretch pretty much to himself. He could see the church spire in the distance. He knew if he headed in that general direction he would end up where he wanted to be.

Although in these circumstances *want* was not really an appropriate term.

The Kemps' holiday home was reached by a narrow, tree-lined lane that ran one side of the churchyard. A more direct route was via the beach—the house boasted a garden gate that gave direct access to the dunes and sand.

Angolos chose the more direct route. The sooner this nonsense was over with, the better, as far as he was concerned. He could not really spare the time as it was.

Angolos was not a man who lived in the past, but under the circumstances it was hard to prevent his thoughts returning to the first occasion he had walked along this stretch of sand.

He had been euphoric after receiving the final all-clear from the hospital earlier that morning. His first thought had been to immediately drive down to the coast to share the good news with the friend whom he owed his life to. If Paul hadn't picked up on those few tell-tale symptoms and cajoled him into having a blood test that had revealed his problem, he'd had no doubt that he would not have been here now.

His plans had been frustrated. Paul and his wife Miranda hadn't been at home. Driving along the sea-front road on his way back to the capital, on impulse Angolos had pulled the car over.

The sea air had filled his nostrils; the sun had warmed his face; he had felt alive...he had been alive.

There was nothing like a brush with death to make a man appreciate things he would normally have overlooked, but even had his senses not been heightened he would have noticed her. Why one pretty girl should have attracted his attention when there were so many pretty girls in the world remained a mystery.

Maybe it was the fact she had refused his impulsive offer of dinner that had made the honey-haired English girl with the golden eyes remain in his mind the rest of the day.

And maybe it had been coincidence that had made him return to the beach late that evening when the light had been fading, but Angolos was more inclined to consider it fate.

And fate was not always kind.

When he'd tried the second time, Paul and Mirrie had been home. They had opened a bottle of champagne to celebrate and had insisted he should stay the night. He ought to have been able to relax—he had been given his life back; he had been in the company of friends—but Angolos had felt strangely restless.

The evening had been sticky and stifling; a few distant rumbles had promised thunder. When he'd announced his intention of taking a walk on the beach, his understanding hosts had said fine, and given him a key to let himself in.

Walking along the pebbly foreshore, he hadn't immediately appreciated that the figure in the waves had been in trouble. Assuming the swimmer had been messing around or drunk, he had turned a deaf ear to the cries.

When he had realised what had been happening he had responded instinctively to the situation. On autopilot he had fought his way out of his jacket as he'd run down the beach, pausing only at the water's edge to step out of his shoes.

He was a strong swimmer and, even hampered by his clothing, it had taken him very little time to cover the hundred or so metres. Even though clearly exhausted, desperation had lent the struggling swimmer strength as she had wrapped her arms around his neck, dragging him down. She had clung like a limpet—yes, even in the desperation of trying to break her stranglehold, he had registered that the body sealed to his was female—and in his weakened condition it had taken him a few worrying minutes to subdue her.

Fortunately she had appeared to have exhausted herself fighting him, and had remained passive as he'd towed her to shore. The undercurrent, which had presumably been too strong for her to negotiate, had been against him on the way back. The swim back had taken its toll on his remaining strength.

The relief when he'd got her ashore had been intense.

It wasn't until he had carried the limp and bedraggled figure from the water and dumped her, coughing, onto the sand that he had recognised her. Lying at his feet had been the golden-eyed girl from earlier.

Something had snapped in his head. That someone like this girl with everything to look forward to could have been so careless of life when he'd known how fragile and precious it was had incensed him beyond measure.

Anger had coursed through his body and brain, causing his vision to blur and his hands to shake. He hadn't been able to recall being this angry in his life—not even when the doctors had given him a poor prognosis. On that occasion he had had to control his feelings, but not now. He had been incandescent with rage.

Dropping down onto his knees beside her, he had taken her small heart-shaped face between his hands, pushing aside the drenched strands of hair that had clung like fronds of exotic seaweed to her face.

He had been able to feel the rapid beat of the pulse that had throbbed in her blue-veined temple. Her taut breasts had lifted as she'd tried to drag air into her oxygen-starved lungs. The black swimsuit had clung to her supple young body as lovingly as a second skin. Her skin, he'd noticed, had an incredible, luminescent clarity, at that moment it had been icy cold.

The image of her lying there was so perfect it might have

happened yesterday. His body responded to the memory as if it had been that night nearly four years earlier. He was rock-hard.

'How could you be so stupid?' he demanded then. He shook her until her eyes opened.

Amazing amber eyes, big and not quite focused, blinked back at him. She was exhibiting classic signs of shock, but he was in no mood to make allowances.

'I didn't think…I…I mean it was—'

'Did you want to kill yourself?' he ranted on, oblivious to her pitiful and barely audible apology.

'Of c…course not.'

'You could have drowned us both.' Her eyes widened; the swimming depths reflected mute horror. 'What the hell were you doing?'

'I was swimming.'

'No, you were bloody drowning!' He watched her full lower lip tremble and without thinking covered her mouth with his own.

Even now, all this time later, he could recall her startled gasp, the salty taste of the soft lips that parted sweetly under his and the softness of her body as she went bonelessly limp. The deep, soundless shudder that sighed through her body would stay with him for ever.

From somewhere he dredged up the strength to lift his mouth from hers when all he wanted to do was explore the sweet, moist recesses. Her fierce little groan of protest as the contact was broken made him forget for several dangerous seconds why this wasn't a good idea.

The tenacious fingers that curled tightly in his wet hair proved infinitely more difficult to resist than the tide that had tried to pull them under.

He grabbed her hands and pinned them above her head, just to stop her touching him. 'You don't want to do this.'

'You're insane,' she contended, shaking.

'Certifiable,' Angolos agreed thickly. The slim body beneath his was burning up. He could feel the blast of heat through the layers of wet clothes that separated them.

'Don't stop!' The husky command wreaked havoc with his already-shredded self-control. She was like fire in his arms, supple, soft and displaying the same sort of savage desperation that thundered through his veins.

He hadn't held a woman for almost a year, let alone had sex.

When he had first been diagnosed, his life had been thrown into utter confusion. He had always known where he was going and how he was getting there. The only restrictions placed on him had been by the responsibilities that had come with the privilege attached to his birth.

His focus and self-belief had always been enough to get him where he wanted to be. Helplessness had never entered the picture; then he had lost control. Someone had moved the goalposts and he had been angry.

He hadn't realised how angry until he had said to the consultant treating him, 'Tell me straight, Doctor, could this thing kill me?'

'Yes, Mr Constantine, it could, but not if I have anything to do with it.'

It was a week later that he had woken up next to a woman, and he hadn't known her name.

It had been a wake-up call. He had never ducked a fight in his life, but that, he'd then realised, was what he had been doing.

He had never been a saint, but he had always been discriminating and one-night stands had never been on his agenda. He had told himself to stop wallowing in self-pity, and had cleaned up his act. Of course later, when the treatment had taken his body to the limits of endurance, escaping into mindless sex had not been an option. He hadn't had the strength, let alone the inclination.

That evening on the beach had been the first time in months that he had felt the stirring of sex…finding the object of his fantasy in his arms, half naked and begging him to kiss her, had transformed those stirrings into a raw, raging hunger.

He must have retained a shred of sanity because he had tried to stop, he could remember loosing her wrists and putting out a hand to lift himself off her, but instead his fingers had closed over the soft curve of one small, perfect breast.

The air had suddenly vibrated with the sexual tension that had erupted between them. Angolos had been immobilised by a wave of lust. In his head he had seen himself pushing aside the black material to reveal the straining pink bud. He had seen himself run his tongue over the straining peak, had heard her soft moan of pleasure…no, the soft moan had been real.

'That feels so…' Mesmerised, he watched her lips form a soundless *oh* as, eyes closed tight, her body arched.

'I want you.'

Her eyes flicked open, tawny and wild. The most beautiful eyes he had ever seen. 'I'm yours.' She reached up and slid her hands under his wet shorts, letting her fingers slide over his skin.

Of course he lost it; what man wouldn't? He pulled her under him and traced the shape of her skull with his fingers, lifting the heavy wet hair from the nape of her lovely neck. The sound that vibrated in her throat as her head fell back reminded him of a cat's purr.

Her eyes opened and he touched his finger to the corner of her wide mouth and traced the full, soft outline. 'You have the most amazing lips,' he told her thickly. 'And such beautiful, beautiful eyes…tiger's eyes.'

'You're amazing all over.'

He allowed himself to kiss her then, driving his tongue into her mouth. He felt her searching hands on his body, sliding beneath his steaming clothes, baring his flesh to the air.

As his body pressed her into the wet sand she was still

shaking and so was he, no longer with cold or anger, but with a wild, frenzied desire. Through the wet clothes separating them he felt the fresh wave of sexual heat that washed over her skin. She wrapped her legs around him and gasped as she felt his erection press into her soft belly.

Angolos wanted to bury himself in that softness more than he wanted to take another breath. He might have done just that, if the night hadn't suddenly been illuminated by a jagged shaft of lightning. Lightning so bright he could see it through his closed eyelids.

He rolled off her with a groan and as he lay there panting there was a roll of thunder that broke directly overhead. The rain began to fall then, cold on his overheated skin.

She touched his shoulder and he shook his head. 'I am not in control,' he told her thickly.

'Me neither. Good, isn't it…?' She sighed. 'You don't have to worry. I'm not afraid of thunder, and the boyfriend…I was lying. I don't really have one. And I don't expect…'

He turned his head. 'You don't expect what?'

'I don't expect it to be…you know…the first time…'

The husky confidence made him freeze. '*Theos!* Can it be true…?' He scanned her face and knew. 'Dear God, it is.'

A man who prided himself on his control, he couldn't believe what he had just done. If it hadn't been for the storm he…

She reached for him and she looked hurt when he jerked back avoiding contact.

He had never wanted a woman so much in his life.

'You're mad with me…?'

He looked at the tears trembling on her eyelashes and cursed slowly and fluently under his breath.

'No, I'm mad with me,' he told her as he picked her up.

She lay passively in his arms as he carried her across the sand dunes to where his car was parked in a quiet lane. The place was totally deserted as he dumped her in the front seat.

'Are you kidnapping me?' There was no alarm in her voice, just a lazy curiosity.

'No, I'm warming you up,' he said, switching on the engine and turning up the heater full blast.

'Maybe I should take off my wet things…?'

The only wet thing she was wearing was a black swimsuit with a zip up the front. 'Maybe you shouldn't,' he said, trying hard not to think about that strategically placed zip. *One tug…*

'I don't think I should have got in a car with a stranger,' she observed absently as he draped a jacket that had been in the back seat over her shoulders.

'You didn't get in. I put you in.'

'So you did. I'm warmer.' She leaned back in the deeply upholstered seat with a sigh. 'You know, I don't think I'm quite myself,' she confided.

That makes two of us. 'You nearly drowned.'

Her eyes, which had been closing, suddenly flickered open. Tawny eyes scanned his face. 'You kissed me.' She pressed a hand to her soft lips. 'I liked it.'

Beside her he didn't dare move; he didn't trust himself to speak. The ferocious tension in his body was so extreme that he remembered the bones in his face aching.

'I noticed,' he admitted.

She lifted a hand and ran a finger down his lean cheek. 'Are you going to do it again?'

'You're in shock.'

'I'm something, but not that. I think you saved my life. How can I repay you?'

He caught hold of her wrist and dragged her hand from his face. 'Well, you can cut that out, for a start.'

She flinched visibly at the cutting response. After a second's hurt incomprehension, a tide of mortified colour washed over her face.

'*Theos!* Don't look at me like that,' he pleaded throatily.

She bit her lip and fixed her eyes on her hands, which lay clenched in her lap.

'I'm s...sorry,' she stuttered. 'I really don't know what came over me.'

'The same thing that came over me. Where do you live? I'll take you home.' And after that he was going to drive away in the opposite direction.

He didn't do virgins.

CHAPTER FIVE

'CAN we have the ball back, mister?'

The request dragged Angolos back from a time he mostly succeeded in blanking from his mind.

To his way of thinking, no useful purpose could be served from preserving the memory of a time when he had allowed himself to be humiliated and deceived, except possibly to learn a lesson. He would never trust a woman again.

Had it amused Georgette to see him oblivious to her affair? Had she laughed with her lover as they had planned to pass the child off as his…?

A muscle clenched in Angolos's lean cheek as he pulled a hand across his brow to wipe off the moisture that clung to his tanned skin. It had started raining and he hadn't noticed; neither had he noticed until now that he was within a hundred yards of the gate that led to the garden of the Kemp house, a slightly battered timber cottage with a tin roof. Bending, he picked up the ball that lay at his feet and threw it back to the family playing a game of beach cricket.

'Good throw,' somebody acknowledged cheerily before they returned to their game.

Angolos headed for the gate. It creaked on the rusty hinges as he pushed it open. His lips curled in distaste as his hand rested on the peeling paintwork. At one time he had found the shabby chic of the Kemp home, so totally unlike what he was accustomed to, charming. Now he just found it, well… shabby.

The family he had never found charming and the feeling was mutual. Her relatives had come across as a bunch of xenophobic idiots who had been appalled at the idea of one of their number marrying a foreigner. Later, when Georgette had confided that her mother had run off with a Greek waiter, her family's attitude had been more understandable.

His critical glance skimmed the semi-screened area. The cottage and garden looked the same as he remembered; the only thing that hadn't been here four years ago was the clutter of children's toys. Angolos's dark eyes were drawn against his will to the evidence of childish occupation…the tricycle, the plastic toy cars, the bucket of shells gathered from the beach.

His classical profile tautened as he averted his gaze and strode purposefully to the door. There was absolutely no point prolonging this.

The door was opened before he had an opportunity to announce his arrival. His raised hand fell to his side as he looked at the woman framed in the open doorway. She was, he judged, somewhere in her mid-fifties, her grey-streaked dark hair was cut in a short modern crop, she had intelligent blue eyes and an interesting rather than attractive face.

She was a stranger to Angolos.

'Hello, I'm—'

'Good gracious, you're Nicky's father.'

Angolos was so surprised by her automatic assumption that his response was uncharacteristically unguarded. 'No, I'm not anyone's father,' he ejaculated bitterly.

'Nonsense, of course you are,' she dismissed, dealing him an amused look.

Angolos was taken aback by this response. 'I will not argue the point with you.'

The woman scanned his face, then threw back her head and laughed, not intimidated by the hauteur in his manner.

Angolos liked that.

In his position there were too many people ready to say what he wanted to hear. They had been saying what he wanted to hear since the day he'd stepped into his dead father's shoes at the age of twenty-two. He valued people who could look him in the eyes and say, 'You're wrong.'

'Well, that would be rather pointless, wouldn't it?'

'It would?'

'Most definitely,' came the robust response. 'You want to see Nicky...of course you do,' she added before he had an opportunity to respond. 'May I be frank?'

'Can I stop you?' he wondered.

The dry intonation brought a fleeting smile to the woman's lips. 'This puts me in an awkward position...' she confided. 'I have no idea what agreement you have...visiting rights and so forth? Actually I didn't think you saw him at all.' She studied the tall man's face. 'I can see you don't want to discuss your personal business with a nosy old woman.'

'I can assure you I have not come to kidnap the boy.'

'I'm glad to hear it, but under the circumstances it might be better if you came back when Georgie is home.'

'But the child is here?' Angolos probed and saw the older woman's expression become guarded. 'The thing is, Mrs...?'

'My name is Ruth Simmons. *Miss.*'

'Miss Simmons, I'm rather pushed for time.'

The woman eyed him with patent disapproval. 'After all these years?'

Angolos supposed he ought to have expected this. Georgette had obviously decided to paint herself as the injured party and him as the unnatural father. His broad shoulders lifted in an infinitesimal shrug. Did she plan to poison this child's mind in a similar manner...poor kid?

'When do you expect Georgette to return?'

Ruth Simmons looked uncertainly at the remote and quite sensationally handsome face of Nicky's father and her brow puckered.

'I really couldn't say.' Was this the sort of man who would turn his back on his own child? He didn't seem the type...

Of course, you could never tell, but the Greeks she had met were very family orientated.

'Couldn't or won't…?' He lifted one long-fingered hand in an unconsciously elegant gesture. 'No matter.' He consulted his watch. 'I will return at a more convenient moment.' And then again maybe I won't… After all, the entire exercise was totally pointless. Better to get in his car and drive back to London.

The tall man's mechanical smile did not reach his eyes; Ruth noticed all the same that it was effortlessly charming. In the flesh this man was even more startlingly good-looking. If I were twenty years younger…? The self-mocking smile that curved her lips vanished as a loud bang followed by an even louder wail emerged from the living room.

'What now?' she cried, hurrying inside.

Angolos stepped through the open door.

A few moments later, with the crying child cradled in her arms, Ruth viewed the damage. It could have been worse. Still, it was a pity that her friend was fond of the hideous ornate Victorian bust that was now lying in fragments on the floor. The overturned chair was a clue as to how the three-year-old had managed to reach the shelf where it had been displayed.

'Did you fall, Nicky?' Her matter-of-fact tone and manner had a soothing effect upon the crying child, who stopped to catch his breath. 'Poor you,' she said, rubbing the obvious bruise that was developing on the child's forehead. 'Did you hurt yourself anywhere else, sweetheart?'

Nicky shook his head. 'Granny will be cross…'

'No, I'm sure she won't.'

'She will,' the child, whose tears had subsided, retorted positively. 'Who are you?' he asked, poking a chubby hand in the direction of the stranger.

'Gracious!' Ruth exclaimed, realising for the first time that the tall Greek had followed her into the room. He was standing there frozen. The only flicker of movement in his body was supplied by his stunning eyes, which were trained on the child in her arms.

Without replying, he continued to draw air into his lungs through clenched teeth, like a man who had forgotten how to breathe. As he squatted, bringing his face level with the toddler, she saw that his gloriously golden skin had acquired a greyish tinge. She saw his lips move; nothing came out.

'Gracious!' she added once more and with feeling. The physical similarity between father and son was truly startling... Nicky began to cry again.

'Nicky...your name is Nicky?' The tearful boy nodded his head.

Georgie walked in through the open door weighed down by supermarket carrier bags filled with groceries. A car, she reflected wistfully, would make life a lot easier, but her budget didn't run to such luxuries.

'Big boys don't cry, Nicky.'

She froze, the blood draining from her face. It was a voice Georgie would never, *could* never, forget.

It was a voice she heard in her dreams and her nightmares.

She stood there oblivious to the eggs that had broken when she'd dropped her bags and were now running stickily over the carpet.

This isn't happening.

Her first instinct was to run as fast and as far away as possible. She subdued her selfish reflex...she couldn't run and leave Nicky. Anyway, running would have been futile if Angolos wanted her. A shudder slid down her spine. When Angolos wanted something he was totally focused and implacable.

Only Angolos didn't want her; he had made that perfectly clear.

Her heart was hammering in her chest and her feet felt as

though they had lead weights attached as she moved towards the living-room door. Her head was spinning but one question amongst the many that chased one another around in her mind was uppermost.

Why had Angolos turned up now?

'I'm not a big boy. I'm lit…ul. Go away!'

Georgie heard the childish treble and her shoulders straightened. Leave him alone, she wanted to yell as she rushed impetuously forward.

She might prefer to walk into a lion's den than voluntarily enter a room that held her husband, but, as she had learnt within two seconds of his birth, for Nicky she would do the unthinkable. Her own needs and desires would always be secondary to her son's best interests…it was being a mother.

As she stepped through the door she almost collided with Ruth, who had offered to look after Nicky while she caught the last post and picked up some groceries and while her mother was staying with Robert. The woman barely seemed to register her presence.

Georgie's eyes moved past her and gasped. Having enough volts to light up a county pass through her body could not have felt more shocking than looking at father and son.

'Oh, my!' she whispered. *His hair still curled on his neck the same way.*

She had never denied to herself the startling resemblance between Nicky and his father but now seeing them side by side it was impossible for anyone to ignore. The sight of the long, lean figure balanced on his heels in front of the child wiped every thought from her head… She felt desire clutch low in her belly.

She grimaced in self-disgust. It appalled her and, yes, *scared* her that, even after all this time and everything he had done to her, she still only had to look at him to be reduced to a screaming mass of hormones.

Georgie took a deep sustaining breath and lifted her chin. 'Come here, Nicky,' she said quietly.

She was aware that Angolos's attention had slewed towards her. The hand she stretched towards her son had a perceptible tremor, but she studiously ignored him and kept her eyes trained on Nicky's tear-stained face.

It was only a moment before the child responded, but during that moment she had to fight back the impulse that urged her to rush over and physically tear him away from the man whose hands lay on his shoulders. Her clenched hands relaxed as Nicky aimed himself at her like a small but determined heat-seeking missile.

Angolos rose to his feet in time to see Georgie bend forward, her softly waving hair spilling across her face. She pushed the silky hank impatiently behind her ear.

'What have you been doing, darling?' Her attention on the child, Georgie didn't see the spasm of something close to pain that contorted her estranged husband's dark, autocratic features as he watched them.

'He had a slight accident. It was my fault...I only left him for a moment,' Ruth interjected.

'With Nicky a moment is all it takes,' Georgie responded as she hugged her son to her. 'Isn't it, champ?' she said, brushing the curly dark hair from his brow as she straightened up with the child's body pressed close to her own. She saw the bruise and sighed. 'In the wars, I see.'

She knew that pretending Angolos wasn't there wasn't exactly a long-term solution to her present predicament, but it was the only one she could think of. Angolos, all six feet four of him, was there barely a metre away from her, looking even more devastatingly attractive than she remembered... Her brain just refused to deal with the reality of the situation.

The muscles in her face ached as she forced a tense smile. 'Now, why don't you go with Auntie Ruth?' She caught the eye of the older woman, who gave an understanding grimace.

'I'm really sorry about this, Georgie.' Her soft apology was accompanied by a sideways look towards the tall man who was silently watching.

'It's not your fault,' Georgie said, handing over her burden. 'This will only take a minute,' she promised, staying one step ahead of her rising panic by sheer force of will alone.

A silent sigh of relief passed through her body as they left the room.

'Do you always reward him for misbehaving?' Angolos's eyes were flat and icy as they scanned her face.

Georgie waited until she judged the child was out of earshot before responding and opened her eyes. 'What would you do—beat him?'

Her sneering suggestion made his face tauten with anger. 'Children need to know what the boundaries are. It makes them feel secure.'

'Hearing you throw around terms like security in connection with Nicky…' She swallowed back the anger that made her want to scream at him and hammer her fists against his chest. Her voice dropped to a low, scornful whisper. 'You lost any right you might have had to criticise the way I bring up *my* child when you effectively disowned him.'

Angolos's head reared as though she had struck him. 'I would never knowingly disown my son.' His low, uneven voice throbbed with sincerity. His mesmeric eyes locked onto hers.

'I stand corrected. You *accidentally* disowned him, which makes it all right, then.' She went to the door and yanked it open. 'You were just passing, I suppose, so feel free to carry on doing just that.'

'You want me to leave?'

Georgie, her expression stony, fixed her eyes on the wall directly ahead. 'The only thing I want more is for you to be kidnapped by aliens, but I'm realistic, I'll settle for the former.'

He dragged his long fingers through his hair. The sheer familiarity of the gesture made her ache.

'We need to talk.'

She turned her head; he was incredible…really incredible! Did he really think she was going to let him waltz in here and mess up her life for a second time?

'Did I really ever find your autocratic mannerisms a turn-on?'

She hadn't realised until he responded in a dry tone that she had voiced her thoughts out loud. 'I don't know, did you?'

Subduing a mortified blush, she gave an indifferent shrug. '*I* don't need to talk,' she told him stonily.

'Then listen.'

Georgie closed her eyes and stuffed her fingers in her ears. Through clenched teeth she began to hum loudly and tunelessly.

'You still haven't grown up, then.'

Georgie's blazing eyes lifted to the contemptuous face of the man who had captured her wrists. '*Me? I'm* not the one who throws away a relationship as casually as a spoilt brat throws away a toy that he's got tired of.'

His breath whistled in a startled gasp through his clenched teeth. 'What did you say?'

'It roughly translates as get the hell out of here and my life… *I hate and despise you!*' She twisted her hands angrily, but instead of releasing her Angolos jerked her towards him.

The breath whooshed out of her lungs as her body collided with a body that had no give. For one shocked moment she stood there feeling the strong, steady thud of his heart, then she began to struggle. She fought the rising tide of sensual inertia so powerful that it threatened to swamp her as much as the strong hands that imprisoned her. She fought because deep down there was a secret part of her that didn't want to escape, a part of her that wanted to melt into him.

'Let me go… How dare…?'

Suddenly she was free.

The brief skirmish had only lasted a matter of seconds, but Georgie was fighting for breath as though she'd just gone five rounds with a contender for the title.

Rubbing one wrist, she glared at him. Angolos had always been lean and hard in a tensile steel sort of way, he still didn't carry an ounce of spare flesh, but that brief contact had revealed that he had bulked out muscle-wise. The treacherous burst of heat low in her belly filled her with intense shame.

'I'd like you to leave,' she told him huskily.

'When I've said what I came to say.'

Georgie gave a frustrated little grunt... Well, that much hadn't changed; Angolos was still as stubborn and incapable of compromise as ever. 'Get your lawyer to write mine a letter,' she suggested. 'Isn't that the way it usually works?'

'You don't have a lawyer...'

'And you don't have a chance in hell of getting me to listen to you.'

He studied her set, stubborn face and stony eyes for a moment before dragging a hand through his already disordered thick dark hair.

'I need a drink.'

'There's a pub around the corner. They're not fussy about who they serve.'

His eyes narrowed. 'The Kemp household still represents the best of British hospitality, I see.'

Georgie hardly heard him; the muscle that clenched and unclenched in his cheek was having a strongly hypnotic effect on her. Dressed all in black, he looked sleek and dangerous and off-the-scale sexy!

'The house and town are the same, but you,' he added, allowing his frowning gaze to move over her slender figure, 'look different...'

Careful not to reveal by so much of a flicker of an eyelash what the critical brush of his eyes did to her, Georgie shrugged and stuck her hands in the pockets of her jeans. She was oblivious to the fact the action stretched the material, lovingly revealing the feminine curve of her slim thighs.

'Designer clothes, you mean?' She gave a contemptuous smile. 'They don't suit my lifestyle and actually they're not me. They never were.'

When Angolos lifted his eyes to her face his natural warm colouring was a shade deeper. 'Actually I meant you look *harder*.' Despite this grim assertion, it was her *softness* that was occupying his thoughts.

You carry on believing that, thought Georgie, pushing her hands deeper into her pockets to disguise the fact they were seriously trembling.

'There was a time when I actually cared what you thought of me...' The memory of her anxiety to please him made her shake her head in pained distaste.

The irony was, the harder she tried to be what he wanted, the farther apart they seemed to drift. All the expensive clothes in the world had not made her fit in with the wealthy, snooty Constantine clan.

From day one his family, or more specifically his mother, Olympia Constantine, had made no attempt to hide her disapproval...at least not from Georgie. Around Angolos his mother had been more circumspect. Olympia had saved her sly digs and outright hostility for when Angolos hadn't been around, which had been most of the time. She had never made any secret of the fact she'd wanted Georgie out of their lives.

And in the end they had got what they'd wanted. Georgie released her breath in a long, shuddering sigh and lifted her chin.

'I'm not the pushover I once was, certainly.' She was faintly amazed to hear her voice emerge steady and even. 'I don't know why you're here, Angolos, and I don't want to know.' She stood to one side and gestured to the open door.

Angolos didn't move. A muscle along his strong jaw spasmed as he picked up a toy car from the floor. She watched warily as he pushed the toy back and forth along across his palm. 'He's my son.'

Georgie's slender shoulders lifted. *'So…?'*

He dropped the toy into an overflowing toy box and lifted a hand to his forehead, rubbing the groove between his dark brows. He continued to look uncharacteristically distracted. *'I have a son.'*

'You say it as if it's news, Angolos,' she mocked. 'You've had a son for the past three years and I didn't notice you breaking any speed records to see him. Not even a b…birthday card.' She lowered her eyes quickly as she felt the warmth of the unshed tears that filled them.

'I thought my lawyers made it clear that if the money I deposited wasn't sufficient I would—'

Georgie's head came up, her luminous, liquid golden eyes levelled contemptuously with his. 'Do you really think I'd touch a penny of your money…?'

Angolos's lip curled. 'You expect me to believe that you haven't touched the money.'

'I never wanted your money!' she flared. 'I wanted…' She stopped dead, dark colour suffusing her pale cheeks. 'If I gave a damn what you believe I'd get out the bank statement.' She had given a damn once, though, and it had hurt her more than she wanted to remember.

'If you haven't used the money, how have you supported yourself?' he demanded suspiciously. 'Or should I ask *who* has been supporting you?'

She sucked in an outraged breath through flared nostrils and watched the toy ball he had aimed a kick at bounce off the wall.

If he thought she had time for a social life, let alone a boyfriend, he really didn't have the first clue about what it took to bring up a child single-handed while holding down a demanding job! But then maybe that was all to the good—she preferred the idea of him thinking she had a wild private life.

'I've been doing what most people do. I've been working.'

His brows shot towards his hairline. *'Working…you…?'*

'Yes, me, working. I was training to be a teacher when we met, if you remember.'

'Yes, but it was hardly your vocation; you gave it up without a second thought.'

Georgie's eyes widened as she scanned his face with incredulous anger. Didn't he realise that she'd have given up *anything* for him…that she'd have done *anything* he suggested without a second thought?

I must have been out of my mind!

'What choice did I have?'

Angolos looked exasperated. 'There is always a choice,' he rebutted.

She swallowed past the emotional congestion in her throat. 'You'd have been quite happy being married to a student, then?' she challenged.

'At no stage did you say your career was so important—'

'You're right, there is always a choice,' she interrupted. 'And I made the wrong one…I married you.'

The skin across his cheekbones tautened; his eyes meshed with hers. 'We both made the wrong choice.'

'Don't dwell on it; I didn't.' If you discounted the endless nights she had cried herself to sleep. 'I went back to college after Nicky was born.'

'A baby needs his mother.'

'That's what I always liked about you; you were so supportive of me.'

Angolos's astonished expression gave her a moment's amusement and for a second she felt like the empowered woman she wanted him to think her.

'For the record, Nicky has his mother; it's his father he

doesn't have,' she retorted, and had the pleasure of seeing a tell-tale wash of colour darken his golden-toned skin.

It would seem that at some level Angolos was aware that he had behaved like a despicable rat.

'*I* didn't reject him,' she continued. '*I'm* not the one who couldn't accept my responsibility.'

Angolos's nostrils flared as his glittering jet eyes locked onto those of his estranged wife.

'I didn't reject my son,' he rebutted thickly.

Georgie arched an ironic brow, outwardly at least oblivious to the waves of strong emotion he was projecting. She might once have turned herself inside out to pander to his moods, but that time was long gone.

'You and I must have very different interpretations of rejection.'

Angolos closed his eyes. The curse that escaped his clamped lips drew Georgie's attention to the sensual curve of his mouth. Her stomach dipped and she tore her eyes away.

'Sorry, but I don't understand Greek. Do you mind translating?'

'You don't understand my language because you made not the slightest effort to learn it.'

'No effort!' she yelped, stung by this unjust accusation. 'I may not have been very good, but it wasn't for want of trying. I only stopped going to the wretched lessons when—'

He looked at her in open amazement. 'Lessons? You did not take lessons.'

'Well, I had to do something to fill my days other than shopping and having my hair done.'

She had no intention of telling him that she had wanted to surprise him. That she had cherished an unrealistic ambition of casually replying to him in fluent, flawless Greek. Her ambition to make her husband proud of her seemed painfully pathetic in light of what had happened.

'So you were not content with your life as my wife?'

'You didn't want a wife, you wanted a mistress! And I'm not mistress material.' She watched an expression of astonishment steal across his face and added as a reckless afterthought, 'I was bored silly.'

CHAPTER SIX

'*BORED...?*'

Georgie turned a deaf ear to the dangerous note in Angolos's voice and nodded. 'Yes, bored. I got bored with you and Greek lessons.'

There was no way in the world she would ever tell him how his mother and sister had made fun of her attempts to converse. Angolos, they had said, would be embarrassed by her awkward grammar and appalling accent. Like all her attempts to fit in, this one had never stood a chance, not with in-laws who had never lost an opportunity to make her feel inadequate.

'I had no idea that living with me was such an ordeal.'

'Neither did I at the time. Now,' she told him calmly, 'I can be more objective.'

His eyes narrowed. 'So now your life is exciting and fulfilling?'

'I have a career and a child.'

'How did you take care of a baby and attend college?'

'I left him in the college crèche. And fortunately the school I work at is happy for him to go to the nursery there.'

'So you qualified...?'

'Amazing, isn't it? I'm actually not the brainless bimbo you and your family thought me, Angolos.'

His dark lashes swept downwards, touching the curve of his high, chiselled cheekbones as he studied his feet. There was a lengthy pause before he lifted his head and replied.

'I never thought you were brainless.'

Georgie did not make the mistake of taking this comment

57

as a compliment. She recognised that she was within seconds of losing control totally. Her assertions, the ones that she repeated like a mantra to herself every night, that she was totally over him, would be out the window if she started to batter her fists against his chest.

Their eyes locked and neither combatant heard the first tentative tap on the open door. The second, slighter louder one got their attention.

'I'll be right there, Ruth,' Georgie promised, pulling the door open.

'No hurry,' the older woman soothed. 'I'm sorry to disturb you, but Nicky is asking for his *cosy*. I wasn't sure what he meant.'

'It's his blanket, yellow…sort of. It's in his bedroom on the chest by the window.'

'He needs a security blanket?'

The faintest hint of criticism and her hackles were up. 'Actually it's a sheet.' So now he was the child expert.

'He has problems…?' A child who had been rejected by his father—why was he surprised? Angolos, a firm believer that a stable family was the only place to bring up a child, knew that if his son had problems the blame lay at his own door. He didn't know how this had happened, but he was a father and he needed to put right the harm he had already done.

'No, he doesn't have problems. He's a normal little boy who…' She stopped and frowned. 'Good grief, I don't know why I'm explaining anything to you of all people.'

'Because I am his father.'

'Biologically maybe…'

She had never expected her dig to evoke any real reaction, certainly not the expression of haunted regret that she saw on his face.

'Look, Angolos, if you've come over with a case of delayed

paternal feelings, I suggest you go take an aspirin or buy a shiny new car. I'm sure it will pass.'

'You think I am that shallow?' he enquired in a savage growl.

'Think? I *know* you're that shallow,' she retorted. 'Shallow and cruel and vindictive…' Something she might remind herself the next time she found herself in danger of feeling sorry for him. The fact was, if she ever started thinking of Angolos as the victim it was time for the men in white coats. 'This is a pointless conversation.'

'It's one we're going to have.'

Fine! If he wanted a war of attrition, she thought, he could have a war of attrition. But he was going to discover that during the time they'd been apart she had developed a backbone, not to mention a mind of her own!

'Why, Angolos? Because you say so? I know it used to work that way, but not any more.' She gave a hiss of frustration as her trained maternal ear caught the sound of her son's cry. A few seconds later Angolos heard it too and turned his head in the direction of the angry sound.

'What's wrong with him?'

'Being a mother doesn't make me psychic.' It had, however, given her the ability to distinguish between her son's cries. The one she had heard suggested tiredness, not pain or distress. 'I've got to go to him.' She started for the door, but he moved and effectively blocked her path with his body. Her nostrils flared as she caught the faint scent of the fragrance he used. Low in her belly her muscles tightened.

'Fine!' she snapped, throwing up her hands in angry capitulation. 'If you want me to listen to you I will, but not now or here.'

'When and where, then?'

She said the first thing that came into her head. 'The beach.'

'Where we used to meet. Where you offered me your innocence…'

His tone, softly sensual, stole the strength from her legs at the first syllable. Falling flat on her face would not be a good move, Georgie decided, reaching casually for the back of a conveniently placed chair. 'The way I recall it, you were pretty eager to take it.' Unfair, but she didn't feel inclined to fairness at that moment. 'I'll meet you tomorrow night at eight…'

Her family would be back then and Nicky would be safely tucked up in bed.

'And this time I won't be offering you anything.'

'Tonight.'

'I can't,' she began, and then saw his expression. 'All right, tonight,' she agreed with a sigh.

For a moment his narrowed eyes held hers, then he inclined his head. 'It would seem we have a date.'

'Hell,' she loudly announced to his back, 'will freeze over first.' She closed the front door and leaned against it with a sigh; she was shaking. With her luck, she thought, Angolos would construe her childish retort as a challenge—that would be just like him.

And what on earth was Angolos up to? she wondered as she sank weakly to the floor. She sat there, her back wedged against the door, her knees tucked under her chin, waiting for her knees to stop shaking. For once Nicky's need for attention came secondary; secondary to the necessity for her to be able to walk without falling over.

When she got to her feet she felt strangely numb, as though her stressed body had produced some natural anaesthetic. She didn't want to think about how she would feel when it wore off.

Georgie went through the rest of the day on autopilot. She tried hard to conceal the anxiety that lodged like a weight behind her breastbone but as the day progressed it got increasingly difficult.

Ruth, bless her, agreed to come over later and sit with Nicky. She didn't ask any questions and, beyond a searching look and a brief, 'Are you all right?' she had not asked anything about Angolos.

Georgie was grateful for her reticence. She knew if Gran had been there she would not have escaped so lightly. Her grandmother had barely managed to be civil to Angolos before they had split up. Who knew how she'd have reacted if she'd been here when he'd turned up?

Why, after years of conspicuous silence, was Angolos here? The question gnawed at her all day. It was when Nicky's lower lip trembled after she had snapped at him over something trivial that she decided enough was enough.

By letting Angolos get to her this way she was allowing him to win. After all, it didn't matter what he had to say, or why he was here, he wasn't part of her life any more. Ironically it was when she stopped looking for answers that she accidentally found one.

She discovered the innocent-looking envelope when she was performing the daily ritual of picking up Nicky's toys from the living room after he had gone to bed. She glanced incuriously at her name, and, assuming it was junk mail, aimed it at the waste-paper basket. It was only when it missed and she went to retrieve it from where it fell that she realised the paper was good quality.

She turned the envelope over. There was no stamp or postmark and it wasn't sealed. She opened it and slid out the contents. She immediately recognised the letterhead of the law firm that Angolos used. Crazy, really, that she should feel shocked—even crazier that she had to blink back the tears. This was something she had been expecting for the past three years. It was the logical step and one that her family had frequently urged her to take.

Angolos wanted a divorce.

* * *

'You look very nice, dear,' Ruth commented as she walked with Georgie to the front door.

'I'm wearing make-up,' Georgie admitted, lifting a self-conscious hand to her lightly glossed lips.

'Charming, but I was thinking of the dress.'

Georgie flushed, and looked down at the pale peach-coloured halter-necked dress she had finally selected. Even with her limited wardrobe it had taken her half an hour.

'It's too much, isn't it?' she fretted, smoothing the light fabric over her slender hips. 'I knew it was. I'll go and change.'

Ruth laughed. 'Don't be silly, you look lovely. Whether it's too much rather depends on what reaction you want to get?'

'I was aiming towards a sharp intake of breath,' Georgie admitted.

'Oh, I think you'll get that. I hope you don't mind me asking, but is there a reconciliation on the cards?'

'I don't mind you asking and, no, there isn't.'

If anyone had asked her yesterday if she nursed any hope of them ever getting back together, Georgie would have been able to give a very definite no way in reply, and mean it.

Yesterday she hadn't opened that envelope.

Reading the contents of a letter that explained with surgical precision that your husband wanted a divorce was a bad time to realise that in some secret corner of your heart you had clung onto hope. Foolish, irrational hope that one day… She took a deep breath. She knew that she was better off without that sort of hope.

'Actually, Angolos wants a divorce.' She had the horrid suspicion that her extremely casual attitude wasn't fooling Ruth for a minute. 'That's why he's come in person. I suspect there's someone else.' Maybe Sonia…? It would certainly please his family if he got back with his first wife.

If not Sonia, there would be someone. A highly sexed and

incredibly good-looking man like Angolos was never going to be celibate. She had come to terms with this.

Sure you have.

'I think it might be serious,' she heard herself say.

Ruth's brow furrowed. 'Now that *does* surprise me.'

'Not me; I've been expecting it.' Georgie gave her best carefree smile and wished she'd not revealed her suspicions to the older woman. 'The only thing that surprises me is it's taken him this long. Actually I think it'll be a good thing…making it official will give us proper closure.'

The other woman nodded and murmured agreement, but Georgie could see that she didn't believe a word. Embarrassed, she turned away. 'I won't be long,' she promised huskily.

About as long as it took to say goodbye.

CHAPTER SEVEN

ANGOLOS watched Georgie walk towards him along the beach with the graceful, long-legged stride he remembered so well. She carried her sandals in one hand slung over her shoulder in exactly the same way she always had. He was not a man inclined to nostalgia, but it was hard not to make a depressing comparison to the past.

Then, when she had caught sight of him her face would light up like a kid on Christmas morning and she would break into a run as though every second apart from him was one too many. Now when she saw him, and he recognised the precise moment, the only place she looked like running was in the opposite direction! You could almost hear her inner struggle as she covered the remaining distance.

Some irrational part of him wanted to make her smile at him that way again. Was it the same irrational part of him that had been tempted, albeit briefly, not to question her pregnancy? Then sense had prevailed and his pride had reasserted itself.

That he had contemplated, even for a moment, living a lie and bringing up another man's child, accepting his wife's infidelity, filled him with a profound self-disgust. Ironically of course it hadn't been another man's child she carried, but at the time he hadn't known that.

'Am I late?' Composed and utterly controlled, she sketched a smile. Her wary eyes, their incredible colour intensified by the soft shading on her eyelids, met his.

'No. I am early.'

Angolos didn't have a clue why her manner annoyed him

64

so much. It wasn't as if he had expected her to throw her arms around his neck and press her slim young body to his.

His eyes drifted towards the slim young body in question and he grew still. The summer dress exposed the soft, creamy contours of her satin-smooth shoulders and slim arms. The locket dangling from a slim gold chain suspended around her neck drew the attention to the firm swell of her breasts. As his glance moved lower the breeze caught the light fabric, drawing it close over her slim thighs.

Georgie had been so gut-churningly nervous that until his dark eyes swept over her she had forgotten that she had dressed to kill, or at least immobilise with lust—until his heavy-lidded, penetrating eyes lifted and met hers.

She had got the reaction she wanted, only this wasn't theoretical lust. A classic case, she remonstrated herself, of not considering the consequences. The smoky heat and raw hunger in his eyes—for a man who could be infuriatingly enigmatic, Angolos had eyes that could be quite devastatingly expressive on occasion—sent a current of sizzling heat through her body.

Experience had taught her how to fan the flames of his desire. She tried not to access the memories that reminded her of how pleasurable the results of her provocation could be. She raised a fluttering hand to her throat and tried to get her breathing under control.

'Can we get on? I'm on my way somewhere.' She was quite pleased with her clever subterfuge; now he wasn't going to think she had got dressed up for him.

She saw his jaw clench. 'I'm so glad you could fit me into your busy schedule.'

'Well, you didn't actually give me any choice, did you?' she reminded him.

'I don't suppose I did.' One dark brow arched. 'Aren't you a little cold dressed like that? Would you like my jacket?'

Her eyes widened in alarm. The thought of having the garment still carrying the warmth of his body, retaining the unique scent of him, next to her skin sent an illicit thrill through her body.

'No, I'm fine,' she promised hastily.

'As you wish. Would you like to go somewhere…for a coffee…a drink? Is that odd little teashop still open?'

The question brought back a flood of memories.

Odd, he had said. Well, as venues for conducting a passionate affair went, the quaint, touristy tearooms run by two elderly sisters had to be one of the most unlikely. They had frequently had the place to themselves. Most people had been outside enjoying the sun that summer, which had been just as well because inconspicuous they had not been—or at least he hadn't!

Not that Georgie had much cared about discretion; as far as she'd been concerned the entire town could talk. She had been too besotted to care about such things, and actually much to her frustration they hadn't actually had much to be discreet about!

After that first occasion when they had come as near as damn it to making love in the wet sand—*and I didn't even know his name*—Angolos had kept her at arm's length. Even though she hadn't been experienced she had sensed he'd been keeping himself under tight control. Georgie, who had fantasised about recreating the wild, primitive night-time encounter—minus the frustration—had bitterly regretted telling him that he was her first lover.

Instead of the passionate love-making Georgie had craved, for two weeks they had drunk tea and talked, or at least that was the way it had felt to her. They had taken long drives and talked. They had taken long walks and talked. It had been sheer agony, but she'd been prepared to endure any torture devised by man to be in his company.

The weekend two weeks later, when he'd disappeared without a word, she had thought that was it, and she had been totally devastated. The idea of never seeing him again had made the future stretch ahead of her bleak and barren.

She had drifted around like a ghost, grey-faced and drawn, but instead of recognising a broken heart her family had been irritated by her lethargy.

Then her grandmother had diagnosed anorexia—*She has all the classic symptoms*… The article she had read had apparently said that sufferers always lied, so Georgie's denials had been ignored.

Consequently, when Angolos had turned up out of the blue at the house two weeks later, instead of looking interestingly pale she had gained seven pounds!

He had formally requested her father's permission to marry her. Superficially it might have seemed a delightfully old-fashioned courtesy, but only *very* superficially.

Oh, he had been polite enough, but he had left no doubt that he had been going to marry her with or without her father's permission. *With* would simply be less problematic.

She was bowled over by his masterful behaviour; it hadn't even crossed Georgie's mind to question the fact he hadn't even asked her. My compliance he took for granted and why wouldn't he…?

She pushed aside the cringe-worthy recollection of her uncritical adoration; she had held nothing back. She hadn't just worn her heart on her sleeve, she had stripped her soul bare!

'No, I don't want tea, I just want this over with as quickly as possible.' She kept her voice cool and unemotional and was rewarded by the surprise flicker in the back of his deep-set eyes.

'You can't spare a few minutes to discuss our son's future…?'

'I would spare a lot more than a few minutes to discuss Nicky's future, but not with you,' she retorted, bristling with antagonism. 'Nicky is nothing to do with you, and don't pretend you're really interested in him,' she sneered.

His expression tautened. 'Be reasonable.'

'Reasonable!' she yelled back, no longer able to contain the anger and resentment that she'd been storing up for these long years. 'Reasonable the way you were when you said you didn't want to know about the baby?' she demanded in a low, impassioned voice. 'Are you on medication, Angolos?'

'Do not raise your voice to me.' His own voice was low and angry.

'If the worst I do is raise my voice you'll leave here a fortunate man.'

He absorbed her angry words in thoughtful silence. 'You have developed quite a temper,' he observed, his glance drifting from her flushed, furious face to her fists clenched tightly at her sides.

'I *always* had a temper.' It was odd, she mused, that a man who knew her more intimately than any other man, a man who was the father of her child, should actually not know her very well at all.

His harsh scowl melted to something far more dangerous as their eyes meshed. 'Maybe you should have revealed this aspect of your character when we were together. It suits you.'

'I should have done a lot of things when we were together, including walking out before you so charmingly threw me out!'

The colour that began low on his throat travelled upwards until his entire face was suffused. 'I could have done that better,' he admitted huskily.

'Is that your version of grovelling?' She gave her head an impatient shake. 'Even if you crawled on your hands and knees I'd never forgive you for what you did.'

His face had that closed, unreadable expression as he said tautly, 'I think I should tell you why I asked you to—'

He's going to say it. *Divorce*…once he said it, it would be real. She suddenly went icy cold. Maybe I'm not ready to hear this after all…?

How long do you need…?

'I know why you're here,' she cut in quickly.

His dark brows drew together in a straight line above his masterful nose. *'You do…?'*

'For goodness' sake, don't drag it out. I need to get back.' She raised her wrist and evinced astonishment at the hour, even though she couldn't see her watch through the warm mist of unshed tears.

'You kept it.'

Her shimmering gaze lifted. 'Kept what?'

Angolos tapped the diamond-encrusted face of the watch he had bought her on their honeymoon. His hand dropped away, but not before the tips of his long brown fingers had trailed lightly along the inner aspect of her slender wrist.

It was barely a touch yet her body reacted like that of an addict given the scent of her drug of choice, only to have it snatched away. Inside the loose cotton bodice her breasts ached and craved the touch of hands and lips. Buried memories resurfaced and the ache low in her pelvis became a physical pain.

'I'm sentimental that way.' Let him never know how true that was.

The week in Paris, their honeymoon, had been utter bliss; she treasured the memory of every single moment of it. She had been a nervous bride the first night, but the moment he had touched her she had quickly lost her inhibitions. Her introduction into a sensual world she hadn't known existed had left her in a daze. Every morning when she'd woken up tangled up with the warm, lithe body of her incredible lover she'd felt as if she had died and gone to heaven.

For a week everything had been magical. Georgie had tried, but had never been able to recapture that magic.

The first cracks had appeared when they'd arrived in Greece. It had been here that the scale of Angolos's wealth had hit Georgie for the first time. They had landed on his private heli-pad, for goodness' sake! In her world people who had two cars were well off; Angolos had casually revealed that he had a yacht, which was presently being refitted.

From the air she had been able to see that the estate, located on a peninsula, covered acres and acres. The main house itself and the gorgeously landscaped grounds with their tennis courts and pools were palatial, and the setting beside the sea was totally stunning.

'Not disappointed, are you?' Angolos had teased.

'It's all incredible.' *So was a museum.*

Georgie, who had been brought up in a standard 1930s semi-detached house, was actually daunted by the sheer scale of everything. She had thought there might be a housekeeper or some help in the garden, but to discover there was an army of live-in domestic help to run the place came as a nasty shock.

This wasn't the sort of house where you nipped down to the kitchen to make yourself a sandwich in the middle of the night. She seriously doubted that Angolos knew where the kitchens were!

Within ten seconds she knew that she wasn't going to acclimatise to her new life overnight. It was going to be a steep learning curve, but she reasoned if she had Angolos there to help her she would be all right. She didn't know at the time that he wouldn't be…that his work would occupy most of his waking moments.

She walked around the place making the right admiring noises, but she couldn't imagine ever thinking of this place as home. And on top of that there was his family, who had been there in force when she'd arrived.

'Sorry about tonight,' Angolos said when they lay in bed later that night. 'They wanted to inspect my new bride, and who,' he suggested throatily, 'can blame them?'

'I don't think they were very impressed.'

'Don't be silly. They'll love you…why wouldn't they?'

Angolos impatiently dismissed her concerns. 'You just need to relax a little.'

'You don't think I was relaxed… Did I come over as—?'

He laid a finger against her lips. 'Forget about my family; it doesn't matter what they think. They'll be gone tomorrow.'

She breathed a sigh of relief. Angolos seemed different in this environment, but she was sure that once they were alone everything would be all right. She couldn't wait.

'Good…that is, I'm sure they're very nice, but there was an awful lot of them.' There was no way she was going to remember the names of all those aunts and uncles and cousins. As Angolos was kissing his way up her neck she was hard-pressed to remember her own name.

'I really don't want to talk about relatives,' he said, pausing halfway up.

'Me neither,' she admitted huskily as he peeled off her transparent nightgown to reveal glowing skin.

'*Theos*, but you are beautiful.'

His words drove everything else from Georgie's mind. She melted.

The sex was spectacular, but the problem was still there the next day in the shape of his mother and sister. They were still there at lunch-time.

Short of packing their bags for them, what could she do?

As she walked out to the helicopter pad with Angolos, who had explained he had to go into the office, she took the opportunity to casually enquire, 'When are your mother and sister going home?'

Angolos threw some instruction to his assistant, a polite, nice-looking young man who was distantly related. As the younger man hurried ahead Angolos directed a puzzled frown at Georgie's face.

'*Home…?*' He shook his head. 'I don't follow.'

'I was wondering when your mother and Sacha were going back home.'

He threw back his head and laughed. 'They are home, *yineka mou*, didn't I say? They live here.'

Somehow the strained smile stayed glued to her face. 'No, you didn't say.' The realisation that they would be sharing a home with his family made her spirits plummet. It had taken about five minutes for her to realise that she and her mother-in-law were never going to be pals, and that her sister-in-law, whom Georgie considered horribly indulged, looked down her aristocratic little nose at her.

'Mother will be a big help while you're settling in, and Sacha is your age—you're bound to have a lot in common.'

Georgie, who seriously doubted either of these claims, responded to the kiss he planted on her lips with less enthusiasm than previously.

'Are you all right?'

Georgie, a big fan of telling it as it was, heard herself lie. 'Terrific…just a bit tired.'

That was the first time she concealed her feelings from him, but not the last time. She even got quite good at it though her acting talents were stretched to the limit when he dropped one particular bombshell on her.

Angolos went to Paris, this time on business and without her. 'I'd love for you to come with me, of course I would, but this is business. You do understand…?'

On his return he casually mentioned, in a 'you'll never guess who I bumped into' sort of way, that he had had dinner with his ex-wife while there.

Georgie, who had already been force-fed a daily dose of Sonia-worship by her in-laws, wanted to scream, but instead she smiled and said quietly, 'How nice.'

The following month he announced he had invited Sonia up for the weekend. That his ex arrived late seemed to be taken for granted. Georgie could have accommodated her tardiness, but she could never forgive their guest for being poised, self-assured and, it went without saying, drop-dead gorgeous. In fact she had all the qualities necessary to be Angolos's wife—heck, she even still had her ring; she'd just swapped fingers!

In other words she was everything Georgie longed to be and wasn't.

She was also very tactile, always touching and stroking. Georgie was forced to watch as she stroked Angolos's arm or ran her fingers over his lean cheek. It seemed to Georgie that every time she walked into a room they were there, laughing in a corner, sharing their jokes and their secrets. Feeling totally alienated, she retreated into her shell.

'You never struck me as sentimental.'

She turned her head towards Angolos and smiled. Unexpectedly recalling the traumatic events made her realise just how much she had changed in the intervening years. It was quite an empowering experience to realise that if she found herself in that situation today she would not creep away to feel slighted and sorry for herself in the corner.

No, she would tell the other woman to lay off. She would confront Angolos—at best his behaviour was insensitive, at worst he still had feelings for his ex. She would demand he decided whom he wanted, because she wasn't playing second fiddle to anyone!

'I was being ironic. The watch—' she glanced at her wrist '—is a good investment, much more likely to rise in value than money in the bank, or so I was told.' By her dad when he'd returned the watch, having taken it to be valued without her knowledge.

'You had it valued?'

She nodded; her father had been shocked that she'd been walking around wearing something that was, as he'd put it, 'worth as much as a two-bedroomed house', without any insurance.

'My finances were tight.'

'You seem to have a more practical attitude to money than you once did.'

'Practical?' She thought about the wild flowers, carefully pressed and preserved alongside other treasures in the velvet-lined box. Angolos had picked them for her the first time they'd walked through the sand dunes. 'I'm working on it. But I don't think I'll ever care about money for its own sake and I don't put a price on things the way you do.'

'Not even your virginity?'

Heat flooded her face as her furious flashing eyes flew to his face. 'Don't you dare make out I held out to make you marry me!' she snapped. 'You always put a higher value on that than I did,' she reminded him. 'You could have had it for nothing, Angolos—you didn't have to marry me.'

In the long simmering silence their eyes locked. His chest lifted as he expelled a long sibilant sigh.

'I know.' She would never know what it had cost him not to accept what she had been so anxious to give him.

'Then why…?'

He pressed his fingers to the groove above his masterful nose and scanned the stretch of beach. It was empty but for a few people walking dogs.

'Why did you marry me, Angolos?'

'Do you want to walk?'

She released a hiss of frustration through clenched teeth. 'You've no intention of telling me, have you?'

The disturbing smile that played around the corners of his sensual lips neither confirmed nor denied her husky accusation. 'Walk…?'

'Walk?' In contrast to the restive energy that Angolos was projecting, she felt utterly drained.

'You know—put one foot in front of the other.'

It really ought to be that simple, but her shaking knees didn't have the strength or co-ordination to move her from the spot. 'You're impossible,' she accused.

'But cute?' he suggested.

She only just stopped herself responding to his smile. 'I never thought I'd hear you say "cute".'

'Is that a yes?'

'No.'

One winged dark brow arched. 'No to cute or a walk?'

'Both.' She sat down rather hurriedly.

'As you wish.'

Angolos followed suit but with less haste and considerably more grace. As she tucked her knees under herself and arranged her skirt around her legs Georgie was aware of his dark eyes watching her. She was aware of just about everything about him, including the warm male scent that made her oversensitive nostrils twitch.

'Don't try and charm me, Angolos. I've got immunity. Anyway, you've no need to butter me up. Like I said, I already know what this is about.'

Her head lifted, their eyes connected. Angolos's expression was wary; it cost her a supreme effort to smile. 'Don't worry, I'm not going to make a fuss, if that's what you're worried about.'

Angolos looked at the envelope she handed him but made no effort to take it.

'I think I've signed all the places I need to.'

He still didn't react, just carried on looking at it with a total lack of recognition in his eyes.

'For heaven's sake.' She leant across and deposited it in his lap. 'I found it, it must have fallen out of your pocket. Did you think you'd lost it?'

He took the envelope and turned it over in his hand cautiously as though he expected it to burst into flames. Georgie found his manner bewildering.

'*Dios*, I had totally forgotten about this.' After his meeting with Paul he had contacted his lawyer. The papers were already prepared; they had been for two years.

'How long will it take to be…final? The d…divorce.'

CHAPTER EIGHT

ANGOLOS'S glance lifted to Georgie's face. There was a strange look in his deep-set eyes that she couldn't interpret. *'Never!'*

The forcefulness of his explosive retort made her stare at him in confusion. 'I don't understand.'

'Then understand this.' Georgie gave a grunt of shock as he began to tear the envelope into pieces with slow, deliberate thoroughness before tossing them up into the air.

She watched in open-mouthed astonishment as the fragments went flying down the beach in several directions, drifting like confetti on the air currents.

'Have you gone mad?' She turned her astounded eyes on him. 'Why make the effort to bring that here personally and then do that?'

'I never intended...'

'Never intended what?' she prompted.

His jaw tightened. 'We're not getting divorced.'

She pressed her hands to her head, the dull throb in her temples had turned into a blinding headache. 'But you came here to...and I *want* to get divorced!' she added on a note of escalating misery.

'Too bad.'

'*You* want to get divorced.' The squally sea breeze suddenly caught her skirt and lifted it. It took her several moments to smooth it back down, and when she looked up she saw something in his eyes that made her sensitive stomach flip.

'You saw Paul at his surgery.'

Georgie didn't want to talk about Paul. 'So that's how you knew we were here.'

Angolos inclined his dark head.

'I know some people think strong and silent is attractive, but ask them how they feel about it after they've lived with strong and silent for a few weeks. I think you'd find they'd have changed their tune,' she predicted grimly. 'For goodness' sake, don't just look all brooding and beautiful—*say something*!'

His only response to her emotional outburst was a raised eyebrow—one of these days she would swing for this man.

'What would you like me to say?'

'I give up!' she declared. She slid an exasperated sideways glance at his lean, saturnine profile. 'What were you doing discussing me with Paul anyway?' she demanded crossly. 'He has no right to discuss me; there's such a thing as patient confidentiality.'

Angolos dismissed her complaint with an impatient motion of his hand. 'I'm your husband.'

'On paper.' Paper that was even now blowing across the ocean...her divorce would probably end up in Normandy. 'And even if we were together, that doesn't give you a right to know my medical details.'

'He didn't divulge any private details, medical or otherwise,' Angolos cut in impatiently. 'He told me I have a son.'

She dug her toe into the sand and vented an ironic laugh. 'That was news...?'

'To me it was.'

'How can you say that?'

He ignored her exasperated exclamation. 'Now I know that Nicky is mine, obviously things must change.'

Her eyes narrowed. 'Two words I'm not liking there... "must" and "change".'

'Don't be obtuse, Georgette. You know where I'm going with this.'

She shook her head. 'Not a clue.'

'Then I'll spell it out: we will be a family.'

The bad feeling in her stomach coalesced into straightforward panic. 'I have all the family I need.' He wasn't…he just *couldn't* be suggesting what she thought he was!

'A family requires both parents. You and Nicky will come back to Greece with me and we will be a family.'

A hoarse laugh was drawn from Georgie's aching throat. 'And to think I used to be intimidated by your vast intellect. You know, mostly I was scared stiff of giving an opinion in case you laughed at me.'

Angolos looked so appalled by this confidence that under less fraught circumstances she might have laughed.

'But now I know that you may be clever, but you're also stark staring crazy. *Me live with you again…?* The only way you'll get me back to Greece is in a strait-jacket.'

'You're speaking emotionally without considering—'

'I don't need to consider anything. I recognise insanity when I hear it.'

Until he captured her wrists in his she wasn't aware that she had been tugging at her own hair. 'Calm down. You're overreacting.'

He acknowledged her snarling, *'shut up!'* with an infuriatingly tolerant smile.

'Once you've thought about it—' he continued talking across her demand to be *let go!* '—I think you'll come to appreciate that this is the right thing to do. Sometimes being a parent involves sacrifice.'

He really was incredible. *'You're* telling *me* that? Know a lot about being a parent, do you? Gosh, share your wisdom, I'm all ears,' she begged.

Her sarcasm drew a soft expletive from his lips. 'You are—' A dark line appeared across the slashing curve of his cheekbones as he swallowed the rest of his furious retort. 'You can mock as much as you like.' The fingers encircling her wrists tightened and then, much to her intense relief, fell away completely.

'Thanks, but I don't need your permission.'

'But,' he continued as though she hadn't spoken, 'it doesn't alter the fact that a child needs both parents.'

'I can tell you from personal experience that you can get by perfectly well with one.'

'You have your stepmother.'

Her brows lifted. 'And who's to say that at some future date Nicky won't have a stepfather…?'

There was a short, stark silence, during which the muscles in Angolos's brown throat rippled convulsively. Then, capturing her defiant eyes, he smiled and lifted his dark head to an imperious angle. 'I am to say,' he responded simply.

The scornful retort died on her lips as she encountered the chilling determination in his unblinking eyes.

'So now you're going to vet my boyfriends, are you? I'd be interested in how that works.'

'This isn't about you. This is about what is best for our son.'

More absurd than him trying to make her feel guilty and selfish was the fact she actually did! 'I've been doing the best for our son for the past three years. What have you been doing for him? On second thoughts, you staying out of his life probably was the biggest favour you could do him.'

He visibly paled in response to her vitriolic attack, but didn't attempt to defend himself. 'I can understand your anger.'

'I doubt that, I really doubt that,' she gritted. 'And besides, I don't want your understanding.' What did she want from him? Was she going to be happier if he walked away? She fixed him with a resentful glare. 'I wish you'd never come.'

'Has it occurred to you that you are denying him his heritage?'

This change of tack increased her growing sense of unease.

'You're the one who denied him that. Besides, Nicky is perfectly happy where he is.'

'He doesn't even speak his own language.'

'His language is English.' She winced to hear both the defensiveness and doubt in her voice.

'Nicky is half Greek. He will only have to look in the mirror to see that.'

'I'm not trying to hide his heritage from him.'

'Aren't you?'

'No, I'm not. I would never lie to my son.'

'*Our* son.'

Gritting her teeth, Georgie refused to respond to the correction.

'He will know when he goes to school that he does not look like the fair-skinned children in his class. What will you say when he asks you why he is different?'

'You obviously know very little about the ethnic mix in most schools, if you think that Nicky will stand out. Have you never heard of a multicultural society?'

One dark brow angled. 'So what will you do when he asks about me?'

'I…I haven't thought about it.'

'Don't you think it's about time you did?'

She lifted her resentful eyes to his. 'Nicky's happy,' she contended stubbornly.

Angolos studied her face. 'You know I'm right, don't you, Georgette?' Before she had a chance to deny his assertion he added, 'And I can see that Nicky is happy.'

Her hopes rose, only to be dashed.

'However, I will not permit my son to be brought up not knowing who his father is…thinking that he is unwanted…' He swallowed hard, the muscles of his throat contracting as he visibly struggled to control his feelings. 'The boy is being brought up surrounded by women…'

'And what's wrong with women?'

His face relaxed briefly into a slow smile. 'I like women...'

'Tell me something I don't know.' And they liked him. Everywhere they had gone together women's eyes had followed him—that he had seemed for the most part oblivious to the fact had been no comfort to her at the time.

'But a boy needs a male role model?'

Feeling increasingly on the defensive because of his uncomfortable ability to come up with a reply for everything she said, Georgie set her chin on her steepled fingers. 'There are plenty of men in Nicky's life.'

The fire in his dark eyes provided a stark contrast to the icy expression of austere disdain that spread across his lean face.

'I have no wish to be regaled with your romantic adventures. Nicky does not need *men* in the plural...'

The criticism struck her as the height of hypocrisy. 'I'm not the one who has trouble forming stable relationships... And who did you have in mind as a role model?' Her feathery brows lifted. 'You? Don't make me laugh,' she pleaded with contempt.

Angolos's expression was glacial as he responded. 'You have someone you consider more suitable in mind?'

Her chin lifted. 'And if I do?' she challenged pugnaciously.

'If you do, Georgette, I would advise you not to pursue that very dangerous course.'

Her chest swelled with outrage. 'Is that a threat?'

His silky smile sent a shiver down her rigid spine, but it was the fluttery sensation low in her stomach that sent her several steps closer to outright panic.

'Threats are for wimps.'

A hissing sound of disgust issued from her pursed lips. 'That is *exactly* the sort of macho posturing I don't want my son exposed to.'

'*Our* son.'

Their combative stares locked and the seconds ticked by. Georgie was the first to break the lengthening silence.

'You can't just walk back into my life this way, Angolos...' She turned away, her face scrunched up in anguish as the fight drained from her body. 'It's not fair.'

'Only children expect life to be fair.' The unexpected note of sympathy in his voice brought a lump to her aching throat.

'It rather depends on their experience.' Her lips curved upwards, but there was no smile in her eyes as she added, 'You forget that my mother walked out when I was a baby.'

'No, I remember.' He dragged a hand through his hair. 'Your grandmother will be pleased to see us reunited.'

'Don't talk like it's a done deal, Angolos,' she warned, managing a weak smile at his irony.

'But you agree that a stable family environment is the best place to bring up a child.'

'Of course I do; I'm not stupid.' Georgie forced her clenched fists to relax. 'I need time to think. This is just too much...too soon...'

'We were good together...you must remember...'

Her eyes flew wide open as anger surged through her body—other things surged too, but she concentrated hard on the anger.

'So *good*, in fact, that you threw me out.'

Unable to hold her accusing gaze, Angolos brought his dark lashes down in a concealing screen. 'I am not proud...'

'I don't much care about your precious pride or regret or anything else!' she declared hotly. 'The fact is you rejected our baby... So you want to be a family now—' her slender shoulders lifted '—big deal! Next year or next week even you'll probably have changed your mind again. Do you think I'd put my future and that of my son in the hands of someone so...who can't make up his mind what he wants?'

'I know exactly what I want.'

His low, throaty declaration sent a jolt of sharp sexua

awareness through her body. 'Yes, you want your own way,' she contended without looking at him. Looking at him would be a *very* bad idea just now.

'I want us to be a family and I think you do too.'

She angled a narrow-eyed look at his face. 'That was what I thought we were four years ago. Give me one reason why I should ever believe what you say to me? You've never even told me why! All I got was a shrug and a sneer and c…coldness.' She stopped and bit her lip to control the quiver in her voice.

'All I want to know is *why*…'

'Well, for starters, I knew that you were sleeping with someone else.'

A long throbbing silence developed.

'Not *that* again,' she said wearily. 'Not even *you* are that stupid. Sure…sure I had a string of lovers.'

The expression she saw cross his face suggested this wasn't the response he had been expecting. 'I had proof.'

'*That* I would really like to see.'

'You've got nerve, I'll give you that,' he gritted back. 'But you were not as careful as you thought.'

'Come on, Angolos, I'm not listening unless you tell me the real reason you rejected Nicky.'

His beautiful mouth twisted as their eyes touched. 'I was prepared…I actually thought we might be able to get beyond your infidelity,' he recalled. 'I blamed myself for leaving you alone.'

'You were going to forgive me!' This got even more implausible. 'If you seriously thought there was another man you would have torn him limb from limb,' she contended.

He gave an odd, twisted smile. 'You'd have thought so, wouldn't you?'

'So what's the *real* reason?'

Above the sound of the waves crashing softly on the sand

she heard his white teeth grating. 'Be honest,' she recommended.

'*Me*, honest?'

'A baby didn't fit in with your life then, did it?' she claimed, ignoring his raw interjection. 'I don't know what's changed, but now you've suddenly decided—'

He pressed his hand to his mouth and shook his dark head. '*Theos!*' he thundered, eyeing her with frustrated incredulity. His chest rose and fell in tune to his rapid, uneven respirations. 'I knew I couldn't have children.'

CHAPTER NINE

THE only sound to disturb the silence that followed Angolos's driven declaration was the cracking noise as he clenched his long fingers and the audible hiss of his laboured breathing.

'Not have children…?' Georgie shot a sideways look at his taut profile. 'You're not making any sense.'

'I was told that I couldn't have children.'

She just stared at him, hearing, but not able to digest what he had said.

'Do you understand what I'm saying?'

She pressed her fingers to her temples and shook her head. 'No.'

'Evidently I was wrong.'

'But it's silly—you couldn't…' Angolos was so rampantly male he couldn't be… She shook her head positively and without thinking her eyes dropped down his body. 'You're—'

'I am functional,' he cut in. 'You're confusing sterility with impotence.'

Flushing to the roots of her hair at his sardonic intervention, she jerked her eyes back to his face.

'I just didn't think I was capable of fathering a child.'

'But we'd only been together a few weeks. You couldn't know that unless—' *Unless he had already tried to have a baby.* With someone else. With Sonia. The colour suddenly leached dramatically from her lightly tanned skin. 'Oh,' she said swallowing. 'I see.'

So now she had the answer to the question that had puzzled many people at the time. Namely, why should a couple so supremely well suited as Sonia and Angolos get divorced?

This new revelation provided the answer, and Georgie could see how it could have happened. They had desperately wanted a family, and Sonia hadn't got pregnant.

It wouldn't be the first time the strain of that sort of situation had split up a marriage.

She could see it all: Sonia had thrown herself into a mad social whirl, and Angolos had buried himself in his work. They wouldn't have talked, of course…as she knew to her cost Angolos didn't talk.

You had only to witness Sonia and Angolos together to see that they still had feelings for one another. And Georgie had witnessed them together. She hadn't had much choice when the woman had been their house guest barely weeks after they had married.

'So when I said I was pregnant…some men might have thought it was a miracle, but you thought that I…'

Some men hadn't had a letter written by their wife's lover in their possession. Even after all these years the humiliation of that discovery was still with him. 'I suppose some men might, but that is all in the past, now I know…'

'And now you know you can have children.'

Right result, wrong mother.

Was that what he had thought when he realised…? Had he wondered why this couldn't have happened while he was with Sonia?

Georgie pressed the heel of one hand to the centre of her chest where misery had lodged like a solid object behind her breastbone. Would the pain ever go away…?

'Yes, now I know I have a child. I have Nicky, and I want to be his father.'

A furrow appeared in her smooth brow. 'No.' She wouldn't deprive Nicky of his father, but how could she survive with Angolos as part of her life? If she had ever kidded herself she weren't as madly in love with him as ever, she recognised now that this convenient self-delusion was no longer an option.

He slid her a burning look of impatience. 'What do you mean, no?'

'I mean…I don't know what I mean.' She shook her head. 'No, this can't be right. We talked about having a family…we planned…' She stopped and realised that they hadn't talked; *she* had talked. Her stomach lurched sickly as the implications of his confession hit her. 'You knew about this when we got married?'

'I did.'

'And you didn't tell me—you let me think…'

Angolos watched the colour drain from her face; the sprinkling of freckles across her nose stood out against the marble pallor. 'You *can't* love them,' she had always said when he had told her he loved those freckles.

'You let me talk about babies when all along…' A shudder ran through her body as she turned her tearful, accusing eyes to his face. 'Why didn't you tell me? You let me carry on thinking…'

'It was an omission, and I was wrong.' A man with an ounce of integrity would have given her the opportunity to make an informed decision.

In his own defence he had fully planned to tell her before the wedding. He had lost count of the number of times that he had started to tell her only to pull back at the last moment.

He had rationalised it, of course, told himself that she was marrying *him*… After all, her inability to give him a child wouldn't have altered his feelings.

Feelings were the core of the problem…

She had lit up when he'd walked into a room; she had shaken when he'd touched her. Angolos had known full well that she had been infatuated with him. Young and infatuated, but *love*…? Had he dared put it to the test?

'I'm sorry, Angolos.'

His startled eyes flew to her face.

Georgie was pale but composed. As he watched she pushed the hair back from her face with her forearm. It was an intensely weary gesture. The urge to reach out and take her in his arms was so strong that for a moment he couldn't drag air into his lungs.

'What are you sorry for, *yineka mou*?'

'Well, it must have been incredibly hard for someone like you to be told that you couldn't father children.'

'Someone like me…?'

She nodded and as she lifted her eyes to his she caught the strangest expression crossing his face. 'Well, any man, then,' she moderated, tactfully not touching on his overdeveloped male pride. 'When they told you…' Her voice faded as she imagined him sitting in a clinical white office having the shattering news broken to him by an unsympathetic doctor. 'You must have felt like someone had kicked you in…' Her glance dropped and dark, fiery colour rose up her neck until her face was glowing. 'Sorry, that wasn't—'

'You're right, that's exactly how I felt,' Angolos cut in, taking pity on her.

'And I don't expect you discussed it with anyone.'

His smile faded. 'It is not the sort of thing a man discusses.'

His stiff pronouncement was exactly what she had been talking about. 'Point proven. You're really into all this macho stuff in a big way. There's no good denying it,' she added. 'And I know you can't help it. I'm just sorry,' she admitted with sigh, 'that you didn't feel able to confide in me, but then that was always the problem, wasn't it?

'You never treated me like an adult capable of making my own decisions. You always kept me out of the loop. Ours was never an equal relationship,' she reflected, contemplating her neatly trimmed, unpolished nails with a wistful expression that unknown to her had a more dramatic impact on Angolos than the kick she had previously so accurately described.

His expression had grown increasingly shocked as he listened to her matter-of-fact analysis of their relationship. By the time she finished he had the stunned aspect of someone who had just been hit by a runaway truck.

'I never expected you to take it this way.'

'Well, I'm not saying I would have been happy about it. I desperately wanted to have your baby.' She looked up and surprised a stricken expression on his lean face that cut her to the core. 'But it wouldn't have changed anything, not essentially,' she added firmly.

'You think not?'

His scepticism annoyed her. 'Yes, I do. We could have adopted...' Her face brightened. 'There are a lot of babies out there who need a home,' she told him earnestly.

'It would seem,' he said slowly, 'that I underestimated you.'

'When were you going to tell me?'

'I honestly don't know,' he admitted.

Truth be told, he had been willing to ignore every precept of decency that had been instilled in him all his life in order to marry a woman he hadn't even believed loved him, and now it seemed that woman's feelings had been deeper and less selfish than his own.

And he had blown it big time.

'At the moment our feelings for each other are not important,' he began in a voice totally devoid of emotion.

She pulled herself onto her knees and brushed the sand from her skirt with slow, deliberate strokes. 'Neither are they any mystery,' she said dully. To her way of thinking, if he had ever felt a shred of true feeling for her, he would never have sent her away.

She experienced a sudden swell of emotion. After everything he had done she still loved him and would continue to love him to her dying breath. The injustice of it all hit her.

Why should he not know what he had done to her? Why should she spare him?

'Do you want to know how I feel about you?'

A muscle along Angolos's taut jaw clenched. 'We will discuss your feelings for me at a more appropriate moment, when you are less emotional.'

'Which, roughly translated, means when you say so—no change there, then.'

The muscle clenching in his lean cheek reminded her of a ticking time bomb. Georgie supposed she *ought* to be grateful that his response had spared her from making a total fool of herself. All the same she couldn't help but think that it would be an enormous relief to get it all out into the open.

'Our son's future is what we must decide.'

'Nothing to decide.' Externally at least she maintained the appearance of control.

Actually his comment had terrified her. If there was one thing she had learnt from her short time with the Constantine clan, it was not to underestimate the power of money! Angolos might never get custody of Nicky—access was another story—but he could tear her life to shreds while he was trying.

'I beg to differ.'

'You never beg,' she cut back bitterly. 'You had your chance to be a father, Angolos, and you blew it. And look at it this way—there's nothing to stop you going out there and making babies with someone else.'

Her comment brought a gleam of pure fury to his eyes. 'You think I'm going to leave it like this?'

Her slender shoulders lifted. 'Why not?'

'I don't want babies, I want…Nicky.'

She drew her knees up to her chest and rested her chin on them. 'You don't always get what you want, Angolos.'

'Wake up, Georgette,' he recommended harshly. 'This is the real world.'

'No, your world isn't my reality. My world doesn't have designer dresses and glitzy first nights, or people who judge you by how much money you have and who your parents are!' she declared hotly. 'My reality is making ends meet, a good day at work, a parking space in the high street, scraped knees, temper tantrums and doctor's appointments.' She stopped to catch her breath. The incoherent inventory of her life made it sound less attractive than it actually was.

'All I'm asking for is a chance to be part of that world.'

It would seem Angolos hadn't picked up on the unattractive part.

Taken aback by the intensity of his unexpected request, she stared at him warily. Perhaps I should have added sleepless nights and guilt. Guilt was a major part of parenting that all the literature skimmed over.

'This isn't a glamorous world we are talking here.'

'*Glamour!*' He dismissed it with a contemptuous click of his long fingers. 'If anyone was seduced by the so-called glamour of my world, it was you,' he contended.

Her eyes widened in protest. 'That's a stupid thing to say.'

'Wasn't the fact I came from a different world than you part of the attraction?' he challenged. 'You put me on a pedestal!' he accused. 'And I exploited it.'

'I didn't feel exploited.' She didn't like the idea his comment created that she'd been some sort of victim walking blindly to her fate.

'The moments from our time together that remain clearly in my mind are not the lavish parties or dinners.'

'What are they, then?' She was probably going to regret asking, but if she didn't the question would plague her for the rest of her life.

'That picnic we had sitting cross-legged on the bedroom floor…'

Georgie's eyes widened. It had been the one time when she had dared the wrath of the kitchen staff and made a personal request. When asked what sort of wine she'd wanted with her fish-paste sandwiches she had said any old thing would do…white and fizzy maybe…?

The horror etched on the face of the chef had been comical.

Of course the sandwiches had been smoked salmon, the wine had been champagne, and the cutlery Georgian silver, but she hadn't quibbled. Instead she had pronounced herself delighted, and thanked the staff warmly.

'You remember that?' she asked, astonished.

'Of course I damn well remember. I also remember what followed it—more so…' He studied her unblinkingly through eyes that contained an explicitly sexual message.

It was a message that Georgie received. The pupils of her eyes dilated dramatically until they almost swallowed up the amber. Breathing fast and shallow, she traced the outline of her dry lips with the tip of her tongue and drew a long shuddering breath. Her hand came up in a fluttery gesture and then fell away again, leaving her fingers trailing in the sand.

'*Do you…?*'

'You know I do.' She screwed up her eyes and tried to ignore the slick heat between her thighs. 'We had some good times,' she admitted huskily.

'A bit better than *good*.'

He was right. Good was safe and comfortable; what they had enjoyed had been neither. 'Think about it, Angolos,' she appealed to him. The glint in his eyes suggested he wasn't in the mood for thinking. 'Nothing has changed, not essentially. You came here to get a divorce.'

This did get his attention.

'I came here to find out the truth,' he rebutted.

'And I bet you wish you hadn't found it.'

'Wishes do not enter into it,' he told her, his voice low and controlled. 'I have a son… *Dios mio*!' he gasped, no longer the least bit controlled. His blazing eyes locked with hers. 'My life has changed profoundly. If you imagine even for one second that I would prefer to live in ignorance you are insane. I have a son. I may be slow but I do recognise a miracle when I see one.'

'You can have more children. Like I said, go and have a baby with someone else,' she recommended, fixing him with a belligerent glare. 'That's what you really want,' she contended. 'Nicky already has a family.'

She knew enough Greek to recognise that the low, impassioned flood that issued from his lips would have been severely censored by even the most liberal of censors. 'You think a solution would be for me to go away and impregnate another woman?'

'Frankly I'm amazed you haven't already. Or,' she added with a sneer, 'have you been waiting to be officially single?'

His nostrils flared as he scanned her face with distaste. 'Yes.'

In the act of brushing a wayward strand of hair from her face, Georgie froze. All expression was wiped from her face. 'I take it that is some kind of joke.'

'Actually, no, it isn't. I take the matrimonial vows quite seriously.'

'Oh, really? Your vows mentioned a bit of cherishing, and I seem to recall when you chucked me out there wasn't much cherishing involved. Don't feel bad about it,' she said. 'Some good came out of it. I have to admit, after not having a say in my own life it came as quite a shock being alone. But I know how to stand on my own feet now.'

Quivering with hurt and fury, she proved the point by standing up in one graceful motion.

The anger in his face was replaced by a grim frustration as he looked at her. Georgie was weeping uncontrollably. There was no resistance in her slim body as he gathered her into his arms.

'Things will be fine now.'

Georgie, who didn't feel as if anything would ever be fine, lifted her head. 'How do you figure that?'

He took her chin in his fingers. 'Look at me, *yineka mou*.'

'I don't have much choice, do I?' she returned with a sniff.

'I will learn to be a halfway decent husband.'

His dark eyes lingered on her face and Georgie shifted uneasily. The movement resulted in one of his heavily muscled thighs becoming wedged between her legs. Painfully aware of the lean, hard length of the body so close to her own, she shivered.

'You're serious, aren't you?' It occurred to her that from a distance they would look to passers-by like lovers embracing.

'Deadly serious.' His thumb moved to the full curve of her lush lower lip. Georgie swayed, nailed to the spot by a wave of intense longing.

'This isn't fair,' she whispered.

'I love your mouth. I always did…'

Georgie swallowed hard. 'I don't think my mouth is relevant to this conversation.'

His restless glance continued to move hungrily over her soft features. 'At night I think about your sweet lips on my body and I ache. I ache for you.'

He thought about…he ached for her…! And she ached for him too.

She felt his warm breath touch her sensitive earlobe and sighed, fast losing the fight against the raw urgency that coursed through her pliant body.

Angolos must have sensed her surrender because she could hear the male triumph in his voice as he promised, 'It will be even better than it was when we are together…'

She turned her head and their lips were almost touching when his comment penetrated. With a cry of disgust she pulled away, breathing hard. 'You are such a control freak!' she accused, backing away with her hand pressed to her throat. Her skin felt hot and sticky. 'Well, your tactics won't work this time.'

'Firstly, it wasn't a tactic.'

She focused on his face and saw that there was a damp sheen to his olive-toned skin that made it glisten; the heat in his eyes was fading, leaving a raw frustration in its place.

She decided not to ask what it was. 'And second?'

'Second, it almost worked. Can't you accept that I just want you, and for that matter you want me? It was not part of some sinister plan. I would not take your compliance to mean you'll come back to me. And it's not as though I was about to drag you down onto the sand. It was just a kiss…' His attention shifted to her mouth. '*Almost* a kiss.'

The husky afterthought made her stomach muscles quiver frantically.

Her hands clenched at her sides. '*Angolos…*'

Against all the odds he responded to the anguished appeal in her voice. 'Fine, you want to concentrate on the practical— have you considered the financial aspect of this?'

'What do you mean, ''financial''?'

'My son will one day inherit all that I have.'

Her eyes widened; Angolos had a lot! 'I hadn't thought about that…'

'He will be an extremely wealthy man,' he slotted in quietly. 'But he will also inherit responsibilities,' he continued in a matter-of-fact way. 'Wealth and power can be the ruin of some people…I've seen it happen. Nicky will need guidance…not heavy-handed, but loving, parental guidance.'

A stark silence followed his comments.

'You've given me a lot to think about,' she admitted. They were very powerful arguments and she couldn't pretend otherwise.

'Then go away and think…until tomorrow.'

'Tomorrow?' She shook her head. 'That's not long enough,'

she protested. 'I couldn't possibly come to such a major decision so quickly.'

'I'm bending over backwards to be reasonable here, Georgette, but don't push it. Tomorrow.'

Reluctantly she shook her head. 'I should be getting back; Ruth is looking after Nicky.'

'He's a beautiful child.'

Their eyes touched. 'He takes after you.' The moment the unthinking but heartfelt words were out of her mouth she wished she could retract them.

'Georgette, you'll make me blush,' he teased, revealing a set of perfect white teeth as he laughed out loud at her visible discomfiture.

'I'm not telling you anything you don't already know,' she retorted, with as much dignity as she could muster. She had touched his perfection on more than one occasion. Thinking about just how unstinting she had been with her praise made her cringe with embarrassment.

Though, in his favour, for a man who had been endowed with such incredible good looks he really wasn't vain. In fact she had more than once seen him irritated by the attention he got, though mostly he tuned out strangers who gawped.

'Shall I call at the house tomorrow?'

She shook her head. 'Best not.' Tomorrow Dad and Mary were driving Gran back up. 'By the church, about one…'

'I'll be waiting.'

CHAPTER TEN

ACTUALLY he wasn't waiting, she was.

When Georgie arrived there was no sign of Angolos. She might have followed her first cowardly impulse and left if she hadn't known that he would come looking for her.

With a sigh she walked through the gate into the small churchyard. Thoughts far away, she began to wander down the interwoven stone paths past the moss-covered gravestones. Georgie had never found this place at all gloomy, and had often remarked on the tranquil atmosphere.

She stopped, her eyes drawn to a lichen-covered memorial. The weathered inscription in the stone revealed the woman born over three hundred years earlier had had a long life. Georgie's curiosity stirred; had she been happy, this woman born into another century?

There were several wars, an industrial revolution and a sexual revolution separating her from this woman. Her own life was light years away from the one this woman had lived, yet the essentials, the things deep down most people wanted, weren't.

To love and be loved.

'Were you loved…?' Georgie squinted at the worn letters. 'Were you loved, Agnes?' she whispered softly.

If anyone had heard her they would have concluded she was crazy, and maybe, she reflected, they wouldn't be far wrong. She had thought she had been loved; she had discovered that she hadn't been in the cruellest way imaginable.

Georgie turned her back on the gravestone and wished her own past were so easily dismissed.

Eyes closed, she inhaled deeply. It had never crossed her

mind that Angolos wouldn't be as thrilled as she was about her pregnancy. Of course, she hadn't known then what she did now.

Georgie had planned the evening down to the last detail. She'd wanted everything to be perfect, but from the start nothing had gone right.

To begin with the party that Sacha and Olympia had been going to attend had been cancelled at the last minute, so the romantic meal she had planned had become a family affair. Georgie had wanted to scream with frustration, especially when Angolos hadn't turned up.

When he had arrived an hour later than he had promised, he'd seemed distracted and had even been terse with his mother, who had been unwise enough to remonstrate him on his tardiness. Georgie had caught him looking at her so strangely a couple of times that she'd started to think that he had guessed about the baby. That would have accounted for the suppressed tension emanating from him.

The meal had been a stiff, formal affair, but that hadn't been unusual, and had seemed to last for ever. When they had finally retreated to their own suite of rooms she hadn't known what to say. Suddenly her planned speech hadn't seemed right.

Angolos hadn't helped; he'd seemed strangely remote and unapproachable. She had noticed that he had drunk more at dinner than he generally did, and the fine lines bracketing his mouth had suggested he was under some strain.

'Did you have a bad day?' She laid a tentative hand on his arm.

His dark eyes immediately slewed in the direction of the fingers curled lightly over his arm. Though there was no discernible expression on his lean features, Georgie withdrew her hand awkwardly.

His mouth twisted. 'You could say that.'

Hurt and bewildered by the underlying hostility in his manner, she retreated to a chair beside the bed.

She watched as he removed his tie and fell backwards onto the bed. He lay for a moment spread-eagled with his eyes closed. Then from his prone position he began to unfasten the buttons of his shirt.

The action revealed the golden skin of lean-muscled torso and Georgie's breath snagged in her throat. He was simply stunningly beautiful.

He looked at her through heavy-lidded, half-closed eyes.

'You were quiet tonight,' he observed.

'Was I?' *What would he say when she told him?* She glanced wistfully towards the open double doors that led out to the balcony and adopted a coaxing tone. 'Why don't we sit outside? I love to look at the moonlight on the sea.' And what could be a more romantic spot to tell him her news?

'You sound like a tourist.' Before she had an opportunity to respond to his dismissive comment he added thickly, 'And anyway, I prefer to look at you. You look particularly glowing this evening.'

'Do I?'

'Yes.' His long fingers closed around her wrist. 'Tell me what you've been doing with yourself today. Have you missed me?'

Only every other second. 'I've been pretty busy, actually.' She had taken his recent hints about being more self-reliant to heart.

She didn't want to become a clingy wife. It had helped that Alan had come over and had been staying in the nearby village with his friend.

Georgie willingly responded to the gentle tug on her arm and fell in a happy heap beside him. She flipped over onto her tummy and, with her chin propped in her hands, smiled at him. He didn't smile back. 'Alan went home today.'

'How sad.'

'Don't be mean about him,' she begged.

'*Mean…?*'

'Well, you're—' She gasped as he turned her wrist over and pressed his lips to the pale-skinned inner aspect; she shivered as all the fine hairs on her body stood on end.

'Have I ever told you that you're the most beautiful man that ever drew breath?'

'Not recently.'

His husky velvet voice sent a shiver along her hopelessly sensitive nerve endings. 'I suppose I have been a bit moody lately,' she admitted. When he realised why, she hoped he would forgive her recent crankiness and mood swings. 'I didn't know why myself until today.'

'Are you going to let me in on the secret?'

'Soon,' she promised as with her best enigmatic smile she hitched up her long skirts to her waist and straddled his body.

'What are you doing?'

'I'm just doing,' she told him primly, 'what any dutiful wife would.' She frowned as she concentrated on slipping the remaining buttons of his shirt. Within seconds she had exposed all of his lean, hard torso. She ran her fingertips over the silky, hair-roughened surface and felt his stomach muscles contract. His skin was like oiled silk. She gave a voluptuous sigh of pleasure.

His hands tightened possessively over the smooth, bare skin of her thighs. 'What has brought this on?'

'Don't you like it?'

'Oh, I like it. I'm just wondering why you should decide to take the initiative tonight…'

Did that mean he found her unadventurous and boring in bed? The thought took the edge off her pleasure and dented her newly discovered confidence.

'Tonight's special.'

'I think you'll remember it.'

Georgie, rehearsing what she was going to say in her head,

barely registered his cryptic response. 'Angolos, I've got something to tell you.' She leaned forward, her eyes glowing with anticipation, her cheeks gently flushed. With a grunt of irritation she pinned the strands of her hair that brushed his face behind one ear. 'Sorry.'

'I like your hair on my skin. It feels…' He closed his eyes and muttered something angry in Greek under his breath.

'I think what I've got to say will cheer you up.'

Considering what had followed, that was probably the silliest comment she had ever made, Georgie reflected grimly.

'You're going to be a father, Angolos. I'm going to have a baby.'

His eyes stayed closed—she began to think he'd not heard her—then, dark, deep and impenetrable, they flickered open. *'Pregnant?'*

She nodded, and experienced the first stirrings of fear. Something was badly wrong, but she had no idea what… Perhaps he felt it was too soon, which didn't make sense because he was the one who had just shrugged when she had mentioned precautions…

'I know we weren't trying…and we didn't discuss it, but I thought you might be happy. You are happy?'

'Happy? I'm bloody delirious,' he contended grimly. 'Can't you tell, *yineka mou*?'

'I d…don't understand…' she stuttered.

Angolos rounded a corner in the lane and stopped. He could see her sitting on the wall, oblivious for the moment to his presence. He took the opportunity to study her undetected.

With her hair tied back in a pony-tail and her face innocent of make-up she looked more like a teenager than the mother of a child—*his* child. The idea still seemed strange to him. Strange as in bordering on miraculous, though he didn't expect Georgie to share his sense of wonder.

'You were far away.'

Georgie jumped at the sound of his voice. 'You're late.'

He didn't react to her shrill, accusatory tone. 'Have you come to a decision?'

'I have.' She had thought long and hard; she had thought until her brain felt as if it would explode.

One dark brow lifted. The casual observer, looking at his face, would have said her reply was in no way important to Angolos. But Georgie was not a casual observer; she knew that Angolos cared very badly about her reply.

'*And…?*' The muscle in his tense jaw continued to click steadily as he held her eyes.

Not into playing games, she replied immediately. 'I agree that I have no right to deny Nicky his heritage. I can protect him now, but I won't be able to always. I'll just have to teach him to look after himself. I think you'd be good at that, Angolos. So I will come to Greece with you, on trial basis.'

She saw the muscles of his shoulders relax. 'Thank you for that, Georgette. For my part I swear that I will do my best not to disappoint you.'

The palpable sincerity in his voice brought an emotional lump to her throat. 'I don't think you would, but you didn't let me finish. There are conditions.'

'Whatever you say,' he said immediately.

'Don't you think you ought to hear what they are first?' she asked him.

'Bring on your demands. It doesn't matter what they are. I will do anything it takes to develop a relationship with my son.'

'I understand that.'

One dark brow arched in sardonic enquiry as he scanned her face. 'But you have your doubts? You don't think it will work out?'

This drew a reluctant laugh from her. 'Only a couple of thousand.' Her expression sobered as she lifted her face to his; she could almost feel his impatience. 'It didn't work last time.' Feeling her control slipping, she turned and began to walk towards the church.

Angolos cursed softly under his breath as he fell into step beside her. 'The situation isn't the same.'

That much was true. Last time he had loved her, or professed to at least. This time there was no pretence that his feelings for her were what they once had been; this was all about wanting to be a father to his son.

'I know that, but everything else is. You...' She stopped and smiled at an elderly couple who walked past hand in hand.

'Lovely afternoon.'

'Marvellous,' she agreed.

'Why are the British obsessed with the weather?' Before she could defend the national obsession he added, 'Why are you determined to be negative about this?'

'I'm not being negative,' she protested. 'I'm being realistic. We're going back to the same house. You're the same man, your mother will still resent me.'

'My mother did not resent you!'

Georgie smiled and looked away. 'If you say so.'

'Perhaps you have left out the most significant obstacle.'

She paused and ran her fingers along the moss-covered wall beside the church gate. Her glance lifted to the tiny church with its square Norman tower. As a young girl she had spent many an afternoon imagining herself walking up the aisle here, and standing underneath the big horse chestnut having her picture taken in its shade.

The reality could not have been more different: an anonymous register office. Angolos had let it be known that he hadn't actually wanted a big wedding. 'Been there, done that...but, of course, if you want...?' he added.

'No, I hate big weddings,' she lied dutifully. 'It's the next twenty years that counts, not the day itself.'

He laughed at her earnestness and called her a hopeless romantic, but she was happy because she had pleased him.

With a sigh she rested her back against the wall now. 'And what is that?' She stretched out her hand and languidly watched the dappled light play across her skin.

'You're still the same person too.'

She shook her head, but didn't look at him. 'You're wrong, Angolos. I'm not the same person at all.'

'You mean you won't grow discontented this time.'

This time she did look up. *'Discontented…?'*

'You never made any effort to fit in.'

'Fit in!' she exclaimed in heated response to this monumentally unfair claim. 'Short of changing my identity, that was never going to happen.'

'What are you talking about?'

As if he didn't know.

'Tell me, Angolos,' she began with vibrating antagonism. 'How long had we been married before you began regretting it? A week…two…?' *Now* he was prepared to put his life on hold to be with their son; back then he hadn't even been able to free a weekend to spend time with her! If her friend Alan hadn't arrived she would have felt even lonelier.

'This,' he said heavily, 'is getting us nowhere.'

'Maybe someone is trying to tell us something,' she murmured as she levered herself up onto the wall.

'It's not exactly constructive raking up the past every five seconds.' Angolos's gaze moved from the small hands folded primly in her lap to her neatly crossed ankles and his jaw clenched.

'You look like a child,' he accused throatily.

She continued banging her heels against the stone as he set his hands against the uneven wall either side of her. But it was an uphill battle to continue to act as if her pulses weren't racing like crazy and she weren't painfully aware of the proximity of his warm male body.

'I'm not, and I've got the stretch marks to prove it.' Without thinking, she moved her hand to hover above the area low on her belly, where the silvery lines were a permanent reminder of her motherhood.

'I'm well aware you're not a child.' He exhaled a long shuddering breath that sucked in the muscles of his flat belly and expanded his impressive chest. He dragged a hand through his dark hair. 'I used to know your body as well as I knew my own.'

The accusing throaty addition brought her startled glance to his face. Their eyes meshed and her insides dissolved.

'The attraction is still there.'

'I don't know if Greece fell short of your expectations or I did? But it is my home and once,' he added, 'it was yours. I would like for my son to have the opportunity to learn to love it also.'

'It was never my home.' The sadness in her eyes was tinged with resentment. 'I was always a visitor and not a welcome one at that.' His mother, the daunting Olympia, had made sure of that.

'That's ludicrous. This melodrama isn't helping anyone,' he retorted impatiently.

Georgie didn't respond. She knew perfectly well that he would never believe that his family had loathed her; in front of him they had been sweetness and light.

'I don't want to share a home with your mother and sister.'

'Is that a fact?'

She could tell from his expression that he didn't take her seriously. She took a deep breath. If she was going to do this, she was going to do it on her terms. 'Let me rephrase that. I *won't* share a house with your mother and sister.'

Eyes narrowed, he scanned her face. 'You're serious?'

'Deadly serious.'

His expression changed. 'You expect me to throw my mother and sister from their home?'

Georgie could see he was totally outraged by her suggestion. 'They're hardly going to be homeless, are they?' His mother owned a palatial villa a few miles away and a town house in Athens and they were only the ones Georgie knew about! 'As for Sacha, if you let her stand on her own feet instead of fighting her battles…'

'She got married last year.'

'Oh, that's great.'

'They had a falling out and—'

'Let me guess—she came back home.'

Angolos's expression grew defensive. 'And why should she not?'

'Hasn't it ever occurred to you that she's never going to sort out her own problems while she knows you're always going to ride to the rescue when the going gets tough?'

His eyes narrowed. 'Do you dislike my family so much?'

She released an exasperated sigh. 'I don't dislike them at all,' she protested. 'They're not keen on me. Actually I think they'd dislike anyone who wasn't Sonia.'

'That's nonsense.'

She felt her anger mount at his dismissive attitude. 'They still think you'll get back together.'

'That is totally ridiculous. We divorced years ago. Who knows why we ever got married…?' he added half to himself.

Angolos knew from personal experience that youthful infatuation might feel intense, but was by nature a transitory thing doomed to fade as the people involved matured. Maybe it was the fact he and Sonia had both wanted out of the relationship that they had remained friends—whatever the reason, the civilised arrangement owed more to luck than good judgement.

'It could have something to do with the fact she's beautiful, talented, sexy and can't keep her hands off you.'

'Were you jealous?'

Georgie laughed. She couldn't help it, he sounded so startled. 'You really are not the sharpest knife in the drawer, are you? Of *course* I was jealous. What wife wouldn't be?'

'One that did not have a self-esteem issue.'

When he got that smug, self-satisfied look she wanted to hit him. 'Your ex-wife told me I was just the sort of quiet, homely wife you needed.'

'Sonia didn't mean anything by it, I'm sure. She just says the first thing that comes into her head. She's very spontaneous.'

The speed with which he flew to the other woman's defence brought a bitter smile to her lips. If he had been half as eager to defend me... She pushed aside the unfinished thought and squared her jaw.

'If I asked the staff to do anything they checked first with your mother before.'

'Ridiculous.'

'It was ridiculous that I put up with it, but I was very young and naïve.' The observation made him flinch, but Georgie was too caught up in her own recollections to notice. 'That was bad enough,' she recalled, 'but when they automatically deferred to Sonia as well I felt as if I was a poor relation... No, that's not right, I didn't feel as though I was a relation at all.' She swallowed and gave a grim smile.

'You're exaggerating.' Despite this claim, she saw for the first time a flicker of uncertainty in his eyes.

'How would you know? You were never there.'

'I had been away from work for a long time. I had a lot of catching up to do and my mother went out of her way to make you feel at home,' he told her stiffly.

Sure she did, Georgie thought as she tactfully conceded the point with an inclination of her head.

Angolos's face was a rigid mask of constraint as he replied. 'If I had wanted Sonia I would have stayed married to her. I wanted you.'

Georgie's stomach flipped. Her covert glance at his hard,

male, deliciously streamlined body resulted in an adrenaline surge of huge proportions. She inhaled deeply and nearly fell off the wall.

'And you wanted me…' Her heart was hammering so fast she could barely breathe. Her knees had acquired the consistency of cotton wool.

'And you wanted me.' He said it again.

A scared sound rasped in her throat and her eyes lifted. 'Things change,' she croaked defiantly.

Angolos studied her flushed face, lingering on the softness of her trembling lips. 'And some things don't.'

Silently she shook her head.

He took her chin in his hand and tilted her face up to him. There was anger in the dark eyes that moved hungrily over her delicate features. 'Why can't you admit it?' he rasped.

'Because I don't want to feel this way…when you…' Without warning she slid off the wall and under his restraining arm. Eyes blazing, her breasts heaving, she stood defiantly glaring at him.

'I'm not an impressionable kid. Getting me into bed won't change my mind.'

'It might make you feel less frustrated, however.' Georgie was about to respond angrily to this supremely arrogant suggestion, when he added, 'I know it would make me feel less frustrated. Where you are concerned I've never had any self-control…' He watched her eyes widen with shock and his lips twisted in a self-derisive smile. 'You haven't the faintest idea what it does to me to be this close to you and not touch…' he said thickly.

A surge of heat travelled through her body. *'Tell me…'* she demanded throatily, then almost immediately started to backtrack as though her life depended on it. 'No…no, I didn't mean that.'

He responded to her denial with a disturbing smile. 'Are you sure?' His smouldering glance dropped to her parted lips.

Georgie heard a soft moan and realised with a sense of
shock that she had made it. Ashamed of the desire that
drenched her shaking body in a wave of intense sexual heat,
she tried to turn away, but her knees gave and she stumbled.

His arm shot out to steady her. Heads close together, their
eyes meshed. 'Do you like the idea of me wanting to touch
you, Georgette?'

. An image of the last time they'd made love flashed into
her head. He had walked into the bedroom and she hadn't
heard him. She hadn't known he was there until she'd turned
around and found him standing with his shoulders against the
door-frame, staring at her.

He'd looked so immaculate in an open-necked shirt and
tailored trousers that she'd immediately wished that she had
not delayed taking her shower. 'How long have you been
there?' He didn't reply, just carried on looking at her. 'I was
clearing out the drawers of this—'

He levered himself off the door and moved unhurriedly
towards her, tall, lean and shockingly sexy. 'There are people
to do that sort of things.'

He reached her side in seconds, and since his eyes had
locked onto hers his unwavering stare had not left her face
for an instant.

'I keep forge—'

The rest of her sentence remained unspoken as he bent
forward and, taking her face between his hands, he fitted his
mouth to hers. He kissed her with a driving desperation that
bent her body backwards. She clung to him, shaking violently
with need. She gasped and moaned his name as his hands slid
under her skirt, pushing back the lace of her pants to touch
the damp heat between her legs.

'Whenever I touch you, you are ready for me...'

'*Georgette*...?'

The sound of Angolos's voice dragged her back to the present. Disorientated, she blinked.

'Are you all right?'

'You asked me if I liked the idea of you wanting to touch me…?'

The dark colour scoring his high cheekbones deepened. 'You're right. This isn't the place or time—'

'Thinking is good, doing is better.'

And Angolos had been very good at *doing*. When she closed her eyes she could see him above her, his skin glistening as he drove deep into her again and again. Her cries urging him on and on.

With a frightened gasp she opened her eyes. *'What am I doing?'*

He caught hold of her chin and angled her face up to his. 'I don't know, but if you don't stop doing it I could end up getting arrested.' His eyes gleamed with laughter but, under the laughter, darker, more dangerous emotions lurked. The darkness in his eyes exerted a powerful fascination for her. It always had.

As she lowered her mortified gaze she caught sight of a bead of sweat running down the brown column of his throat. She followed its progress, unable to tear her eyes from it.

'I didn't mean to.' She gave a self-condemnatory groan. 'That sounds so stupid! But I just do and say things around you that I wouldn't even think around anyone else… I'm really sorry.'

'Do I look offended?'

Her eyes lifted. She shook her head and restlessly twisted her hair into a knot on the nape of her neck.

Don't even think about telling him how he looks, she cautioned herself.

'You still want me. This is not to my mind a cause for repentance.'

'Well, there's no need to act as if you didn't already know,' she returned, centring her cross frown on his dark, devastatingly handsome face.

'I didn't consider it the foregone conclusion you seem to,' he contended drily.

His eyes strayed to the exposed length of her slender throat and stayed there. Flushing, she let her hair fall and lowered her arms. Crossing them in front of her chest, oblivious to the fact the protective action pushed her compressed breasts upwards, she pursed her lips in a scornful grimace.

'I bet you were a bundle of insecurity.' Angolos, a victim to fragile self-esteem...? Oh, sure, that was *really* likely.

'The flame that burns brightest does not always last the longest. You were very young—'

'And stupid,' she cut in angrily. 'Yes, a lot of people think that, and it just goes to show that a few more years on the clock don't necessarily make you any less stupid!' If anything she wanted him more now than she had then.

'So that aspect of being back with me does not fill you with disgust?'

'The sex was always pretty fantastic,' she grunted, avoiding his eyes as though her life depended on it. 'It was the other stuff we were terrible at.'

'So, we will work on the ''other stuff'', and enjoy the sex,' he announced, sounding pleased with himself, which, considering she had just told him she fancied the pants off him, was not surprising. Why *did* her mouth detach itself from her brain when she was around this man?

'That remains to be seen,' she replied as he fell in step beside her, moderating his long stride to match hers.

'Where are we going?'

'I'm going to pick up Nicky from Ruth's, and then—'

'I'll come with you.'

CHAPTER ELEVEN

GEORGIE walked into a room full of people and blinked.

'Look at her,' Robert Kemp teased. 'She forgot we were coming.' He enfolded his startled daughter in a bear hug.

'No, of course I didn't, Dad,' Georgie lied. 'How are you?'

'We're fine...but never mind us. How's my favourite grandson? More to the point, *where's* my favourite grandson?' he asked, looking around the room expectantly.

Her more-observant stepmother laid a concerned hand on Georgie's arm. 'Is anything wrong, Georgie, dear?'

'I'm fine, thanks, Mary. He's in the garden, Dad.' On cue the sound of Nicky's high-pitched laughter drifted in through the open door. 'No, don't go yet,' she added, catching her father's arm as he headed towards the French door. 'I need to tell you something.' *Deep breath...keep calm, be firm...don't get apologetic.* 'No, actually I need to tell *everyone* something,' she corrected.

'Well, go on, then, don't keep us in suspense,' her father urged impatiently.

'Sit down, Robert,' his wife, her eyes on Georgie's tense figure, instructed sharply. 'Can't you see there's something wrong?'

'There's nothing *wrong* exactly, I've just made a decision.'

Her grandmother spoke for the first time. 'It's that man, isn't it? You've seen him again. Oh, yes, and I've heard that he's been here. You can't drive around in a flashy car like his and not get noticed.'

'What man?' Robert Kemp demanded in exasperation. 'Will someone please tell me what's going on?'

'The Constantine creature.'

112

Robert turned to his daughter, his face stern. 'Tell me this isn't true, Georgie.'

Georgie scanned the three faces staring accusingly at her. No wonder I feel as if I'm on trial, she thought wearily. 'Angolos has a right to see Nicky, Dad.'

Her father groaned and clutched his head in his hands. 'He's sucked you in again, hasn't he? That man has caused this family nothing but heartache since the moment he appeared and I for one wish you'd never laid eyes on him.'

'Well, if I hadn't I wouldn't have Nicky, would I?'

'Don't be smart with me, my girl. I hope you've told him we don't need him.'

'Not exactly,' Georgie admitted uneasily. 'Actually,' she added, 'I agreed to go back to Greece with him...'

There was a stunned silence.

Her father was the first to recover his voice. He jerked his head towards the window. 'Is he here now?'

'Dad, please...?' Georgie begged.

'Were you born stupid?' he wanted to know.

Her grandmother reached for her pillbox and popped a pill with her hand pressed significantly to her heart. 'If that man suggested you jump into the nearest lake you would.' There was nothing frail about her contemptuous observation. 'All he has to do is get you into bed and you'd sell your own soul or, in this case,' she declared dramatically, 'your son.'

Georgie flushed at the accusation. 'Nicky has a right to know his father, Gran.' *Does he? Didn't he lose those rights...?*

'This isn't about Nicky, it's about you,' the old lady retorted.

Georgie coloured guiltily. This was a charge she had levelled at herself. And she still couldn't swear, hand on heart, that there wasn't an element of truth in it. She wanted to do the right thing for Nicky, but, when the *right thing* involved being back with the man who was the passion of her life, could she ever be sure her decision was totally objective?

'If that man goes near my grandson I'll…' Robert added.

Georgie lost her patience. Her family had been there when she'd needed them, but this was her life they were discussing.

'You'll what, Dad?' she asked. 'Teach him a lesson? Do you really think you could? Sorry.' She bit her lip. 'I shouldn't have said that. I know you have my interests at heart, but this is my life. This isn't an impulse, you know. I've given it a lot of thought.'

'Well, in that case there's no more to be said.'

Georgie heaved a sigh of relief. 'Thank you, Dad. I really appreciate this.'

Robert looked at the hand extended to him and deliberately ignored it as he walked to his wife's side and placed an arm around her shoulder. 'You go to Greece with your so-called husband if that is what you want, but if you do you are no longer my daughter.'

'You can't mean that, Dad,' she said, even though she knew he did.

'Robert!' her stepmother protested. 'You can't make her choose this way… He doesn't mean it, Georgie, dear.'

'I do mean it. You go to Greece and I wash my hands of you.' He patted his wife's hand. 'Sometimes tough love is called for, Mary. This is a matter of loyalty.' Face set in stone, he turned to his daughter. 'What is it to be, Georgie? Your family or this man who cares so much about his son that he's been too busy for the last three years to notice he's alive?'

'I've made my decision, Dad.'

An expression of blank amazement spread across Robert Kemp's florid face. 'You're going to Greece?'

Her grandmother, who had been watching proceedings from her armchair, reached for her walking stick and rose majestically to her feet. 'You ungrateful child.'

'Please, Gran…' She slid an anguished look in her father's

direction. 'I know what it's like not to see a parent. I don't want Nicky—'

'You think your father stopped your mother seeing you?'

'I don't blame Dad. I know Mum hurt him badly.'

'Your father is too soft to tell you. He didn't. The fact is she didn't want to. My daughter-in-law didn't care about you at all,' the old lady spat contemptuously. 'The only thing she cared about was her pretty-boy waiter and he didn't want a baby. I think,' she added, her normal strong voice quivering, 'this could be called history repeating itself.'

Shock had drained the colour from Georgie's face. Her eyes darted from one person to the other without really seeing them. Silly, really. She knew that if her mother had wanted to contact her she would have, but like any child she had nursed her fantasies. And those images had persisted into adulthood: her mother a victim of cruel fate, separated against her will from the daughter she loved.

'I wouldn't leave Nicky, not ever, not for anything.'

'Of course you wouldn't, Georgie,' her stepmother soothed. 'You're a marvellous mother.'

'I couldn't agree more.' Angolos waited until every eye in the room was fixed on him before continuing. 'Georgette has been doing the job of two parents for three years. I think it's time she was relieved of some of the load.'

Georgie turned towards the sound of that deep, confident voice. She experienced a wave of inexpressible relief as their eyes connected.

'Angolos, I...' How much had he heard?

'I think this young man needs a clean-up.' Acting as if there weren't an atmosphere you could cut with a knife in the room, Angolos slanted an amused look at the grubby figure in his arms. The love in his face was so palpable that Georgie couldn't believe she was the only one who could see it.

That was why she was doing this.

Angolos shared his smile between the three other occupants of the room. 'I will wait here.'

'I don't think that's such a good idea,' Georgie said dubiously as he transferred their restless son to her arms.

'You've got him?'

She nodded. 'I think it might be better if you just went. You can ring me later.' He simply couldn't be oblivious to the hostility aimed at him, but from his manner you'd never have known it.

Her father, apparently sharing her view, muttered under his breath, 'He's got a nerve.'

'You haven't changed a jot, Robert—are you working out?' While the other man pressed a hand to his expanding middle and turned dark red with incoherent rage, Angolos turned calmly to Georgie. 'Go on,' he urged. 'It will be fine.'

Throwing a last worried frown over her shoulder Georgie mounted the staircase.

Angolos's smile lasted until he heard the sound of a door opening and closing upstairs. 'Right, you can't stand the sight of me—I can live with that. I have an incredibly thick skin and I am not at all sensitive,' he admitted. 'The only person your insults hurt is Georgette and I don't actually think you want to do that…?' He arched a dark brow and levelled a questioning look at his father-in-law, who glared at him with venomous dislike.

'In your place,' Angolos admitted, 'I would probably feel the same way. You would like me to disappear from your lives. It isn't going to happen, so I suggest you get used to it.'

'*Never!*' Robert Kemp grunted.

'I have no particular fondness for you either, but I am prepared to tolerate you for Georgette's sake. You are my son's grandparents and I hope you will remain an important part of his life. I realise that you spoke in the heat of the moment and you have no wish to disown your daughter or grandson, so I think it will be best all around if we forget you ever said it.'

'You…*you* think…?' Robert blustered, ignoring his wife's agonised aside to leave it be. 'What makes you think I give a damn what you think?'

'I don't. But I think you care about what Georgette thinks. Perhaps we should concentrate on what we have in common.'

'And what would that be?' Robert sneered.

'We both want Georgette to be happy. I can make her happy.' With that he walked out of the room leaving a stunned silence behind him.

Though his approach had been silent Georgie sensed his presence at her shoulder. 'He fell asleep.'

'So I see,' Angolos said, looking at the sleeping child. 'Amazing,' he breathed softly. 'How are you?' he added, not taking his eyes from Nicky's cherubic face.

'As well as could be expected considering my family have cast me off.' Despite the tough words, he could feel the waves of hurt emanating from her.

'And that would bother you…?'

Narrow shoulders hunched, she picked up a stuffed toy from the floor and tucked it in beside the sleeping child. 'Do one thing for me,' she husked, not turning around.

'It's possible I might do one thing for you.'

'Please don't be nice,' she pleaded from between clenched teeth.

His expressive lips quirked. 'You want me to be unpleasant?'

'I want you to be yourself, which amounts to much the same thing.'

'I will do my best to behave with the callous lack of consideration you expect of me.'

Georgie whipped around and promptly forgot the acid retort that had hovered on the tip of her tongue. He was closer than she had anticipated…*very much closer.* Close enough to feel the heat rising off his skin, smell the warm, male, musky scent of him. She couldn't summon the strength to fight as she felt herself sink beneath a wave of enervating lust.

'I only want you to hold me because I'm temporarily feeling alone and sorry for myself.' *Did I really say that out loud?*

Angolos cupped her face between his big hands. 'You're not alone,' he rasped.

Yes, I said it! 'I'm not normally a needy person,' she promised, feeling weak tears squeeze out from her closed eyelids. 'I just need a tissue and possibly a drink.'

Something flickered in his deep-set eyes. 'But not me?'

'I make mistakes,' she told him. 'But not twice,' she added grimly as she pulled back from him, back in control—or as much as she ever was around him—of her feelings.

His expression hardened. 'I will make the flight arrangements and contact you with the details. I'm assuming you don't travel light with a child?'

'What flight arrangements?'

He looked irritated. 'What flight arrangements do you think I mean? I will fly over later tonight and organise things that end, then—'

'You think I'm going to drop everything and leave immediately?'

'Not immediately, but I see no reason to delay.'

She stared at him incredulously. 'No, of course you don't.' How could I have forgotten how selfish and single-minded he is…?

He shook his head and sat down on the bed. Something she immediately wished he hadn't done. 'What is your problem? I have acceded to all your demands, placated your family… Do not push your luck, Georgette,' he advised.

'Oh, the ''I'll do anything to be with my son'' didn't last very long, did it?' she observed with withering scorn. 'I have commitments here.'

Angolos's facial muscles clenched, giving his face the appearance of stone as he asked in a voice devoid of all emotion, 'Does he know you are married?'

Georgie shook her head, frowning. '*He…?* Will you stop talking in riddles…?' Then as his meaning hit her angry heat flooded her face! 'I don't believe you! Do you really think I'd be stupid enough to commit to another man? After you!' she stressed.

'You don't have a boyfriend.' He sounded cautious, but not unhappy with this information. 'Then what commitments are we talking about?'

'I have a job, I'm contractually obliged to give the school notice and even if I wasn't I wouldn't dream of leaving them in the lurch.' She made a quick mental assessment. 'I won't be able to leave until half-term at the earliest.'

'And when is half-term?'

'The end of October.'

'That is not acceptable.'

She shrugged and thrust her hands in the pockets of her jeans. *'Tough.'*

'You really have changed.'

'I'll take that as a compliment.'

'I'm sure I would be able to get the school to release you immediately.'

Georgie had no doubt he could, though he would probably delegate the task. 'And I suppose that would involve throwing sacks full of money at them.' Sometimes the Constantine name was enough.

'Not *sacks* full.'

'Typical!'

The way he was looking at her made it obvious he was totally mystified by her anger. 'Don't take that "I'm being reasonable and you're being irrational" tone with me; I always hated it!' she told him.

'Thank you for sharing that with me.'

'I'm not your sister. I don't want, or need, you to make my problems go away by producing your cheque-book. Besides, this time I'm not burning my bridges. If things don't work out I'm going to need a reference.'

'To anticipate failure is hardly a positive attitude.'

'Maybe not, but it's a practical one,' she said, responding to his criticism with a careless shrug. 'I'm a mother now. I can't act on a whim—I have to consider the consequences of my actions.'

'And you married me on a whim—is that what you're saying?'

Her mouth twisted in a cynical smile of self-derision. 'I like to think of it more as temporary insanity.'

Oblivious to the fact that her confidence had caused Angolos to stiffen, she took the top item on a pile of freshly laundered clothes waiting to be put away and began to fold it with geometric precision. The mundane action helped steady her nerves.

'It's a pity really we didn't just have sex as my dad suggested.'

'Your father told you to sleep with me?'

His outraged tone brought her head up and she found herself looking into eyes that had narrowed into icy, incredulous slits.

'Well, wouldn't you prefer your daughter to sleep with the wrong man rather than marry him?' she charged impatiently.

'If my daughter was involved with the wrong man I would not advise her to have sex with him,' he assured her grimly.

'What would you do?' she asked, even though she could hazard a guess from his expression.

'I would remove the man from her life.'

'And if he didn't want to go?'

He looked astonished that she needed to ask. 'I would not give him a choice.'

She shook her head. 'I think it's just as well that Nicky wasn't a girl.'

'Our next child might be, though.'

The colour drained from her face. 'What did you say?' she choked.

His brows lifted. 'Would you condemn Nicky to be an only child?' he wanted to know.

'*Me condemn…!* You really are a piece of work. Don't you *dare* try and use moral blackmail on me.'

'Moral blackmail.'

'Don't give me that innocent look. I've seen wolves who looked more innocent than you.'

The accusation drew a grin from him. 'I believe that wolves suffer from a very bad press. They are not the bad guys of popular fiction. Did you know they mate for life?' he asked.

'I'm willing to give wolves the benefit of the doubt,' she gritted. 'But we both know that you'd do whatever it took to get what you wanted.'

'*You* don't want another baby?' Despite his mild tone his eyes were fixed with a curious intensity on her face.

She blinked; the question took her aback. Did she want another baby? 'That's not the point—'

'I would say it's very much the point,' he inserted drily.

'It's far too early…' She stopped and angled a searching look at his lean face. 'Do *you* want a baby?'

'And if I said I did, would it make a difference to you?'

She looked from the sensual curve of his mouth to the velvety darkness of his eyes and felt her concentration slipping… Her expression hardened.

'You expect me to believe you give a damn about what I think?' She released a scornful trill of laughter and saw the anger flicker in his liquid dark eyes. 'Let's not drift into fantasy land here…'

Angolos cut across her. 'Actually I don't feel that having a baby at this time would be a sensible idea.'

The colour in her cheeks receded. She ought to welcome his comment, she told herself crossly. Anyone would think I *wanted* to have his baby. 'When we don't even know if we'll be together in two weeks' time, let alone two years, I couldn't agree more,' she contended coolly.

'The positive attitude again. You know, Georgette, cynical doesn't suit you.'

'Get used to it, Angolos,' she suggested, maintaining her indifferent pose.

'Do you realise that the moment I start to get close to you…' He took an actual step towards her and without thinking Georgie retreated two steps. 'I was going to say, you push me away, but maybe that should have been you run away.'

A defiant frown formed on her face as she met his ironic smile. 'I'm really not in the mood for your silly games.'

'I'm not playing games, Georgette. I know you want to punish me,' he revealed in a harsh voice, 'but hasn't it occurred to you that I'm not the only one suffering here? You're hurting too. You want me, Georgette. We both know that.'

She opened her mouth to angrily rebut this claim and stopped. She released a long, slow, shuddering breath. 'I am hurting, but there's not a lot I can do about it. And I doubt very much if getting into your bed is going to make that hurt go away. I will probably sleep with you, Angolos.' She saw triumph flare in his eyes and added with a self-derisive shrug, 'You're right—I have very little self-control where you are concerned. But I can't let myself trust you again, Angolos; you hurt me so much.'

The taut silence lengthened. Angolos walked over to the window. 'That cuts both ways.'

Bewildered, she stared at his broad back. 'I hurt you…?'

Angolos turned back; he didn't want to hear another denial. 'I really think there is no point dissecting what went wrong between us.'

On one level he could recognise how the situation could

have driven her into another man's arms: she had felt isolated; he had been too busy with work to give her the attention she needed…recognise but never forgive.

'I thought you wanted to talk,' she protested, bewildered by his swift change of mood.

'I think we should talk about the future.'

'Suits me.' She shot him a wary glance. 'But let's not go over ground we've already covered,' she cautioned.

'What ground would that be?'

'Babies,' she elaborated.

'I was not…I actually think you're a marvellous mother.'

Georgie's eyes widened. Coming from Angolos, who didn't throw around the compliments, this was praise indeed. 'I'm a fairly all right mother,' she corrected. 'I'm a long way from marvellous. I make loads of mistakes. I expect you will too. It's a steep learning curve so don't expect to get it right the first time. I suppose it's not unlike riding a bike or…'

'Or?'

'I forget,' she said, unable to think on the spur of the moment of a more convincing lie. Angolos didn't look convinced.

She released a hiss of angry frustration and she shot him a look of fulminating frustration. 'I was going to say making love, but I'm sure you were always perfect at that, *damn you*!' she added with a resentful sniff.

The look of astonishment that spread across his face was swiftly supplanted by a slow, sensual smile. 'There's no need to look so smug.'

'I don't feel smug. I'd just forgotten how much you always made me laugh.' Then to her dismay he did just that in a loud and uninhibited way.

Hell, she thought, he really did have the sexiest laugh in the world.

'Shut up,' she hissed, 'Nicky will wake up, or someone will come up to see what's going on.'

'Is this better?' he asked.

Georgie studied the sober face he showed her. 'Your hair's sticking up,' she said. It wasn't, but it helped her not say what she wanted to. *You're beautiful* might take this conversation in a direction she really didn't want to go!

'Thanks,' he said, drawing a hand over the neatly trimmed pelt. 'Has your family got something against laughter?'

'No, just you.' The rueful smile created a brief sense of unity. 'Do you remember…?' she began, then stopped.

'What?' he prompted.

'I was just thinking about the first time you met the family, and your face when Gran asked you if you worked in a bar. You looked so astonished.' She shook her head. The memory of his aghast expression was so strong that it was hard to keep the quiver of amusement from her voice. 'And you said no, but you thought that you might own a vineyard, but you'd have to ch…check.'

'I did check and I own two, but they are very small.'

CHAPTER TWELVE

'YOU'LL wake him,' Georgie reproached Angolos again before stuffing her fist on her mouth to stifle her own laughter. She laughed until her ribs ached and when she stopped she wiped away the tears from her cheeks. A quick peek revealed that Nicky was still sound asleep.

'It's lucky he's a...' She turned towards Angolos and promptly forgot what she had been about to say.

There was no lingering amusement on his face. Under the sweep of his dark, luxuriant lashes his eyes glittered. The expression on his lean face was intense and raw.

The air between them suddenly buzzed with an almost visible electric charge. It made the fine hairs on her arms stand on end and caused a tell-tale, quivery ache low in her belly.

If she didn't do something and do it quick things were going to happen. And she didn't want that, *did she*?

'You're staring,' she accused with a weak little laugh that fooled nobody, especially herself.

He carried on staring.

She looked at his mouth, seeing it against her breasts. Inside her shirt her nipples grew hard as though his lips had actually brushed over them.

'This is a trial,' she began, calling on every ounce of her will-power to control her voice. 'I was explaining, before you hijacked the conversation, that I'm going to give work my notice.'

There was a long uncomfortable silence while he studied the rigid lines of her determined face.

'They've always been good to me at the school. Nicky has a free place at the nursery,' she continued.

'So it's non-negotiable?'

Her shoulders sagged in relief. 'Yes.'

'In that case I suppose I'd better rearrange my schedule.'

Georgie, who had been expecting something along the lines of, *Over my dead body,* raised suspicious eyes to his face. 'What do you mean?'

'I mean that now that I've found my son I'm not about to wait to be his father. I will relocate.'

'But your work!' she protested.

He dismissed his multimillion-pound company with a casual shrug of his shoulders. 'If necessary I will work from home.'

'Don't be ridiculous. You don't even know where I work and you can't possibly run an international company from a Sussex village.'

He gave her a mocking look. 'Anyone would think you didn't want me to move in with you, *yineka mou,*' he drawled.

Anyone would be right. Her body grew rigid as the full import of his comment penetrated. *'Move in…?'* She echoed sharply.

'I think we should start as we mean to go on. This is to be a marriage in every sense of the word.'

Her shoulders suddenly relaxed as she realised that what he suggested was impossible. 'That would be sensible…the starting as you mean to go on bit, I mean,' she agreed. 'But unfortunately my flat is tiny, one bedroom.' Her glance came to rest on his broad-shouldered frame. 'You wouldn't fit in…and I mean that in the literal sense.' She actually meant that in *every* sense.

'I am very adaptable.'

'Trust me, not *that* adaptable. My kitchen is about three feet square.'

'Compact.'

She gritted her teeth. 'The idea of slumming it might seem

amusing to you now, but I think the novelty would wear off rather rapidly.'

'You think I am spoilt? That I am incapable of roughing it?'

'Frankly, yes. When I said there was one bedroom...'

'Cosy.'

Her stomach muscles tensed. 'Very cosy with Nicky's bed in there too.'

'Nicky shares a room with you?'

She nodded. 'And I don't need to turn my TV on; I can hear the one in the flat next door.' A sweet couple, but noisy. 'I can hear a door close, and as for what I can hear through the bedroom walls! Even with a pillow over my head...not that we'd—' She broke off, blushing madly.

'You don't think that our love life would be as uninhibited as that of your neighbours?'

She flushed and hissed, 'I'm really not interested in other people's sex lives.'

'You never used to be a prude.'

She shot him a look of anguished embarrassment. 'I'm not a prude,' she denied indignantly. 'I just happen to think that what goes on between two people behind closed doors should be private,' she said. 'As for uninhibited, I seriously doubt that anyone could be as uninhibited as you!' As a lover Angolos had been not only passionate, but inventive. Thinking about how inventive made the colour fly to her face.

Her agonised observation made his lips quiver. 'You never seemed to mind and I always considered you the noisy one. There was that sound...' Eyes half closed, he drew a deep, shuddering breath. 'You know the one I mean, when I—'

Georgie pressed her hands to her burning cheeks. 'You're disgusting!' she hissed. 'You probably *like* the idea of people listening.' She could cope with being embarrassed; it was being aroused by his taunts that she couldn't deal with.

He was oblivious—*she hoped*—to her internal struggle; her embittered accusation caused his white grin to broaden.

'I never found I needed to resort to other forms of stimulation when you were in my bed, *agape mou*, but I'm always open to suggestions. In fact, you almost make me want to share your flat. However, you are right: it is not a practical solution.'

She regained enough control of her breathing to be able to respond with simulated calm. 'Exactly, and three months isn't very long. You can still see Nicky during that time…take him to the park and so forth.'

The way Angolos felt at that moment three months was a lifetime! If he didn't get Georgette back in his bed, and soon, he might well explode. He would certainly be incapable of functioning.

There was not a shred of his rampant frustration in his voice as he responded. 'That would be one solution, certainly. However, I favour a less…passive approach.'

'What *approach* did you have in mind?' she asked suspiciously.

'I'll get onto a local property agent.'

'There's virtually no rental property in the area,' she inserted quickly.

He looked amused by her intervention. 'I don't intend to rent; I intend to buy.'

'Buy!' she echoed, startled. 'That's crazy. It's only three months. Think of the expense.'

'*Expense…?*' He looked amused.

'All right, you have money to burn,' she conceded crossly. 'But it takes ages to find a suitable house, let alone buy one.'

'If you want something badly enough you make it happen.'

Their eyes connected and she knew that she hadn't imagined the undercurrent in his voice, the one that had sent a prickle of heat through her body. 'Now,' he continued, adopting a businesslike attitude, 'are there any areas you prefer? Is the distance to your work a factor?'

Georgie sighed and decided to go with the flow. When Angolos made up his mind about something, it was the most sensible thing to do.

With any luck the agent wouldn't have anything suitable on his books.

The agent did.

Two days later they drew up outside their new home.

It wasn't until the moment when Angolos opened the car door and stood back impatiently waiting for her to get out that the enormity of the step she had taken struck Georgie.

She was going to move in with the man who had broken her heart.

Angolos expected her to share his bed. She wanted to share his bed. It was inevitable, so where was the problem?

She slid from the front seat and stepped out onto the gravelled forecourt.

'So do you like it?' He sounded impatient to hear her opinion.

She flashed him an incredulous look. Like the place...? It was gorgeous. Georgian, faced in local brick, it had a gated approach, swish circular drive and, as she later discovered, private gardens in the rear that led down to the river.

'You've bought *this*?'

'I would have preferred for you to see it first, but there was a lot of interest. I had to act swiftly to secure it. It's small, but you were right—there isn't much on the market.'

'*Small!*' She released a slightly hysterical laugh as they walked up the steps that led to the porticoed entrance. Her entire flat could have fitted into one small corner of the massive hall revealed when he opened the door. She swung back to him. 'It's massive.'

'It's workable,' he conceded. 'And it's basically sound. I hope you didn't mind that I bought the furniture *in situ*...

It is not something I would normally do, but it is only a stopgap.'

She was unable to repress a laugh. 'You have a very unique take on stopgap, Angolos.' She ran a finger over the back of a carved oak chair. 'And I like the furniture.'

'Would you like to look around?'

She nodded eagerly and followed him into the drawing room. As they explored she couldn't hide the fact she was enchanted with the place. A satisfied expression appeared in his eyes as she began to plan out loud what she would use the rooms for.

'This can be Nicky's room,' she cried immediately when they walked into a light and airy south-facing room on the first floor. 'It's big, but not too big, and he will just *adore* the garden.' She gazed happily through the window. 'I wish we'd brought him with us.'

'I'm sure he will enjoy his little friend's birthday party.'

Absently Georgie nodded. 'I can just see him on his little trike out there.' Without thinking about it she leaned back into Angolos's body.

The contact with the hard warmth of his body sent a sharp shock through her own that sizzled down to her toes. She stiffened and then allowed herself to relax.

After a moment his arms came around her, drawing her closer as they tightened across her ribcage. Georgie, aware of every hard inch of him, pretended not to notice. If she acknowledged the embrace she would be obliged to do something about it, and she didn't want to.

'I always wished that I could afford somewhere with a garden,' she admitted with a wistful sigh.

'You could have if you hadn't been too proud and stubborn to use the money in the bank.'

'I couldn't take anything off you when you didn't believe that Nicky was yours.' Still in the circle of his arms, she turned her head and caught a stricken expression on Angolos's lean face. An expression that vanished the moment their eyes connected.

Without thinking, she half turned and reached out. 'It's *now* that's important, isn't it…?'

Angolos looked at the small hand laid on his arm and the muscles around his stern mouth relaxed. 'Yes,' he agreed.

The smile in his eyes as he looked into hers made her own smile fade. The emotions she'd been working so hard at keeping in check flowed without warning over the barriers she'd constructed.

Angolos watched the tears well in her eyes and his expression grew alarmed. 'Are you unwell?' Bending forward, he brought his face to her level and cupped her chin in one big hand. 'What is it? Tell me?' he demanded with increasing urgency.

She shook her head mutely and managed to mouth a barely intelligible, 'I'm fine. It's just…' Mutely she shook her head. 'I wish sometimes.'

'You wish things had been different?'

'I wish things could be like this all the time.' With a sigh she let her head fall against his chest. 'Sometimes I get so tired…'

'Things will be better when you have help…a nanny.'

'Not that sort of tired.' She closed her eyes as he lifted her hair off the nape of her neck and touched his lips to the gentle curve of her throat. 'And I don't need a nanny.'

'We are rarely alone.'

'That's part of being a parent.'

'I'm not complaining. It makes stolen moments all the more precious.'

Georgie gave a low, broken gasp of pleasure as she felt his tongue flicker moistly over her ear. Things low and deep in her belly shifted and tightened. 'Is that what this is?'

'It's whatever you want it to be.'

The sensual promise in his voice made her shiver. Their

eyes met and suddenly she was scared. Her eyes dropped from his but she extended her hand to him. 'Come on,' she said huskily. 'I want to see what's through there.'

After a moment Angolos took her hand and allowed himself to be led through the door into an adjoining room.

Georgie stopped dead. This was obviously the master bedroom.

'I've never slept in a four-poster,' she said, gazing at the impressive centrepiece of the room with its heavy canopy and elaborate carvings.

Angolos's voice above her head had a strained, husky quality to it. 'It isn't something I have had strong feelings about—until now. Suddenly I want very much to sleep in a four-poster bed.'

'Me too.'

His breathing was audible in the quiet room.

Georgie was hardly breathing at all as she turned around and lifted her face up to him. His was a dark blur as his warm lips immediately came over hers, hard and hungry. It felt so good, it felt so right, and most of all it felt mind-blowingly exciting.

'I convinced myself that I was over you,' she confided against his mouth as the deep, hungry assault morphed seamlessly into a series of soft, biting kisses.

She felt the muscles of his upper arms bunch beneath her hand and he slid his fingers into her hair, pushing through the slippery strands to mould the shape of her head. 'And are you?'

'I'll tell you on the condition you don't stop doing what you're doing if you don't like the answer.'

'I doubt I could stop if I wanted to,' he retorted. His throaty laugh did not reach his dark eyes; they remained intense and hungry.

'I was only over you in my dreams…and actually not there either.' Her dreams had always been filled with Angolos.

She was barely breathing as he leaned forward and slipped the buttons on her shirt. His eyes held hers as the fabric parted.

'Take it off for me.' Arms folded across his chest, he took a step backwards and waited.

The sensual request shuddered through her. Her eyelashes fluttered against the flushed curve of her cheeks as she lifted her gaze to his. 'You want me to…?'

'I just want you,' he inserted throatily.

Her breath snagged in her throat as he added, 'I always did and I always shall. From the first moment I laid eyes on you I was bewitched,' he imparted thickly.

The air felt cool against her overheated skin as she let her shirt fall to the floor. Thrusting one hip forward in a consciously provocative pose, she stretched her hands behind her back until her fingers found her bra clasp.

Sexual challenge glittering in her wide-spaced tawny eyes, she looked directly into his eyes. 'This too?'

He swallowed and nodded.

Georgie didn't watch the lacy scrap fall to the floor.

She watched Angolos.

Her heart felt as if it were trying to batter itself out of her chest. Her breathing was fast and shallow, her mouth dry. They weren't touching but she was so aroused she could barely breathe.

As her pink-tipped breasts sprang free of their confinement his eyes dropped. She heard his sharp intake of breath from where she was standing and she simply dissolved.

In one stride he was at her side. He carried her to the bed and fell with her onto the mattress. Before her head had hit the pillow his hungry mouth was on hers. He pulled her under him and she moaned into his mouth, squirming, relishing the heat and weight of his body pressing her down.

'I can't get enough of you,' she gasped when his mouth lifted momentarily from hers.

'You can have as much of me as you want,' he promised throatily.

'Don't stop, I'm...' she protested as he rolled away and pulled himself onto his knees.

A slow, predatory smile spread across his face as he looked down at her pale body, naked to the waist. 'You really are the most perfect thing.'

He cupped one breast in his hand. The feverish lines along his cheekbones drew attention to the glitter of his inky dark eyes as they moved over her skin like a caress. 'You're softer and fuller,' he marvelled, his eyes riveted to the quivering rise and fall of her breasts with their tightly engorged nipples.

'A baby, breast-feeding.' She was afraid the admission would break the mood, but it had the opposite effect on Angolos, whose breathing became even more ragged and uneven as he started to rip off his own clothes.

Her pulse was pounding in her ears as she watched him through the screen of her lashes. Halfway through he changed his mind and, leaving his shirt hanging open, he began to slide Georgie's jeans down her thighs.

Georgie eagerly kicked her way free of them. The sight of his dark head outlined against her breasts was an image that had featured in her dreams on countless lonely nights. The reality, the scalding pleasure that convulsed her body as his tongue moved back and forth, relentlessly over the rosy areola, surpassed any dream Georgie had ever had.

As he licked his way down her stomach she tangled her fingers in his dark silky hair.

Angolos lifted his head when he reached the barrier of her underwear. He smiled, a smile of predatory promise as he watched her face. Georgie's eyes closed and a keening cry was drawn from somewhere deep inside her as he slid his fingers under the lacy material. She released a second long moan of naked pleasure as he slid a finger over her slippery heat and inside her.

'This is…I can't…Angolos, I need you…now…now…!'
She reached up and grabbed either side of his shirt. A determined tug brought him down on top of her.

The skin-to-skin contact as her breasts crushed against his
hard, hair-roughened chest was almost too good to bear. She
moved and the searing pleasure created by the friction of his
sweat-slick skin against her own wrenched a series of sharp
whimpers from her dry, aching throat. Her head was spinning,
her starved senses reeling from sensual overload.

They kissed with frantic hunger.

But there was only so much of the kissing and touching
Georgie could bear; she wanted more, much more.

Angolos responded to her loud announcement to this effect
by grabbing her hair in one hand and forcing her head back
onto the pillow. She listened to the passionate flood of words
that flowed from his lips. He seemed unaware that he was
speaking in his native tongue and Georgie didn't care. The
expression stamped on his dark, driven features told her everything she needed to know.

As he rolled a little to one side and tugged at the zip of his
trousers her eyes followed the sound.

'Oh!' she gasped as she saw the hard column of his engorged erection brush against his flat, hard belly. Her body
was flooded by a tidal wave of hot longing that made her feel
faint.

Watching her reaction with glittering eyes, his own dark
features taut and strained, Angolos kicked aside his pants and
reached for her.

Lying on top of him, she took his dark head between her
hands and kissed him. She let her tongue dart into his mouth
and felt the satisfying pulse of his rock-hard erection grind
into the softness of her belly.

'Theos…!' He groaned an electrifying raw sound against
her mouth, and flipped her over. Parting her legs with hands
that trembled, he slid into her in one smooth, thrusting motion.

'Look at me!' he instructed throatily. 'I want to see you…I want to see you feel me.'

Georgie opened her eyes; his face was a dark blur above. 'Anything,' she sobbed as he moved inside her. 'Anything. I'll do anything for you.'

CHAPTER THIRTEEN

GEORGIE and Nicky were installed in the house two days before the start of term. Angolos was called away on urgent business and it was all terribly rushed so when her father phoned out of the blue and offered to help, after she had picked herself up off the floor Georgie said, 'Yes, please.'

'I don't know what you said to him,' Georgie said four days later as she sat on the edge of the desk in the room Angolos had done out as an office.

The place was full of space-age technology that made her nervous and the room next to it was occupied by his PA, a pleasant young man called Demitri.

'But Dad was being *really* nice. Not a single snide remark…and he made admiring noises about the house.'

'Say…? What makes you think I had anything to do with it?'

'Well, the last time my dad backed down was…' She pressed a finger to the faint dimple in her chin and pretended to consider the matter. 'Let me see…*never.*'

'Nothing to do with me,' Angolos insisted. 'Maybe…?' he began closing the laptop in front of him.

'Maybe what?' she prompted when he didn't continue.

Angolos looked up, his dark eyes grave. 'Maybe he could see you are happy…?'

Without warning Georgie felt her eyes fill. She blinked and swallowed past the emotional constriction in her throat.

'Maybe he could,' she admitted quietly.

In reply Angolos simply nodded, but she saw the flare of fierce satisfaction in his eyes before he opened his laptop once more.

This was the closest either of them had come to discussing whether their arrangement was working out. For her part, Georgie was afraid that admitting out loud that things were going well would be tempting fate.

Of course there had been awkward moments, and she wasn't totally at ease with being around him, but there had been none of the *major* difficulties that she had expected—*not yet*. Maybe, she mused, there had been so few disagreements because they were both being terribly diplomatic…?

And for Georgie there was the added complication of knowing that if she started speaking without first carefully thinking about what she was going to say the *love* word might inadvertently creep out.

Such behaviour was clearly out of the question when your husband wanted you back in his life because you were the mother of his child, not because you were…well…you. She was sure that someone as controlled and in charge of his emotions as Angolos would not welcome overt emotional displays.

It made her cringe to remember how as a newly-wed she had been all over him like a rash—well, he wouldn't be able to complain about that this time around.

Nicky, on the other hand, wasn't trying; he was just being Nicky. He had had no problem accepting Angolos's presence in his life. Angolos for his part was touchingly eager to be with his son. Even the most cynical observer, seeing them together, could not doubt Angolos's devotion to the child.

'I'll leave you to it, then,' she said, sliding off his desk.

'No need to run away.'

'You're busy and I should…' Their eyes locked and she paused.

'Wash your hair…?' he suggested. His eyes touched the silky waves and he decided it didn't look as though it needed washing; it looked shiny, slippery clean. He felt the urge to bury his face in it and inhale at the most unorthodox of moments.

'There's no need to be sarcastic.'

'And there's no need for you to be so painfully polite. The only time you actually relax around me is in bed.'

She refused to blush at the allusion. At night she didn't have to watch her tongue because it was a well-known fact that people said things they didn't mean in the slightest when they were in the grip of passion. She meant them, of course, but so far Angolos hadn't caught on. And anyway he said some things he didn't mean too, once the lights were out. Fortunately she didn't take them seriously.

'I don't want to intrude. I'm still feeling my way.'

I know my way pretty well around his body.

'Anyhow,' she added, her colour significantly heightened, 'you're not exactly acting normally around me, are you? If you were you would never have sat and watched that weepie movie with me last night.'

'That was compromise, not unease, and I wasn't watching the movie, I was watching you.'

'Oh!'

'I like watching you,' he added.

Georgie licked her dry lips; her heart had started thumping very fast. 'That's really strange. I'm not exactly—'

'Shall I tell you what you are?'

Angolos had half risen from his chair when his assistant walked in through the connecting door with a computer print-out in his hand. He was speaking in Greek, and frowning at the page in his hand.

Angolos replied in the same language and the young man looked up, flushing darkly.

'Sorry, I didn't know you were busy. I'll—'

'No,' Georgie said, leaping to her feet. 'I was just leaving.' Carefully avoiding her husband's eyes, she swept out of the room.

*   *   *

The headmistress was flatteringly reluctant to accept her resignation, but when she saw that her mind was made up she promised Georgie an excellent reference.

'You've been an invaluable member of the team,' she told Georgie warmly. 'And we're all going to miss you.'

Georgie, touched by the genuine warmth, left the office close to tears. Part of her felt sad and scared that this chapter of her life was ending. She wondered for the hundredth time if she was doing the right thing...

The news spread around the staff room the way secrets always did and by the end of the day at least six people had asked her if it was true.

The next morning at coffee she made an announcement.

'Yes, the rumours are true. I've handed in my notice and I'm leaving at half-term. My husband...'

The rest of her rehearsed speech was lost as the room quietly erupted.

'Oh, didn't I mention I was married?' she said when the hubbub had died down. She gave them a carefully edited version of the events that had led to their reconciliation.

They all thought it was dreadfully romantic and wanted to know when they were going to meet the man himself. Georgie was deliberately vague and not encouraging.

'He's snowed under with work. I don't expect I'll see him much myself.'

She did see him only a few hours later; so did the rest of the school. He made quite an impression—*big surprise!*—as he strode into the playground with Nicky perched on his shoulders. About to go back in the building after her stint on playground duty, she ushered the last child inside and closed the door.

'Hello, sweetheart.' Her smile faded as she shifted her attention to the elder Constantine male. 'What,' she demanded, 'are you doing here?'

'Are you this stern with the children?'

'Nicky should be in nursery and,' she added grimly, 'they shouldn't have let you just take him. You could have been anybody!'

'Not according to staff there. They were of the opinion that Nicky and I were—what was the expression?'

'Two peas in a pod?' she suggested drily.

'That is it,' he agreed with a complacent smile. 'They were charming.'

'I've noticed you have a way with women of a certain age.'

His dark eyes danced with amusement as he clicked his tongue in reproach. 'Animals like me too and I am asking your permission to take Nicky here out of nursery early. That children's theatre group you mentioned, they are putting on an afternoon performance. I thought I might take him. Don't look now,' he added, 'but I think we are being watched.'

'Of course we are being watched!' Maintaining a fixed smile was making her facial muscles ache. 'Could you be any more conspicuous if you tried?' she demanded, eyeing his tall, supremely elegant figure with exasperation.

'Is there something wrong with the way I look?'

Her eyes skimmed his tall, powerful body; he looked incredible, but no more incredible than he always did. Dark jeans that matched the cashmere sweater he wore clung to the powerful muscles of his long thighs. They were simple clothes if expensive, but when he wore them they became something special.

'No,' she gritted grimly. 'That's the problem. Have you any idea what I'll have to put up with now? They'll all be talking about you,' she predicted gloomily.

They were, and more than a few envious glances were cast in her direction.

She smiled through the questions, the favourite being: 'He's gorgeous. How on earth did you catch him?' To her relief as the term progressed the excitement and teasing died down, though when Angolos appeared to collect her or Nicky he always caused a minor sensation amongst staff and mothers alike.

To Angolos she grumbled about their behaviour; privately she understood it—didn't her own pulses leap every time she saw him…?

It wasn't until the landlord contacted Georgie and said he had a new tenant for her flat that she realised she still had several boxes of her stuff sitting there. He went on to explain he needed her to clear the place by the end of next week.

'You really don't mind?' she asked the next day as she climbed into the Transit she had borrowed from the school secretary.

'You kidding?' Her friend Alan said, swinging Nicky high above his head, much to the child's delight. 'We're going to have a ball. Isn't *Daddy* helping you move out?'

Georgie grimaced; she didn't want to get into this.

Alan had made no secret of the fact that he thought her decision to move back to Greece with Angolos was crazy. 'The guy made you as unhappy as hell the first time, Georgie!'

But, being Alan, once he had said what he thought he had been as supportive as ever.

'Don't start, *please*,' she appealed to her friend with a warning look in Nicky's direction. 'Angolos is in Athens; he's not back until tomorrow.'

She had expected to be able to empty the flat in one go, but when the Transit was full there were still half a dozen boxes sitting there. She left with the intention of picking them up after school the next day.

Around lunch-time she received a call from Alan who offered to pick the stuff up for her.

She gratefully accepted the offer. 'That would be brilliant. I've got a parents' night after school that I totally forgot about and—'

'Just call me your guardian angel. Key in the usual place?' he asked cheerfully. 'And remember you owe me a pint.'

'At least,' she laughed. 'Do you mind keeping the stuff at your flat until tomorrow?'

'No problem.'

The parents' evening went on longer than usual and it wasn't just Nicky who felt cranky by the time they left for home. Her fatigue suddenly lifted as she saw the top-of-range Mercedes that Angolos drove parked in front of the house.

He was home early.

It was with a strange mixture of excitement and trepidation that she entered the house. The indomitable Emily, Angolos's half-Scots half-Greek ex-nanny, who, despite Georgie's initial doubts, was fast becoming indispensable, stepped into the brightly lit hallway as they walked in.

'You look exhausted.'

'It's been a long day,' Georgie admitted.

'Why don't you go and put your feet up? I'll give the little one his supper and bath.'

'Would you?' Georgie sighed. 'That would be marvellous,' she admitted, handing Nicky over into the other woman's capable hands. 'The car…?'

A broad smile spread across the older woman's homely features. 'He's in the study, dear.'

Georgie paused outside the study door and glanced at her flushed reflection in the mirror. The face that stared back at her was lit up from within.

His back to her, Angolos was looking out of the window. Despite her rigidly enforced restraint, she couldn't help the way her senses thrilled at the sight of his broad-shouldered, narrow-hipped figure.

'This is a surprise. I didn't expect you until much later.' Amazingly—at least it amazed her—nothing of what Georgie was feeling seeped into her voice.

'*Obviously.*'

The moment he opened his mouth she knew something was wrong. When he spun around to face her she saw she had not been mistaken...Angolos was in a foul humour.

'What's wrong?' She slid her bottom onto the arm of a chair and gave a sympathetic grimace. She lifted her hands to the log fire crackling in the hearth. The warmth it threw off didn't compensate for the inexplicable iciness in Angolos's manner. 'Did your meetings not go well?'

'I cancelled them,' he said curtly.

Her eyes widened. She knew from what he had told her they had been important—very important. 'Why?'

'Because I couldn't bear to be away from my loving wife.'

Hurt, Georgie flushed. 'Don't tell if you don't want to, I was only trying to take an interest. There's no need to be sarcastic.'

'Where have you been...or should I not ask?'

The question and his attitude brought a bewildered expression to her face. 'Of course you can ask. Do you have to pace around like that?' She watched him; how could she not? Everything he did, including pacing like a caged tiger, was rivetingly graceful.

One brow lifted to a satirical angle as his unfriendly dark eyes raked her face. 'I'm sublimating...what I actually want to do is wring your faithless neck.'

Georgie looked at him in astonishment. 'I've not the faintest idea what you're talking about, but I know I've had enough of this,' she said, getting to her feet. 'And you,' she flung over her shoulder.

'Don't walk away while I'm talking to you!'

She swung back. 'You're not talking, you're yelling at me, you're glowering and you're being generally incredibly unpleasant. But you're not talking to me.' She lifted a hand to her head in an intensely weary gesture. 'Shall I tell you something funny? When I saw your car I was excited...happy.' She stopped, hating the wobble in her voice.

'He didn't ring you, then. I thought he would…'

'He…?'

'Theos!' he raged, raking an unsteady hand through his hair. 'I may act like a fool where you are concerned, Georgette, but I would not advise you to treat me like an idiot,' he recommended in a low, throbbing voice.

'I've no idea what you're talking about,' she protested.

'I am talking—' he began advancing towards her with a slow, measured tread that reminded her of a panther menacing its prey '—about my visit to your flat.'

'You visited my flat…?'

Angolos watched her face; surprise but not the faintest trace of guilt was written there. He frowned as if her response was not what he had anticipated. 'You're a much better actress than I gave you credit for.'

'I take it that wasn't a compliment…'

He sucked in his breath through flared nostrils but didn't deign to respond to her comment.

'Why,' she asked, feeling her way, 'did you go to my flat?'

'I went because a person who said he was your landlord rang and said you still had property there and you had promised to vacate by today…but the why is not important—'

'Today! I've got until the end of the week!' she exclaimed indignantly. 'I'm sorry you had the bother. Alan's going to pick it up for me.' Surely the fact he had had a wasted journey could not account for his atrocious mood.

He shot her a look that simmered with hostility. 'So I understood from him.'

A sliver of caution crept into her manner; the antipathy Alan felt for Angolos was fully reciprocated. 'He was there…?'

'Oh, yes…he was there.'

She sighed. 'I suppose things got a little awkward?'

His brows lifted. 'Awkward…?'

'Well, I know you never took to him…'

A choking sound emerged from Angolos's brown throat. 'And this surprises you?' he enquired.

'Not really,' she conceded with a sigh. 'But I wish you'd make a bit of an effort. Actually it's just as well he was there or you wouldn't have been able to get in. You don't have a key.'

'I must admit that I had not quite realised my good fortune until this moment.'

The inflection in his voice made her wince. 'Please don't be like that. I've had an awful day.'

In the act of raking his fingers through his hair he stopped and grabbed a hank of the dark silky strands in his clenched fingers. 'Mine hasn't been too terrific.'

'Do you want to talk about it?'

Her attempt to be an understanding wife was greeted with a look so hostile that she physically recoiled. 'I'll take that as no, shall I? Did Alan leave a message?'

'No!' The explosive negative emerged with the force of a bullet leaving a pistol. 'He did not leave a message and unless he is even more stupid than I think do not expect to hear from him any time soon.'

'You were horrible to him, weren't you? I'm going to have to ring him and apologise now.'

'Apologise…?' he echoed hoarsely, incredulous. 'Apologise for me?' His outraged gaze locked onto her. 'You will not apologise for me. In fact you will not speak to that man again. Nor will you see him. I made it very clear to your…*Alan*…that if he comes anywhere near you I will break every bone in his body!'

'You did *what*? Are you mad?' she demanded. No other immediate explanation sprang to mind for his extraordinary behaviour.

His lips twisted as he gave her question a moment's consideration. 'There is every possibility I am mad. I'm mad because I married you and I'm mad because I didn't break his neck. Nevertheless, I think the spineless jerk got the message. He knows what I'll do if I find him creeping around you again.'

She went white with a combination of fury and shock.

'Oh, for goodness' sake!' She was literally shaking with outrage as she stepped right up to him. 'Do you think this sort of stuff intimidates me?'

Angolos's eyes remained glued to the finger that was being jabbed into his chest.

'Because I can assure you it doesn't. It just shows you up for the nasty bully you are. How dare you sneer at my friends? And what makes you think you can tell me who I can or cannot have as a friend...?' She closed her eyes and shook her head. 'And to think I thought this might actually work!'

'What really offends me is that you brought my son in contact with that man!'

Eyes closed, she shook her head slowly from side to side. 'Contact? Nicky has known Alan all his life. He's marvellous with him.' Her eyes blinked open, bright gold and filled with sick, shocked comprehension. 'That's what this is about, isn't it? I thought you were a lot of things, but I never had you down as homophobic. Well, I don't care about your prejudices, but I won't have you pass them on to Nicky.

'For your information, Alan has been a good friend to me over the years and I don't intend to give him the push just because you're a nasty, narrow-minded bigot!' she finished breathlessly.

Angolos did not react to her impassioned outburst immediately. He didn't just not react—he didn't do anything. Not even an eyelash flickered as he stood there motionless, his dark liquid eyes trained on her face.

'What did you just say?' There was a strained quality to his accented voice.

'I don't remember,' she admitted miserably. The emotional aftermath of her outburst had left her literally shaking.

'*Homophobic…?*'

'Well, can you deny it?'

'Of course I can damn well deny it!'

'Really?' She gave a sceptical sniff. 'Well, what other reason could you possibly have for the way you're acting? *Well…?*'she added as he showed no signs of responding to her challenge.

Actually closer inspection revealed that his skin had acquired an unhealthy greyish tinge and the tension that held every muscle of his body rigid was scary.

'Are you all right?' she asked, her voice roughened by a concern she felt awkward revealing. In the space of seconds she had gone from wanting to hit him to wanting to hug him… She doubted there was another person in the world capable of drawing such an exhausting, extreme response from her.

Without saying anything, he walked over to his desk and opened the big diary that lay there. For several tense moments he stood there staring at the blank page. Still staring at the page, he said, 'I thought he was your lover.'

At first she thought she had misheard him. '*What…?*'

A great sigh shuddered from the depths of his chest as his eyes lifted to hers. 'I thought you were sleeping with the guy. What else was I to think?' he demanded, suddenly angry. 'He had a key and wherever you are he always turns up…'

'That's what friends do,' she reminded him. 'But he's gay.'

He slanted her a look that seethed with frustration. 'I know that now, but quite obviously *he* didn't know when he was in Greece.'

'You thought that I was sleeping with another man?' She lifted her eyes to his face expecting him to deny it. He didn't. She gave her head a tiny shake. 'This is mad…' she contended huskily. 'How on earth could you have thought even for one minute that…Alan…?'

'Stop this, Georgette.' The anger seemed to have drained

from him, leaving only a sense of immense weariness. 'I know what went on between you in Greece.'

'What are you talking about, *what went on*? I don't understand.'

Angolos studied her bewildered face and released a hard laugh. 'Then I'll explain, shall I? It means that you can stop pretending.'

'I'm not—'

'Enough!' His voice was like a clap of thunder. 'I found the note he wrote you. The day you told me you were pregnant.' He closed his eyes and quoted in a flat voice. '"I'm sorry. I thought I was ready, but I'm not. Sorry I'm not strong, love you always, Alan."'

'You remember it word for word?' Georgie was amazed by his perfect recall.

'Of course I bloody remember it word for word. I had the damned thing in my pocket when you told me you were pregnant. To me it seemed obvious that your lover had let you down so you were trying to pass off his baby as mine, because I knew that I couldn't father a child.'

Georgie stood stock-still, unable to believe what she was hearing. He scanned her marble-pale face and gave a twisted smile.

'But you could,' she whispered.

'Yes, I could. As a matter of interest, did you know who was the father before Nicky was born? Or were you relieved to have the matter settled when he looked so like me?'

Tears formed in Georgie's eyes. Not of anger—she had gone way past anger by this point. 'Yes, I knew who the father was. There was never any question of who the father was.'

'No contraception is foolproof,' he stressed.

It took several seconds for his meaning to sink in. For reasons that were now obvious, Angolos had never used contraception and had changed the subject whenever she had awkwardly broached it.

'I suppose I should be grateful you had safe sex.'

'Right now I want very badly to hit you.'

Angolos looked slightly disconcerted by her low comment voiced in an almost conversational tone.

'Alan came out to Greece because I asked him to. I was lonely.'

An explosive sound erupted from Angolos's throat as he began to stride towards the door. 'Are you trying to rub my nose in this, Georgette? Because—'

'What I'm trying to do is set the record straight,' she cut in. 'That letter you memorised would read slightly differently if you knew that I had persuaded Alan, or I thought I had persuaded him, to tell his parents about his sexuality.'

His back turned to her, Angolos froze. Slowly she saw his fingers unpeel from the door handle.

'He decided at the last minute that he couldn't go through with it,' Georgie told his broad back. 'It was another six months before he confronted them, and you know what was funny…?' She paused and brushed away the tears that were silently streaming down her face. 'They knew all the time. They had been waiting for him to tell them. Now you have to admit that that is classic.'

Angolos turned. The strain etched in the strong lines of his face was echoed in his eyes. 'Is this true?' he asked hoarsely. 'You were never lovers?'

'You're the only man I've ever slept with. My secret lover was only ever a figment of your sordid imagination.'

The accusation made the last dregs of colour leach from his face. The knuckles on the fist he had clenched against his mouth went white. With his other hand he wiped away the sheen of moisture from his forehead, but almost immediately beads of sweat bubbled up to replace it.

'What have I done?' He swallowed convulsively and

pressed his hands to his head. 'I thought you had made a fool of me... My damned pride. I thought another man had given you what I couldn't.'

Georgie stood there. She knew that seeing him go through such agonies of remorse should be making her feel better, but it wasn't. Seeing him suffer gave her no glow of satisfaction at all. It just made her feel wretched, because when Angolos hurt so did she.

Angolos's shoulders suddenly straightened. He looked directly at her. 'I will of course apologise to your friend.'

All her instincts made her want to run to him and throw her arms around him, but his manner was so distant and formal that such a thing was unthinkable.

'Thank you.' She didn't know what else to say.

He shot her a pained look. 'You don't have to thank me. Because of me you have spent the last three years struggling to bring up a child alone.'

'It wasn't a struggle, it was a pleasure, and I wasn't alone, I had my family.'

'I will make it up to you. If it takes me the rest of my life I'll make it up to you,' he vowed, grinding one clenched fist into the other.

'You think I want our marriage to be a penance?' She let her head loll back to release some of the tension in her neck muscles.

'What do you want our marriage to be?'

At last a question that she actually knew the answer to without three hours' soul-searching. 'What I always wanted it to be: a partnership of equals.' *Loving* equals, she silently qualified.

He studied her in amazement. 'You still want that?'

'What has changed?'

Angolos stared at her, as far as he was concerned, everything had.

Five minutes earlier he had been comfortably occupying

the moral high ground. She had betrayed him but he had been prepared to put that to one side in order to preserve their marriage and create a stable home for their son.

Now he knew everything he had been thinking had been based on a lie. He had punished the woman he loved because he had been blinded by jealousy.

'I hope one day you will be able to forgive me for what I have done.'

'I do...'

'That isn't possible.'

She gave an exasperated sigh. 'Will you stop telling me how I feel? You're as bad as my family. It's true,' she added as he looked about to protest. 'You are. I know you feel bad, but that's not the important thing, is it...?'

'It isn't...?'

'We got back together because of Nicky, didn't we?'

Angolos, who was pacing restlessly around the room, stopped mid-stride. His face turned to hers; his dark eyes moved over her pale but resolute face. 'Is that why we got back together?'

She put down the strangeness of his tone to the discovery she had not been unfaithful. 'Well, obviously.'

He suddenly flopped down into an armchair. 'Of course it is.'

'Well, given that, does any of this really matter? You were wrong but the fact remains you can't change the past. So shouldn't we be concerned about making the future we want for our son? I'll sleep with someone if that will make you feel better.'

The smile died on her lips as he rose with one fluid motion to his feet, his face contorted in a mask of livid fury. 'No that would not make me feel...*better*.'

'For heaven's sake, Angolos, it was just a joke. You don't think I'd actually...well, no, you do think I'd...' She stopped and closed her eyes in despair. This was all coming out wrong.

Her eyes flickered open as she felt the light touch of his hands as they closed over her shoulders. 'So you want us to stay together for Nicky?'

I want us to stay together for us… 'Well, we can't give up at the first little problem, can we?'

'Little problem,' he repeated. 'You really have a novel outlook on life.'

'I have a practical outlook on life.'

'So we will do the practical thing and stay together.'

She nodded. She had got her own way and suddenly all she wanted to do was cry her eyes out.

CHAPTER FOURTEEN

THEY arrived at Paul and Mirrie Radcliff's the day before the christening, and were shown to the pretty guest room. It was charming and Nicky was equally happy with his camp-bed, which had been put up in the adjoining dressing room. Watching him playing with the Radcliffs' dog, a large animal of very mixed ancestry, Georgie wasn't at all surprised when Nicky introduced the subject of a dog of his own.

Angolos entered their bedroom as she was fastening the antique pearl choker around her neck. A glance in the mirror told her it was the exact finishing touch the outfit she'd brought for the christening needed.

'I suppose you know that Nicky thinks you're a soft touch. Damn,' she muttered as the catch eluded her. Angolos's silent scrutiny made her clumsy.

'*A soft touch…?*' She was soft…thinking of her softness made him hard. Around Georgette his normal self-control was non-existent.

Watching him lever his long, lean frame from the wall, she doubted that there was an adjective *less* appropriate. Everything about him was hard, including his impenetrable expression. He wore that expression a lot just lately. The only time he was spontaneous was in bed!

'Nicky says you said he can have a dog…a big dog,' she added drily.

'A boy should have a dog.'

'Did you?' she asked, giving up on her attempts to master the clasp as her arms began to ache.

He shook his dark head. 'My mother considered pets in the house to be unhygienic. But do you have any objections…?'

154

'No, I don't mind a few dog hairs on the furniture and I think you're right—a boy should have a dog.'

'You think I'm right? Be careful, Georgette,' he mocked. 'This is getting to be a habit. Let me,' he added, taking the choker from her unresisting clasp.

She stiffened as he brushed her hair from the nape of her neck, then as his fingertips brushed her skin she released a long, sibilant sigh.

'Problem?' he asked.

The enquiry made her eyes snap open. He had to know what his touch did to her. 'Give that to me,' she snapped, snatching the pearls from his grasp.

Hands up, Angolos took a step backwards. 'What did I do…?'

Georgie observed this display of bewilderment with exasperation. 'Nothing, that's the point,' she admitted, succumbing to a bout of ill-timed frankness. 'You don't have to do anything, you just,' she emphasised, stabbing her finger accusingly at him, 'have to be…*you*,' she finished lamely.

'Who would you like me to be? Do you find living with me such a burden?' he asked in a driven undertone.

'It's driving me crazy!' she admitted. 'Breathing the same air as you drives me crazy.'

'Then there is no more to be said.'

His air of cool finality made her want to scream. 'There's a great deal more to be said,' she yelled. 'I'm fed up with walking into a room and you not looking at me. The only place you want me is in bed,' she accused.

An expression of total astonishment swept across his face. 'That is totally untrue!'

'*I don't think so,*' she retorted bitterly. 'Did it ever occur to you that simply looking at you turns me to a…?' She suddenly buried her face in her hands. 'Look at me—I don't even know what I'm saying any more…'

Angolos, who had been staring at her, suddenly shook his

head as though to clear his thoughts. 'I am looking at you. I'm always looking at you... I can't stop looking at you. I want to touch you.'

The catch in his deep, driven voice penetrated her misery. Blinking, Georgie lifted her head. 'You only have me in the house because Nicky and I are a joint package.'

His jaw tightened. 'That is a ludicrous thing to say... At times,' he told her through gritted teeth, 'I could shake you. *You're my wife.*' He grasped her chin in his hand and drew her face up to his. 'I shouldn't have to apologise for wanting to look at you, but I feel as if I do.'

'I'm your mistress,' she contended stubbornly, 'in all but name—you only want me in your bed!' she accused.

'Sure, I want you in my bed. You in my bed is the only thing that's keeping me sane.' He dragged a visibly unsteady hand through his hair.

Georgie was mesmerised by the deep, hot flame that seemed to smoulder in his dark eyes.

'But I also want you to be my wife in every other sense. I just thought that since I... I thought that you would prefer it that way.'

Her lips quivered. 'Well, I don't,' she rebutted bluntly. 'Just because you're on some sort of stupid guilt trip and want to go around looking all stupidly noble I don't see why I should suffer.'

He looked disconcerted and slightly dazed by her forceful pronouncement. 'You are suffering...?'

She lifted her glowing eyes to his. 'Of course I am, you stupid man! I want to be able to talk to you about something that isn't to do with Nicky without being frozen out. I want to be able to yell at you, and hug you and—'

There was a knock on the door. *'Ignore it.'*

Georgie, who was struggling to catch her breath, was more than willing to follow his tight-lipped advice, but the second knock followed by an apologetic voice was harder to ignore.

Angolos cursed softly under his breath, said *'Later,'* and strode to the door.

'About time to go to the church, if you're ready…?' Paul, oblivious to the electric atmosphere, popped his head around Angolos and gave a thumbs-up sign. 'Looking good, Georgie,' he called cheerily.

Georgie, almost laughing at Angolos's expression, said thank you primly and promised she was ready.

Seeing Angolos with Paul and his wife had been a revelation to Georgie. She had never seen him as relaxed as he was in this informal setting. She had found it difficult to hide her amazement when she had seen her elegant husband roll up his sleeves and do the dishes.

The last of the guests left and Paul came out into the garden to join the two women, who were chatting cosily at the now deserted table. 'Well, I think that went very well…other than the Uncle Tim, vicar incident.'

'I think the vicar has heard the odd naughty joke in his life,' his wife laughed.

'Could be right. I heard he had quite a colourful life before he donned a dog-collar.' He pulled up a chair. 'Where's Angolos?'

'He's gone to check on Nicky,' Georgie explained.

'Right. Quite a live wire, isn't he, that boy?' He glanced down at the baby sleeping in the wicker crib set on the grass beside the women. 'I wonder if this one will be like that.'

'Worse, probably,' his fond mother suggested comfortably. 'Leave those, Paul,' she added as her husband began to gather up stray glasses. 'We can do them later. He isn't always so domesticated,' she added to Georgie. 'I think he's showing off for your benefit.'

'I like that,' said her indignant spouse with a grin as he dragged up a chair and proceeded to pour the last dregs from a champagne bottle into his glass. 'I'll say this for Angolos, he knows his wine, though I suspect most of our guests would have been just as happy with any old fizz.'

'Don't be rude, Paul—offer Georgie a drink. I know you've still got a crate of the stuff in the kitchen.'

Georgie raised her glass of mineral water. 'No, I'm fine, thank you.'

'When is it you move over to Greece?'

Georgie grimaced. 'Tuesday. I'm pretty nervous,' she admitted.

'Don't be. I'm sure you'll be fine. It's easy to see that you and Angolos are solid.'

'You think so?' Georgie asked, unaware of the wistful note in her voice or of the glance the married couple exchanged. 'To be honest I'm not Olympia's favourite person. Have you met…?'

Mirrie laughed. 'Oh, yes, we've met Olympia. Scary lady. But, Georgie, you're older and wiser now and, more importantly, you have Nicky. I predict that you've done the one thing that will grant you a place in that lady's heart. You've given her a grandson, lots and *lots* of Brownie points, girl. I think you'll find the balance of power has shifted.'

'I don't know about that,' Georgie said softly as she abandoned her seat and walked over to the crib.

Angolos emerged from the house just in time to hear her say, 'They're really lovely when they're this age, aren't they?'

'Worth all the hard work and pain,' Mirrie agreed, watching the younger girl with a thoughtful expression. 'And I had an easy labour, or so they told me. How about you?'

'Long,' Georgie said, her mind drifting back to those unendurably lonely hours when she had called out Angolos's name. He hadn't come and the doctor, whom the midwife had called when she'd become worried by the monitor readings, had been sympathetic but firm.

You can cry later; just now we need to get this baby out.

She gave her head a little shake… She never thought of

that. 'But that's par for the course with the first baby, so they tell me.'

The other woman grimaced in sympathy. 'Would I be wrong in thinking you're just the tiniest bit broody?' she probed gently.

Across the garden Angolos paused.

Georgie's head came up with jerk. 'Angolos doesn't want another baby just yet,' she said abruptly. Then, realising she'd made it sound as though Angolos had made the decision unilaterally, she added quickly, 'That is, we decided…' She lifted her slender shoulders in an awkward shrug.

'The mystery is to me that anyone ever has more than one,' Paul interjected, shaking his head. 'I know I couldn't do it again.'

'Do what, exactly, Paul?' his wife teased, winking at Georgie. 'Seriously,' she added before her husband could retort, 'I don't know what I'd have done in labour without this one.' Mirrie caught hold of her husband's hand. 'Just having him there to give me support made such a difference, but then I'm sure you know what I'm talking about.'

'*Mirrie!*' her husband muttered, elbowing her in the side.

'Ouch! I…' she began indignantly, then she saw Angolos standing there looking as if someone had just slid a knife between his ribs. His eyes were trained on Georgie, who looked equally stricken. Her hand came up to her mouth. 'Oh, I didn't mean…'

'Right, I think it's time to open another bottle,' Paul said, clapping his hands.

Angolos's gaze flickered to his friend. He exhaled the breath that had been trapped in his chest and smiled. 'Not for me, thanks, Paul,' he said quietly. 'But I wouldn't mind a coffee. Shall I…?'

'Are you saying I can't make coffee?' Beneath the teasing his friend looked concerned as he followed him back into the house.

*   *   *

Mirrie sought her bed early and Georgie wasn't far behind. The two men stayed up later, talking about, Georgie presumed, what men talked about when they stayed up late into the night.

Did Angolos discuss her? Did he talk about his marriage? Did his friend know that if it hadn't been for him discovering Nicky they would by now be divorced?

When Angolos did come to bed she lay there in the darkness listening. She heard him go into the dressing room, presumably to check on the soundly sleeping Nicky. When he came back the soft rustle of clothes indicated he was undressing.

'Did I wake you?' he asked when he slid between the sheets.

'How did you know I was awake?' she asked, her voice muffled by the pillow she was clutching to her chest.

Not that there was any chance of her falling asleep before he came to bed. Considering the fact she had slept alone for so long, her inability to sleep when he wasn't there was all the more perverse.

'I didn't.'

Georgie could hear the smile in his voice.

'Come here.' When he reached for her she allowed herself to be hauled up against him. She felt his breath warm on the back of her neck just before he kissed her ear.

'You're naked…' he discovered.

'I was hot.'

'This is something I have noticed about you,' he agreed.

She sighed and flipped over so that they lay chest to chest, thigh to thigh. She rubbed her cheek against his rough stubble. In the darkness a secret smile curved her lips as she felt his instant response.

He muttered something in Greek and then rolled away from her. A moment later there was a click.

She blinked as light from the bedside lamp illuminated the room. Her expression was a fair reflection of the seething sense of frustration she was feeling.

'What's wrong?'

'You have a very attractive pout.'

Angolos was lying propped up on one elbow, his eyes trained on her face. The sheet had slipped down to waist-level exposing each smooth muscle and hard angle of his taut torso. His skin gleamed like oiled silk in the subdued light. Georgie caught her breath as a spasm of sexual longing so intense she could taste it pierced to the core of her.

'We need to talk.'

'Now…?'

'Did you have a difficult labour?'

Georgie frowned and plucked at the sheet, pleating it between her fingers. It had been the very last thing she had expected him to say. 'Labour? What brought this on?'

He ignored her bewildered question. 'Was your grandmother there…or a friend?' He waited tensely for her reply; the idea of her being alone was intolerable.

She shook her head. 'Gran—can you see that? Gran's idea of being supportive would have been to tell me to pull myself together and get on with it.' When he didn't smile she added, 'No, I was alone.'

He closed his eyes and, alarmed by the expression that drew his skin taut across the marvellous bones of his face, Georgie pulled herself into an upright position, bringing the sheet with her.

'If you don't count a room full of medical staff.' *Where was this coming from?*

His dark lashes lifted. 'Do not make this a joke,' he reprimanded severely.

'I wasn't…' She released a sigh. 'I was just trying to…'

'Be very British and stoical,' he suggested.

This accusation drew a small smile from her. 'If you really

want to know I had a very long labour. Nicky was a big baby and I...'

Angolos's eyes followed the direction of her gaze and he added huskily, 'You are not.' *She was slender and delicate and...*

She nodded. 'That's what the midwife said,' she agreed. 'It lasted a long time and I was pretty tired. I tried but... She got worried when Nicky's heartbeat slowed. The doctor was called.'

'The doctor,' Angolos exploded furiously, 'should have been there all along!' If he had been there he would have made sure that she had not been neglected. He caught her expression and made a visible effort to control himself. 'Sorry...go on,' he said tautly.

'There's not a lot to say.'

'You mean you don't want to tell me. I always know when you're hiding something, Georgette.'

If that were true, Georgie reflected, she was in big, *big* trouble! 'Not hiding, it's just everything was fine in the end. The doctor just thought it might be necessary to do an emergency section if things didn't move along.'

Georgie retained a distinct memory of grabbing the poor guy's arm and yelling, 'I don't care so long as my baby's all right.' The memory made her smile.

'But things did happen and it wasn't necessary.'

Angolos studied her in silence for a moment. 'You make light of it. I know you do,' he added impatiently as she opened her mouth to rebut the claim. 'But it must have been a terrifying experience.'

'I was very tired,' she admitted quietly. 'But a lot of women have it a lot worse than I did.'

'You were all alone and afraid.' Hand pressed to his forehead, he fell onto his back on the mattress. On the pillow his head turned towards her. 'You must have hated me.'

'Would it make you happier if I said I did? I don't know

why you're suddenly so determined to beat yourself up over this…it all happened a very long time ago.'

A spasm of self-disgust contorted his features. 'Of *course* you hated me!' A bitter laugh was drawn from his throat. 'How could you not? I rejected you and left you to give birth to my child alone. If I had been a bigger man I would…' Angolos flinched and turned his head to look at the small hand on his shoulder.

She simply couldn't bear the pain in his voice.

'You missed out too, Angolos,' she told him in a voice thickly congested with emotion. 'You,' she added swallowing, 'didn't see your son born.'

'And I will regret that to my dying day,' he admitted.

'I'm so sorry,' she said.

'Sorry…?'

Unable to bear the intensity of his scrutiny, she looked away. 'Yes, I am.'

A strangled expletive escaped his clenched teeth. 'The thing is you really are, aren't you? It's incredible. You haven't got a vindictive bone in your body.' Inexplicably—at least it was pretty inexplicable to Georgie—he sounded as though the discovery made him angry.

Georgie, thrown by his shift of mood, didn't know how to respond to this allegation. The silence between them stretched as his dark gaze seemed restless, but it always returned to her face. Sheet tethered in one hand, she reached across him for the lamp switch.

'Would you like another baby, *agape mou*?'

She flushed and looked at the big hand covering her own. The tender endearment was like a blade piercing her aching heart.

Not *a* baby; *your* baby.

Obviously she didn't voice her thoughts, though for a split second she had come close. How could she tell him how she felt when even she knew her feelings defied all logic? Turning her head slowly, Georgie met his eyes; his regard was too searching for her. Catching her full lower lip between her teeth, she looked away and with a sigh drew her knees up to her chin.

'That is a forlorn sound.'

'You heard what Mirrie said. I thought you must have.'

'And was she right?'

'We discussed this…'

'Did we?' he inserted.

'You know we did.' Her determination to convince him of her sincerity made her voice higher than usual.

'Maybe we should discuss it again.'

'I don't think so. Let's face it, our marriage is not what you'd call solid, is it?' Her laugh had a pretty hollow sound.

There was a long, dragging silence before Angolos responded. 'This is about our conversation earlier…?'

She shrugged.

'I am making you unhappy…?'

'That's not what I'm saying. It's just ours is a marriage of convenience. We're together for Nicky's sake. Sure, the sex is good…actually it is sensational,' she admitted, lifting her chin. 'But sex isn't enough.'

The problem was that, being with Paul and Mirrie and seeing what they had, that magical element…the fact was she had caught herself experiencing jealous pangs on several occasions. Was it greedy of her to want more?

'You're not getting all that you want from our marriage?' From the expression etched in the taut lines of his strong face, she assumed he was angry.

'It isn't about what I want.' She could never tell him what she wanted. 'A child should never be used to paper over the cracks in a relationship, and we have some gaping chasms. I mean, in case you had forgotten, if things had gone differently we would be divorced by now.'

'*Theos!*' he gritted. 'I am hardly likely to forget when you so obligingly remind me of the fact on a daily basis.'

'I don't…'

'Life is precious and, although it is clichéd, you should live every day as though it were your last. You live your life in the expectation of there being something cataclysmic around the next corner.'

'Maybe experience has taught me to expect things to go wrong.' The moment the bitter observation left her lips she regretted it. 'I'm sorry. I didn't mean to say that.'

He looked at the hand she laid on his arm and then looked away; a muscle along his jaw clenched. 'But you think it.' His dark glance swept across her face. 'Do not deny it. I am capable of accepting the part I have played in making you afraid to live life, *yineka mou*. Surely,' he added, 'the point is we are *not* divorced, and we are not going to be.'

'You can't *know* that.'

'Certainly I can *know* that,' he proclaimed. 'Unlike you, I am *totally* committed to this marriage.'

'Because of Nicky,' she said, as much to remind herself of this as to show him that she understood his motives and was all right with them. Actually she wasn't at all all right; actually thinking about him staying with her because of Nicky filled her with an inexpressible sadness.

'What other reason could there be, *agape mou*?'

Once again his volatile mood swing took her unawares. For some reason he sounded and looked utterly furious. She shrugged noncommittally, but on this occasion it did not lessen the intensity of the emotions he was projecting.

'The only thing that will take you away from me…' he reached across and framed her softly rounded chin between his thumb and forefinger; his other hand he fitted into the curve of her neck, pulling her close so that their faces were inches apart '…is an act of God,' he completed thickly.

He made it sound like a jail sentence. Was that how he

thought of it? 'I *am* as committed to this marriage as you are!' she protested.

He raked a hand through his dark hair. 'But it makes you shudder…?' He said it so softly that Georgie barely caught his bitter observation.

She laughed.

'What is funny?' he asked, with the air of someone who was very close to losing it.

Losing it was not something Angolos did often, but Georgie was far too preoccupied with keeping a grip herself to notice.

'Maybe the day will come when I can be naked in bed with you and not shudder when you touch me.' Her restless gaze roamed unrestrained over the firm, taut skin of his bronzed torso. She gulped and added huskily, 'But I suspect the day when you won't touch me will arrive a hell of a lot sooner…'

Angolos leaned across and pressed a finger to her lips. Georgie couldn't believe what she had just said, but she knew she had said it because he was looking unbearably smug.

'We were talking about extending our family, I believe? You agree that Nicky needs a brother or sister.'

'But you said—'

'Forget what I said. It is not a matter of not wanting. I felt that after being deprived of a father for the first years of his life Nicky deserved to have all my attention, but I have since come to realise that the best thing I can do for Nicky is give him a family life.

'A family life that involves all the rough and tumble and sharing that having siblings involves. The only problem I foresee is that addressing this problem will require me being naked in bed and possibly out of bed quite a lot.' He angled a questioning glance at her flushed face. 'Do you think that you could cope with that?'

Georgie managed to convince him that she could.

CHAPTER FIFTEEN

To GEORGIE'S amazement Mirrie's prediction turned out to be true. The dreaded Olympia took one look at Nicky and burst into floods of emotional tears.

As Angolos promptly walked out of the room, it was left to Georgie to comfort her. Suddenly Georgie found she was the flavour of the month. She had given her a grandchild—and he was a boy and there was no more talk of Sonia.

Georgie also found her mother-in-law easier to cope with when she lived ten miles away, though, as she doted on Nicky, she did visit frequently. In fact, the entire set-up was a lot less daunting the second time around. She could see now that half the problem before had been her lack of confidence.

Even though she was no longer that inexperienced girl she did have a few things to prove to herself, hence the party. For good measure she added Sonia to the guest list.

The day arrived.

What, she asked herself, possessed me? I'm not a society hostess. I can't do witty conversation... I'm not even totally sure what fork to use half the time. I knew all these things and yet I still thought it would be a good idea to invite a selection of rich, powerful people for dinner.

Clearly I have lost my mind.

The obvious solution is to cancel, she told herself. After all, it's not like I've got anything to prove.

Not much...!

She marched through the house to Angolos's study, and entered without knocking. She opened her mouth and saw he had his ear pressed to a phone.

Angolos motioned her to a chair, which Georgie sat down

in, feeling cheated out of her big entrance. The conversation was in Greek, but one word she did catch...*Sonia*.

She walked over to the wood-panelled wall and with a decisive motion yanked the phone cord from its socket.

It took Angolos a second or so to realise that the phone was dead. When he did he frowned and slammed it down on its cradle.

'There must be a fault on the line,' he began, turning, then he saw Georgie. He looked from the cord she was casually swinging back and forth to her face. 'Just what the hell are you doing?'

'Getting your attention.'

Angolos flopped down with fluid grace into a deeply padded leather swivel chair. He planted his chin on his interlaced fingers and looked at her through his lashes. 'You have it,' he promised.

'I came to tell you that I'm cancelling this dinner tonight.'

His brows lifted. '*And...?*'

His reaction threw her off stride. 'There is no and.'

'Right, no dinner.'

Her brows knit as she looked at him. 'Is that all you've got to say?'

'What else would you like me to say?'

'Don't patronise me!' she gritted back. 'In case it has escaped your notice I've been planning this dinner all week. A lot of very important people are coming and all you can say is, *Fine...?*'

'I said right, actually.'

'I don't care what you said.'

This contradictory statement caused him to massage the groove between his darkly delineated brows.

'I know you think I'm a total failure...I'm a social liability.'

'I never wanted the party anyway.'

'Don't humour me, Angolos.'

'I don't enjoy formal dinners.'

'Well, tough, because this one is going to be a great success!' As she slammed the door she could hear him laughing.

The preparations were going quite well when mid-morning she got a phone call.

'Emily, I've got to go out for a while. Can you hold the fort?'

She drove herself to the office and was ushered straight in. She brushed aside the offer of refreshment and got straight to the point.

'You've located my mother?'

The man looked at her with sympathetic spaniel eyes; he didn't look Georgie's idea of a hard-bitten private investigator at all. 'Your mother died two years ago.'

Georgie sank into the chair. 'I see...'

The sympathetic man handed her a thick file. 'It's all in there. She married the man who she...ahem. He is still alive; he owns a hotel chain and runs it with his eldest son.'

'Son! You mean I have a half-brother?' This was something she had not even considered.

'Yes, and two half-sisters. The details are all in there.'

By the time Georgie got back home her head was pounding. She had a family she didn't know, who probably didn't even know she existed. The choice as to what she should do with the information in the file was for later. Right now was for getting her head around the fact her mother was dead. It was silly—she hadn't known the woman and she still felt... Actually, she didn't know how she felt.

She would discuss it later with Angolos and see what he said, she decided.

Angolos had a lot to say, it turned out the moment she walked through the door.

'Where have you been?'

She was emotionally exhausted; his accusing tone was the last straw. 'Out?' she said shortly.

'Out somewhere with a man.'

Her eyes flew wide open. 'Pardon?'

'He rang to say he had something that belonged to me and, not to worry, he would make arrangements for me to get it back. When I asked who he was, he hung up. What was I supposed to think?' he asked grimly.

After this morning this was as much as she could take. She gave a contemptuous sniff and drew herself to her full height. 'The worst thing possible, I would imagine. After e…everything that has happened,' she added in a shaking voice, 'I can't believe you would still think that I would cheat on you. It was my purse that…'

'I thought you had been abducted…kidnapped…'

Georgie's jaw dropped. *'You're not serious…?'*

'I was within this…' he held his thumb and forefinger a whisper apart '…of calling the police.'

'But that's ridiculous!'

His response was a frigid, 'I'm glad you think so.'

A giggle escaped her compressed lips, then another and another…until she was laughing helplessly, tears streaming down her face.

Georgie's head continued to pound long after Angolos had walked out. She had not the faintest idea where he was or if he would even turn up for the wretched dinner party that night, and, she told herself angrily, she didn't care!

Actually the truth was she did care, and not just because the guest list for the dinner party was enough to make an accomplished society hostess nervous! Without Angolos to steer her through the evening the occasion would no doubt be a total disaster. And what was she supposed to tell them when they asked why he wasn't there?

She could see now that her laughing might have upset him; it had just been the shock of hearing him say what he had coming right on top of everything else that had set her off.

Angolos had been livid.

'Don't you walk away when I'm talking!' she yelled. Then, seeing her words had no effect on him, she added gruffly, 'When will you be back?'

He stopped then and looked at her through the mesh of his incredibly long lashes. 'When I can trust myself not to strangle you.'

Who knows when that might be? she thought gloomily now. From the way he had looked when he'd said it, it could easily be never.

With her personal life falling apart she had totally forgotten to tell the chef that one guest this evening was vegan and another had a dairy intolerance.

The chef, who had always regarded her with deep suspicion since he'd caught her making beans on toast one evening, received the information in silence.

At least, she reflected, he hadn't walked out too—not like some people. She hastily blinked away the tears that filled her eyes as Nicky appeared with Emily. He was wearing his swimming trunks.

'Oh, I'm sorry, darling,' she said, scooping him up. 'I know Mummy said she'd come swimming with you after lunch, but I'm really busy.'

Nine out of ten three-year-olds would have sulked at having a promised treat denied, but Nicky gave a philosophical little shrug that was heartbreakingly familiar.

She gave him a rib-cracking hug back. 'I promise I'll come tomorrow. Make him keep on his sun hat, will you, Emily?' she reminded the older woman.

'I will, my dear,' she promised.

It was half an hour later when she was giving her opinion of the flower arrangements in the formal dining room that Kostas the gardener rushed into the room unannounced.

'It is the little one!' he yelled.

'Nicky...?'

The man gestured towards the door. 'Come.'

Thomasis, the major domo, came up behind Georgie and spoke to Kostas in Greek.

'It is the little one,' he explained. 'Kostas says he slipped and hit his head on the side of the swimming pool. He is unconscious. I will call an ambulance...'

Before he had finished speaking Georgie was running. Halfway down the steps she ripped off her high heels and ran on barefoot down the flower-filled terraces that led to the tree-shaded pool area.

It was one of Georgie's favourite spots on the estate but at the moment she had no eyes for the panoramic views over the sparkling Aegean. Today all she saw was the tiny figure lying on the ground.

He looks so small.

'I'm so...sorry, he ran and...'

Georgie tuned out Emily's tearful explanation as she dropped down onto her knees beside Nicky.

'He's breathing,' she said as she brushed the tears streaming down her face away with the back of her hand. 'Thank God!' She touched the skin of his face and bit her lip. 'We can't leave him here; we should move him to the house.' She took his hand between her own and chafed it. 'Wake up, Nicky, sweetheart.'

'No, to be on the safe side I don't think we should move him. The ambulance will be here directly.' From somewhere Thomasis produced a blanket and tenderly placed it over the unconscious child.

'No, no, you're right,' she agreed. She screwed up her eyes as she made an effort to focus her thoughts. Despite these efforts all she felt as she spoke again was blind fear. 'Do you think he's...?'

'I think he's going to be fine, *kyria*,' Thomasis replied.

Georgie was vaguely conscious of Emily being led away weeping. 'He looks so small.' She took a deep breath and fought back the panic that threatened to overwhelm her. 'I want Angolos. He will know what to do.' She knew it was totally irrational, but she was sure that if Angolos were here he would make everything all right.

'We are trying to contact him,' came the soothing response.

The minutes while they waited for the ambulance seemed like a lifetime to Georgie and the journey to the hospital was a blur. She protested as Nicky was taken away, the language barrier made it worse and what little Greek she had acquired deserted her totally.

To her relief the doctor spoke perfect English.

After he had given her a consent form to sign and explained what they were about to do he looked at her marble-pale face. 'You do understand what I'm saying…?'

'Yes,' said Georgie, who had only taken in one word in three. 'Perhaps we should wait for my husband…?'

'I'm afraid that a delay would not be a good idea.'

Georgie swallowed. 'Fine, do what you must.'

When her mother-in-law made her sweeping entrance twenty minutes later Georgie was sitting there with her white-knuckled fingers closed around a cup of coffee someone had brought her fifteen minutes earlier. It was untouched and stone-cold.

Olympia wasn't alone; she never went anywhere alone. Her secretary, an elderly cousin who was her companion, and a liveried chauffeur accompanied her into the hospital.

By magic a comfortable chair appeared.

Olympia ignored it. 'I do not want a chair. I want to see a doctor. My dear,' she added, going straight to Georgie and enfolding her in a fragrant embrace. 'Have they told you anything?'

Georgie shook her head. 'They took him to Theatre; they said he had raised inter-cranial pressure. I think they're going to drill…' She couldn't bring herself to tell the older woman that the doctor hadn't given her a straight answer when she had asked if there was a chance of brain damage.

'*Theos…!*'

'How did you know? Is Angolos here?' Georgie asked her mother-in-law.

'No, I'm afraid we haven't been able to locate him yet, but do not worry, he will be here. Thomasis rang me. At a time like this you need family around.' She gave an understanding nod at the tears that began to silently run down Georgie's cheeks.

'You must put your faith in the doctors. They know what they are doing,' she said, gently taking the cup Georgie was still clutching from her hand. 'Sit down, my dear.' She looked at her daughter-in-law's bare feet but said nothing.

Georgie did as she was urged. She felt numb and strangely disconnected from the things going on around her.

'I want Angolos,' she said.

'Of course you do, and he will be here presently.'

'It's my fault…if I had gone swimming with Nicky none of this would have happened—'

'I do not want to hear that.' The imperious older woman cut her off mid-sentence. 'Accidents happen. There is no point in dealing in "what ifs". From what I have seen you are an attentive mother.'

The unexpected tribute brought fresh tears to Georgie's reddened eyes, but she knew that if Nicky's grandmother didn't blame her his father would. 'Angolos would never forgive me if anything happened to Nicky,' she predicted tragically.

'My son is a bigger man than that.'

'I know, but we argued,' Georgie admitted, biting her lip. 'He left; he was furious with me.'

The older woman took Georgie's hand between her own. 'Angolos is a man with a hot temper, but a big heart, and he loves you.'

Astonished, Georgie stared back at her mother-in-law.

'And I think you love him also…yes…?'

Georgie nodded.

'Then if you talk things will be all right. First,' she added briskly, 'we must find him, but I have people looking for him so do not worry. He will be here.'

And what will he find when he gets here…? Georgie hardly dared think that far ahead.

The two women sat in silence as the minutes ticked by.

'Why doesn't he come…?'

The rheumatic fingers around her own tightened. 'He could do nothing if he was here. Waiting is hard, I know…' The older woman heaved a sigh.

'What will I do if he doesn't get better? I can't bear…' Georgie's face crumpled. 'He's so little,' she wailed.

Olympia seemed to have no problem following this disjointed, sorrowful sentence.

'I thought we had agreed there is no point worrying about something that hasn't happened yet, and Nicky may be little but he is a Constantine and he is a fighter just like his father.'

'Yes, yes, he is, isn't he?' Georgie said eagerly. She gave a wan smile and wiped her damp face.

'And you are a Constantine now too, so you must be brave. Be brave for little Nicky; he will need his mother.'

Georgie swallowed and lifted her chin. 'Thank you,' she said thickly.

A nurse approached. 'Mrs Constantine?'

Both women got to their feet.

'Is there news?'

'Well, the doctor will explain, but…'

Georgie managed to hold back her emotion until she had spoken to the doctor and seen Nicky come round briefly after his operation. But when she left him sleeping peacefully again, then it all spilled out. She leaned against the wall, her body shaking with silent sobs as tears ran unheeded down her cheeks.

'*Theos…!*'

She opened her eyes and found herself looking up into the

dark eyes of her husband. Weak with relief, she staggered into his arms.

'Angolos!' she breathed as his arms closed tight around her. She felt his mouth in her hair; his breathing close to her ear was uneven and laboured.

'I'm so, so…sorry,' he said, his voice an agonised whisper. *'Is he…?'*

Then she realised he didn't know that Nicky had come through the operation and there would be no lasting damage. She lifted her head and took his face between her hands. The depth of pain inscribed in those proud lines shocked her deeply.

'Nicky is going to be fine, Angolos,' she told him. 'The operation was a total success.'

He froze, hope suddenly flaring in the shadowed depths of his eyes. 'But I thought, they told me, and when I saw you breaking your heart I thought he was…'

'It was relief; I was crying with relief.'

'This is true?' The big hands that took her shoulders were shaking. 'Nicky is going to be well…?'

She nodded, unable to speak past the emotional constriction in her aching throat. 'He was bleeding…' she touched her own head '…inside. They relieved the pressure.'

'Will there be any complications?'

She shook her head. 'No, they say he'll be a hundred per cent.'

She stood to one side and gestured towards the door. 'He's in there. Would you like to see him?'

The brown muscles in Angolos's throat worked as he nodded.

The nurse who was sitting beside the small figure whose head was swathed in bandages rose as they entered.

Angolos said something in Greek to which she replied in the same language. With a nod towards Georgie she moved away from the bed to make room for them.

'She said he'll sleep for a while yet,' Angolos said, his eyes trained on the sleeping figure.

Georgie nodded. 'He did wake up, though.'

'Did he ask for me?'

She shook her head. 'No,' she replied with a smile in her voice. 'He asked for a dog…a big dog and he also said that it wasn't his fault.'

The admission drew a short laugh from Angolos. He exhaled and dragged his long fingers through his dark hair. 'He looks so small.'

'I know.'

Angolos turned and looked at her. 'I'm so sorry,' he said thickly.

'*You're* sorry?'

'I wasn't there for you when you needed me.'

The self-recrimination in his voice made her shake her head in denial. 'But you couldn't know, and your mother was here.'

He looked astonished. 'My mother?'

She nodded. 'Yes, your mother, and actually she was pretty fantastic, a real hero. She stayed until Nicky woke up and then I made her go home. She looked exhausted; she left cousin Sabine with me.'

Angolos grimaced. 'That was kind of her,' he said drily.

Georgie's lips twitched. 'She is really a very nice woman.'

'She's a nitwit,' he retorted.

'She has a kind heart, actually, and she hates hospitals so it's very kind of her to offer to stay.'

'More like she's too scared of my mother to disagree.' Head turned slightly from her, he pressed the heels of his hands against his eyes. For the first time she registered the lines of exhaustion scoring his handsome face. The ache in her chest became a physical pain.

'I was going to get a coffee when you arrived. Would you like me to fetch you one…?'

At her soft words Angolos's head lifted. He looked at the

small hand curved over his arm and then at her face. A slow smile that made her heart flip spread slowly across his impossibly gorgeous face.

'Actually, I think I'll come with you. Nicky will not wake yet for a while…?'

She shook her head and turned to the nurse. 'That's right, isn't it?'

The nurse nodded.

'And if he does they've given me a bleeper,' Georgie added, producing the item from her pocket.

Angolos nodded and placed a hand on her shoulders and steered her towards the door. 'There are things we need to talk about.'

A finger of dread traced a path down her spine. *Oh, no…!*

'Are you cold?' asked Angolos, who felt her shiver.

'No.'

Up to this point Nicky's condition had been the only thing occupying Angolos's mind. Now that he knew Nicky was out of danger, Georgie, who knew the way his logical mind worked, knew that he would move on to the next obvious question—namely who was responsible for Nicky's accident?

'The café is this way,' she said when they got out into the corridor.

Angolos shook his head. 'If you don't mind I'll take a rain check. Hospitals,' he confided, 'are not my favourite place. Maybe we could sit outside…?'

'Sure.'

Angolos shot her an enquiring look when she hung back instead of following him.

'I know what you're going to say.'

His darkly defined brows drew together in a frown. 'That I seriously doubt,' he said drily.

'I do. And I just want to say that nothing you can say could make me feel worse than I already do,' she stressed in a tremulous voice. 'If I hadn't been busy with that wretched party

I would have gone swimming with Nicky as I promised and none of this would have happened.'

'If *I* hadn't flounced out of the house like an adolescent...if we had never met...'

She went pale. Was that what he wished...?

'You see how foolish and futile it is to think that way?'

'I suppose so,' she said in a small voice. 'I don't blame you for walking away. I was mean to you. The party was a stupid idea anyway. I only arranged it because I wanted to impress your mother and your friends and,' she admitted, 'Sonia.'

'Why?'

'Because I wanted to show you I was as good as her.'

He looked astonished. 'What on earth gave you the impression I wanted you to be like Sonia?'

'She's beautiful, and *she* knows what to say to important people, and your family thinks she was the perfect wife for you...also I suffer from terminal stupidity,' she added with a shrug. 'Actually I stopped caring about Sonia some time earlier this evening.' She took a deep breath and met his eyes. 'This morning I left my purse in the office of a private investigator I employed to trace my mother.'

'You did what?'

'I was going to tell you but there didn't seem much point if he didn't find anything.'

'And did he?'

She nodded. 'He told me she died two years ago and I have a half-brother and two half-sisters.' The words emerged in a rush.

He held open his arms and she walked into them. 'You did that all alone and then I shouted at you... I was frantic when I thought you were in danger. I'm so sorry.' She felt his lips in her hair.

'I don't know why I laughed...I just couldn't stop...'

'Hysteria, I should imagine.' He framed her face in his hands and turned it up to his.

The kiss was hard, hungry and at the same time breathtakingly tender. It drove every thought from her head.

'Oh, gracious,' she gasped shakily before he kissed her again.

When they disengaged he was breathing hard, but nothing else in his demeanour suggested he had done anything more extraordinary than say hello. Georgie's legs were shaking so much she could hardly walk but Angolos led her through a door and out into a quadrangle. It was an unlikely oasis of greenery in the middle of the miles of antiseptic corridors.

She touched a lemon tree. 'How did you know this was here?' She was pretty sure there had been no signposts in any language, and a person could walk this way a hundred times without discovering it.

'Insider knowledge?'

'Insider...?'

He nodded. 'It used to be just a few paving stones and benches. I had a landscape architect friend of mine make it over.'

'It's beautiful, and a lovely gesture, Angolos.'

She had already learnt that though Angolos donated generously to several charities, he did so on the strict proviso that his contributions were never made public. This, though, felt different. It was somehow...*personal*...?

'That door over there...'

Georgie's eyes followed the direction of his finger.

'It leads to the oncology unit.'

In her chest, her heart started beating fast. 'That's cancer treatment.'

His dark eyes held hers. 'That's right,' he confirmed.

'Did you know someone who was a patient here, Angolos?'

'In a manner of speaking. I had most of my treatment in London, but I did spend some time here when...well, I won't bore you with the details. I was here for a few weeks on and off.'

'You were ill?' The world started spinning in a sickening fashion. 'You had c…c…?'

'Cancer. I had cancer.'

She looked at him, but his dark lean face—the face she loved more than life—kept slipping in and out of her focus. There had to be some mistake. Yes, that would be it—she had misunderstood. Angolos was strong, he was… She was not conscious of the choking sound that emerged from her bloodless lips in the second before Angolos helped her sit down on a slab of smoothly polished tree trunk.

'This is nice,' she said vaguely, running her hand along the smooth wood that had been carved to provide a seat.

Angolos dropped to his knees before her.

'I didn't mean to shock you,' he said, taking her hands and fitting his long fingers to hers.

She looked at their interlinked fingers. Fear was a metallic taste in her mouth. 'You're well now?' she said, lifting her terror-filled eyes to his. 'It went away?'

'It went away,' he confirmed.

A tremulous breath hissed from her parted lips. Obviously it had; the man literally oozed vitality. 'When did it happen?'

'I had just been given the all-clear the day we met.'

She disentangled her hands from his and wrapped them around her shaking body in a defensive gesture. This shock fresh on the top of the previous one had an oddly numbing effect. With her eyes closed she suddenly saw his beautiful, fallen-angel face exactly as it had been that day.

'That's why you were so thin.' She suddenly turned accusing eyes on him. 'You jumped in the sea to rescue me and you were ill.'

'Not as ill as you'd have been if I hadn't jumped in.'

'This isn't a laughing matter,' she rebuked. 'Oh, I should have known…why didn't I know?'

'I had come down to give Paul the news.'

If it weren't for him… His shoulders lifted. 'Basically if it hadn't been for Paul I'd be dead.'

'Don't say that!' she pleaded. The idea of a world without Angolos in it was too appalling to contemplate. 'I always liked Paul.'

He grinned.

It suddenly struck her what all this meant. 'Basically when you met me you'd just had a death sentence lifted.'

'In a manner of speaking I suppose I had.'

'And you weren't what most people would call in your right mind… Oh, that explains a lot.' In fact it explained everything.

A dangerous expression entered his eyes as he watched her putting two and two together. 'What does it explain?'

'Do me a favour, Angolos. In your right mind you'd never have looked at someone like me twice let alone marry… No wonder all your family and friends disapproved.' She let out a weak laugh and covered her face with her hands.

He had got rid of her as soon as he'd recovered his senses and that situation would have been made official if he hadn't discovered he had a son. Why was she making this such a big thing? It weren't as if she hadn't always known that the marriage was all about Nicky.

Angolos took hold of her wrists and prised her hands away. 'Look at me!' he commanded.

She shook her head and heard his frustrated curse.

'Nobody goes through an illness like I did without it changing them, even profoundly changing them,' he conceded.

She lifted her chin. 'I'd say I can imagine, but I can't,' she admitted.

'It makes a man…or at least it made me,' he corrected, 'reassess things. I discovered that I didn't much like the person I had become. I was wealthy and what was I doing with my wealth? Making it grow… Yes, I'm good at making money, but was it making me happy?' He shook his head. 'I decided that if I got a second chance things were going to be different. Far from suffering from some sort of temporary insanity, I think the day I walked along that beach and saw you…I think that I was the sanest I had ever been.'

'Why didn't you tell me, Angolos?'

'Because I didn't want to see you look at me differently.'

'I wouldn't have…' she began to protest.

He looked at her. 'Are you sure?'

She sighed. 'Maybe you're right,' she admitted reluctantly. 'When you're ill people don't see the person, they see the disease. And some don't know how to deal with it; maybe it reminds them of their own mortality. With you there was none of that. They told me that the likelihood was the treatment would make me sterile. A trade-off, they called it. Basically I think the reason I didn't tell you was I knew you weren't really in love with me and I couldn't risk losing you, *agape mou*…I couldn't.'

The pain in his voice brought tears to her eyes. 'But you wouldn't have lost me, darling,' she protested. 'Of course I loved you. I always have and I always will.'

'I should have let you go… Hell, I tried, but I couldn't…'

'I didn't want to be let go. I wanted you.'

He shook his head. 'You were in love with the guy who saved your life. You were in love with a hero figure who could walk on water. I wasn't that man, but,' he added bitterly, 'I wanted to be, for you.'

'I didn't want a hero, I wanted a husband.'

'A husband who had had his body pumped full of chemicals? A husband who couldn't give you a baby? You asked me why I didn't tell you, why I didn't give you the opportunity to say, Thanks, but no, thanks.'

'I wouldn't have!'

He stilled her instinctive protest with a brush of his pain-filled eyes. 'The truth is—' He paused, swallowing hard, and

Georgie, who couldn't bear the pain and self-loathing in his voice, pushed her fist in her mouth to stop herself crying out. 'I knew if I told you the truth there was a good chance I would lose you. My behaviour from the moment I met you was totally reprehensible. I fell in love with you at first sight.'

'You…with me…' Somewhere inside her there were fireworks of pure joy exploding.

'Totally, and completely. I took advantage of your youth and inexperience. You were so young and I knew full well that what you felt for me was a crush. I knew you weren't ready for marriage…'

Georgie could hold her tongue no longer. 'That's the biggest load of patronising rubbish I've ever heard.' He blinked and she smiled at him with total confidence. 'I may have been young, but does that make what I felt any less valid? Angolos, I wasn't a teenager, and don't you think I'm in a better position than you to know if I was ready for marriage?'

'The truth is, Georgette, I was scared out of my mind of losing you,' he confessed huskily.

She brushed the tears from her cheek with the back of her hand and sniffed. 'Well, you're not going to lose me now,' she said firmly. 'You're stuck with me for ever and this time you're going to be there when this baby pops out.'

An expression of shock froze his mobile features. '*Baby…?*' His eyes dropped.

She nodded and, taking his hand, laid it on her flat belly. The feeling of his hand there warm against her was the best feeling in the world. 'Baby…I was sort of planning to tell you after the party tonight.' Her eyes widened in sudden horror. 'Oh, no, the party—all those people!'

'To hell with those people,' Angolos said with callous disregard for their comfort or her reputation as society hostess. 'A baby…now *that's* amazing.'

'Not really, considering the amount of effort you've put into the project. What's amazing is that you love me!'

He ran a finger down the curve of her cheek. 'No, what's amazing is that you can love me after all the pain I've caused you.'

'And all the pleasure, Angolos…all the pleasure. You gave me Nicky… Talking of Nicky, he's awake!' Laughing, she extracted the vibrating pager from her pocket and handed it to him. 'This is what life is like as a parent at the beck and call of children twenty-four seven.'

The prospect of this life illuminated Angolos's face with joy that brought a lump to her throat. 'I'm a man who thought I had no life. Now I have the woman I was born to love and a son and another on the way. What,' he demanded, pulling her to her feet, 'could be better?'

'A daughter?'

'That would be acceptable,' he conceded. 'Now, twins would be something…'

'Don't,' she begged, laughing, 'even *think* about it.'

'Shall we tell Nicky he's going to have a brother or sister?'

'He'll say he'd prefer a dog,' Georgie predicted.

Laughing, Angolos drew her to him. 'I love you,' he said, gazing tenderly into her happy, glowing face.

The future, Georgie thought, looked good, but she was content to enjoy the golden present. 'I love you too.'

'I loved you first,' he retorted.

'You always have to have the last wo—' Her husband silenced her retort in the time-honoured manner and Georgie… she didn't mind a bit!

HIS PREGNANT PRINCESS

by

Robyn Donald

Robyn Donald can't remember not being able to read, and will be eternally grateful to the local farmers who carefully avoided her on a dusty country road as she read her way to and from school, transported to places and times far away from her small village in Northland, New Zealand. Growing up fed her habit; as well as training as a teacher, marrying and raising two children, she discovered the delights of romances and read them voraciously, especially enjoying the ones written by New Zealand writers. So much so, that one day she decided to write one herself. Writing soon grew to be as much of a delight as reading – although infinitely more challenging – and when eventually her first book was accepted by Mills & Boon she felt she'd arrived home. She still lives in a small town in Northland with her family close by, using the landscape as a setting for much of her work. Her life is enriched by the friends she's made among writers and readers, and complicated by a determined corgi called Buster who is convinced that blackbirds are evil entities. Her greatest hobby is still reading, with travelling a very close second.

Don't miss Robyn Donald's exciting new novel, *Rich, Ruthless and Secretly Royal*, available in September 2009 from Mills & Boon® Modern™.

PROLOGUE

HUNT RADCLIFFE looked from the window of the private jet, metallic-blue eyes half-hidden by thick long lashes as he watched the desert inch past thousands of feet below. A glance at his watch confirmed that in just over an hour he'd be landing in the small Mediterranean island of Dacia.

He picked up a magazine his PA had handed over with a grin just before Hunt had boarded the plane at Capetown.

'Since when have I read society magazines?' Hunt enquired after a disbelieving glance.

The younger man's grin widened. 'I thought you might like to do some more research. It features official photographs of the Prince and Princess of Dacia at their wedding.'

Hunt already had a signed portrait of the royal couple, so he'd tossed the magazine onto an empty seat in the private jet, but now that he was almost there curiosity drove him to open it.

The formally posed shots had been taken in one of the rooms of the Dacian royal palace. Although Prince Luka and his bride, Alexa Mytton, looked cool and composed, nothing could hide the transparent happiness that radiated from them. A half-smile creased his face. No doubt, Alexa had fallen headlong in love, and it certainly looked as though the prince had met her more than halfway.

A prior engagement had kept Hunt away from the wedding, but he was now fulfilling a promise to visit his old friend and her new husband.

Hunt turned the page. His eyes met a pair of amber ones,

5

staring straight at the camera with the kind of haughty aloofness that set his teeth on edge.

Princess Lucia Bagaton, he read, distant cousin of the
ruler of Dacia, and until his marriage his hostess.

The Ice Princess…

She was one of Alexa's bridesmaids, and by the look on
that remote, beautiful face, hating every moment of it.
Hunt's black brows drew together. She probably thought her
precious cousin had married beneath him. God, he loathed
snobbery!

With a contemptuous flick of his fingers, he tossed the
magazine onto the seat beside him.

Yet a moment later he picked it up again and opened it
at the same page. He'd never met Lucia Bagaton, although
he'd heard enough about her from a business associate
whose son had met her, fallen in love with her and eventually died because of her.

Three months previously, after the royal wedding, Hunt
had kept a quiet wake with Maxime Lorraine's father as the
Frenchman mourned the death of his only child. Years before, the tall New Zealander had reminded the middle-aged
industrialist of himself as a young man, determined to forge
a future in alien territory. Kindly Édouard Lorraine had
helped Hunt negotiate the tricky protocols of European social and business arenas.

'She targeted him,' Édouard said wearily in his heavily
accented English. He put his empty glass down on the side-
table with a shaking hand. 'And then, when he asked her to
marry him, she threw him over.'

'Snobbery?'

'Possibly. The Bagatons have a pedigree that goes back
a couple of thousand years, whereas I, as you know, am a
nobody. But more, I think, because of money.'

Hunt's brows shot up. 'So what was the problem?' he asked bluntly.

The older man picked up the superb cognac. 'For you too? No? I'm sure you'll grant me this indulgence for once.' He poured himself another glass, then said bleakly, 'Oh, she might have fallen in love with him, but she wanted the money more. She has none, you see. Or only a pittance.'

'I thought the Bagatons were rich,' Hunt said, frowning.

'The prince is, but her father and grandfather were charming playboys who ran through their inheritance as though they owned a goldmine. As Prince Luka's hostess she has a settled position, but when he announced his engagement to your countrywoman, Princess Lucia must have realised that her days of influence in Dacia were over. Titles, even titles as exalted as princess, are two a penny nowadays, but they do have commercial value. Looked at logically, her best bet was to find a very rich man and marry him.'

'Barter her social cachet for his money,' Hunt said with distaste.

'She has assets that push her price higher.' Édouard smiled cynically. 'That beautiful face and slim body are added value, and so is her discretion—she has figured in no scandals.'

'Have you met her?'

The older man nodded. 'Of course, as soon as Maxime told me that he had fallen in love with her I went to Dacia. She is pattern-book royalty—intelligent, exquisitely mannered, always gracious, with an endless fund of small talk.' He sipped some more of the cognac. 'I liked her very much, and it seemed to me that she liked my son, although she revealed very little of her thoughts.'

Hunt made no comment.

His host said, 'Maxime asked her to marry him the day after the Cortville deal blew up in my face. You remember it; some commentators were sure that Lorraine's would come crashing down with it.'

'I remember. They were wrong, of course.'

The older man drank half his brandy then set the glass down and finished fiercely, 'But it was touch and go for a week or so, during which the Ice Princess turned my son down. He came back shattered, and then—then he decided to join this expedition.'

Hunt frowned, but said nothing, and after a few brooding moments his host said, 'If she hadn't been so greedy, if she had waited only a few days, she could have had my son and the money, a life with as much privilege as the one she left behind. But she didn't wait and now he is dead, lost in an imbecilic attempt to discover a dinosaur in the swamps of Africa. He would never have gone if she hadn't rejected him.'

Hunt wondered. Maxime hadn't been the classic spoiled rich kid, but he'd been young enough to still feel bullet-proof. Until the break-up of his affair with the princess he'd contented himself with the usual dare-devilry, skiing the most dangerous pistes, sky-diving, racing his huge motor boat. Awash with humiliation and frustration, he'd probably jumped at the chance to go to Africa.

Now, less than an hour from meeting her, Hunt scruti-nised the lovely, aristocratic face that gazed so calmly from the magazine page. Although still intensely sorry for Édouard and angry at the waste of a young life, it was none of his business if Princess Lucia of Dacia was despicable, a woman who substituted cunning and venal self-interest for integrity.

Yet his eyes lingered on her soft red mouth, wildly pro-vocative in that aloof, controlled face.

His body stirred, hormones purring into predatory mas-culine alertness. She was truly lovely; blue highlights softened the black hair sleeked back in a regal coronet of braids, skin the softly burnished gold of a Mediterranean dawn, and eyes like a tiger's, amber with gold streaks in them...

In spite of her regal composure, Princess Lucia oozed a subtle sexuality. For years she'd been driving the gossip columnists crazy; no men in her life, no wild parties or romances, nothing but good works and self-effacement. Even her affair with Maxime hadn't reached the columns; on Dacia, her cousin had power enough to keep his family's affairs private.

He flicked over another page, and there she was again, dancing with an obviously besotted man. Beneath the photograph a cleverly worded caption wondered if this was the man in the Ice Princess's life.

Hunt said aloud, 'So she's clever, and discreet and prudent. A model princess ready to sell herself to the highest bidder.'

He had better things to do than lust over a calculating, heartless woman. Yet as he closed the magazine with a snap and tossed it onto the empty seat beside him, that exotic face, almost feline in its beauty, lingered in his mind.

It held secrets, secrets he was privy to. That gracious, seamless façade, a product of rigorous training, disguised a woman who had given herself to a man who loved her, and then cruelly spurned him.

He wondered contemptuously if she ever regretted dumping Maxime Lorraine on the strength of a rumour.

Hunt stretched his long body, a cold smile tilting the corners of his mouth. Some questions would soon be answered, because she'd be meeting him at the airport in Dacia.

CHAPTER ONE

PRINCESS LUCIA BAGATON—known to those she loved as Cia—anchored a wisp of glossy hair behind her ears and replaced her sunglasses, her fine brows drawing together in a faint frown. Automatically her fingers went to the diamond star that rested just below the hollow of her throat. She stroked the pendant as though it was a talisman, then realised what she'd done and dropped her hand to her lap with a tightening of her lips.

Although this meeting wasn't an official occasion, she'd dressed conservatively; Hunter Radcliffe was an important figure in the business world as well as a friend of her cousin's new wife, Alexa.

In fact, Cia thought, fighting back the grey misery that had been her constant companion for months, the last person she'd met at the airport had been Alexa, now Princess Alexa of Dacia.

That meeting had changed Cia's life; this one wouldn't, but it was the last time she'd greet anyone as Luka's representative. A week from now she'd be flying away from the island, the only home she'd known since she was ten.

'We're here, your highness.' The chauffeur's voice murmured respectfully through the intercom as the limousine drew up in a private parking place out of the view of any travellers or passers-by.

'Thank you.'

Before the car stopped she'd relaxed her taut expression; the Dacians expected smiles from her. Bag clasped loosely,

she waited for the elderly attendant to open the door, returned his smile and walked into the airport building.

In the private lift that led to the waiting room reserved
for Dacian royal family, she asked the airport manager, 'Is
Mr Radcliffe's jet on schedule?'

'It will touch down in a few minutes, your highness.'

'Good.' Another smile lilted through her words. 'Excellent, in fact. How is the new grandson?'

He looked gratified. 'A lovely little boy. And so forward!
Yesterday he smiled at me—and even though my wife and
daughter tell me he's far too young, it was *not* wind! I know
the difference between a grimace of pain and a smile.'

Walking ahead of him out of the lift, Cia laughed. 'He
must already realise that he's a lucky baby—he has a special
link with his grandfather.'

She loved children. Sometimes, in the dead of another
sleepless night, she mourned the children she'd never have
now. Once again her hand crept to the pendant at her breast
and touched the five exquisite stones that made the star.
They were cold and smooth against her fingertips. Once
again she dropped her hand abruptly.

The manager opened the door into the suite with a flour-
ish. 'Well, perhaps he's a little young for that,' he conceded
with a half-laugh. 'I trust everything is as you wished it,
ma'am.'

Cia cast a professional glance around the room. 'It looks
wonderful, as always. Thank you.'

He nodded, then looked past her out of the window. 'Ah,
this must be the gentleman,' he said with satisfaction as a
slender private jet touched down on the runway. 'He is a
friend, I believe, of Princess Alexa's?'

'Yes. Like her, he is from New Zealand.' Her voice was
very steady, as warm as she could make it—entirely normal.
She'd had enough practice—Luka had been married to

his lovely New Zealander for four months now. And for years before that Cia had tried to accept that he'd never see her as anything more than the much younger, very distant cousin who'd become his responsibility when she'd been orphaned.

Most people grew out of their teenage crushes, but she didn't seem to be able to chisel Luka from her heart. Loving someone for almost half of your twenty-five years was a difficult habit to break.

The sleek private jet taxied back towards the building and nestled against the end of the bridge. Firmly pinning her social secretary's smile to her mouth, Cia walked across to the gate, ready to welcome Hunter Radcliffe to Dacia.

All it needed, she thought with black humour, was for him to be in love with Alexa, and they'd have the makings of a modern novel—one of those that ended in tears and disillusion all round.

But the man she'd come to meet didn't look as though he'd ever loved anyone in his life. Watching him walk towards the gate, Cia blinked and her mouth went dry. Photographs of Hunter Radcliffe in magazines and newspapers failed to convey the formidable charisma that burned around him like an aura.

Cia swallowed. The world suddenly seemed to have become a much darker, more vital place.

Tall—taller even than Luka—with broad shoulders and lean hips and the easy, deliberate pacing of an athlete, he strode towards her like a warrior from another world. Skin burned bronze by a sun as strong as Dacia's emphasised boldly chiselled features that revealed only what their owner intended.

Neither his hard face nor narrowed eyes changed when he inspected her. Cia's stomach performed an uncomfortable manoeuvre behind her ribs.

The noisy hum of the busy airport faded. Quickly, she retrieved her slipping smile. 'Welcome to Dacia, Mr Radcliffe,' she said in English, and extended a hand. 'I'm Prince Luka's cousin—Lucia Bagaton.'

He took her hand, enveloping it in a grip judged to a nicety—firm but not crushing. The strength in his fingers and the slight calluses that indicated hard physical labour sent a swift, disturbing shiver down the length of her spine.

'How do you do, Your Highness?' He spoke in a deep, distinctive voice with a New Zealand accent, and he had definitely put capitals on the formal term of address.

Her sharp look examined a face that revealed nothing but bland politeness—if you ignored hooded, metallic-blue eyes and the twist of classically sculpted male lips.

When he continued, 'I'm pleased to be here,' she detected an edge beneath the measured courtesy of the words.

Cia had done her research; growing up motherless, like her he'd been orphaned at fourteen, spending three years in a foster home. By the time he'd reached his early twenties, Hunter Radcliffe had made a reputation on the stock market as a day trader—a route to riches that needed nerves of steel, a vast knowledge of the field, and huge amounts of luck.

Fortune duly made, he'd moved out of that incredibly risky market, expanding his interests until today he was a well-known and respected player in the world's financial scene.

Defying the unwavering impact of his gaze, she decided he was formidable enough to make a success of anything he decided to do. Sensible people probably ran for cover when his eyes, darkly blue as a dangerous midnight, probed for signs of weakness.

She couldn't—and wouldn't—run. When another ironic twist of his mouth reminded her of her manners, she held on to her steady smile. 'My cousin and Alexa send their apologies. Unfortunately they are—'

'At a special meeting of a relief organisation. I know.' He looked up as a porter wheeled his luggage through.

Not a man to waste time, she thought acidly—and with enough presence to power a large city! Why hadn't Alexa chosen to marry *him?*

Not that it would have made any difference; Cia had long been resigned to the fact that Luka would never love her the way she wanted him to.

'They'll be home by the time we get there,' she said politely, wondering if Hunter Radcliffe normally greeted strangers with barely restrained aggression.

Possibly; you didn't rise from his background to become a tycoon unless you were tough and forceful and ruthless, and of course, once you reached his heights you could be as rude as you liked to almost anyone without worrying about the consequences.

As if she cared! In her most courteous voice she said, 'Ah, here are your bags. I'm afraid you'll have to go through Customs and Immigration before we can leave.'

Five minutes later, his passport stamped and his luggage whisked off to the waiting limousine, she indicated the door. 'This way.'

He stood back to let her go out first. 'After you, Your Highness.' A faint, infuriating note of mockery coloured the words.

Straight-backed, Cia preceded him into the corridor. Either he'd taken an instant dislike to her, or he disapproved of the monarchy. It was a method of governance many believed to be on its way out, but try and convince the Dacians of that! After long, terrifying years protected from the territorial ambitions of a neighbouring dictator solely by their prince's marriage to the tyrant's only child, they weren't planning to give up their loyalty to the Bagaton family in the near future.

And she didn't care what this man thought of her. It was surprising, though, that Alexa, who was a darling, should have such a coolly arrogant friend.

At the lift, Cia reached for the button, startled when a lean, tanned hand forestalled her automatic summons. She looked up, and met eyes so piercing she had to stop herself from taking a betraying step backwards. A pulse jumped in her throat and swift, unexpected heat licked the width of her cheekbones as her hand dropped.

The lift doors opened in sighing welcome. Gratefully she stiffened her shoulders and walked in.

Glancing at the control panel, Hunter Radcliffe observed, 'I assume we're heading for the ground floor.' Then added, 'Your Highness,' again edging each word with that flick of sarcasm.

'Yes,' she said shortly.

He pressed the button and the lift began its descent. It was idiotic to let herself be so affected by him.

It was the colour of his eyes, she decided. In Dacia liquid darkness reined supreme, and she was accustomed to the signature tawny-gold of the Bagaton family. Alexa had crystalline grey eyes, and although Cia's English relatives came equipped in various shades of blue, none drilled through her defences like lasers.

Did Hunter Radcliffe's ever warm up? Making love, perhaps…

A suspect surge of adrenalin sharpened her senses. She stared stonily ahead, uncomfortably aware of the faint, vital scent of the man beside her.

Who moved slightly, and smiled down at her. It was a killer smile—sexy, disturbing and mercifully brief. Her stomach lurched again, then contracted into a tight knot.

Fuming and oddly disoriented, Cia clung to her dignity as her composure began to splinter.

'I don't think I've ever been in a lift reserved for royalty until now,' he observed.

Cia forced a tight smile. 'It's actually for private visitors,' she corrected.

He seemed to fill the lift, dominating it as he'd dominated the waiting room, without effort.

It's called presence, she told herself crossly. He had it in spades.

Clad casually in cotton trousers and a shirt that revealed broad shoulders and a splendid chest, the man made her feel ineffectual and ridiculously formal. No silk dress—not even a bronze one that made her skin and eyes glow—could compete with his impact.

It will be interesting, Cia thought loyally, to see him with Luka. Two uncompromising men, both accustomed to power...

As the lift gained momentum she summoned a smile and said lightly, 'It isn't necessary to call me Your Highness. Even in formal situations it's only used once, and after that a simple ma'am will do. Informally, most people just call me Lucia.'

'Thank you for telling me that,' he said gravely.

Cia looked up sharply. When his lips curved into a smile that combined speculation with a taunt, she realised that she hadn't told him anything he didn't know. Hunter Radcliffe rubbed shoulders with the world's power élite, so he'd have learned the intricacies of formal address.

Chagrin chipped away at her crumbling self-possession. She should have realised—she *would* have realised if she hadn't been thrown off balance by his attitude!

Pinning a professional smile in place, she straightened the

diamond star on its chain and dropped it inside the neck of her dress. It looked like being a long week.

Surely the lift was much slower than usual? She seemed to have been shut in it with this overbearing, sarcastic man for hours.

In that distinctive voice, he drawled, 'You'll have to forgive me for any mistakes I might make. In New Zealand we don't often meet royalty.'

Well, two could play at that game. Anticipation simmering through her veins, she countered sweetly, 'Oh, don't worry about it—Kiwis are clearly very adaptable people. Alexa has managed superbly. And I'm sure she told me you had some order or another—I'm sorry, I can't remember which—bestowed on you by your Queen? Perhaps she was wrong?'

His brows drew together in a swift, formidable frown. 'Alexa must keep up with the newspapers from home.'

The lift drew to a stop on the ground floor with Cia savouring a moment's wicked satisfaction. Her delicate insinuation that he'd been bragging to Alexa had grazed his formidable self-possession. Still, she wasn't going to let him off the hook so swiftly, and if the wind-chill factor fell any lower, she'd just wear winter clothes.

'And I'm sure I've seen photographs of you escorting— oh, a princess from another European royal house,' she murmured discreetly, donning her sunglasses like a shield before they emerged into the blinding Dacian sunlight. The doors opened in front of them.

'I didn't expect you to be an eager follower of the gossip columns,' Hunter parried, his voice smooth as silk.

She bestowed a pleasant smile on him. 'I'm related to almost every royal family in Europe, and, as in all families, news travels fast,' she said easily. The princess—her cousin—had confided that he was a magnificent lover.

Even without inside information, Cia would have guessed. His potent male magnetism proclaimed his sexual expertise. But she'd been surprised—and a little sceptical—when the cousin had gone on to say that he'd been faithful while they'd been together.

'This way,' Cia said, automatically indicating the waiting limousine.

Once the limousine doors were closed, the man sitting beside her settled his broad shoulders back into the seat and surveyed her with his particular brand of challenging speculation. 'What exactly do you do here, ma'am? Good works?'

'My name is Lucia,' she said, hiding the sudden heat in her blood with another expertly controlled smile. 'As for what I do—nothing.' And waited for the familiar pain.

It didn't arrive; instead she was zinging with irritation and a kind of reluctant, abrasive awareness.

His sardonic glance cut through her composure. Bewildered by the strength of her anger—with him and with herself for reacting to his unspoken contempt—she added, 'I used to be the palace social secretary.'

Handsome didn't apply to Hunter Radcliffe; the word was too wishy-washy to describe the strong, thrusting bone structure that gave his face such authority. And he didn't possess Luka's spectacular male beauty.

But his was not a face she'd ever forget. Arrogantly compelling, his features gave him a kind of ruthless, patient concentration that made the name Hunter fit him exactly. Although his self-control blazed like a cold beacon, she sensed he'd make a bad enemy.

He turned a simple response like the raising of his black brows into a subtle insult. 'Social secretary? It sounds a riveting career.'

Resolutely Cia kept her face set in an expression of calm

detachment. Not only had he decided he didn't like her, he was making sure she knew it. 'Somebody has to do it, and it was one way I could help Luka.'

'Why did he need help?'

She said briskly, 'He didn't need help—he needed an efficient, reliable organiser.'

'And his need was a good enough reason for you to dedicate your life to smoothing his social path?'

Cia shrugged. 'My mother died when I was ten, and my father wasn't very interested in me, so Luka made sure I spent every school holiday here, and when I left school I came to live here.'

He nodded. 'I thought you had English relatives.'

'They weren't very interested either,' she said evenly. 'Luka and Guy, another Bagaton cousin, made me feel I had a family, but I knew Luka best.'

His acceptance and affection had been a novelty for a girl who'd been the third wheel in a spectacularly unsuccessful marriage. She added lamely, 'I was glad to repay him in whatever way I could.'

Although Hunter was glancing at the passing scenery, she had an impression of a cold, clever mind sifting and sorting facts. Let him think what he wants, she thought scornfully; she didn't care a fig for his opinion.

'I gather the boarding-school was in England,' he startled her by observing. When Cia's brows lifted he went on, 'That would explain your faultless accent.'

Not without satisfaction she replied, 'That, and the fact that my mother was English.'

'So your colouring came from your father.'

The invisible hairs on the nape of her neck lifted in instinctive warning. 'Not entirely,' she said with remote courtesy. 'My mother was part-French and I look like her, but of course black hair and brown eyes are standard in the Mediterranean.'

'Possibly, but skin the colour and texture of pale gold satin, and eyes like hot amber are not.' The words emerged in an abrasive male purr, sensuous yet controlled.

Although the air-conditioning was on, the inside of the car suddenly seemed oppressively humid. Sweat sprang out across her temples; without thinking, Cia touched the chain around her neck, her fingers sliding down to clasp the diamond star.

She flushed when Hunter's blue gaze followed the betraying little movement, and released the pendant, folding her hand firmly in her lap. This man, she thought disjointedly, is dangerous.

It took every ounce of self-possession to say, 'You have an interesting line in compliments. Hot amber—I must remember that. I don't think the Bagaton eyes have ever been described like that before. And I like the idea of skin like golden satin too.' She managed a smile, coolly distant. 'It might make the constant application of sunscreen less irritating. It's the predominant scent of the Mediterranean in summer—sunscreen.'

She surprised a cynical laugh out of him. 'Not yours. When you walk there's a faint drift of very exclusive perfume and a soft whisper of silk. As for your skin—you must know that every man who sees it wonders how it would look against his.'

Awareness, sharp and reckless, clamoured through her body in sensations so powerfully narcotic that she had to stop herself from squirming on the seat. She should give him a disdainful glance and turn the conversation, but she didn't trust her voice.

Silence drummed between them. In the end she managed

a smile that was, she hoped, both amused and repressive, and said, 'I'm afraid I didn't know that until you told me.'

Until the moment she'd seen Hunter Radcliffe walk into the airport she'd had no idea that she could feel a lethal, violent attraction for a man she didn't know and was rapidly learning to dislike. As its dark intensity shafted through her, she realised she had no way of dealing with him. Armoured against all other men by her love for Luka, at twenty-five she was still a virgin.

A virgin turned on by this man! *Live Dangerously* had been the motto of one of her ancestors—it certainly wasn't hers.

Either he was as big a womaniser as the gossip columnists hinted, or he felt that same driving lure. His blue eyes had heated to glinting jewels in his tanned face, and the smile sculpting his wide, sensual mouth was definitely, if reluctantly, appreciative.

Savage, undiluted excitement sizzled through her body. Trying to douse it with common sense, Cia commanded herself trenchantly to grow up. With that indefinable air of sexual charisma, and his power and the money that went with it, he'd had women falling at his feet ever since he'd made the world stage. Probably before; he didn't need money or position to attract attention.

She jutted her chin, frowning when she saw a child trudging along the road ahead. Through the intercom she said, 'Julio, stop, please.'

'Your highness?'

'We'll give her a lift,' she said briskly, ignoring Hunter Radcliffe's quizzical expression.

As soon as the car stopped she got out. 'Well, little one,' she said in Dacian, 'what are you doing away from school?'

The child—no more than six or seven—shrank back until she recognised who had stopped her. Knuckling her eyes, she flung herself into Cia's arms and burst into tears. Cia fished out a handkerchief and set to the business of comforting.

When the swift storm had passed, she coaxed the child into the car and soon extracted the story from her.

It was long and involved, and there were more sobs before it was told, but Cia finally removed her arm from around the thin shoulders and said, 'There, that's enough now, Gracia. Blow your nose again, and wipe your eyes. I think I should take you home and perhaps chat to your mother.'

With a worshipful smile Gracia obeyed, but before the car had gone far she turned to stare up at Hunter. To Cia's surprise he grinned at the child, a humorous flash of white teeth that summoned a shy smile in answer.

'Good morning, miss,' he said in very passable Dacian.

The child giggled and Hunter winked at her, then looked across the small black head to meet Cia's startled eyes. His smile faded as their gazes collided.

Cia's heart jumped in her chest and that suspicious tide of sensation began another rampage. Humiliated by her lack of control, she released herself from the steel-blue trap and gazed stubbornly ahead.

At least he wasn't going to be here long. This time next week he'd have left Dacia.

And so will you, taking off to London to wallow in self-pity and mourn a love you never had, she thought in astringent self-contempt, and began to talk to their small passenger, who reached up and touched the pendant at her breast with a grubby, wondering finger.

'It's so pretty,' the child whispered. 'My mummy has a cross, but it doesn't shine like this.'

'It was a birthday present from the prince,' Cia told her. She glanced up and found Hunt examining the star with hard interest. In English she said, 'How much Dacian do you speak?'

'I can greet and farewell,' he told her, 'with a few other phrases.'

'I see. I told her that my cousin gave it to me for my eighteenth birthday.'

'A very suitable gift,' Hunter Radcliffe said, not looking at it. 'Excellent stones.'

The car drew up outside a small, stone house and Cia said evenly, 'I'll go in with her and tell her mother what's happened.'

Hunt nodded and said to the child, 'God go with you.'

The little girl giggled again at the formal farewell, but said in a low voice, 'And you, sir.'

Hunt watched them disappear into the house, the child skipping along with her hand in Cia's, the princess very much in charge.

Security on Dacia obviously wasn't much of an issue; although the driver got out and gazed around, he wasn't on full alert.

Hunt opened the door and stepped onto the road, drawing in a deep breath of sweet, scented air. He shouldn't be surprised that Princess Lucia was so good with children. That was what female royalty did; smiled a lot, accepted bouquets of flowers from kids, and learned how to make small talk in their cradle.

He hoped Alexa enjoyed it. He also hoped that her husband realised he'd married a real artist with a camera, not just another amateur.

And he hoped to hell he didn't see much of Princess Lucia during the next week. Normally well disciplined, his hormones had rioted into uncomfortable life the moment he'd laid eyes on her, so cool and composed, every hair ruthlessly organised into that sleek bun at the back of her head, her golden gaze remote and assured.

He set his analytical mind to working out just what about her had tugged at the leash on his self-control. Beauty, of course, but he'd seen enough beautiful women to be able to appreciate them without wanting to get them into bed.

And yeah, there was something sleekly tactile about that golden skin, and that trick of lowering her long lashes and then looking up through them sang straight through his defences. Couple that with a soft mouth that suggested a secret voluptuousness wildly at odds with her restrained exterior, and the predator inside him stretched its claws and sniffed the air.

Add a slender body in the right proportions and a smooth voice that went from cool English to warm, soft Dacian, and you had feminine dynamite.

His eyes narrowed. No wonder Maxime had fallen for her.

He watched as she emerged from the house, the child's hand still in hers, the white-aproned mother, with another child in her arms and one at her feet, beaming effusively.

Hunt's body sprang into red alert. Hot Dacian sunlight glowed lovingly across the princess's patrician face, hinted at the soft curves of breasts and narrow waist, the rhythmic movement of her hips as they came up to the car.

His hand clenched on the door as he opened it and got in.

The driver opened the door for her and listened with an expressionless face while she gave him some directions.

As the engine started, Cia gave a cool smile to the man sitting beside the little girl. 'We're taking Gracia back to school.'

The child twinkled up at him, and got that shockingly disarming grin once more.

Hunter said, 'She ran away?'

'She'd rather be at home with her mother and the two little ones.'

'But a royal decree did the trick,' he said softly.

'I promised that if she goes to school every day she isn't ill, Alexa would visit her school at the end of the year and present the attendance certificates.'

Recognising the name of her princess, Gracia turned to Hunter and burst out, 'She is like a fairy princess! I saw her ride in a carriage in her white wedding dress with the prince—she is so beautiful.'

Despising herself for a faint, sour twist of jealousy, Cia translated, before adding in Dacian, 'She won't come to the school in her wedding clothes, but she will wear a pretty dress.'

Hunter said, 'Would you mind telling Gracia that if she stays at school every day, I'll send her a book about New Zealand?'

Gracia beamed and wanted to know where this strange country was, so the rest of the trip was taken up with a three-way conversation in two languages.

When Cia was back in the car, being waved off by the entire class, Hunter Radcliffe said admiringly, 'That was a clever bit of PR. I hope Alexa doesn't mind you making appointments for her.'

Biting back her outrage, Cia gave a last wave to the excited children. 'I'm sure she won't—she knows how important education is for every child.' She changed the subject with considerably less than her usual finesse. 'Luka tells me that you have an interest in forest rehabilitation, Mr Radcliffe.'

'My name is Hunter.'

She paused, then repeated in a colourless voice, 'Hunter.'

'But most people call me Hunt.'

When she remained stubbornly silent he observed, 'As I'm sure you've found out from Alexa, New Zealanders are informal. But determined.'

'Hunt,' she said between her teeth. And suspected that her *hot amber* gaze told him how very appropriate she considered both his full name and the shortened version to be.

CHAPTER TWO

EYES burnished blue as starfire beneath outrageously long lashes, Hunt gave her a smile that skimmed the borders of mockery. 'And yes, I am very interested in forest rehabilitation.'

Cia said doggedly, 'Was there any particular incident that started you off in this field?'

The man beside her fixed his gaze on the hills of Dacia, dark with the trees planted by Luka's father. 'I bought a station in—'

'Station?' She looked enquiringly at him.

'A cattle station,' he enlarged.

'What is the difference between a farm and a station?'

'A station is bigger—often much bigger—than a farm. It's usually on poorer, steeper country, further from civilisation, and whereas farms can produce a variety of produce, stations are usually pastoral—that is, their business is producing food from animals. More than you wanted to know?'

He was giving her a chance to repay his rudeness. Armoured by propriety, Cia managed to resist temptation, but it was a close-run thing. She'd met a range of people in her life, some difficult, some rude, some snobbish; none of them had managed to make her bristle as much as this man. 'Local idioms are very interesting. Is this station your home? Alexa said you live in Northland.'

'I do. The place I'm referring to is several hundred miles further south—steep country stripped of its original cover of bush and rapidly eroding into the sea.'

Cia nodded. 'So naturally you planted it with trees. Did

you choose ones native to that area, or exotic species?' Rather pleased at her smooth, interested tone, she risked an upward glance.

Only to find him surveying her with sardonic understanding; he knew exactly what she was doing. Her heart lurched and missed a beat, but she forced herself to meet those far too perceptive eyes with limpid innocence.

'I chose exotic trees in the most eroded spots because they grow faster, but all the gullies were fenced and replanted with native trees,' he informed her.

Cia gazed blindly out of the window, trying to ignore the deep, potent voice and concentrate on what he was saying. She'd trained herself to concentrate on people who spoke to her, but this man managed to scramble the circuits in her brain so that all she was aware of was his voice, cool and steady with an intriguingly abrasive thread running beneath it.

Startled when he stopped, she flung more words into the small silence. 'Luka's father planted trees here when he realised the soil on the hills was washing down to the sea. It's worked well.'

'He was ahead of his time,' Hunt observed laconically. 'I'm sure I'm boring you—you don't have to make small talk.'

Infuriating though he was, for the first time in months—since she'd realised that Luka loved Alexa—energy rushed through her in an exhilarating surge. And despising herself didn't curb her response; it had nothing to do with her mind or her emotions.

Hunter—*Hunt*—Radcliffe had a powerfully physical effect on her.

Instead of the platitude she'd normally have produced, she murmured, 'Oh, don't worry—small talk is a vital part of my job.'

He showed his teeth—very white, she noticed—in a grin that warned her she was out of her depth. 'Does that mean being bored—or boring people are part of your job?'

'Both,' she said lightly.

That ironic smile narrowed. 'It sounds like hell—coping with boredom, or with people who bore you, while hoping you're not boring them. Why don't you get yourself a proper job?'

'But I meet such fascinating people in this one,' she purred, tawny eyes gleaming.

He flung back his head and laughed with open enjoyment. That suspicious energy surged up another gear, tightening into an acute tension. Cia could have closed her eyes and drawn from memory everything about him—the arrogant jut of his hawkish features, the blade of a nose, the high, savage cheekbones and the ruthless line of his jaw.

As for the disturbing combination of raw strength, discipline and male promise that was his mouth, she suspected it would haunt her for a long time.

'You weren't boring me,' he said lazily. 'I like the way your mouth moves when you talk and the way you use your lashes—are tricks like that all part of the job too?'

No doubt about it, he's a brilliant lover, she thought dazedly.

She endured his piercing gaze for as long as she could, aware with some primal instinct that this was a surrender of sorts. When his eyes narrowed further she realised she was touching Luka's pendant, her fingertips caressing the five superb diamonds that made up the star.

Heat prickled through her, but she lowered her hand in a casual movement and said collectedly, 'The main part of my job is to be inconspicuous.'

'Inconspicuous?' He lifted his brows and surveyed her face with such lazy thoroughness that her hands itched to slap him even while that forbidden sizzle burned through her nerves.

'With that face you'd be conspicuous in a harem,' he drawled.

Disgusted with herself for reacting like a hot-blooded adolescent, she said colourlessly, 'You're too kind,' and grabbed the conversation by the scruff of its neck, firmly re-routing it in a safer direction by pointing out items of interest.

He must have decided that goading her was no longer amusing, because he leaned back with a satirical half-smile, as they passed stone-walled olive orchards. Spring had dusted the grass beneath the branches with a riotous crop of golden crocuses and cobalt grape hyacinths that blended into clouds of irises and brilliant marigolds.

In spite of her taut awareness, Cia discovered that she was enjoying the drive. He had a formidable mind. But then, he was a formidable man—compelling, forceful and too sure of himself.

Remembering Alexa's interest in antiquities, she indicated a church built over the ruins of a Roman temple. 'This is the old road from the port to a Roman emperor's villa in the hills. We're not going to the Old Palace in the city; it's mostly used for ceremonial purposes. Luka and Alexa actually live in the Little Palace, a much more intimate house a few kilometres in the hills. It's cooler there, with lovely gardens.'

Hunt listened to her soft, low voice, his unruly senses stirring at the subtle cadences and the silken, sensuous undernote through each word. Usually his cold, analytical brain could override the urging of his hormones, but this woman's potent allure had pressed every button.

Now he understood why Maxime Lorraine had fled civilisation when she'd turned him down. It was probably the first time the handsome heir to the Lorraine fortune had ever met rejection, and the shock and humiliation would have been impossible for him to bear. Hunt's lip curled. According to the letter Maxime had left before taking off for the Congo, she'd led him on, convincing him that she reciprocated his feelings.

The princess's voice broke into Hunt's thoughts. 'I believe you're an old friend of Alexa's?'

'I've known her since she was a skinny sixteen-year-old in love with a camera.'

No emotion registered in her sultry eyes, set like tawny jewels between thick black lashes. 'She's still in love with it—she has donated some magnificent photographs to an international exhibition that's raising funds for charity.'

When they left the main road and began to wind upwards, Hunt looked out of the window without seeing anything of the passing landscape.

He'd met hundreds of beautiful women in his life. Some—a rare few—had possessed characters that matched their faces. He suspected that Édouard had been correct; this one had had the heart of a siren, cold and scheming and avaricious.

'Exactly how closely related to the prince are you?' he asked lazily.

'Very distantly,' she said on a flat note that warned him she resented the question.

Tough. 'But you're close enough to be a princess?'

'Continental usage differs from English. My great-grandfather was the second son of the then ruler of Dacia. All of his descendants can claim the title.'

'How many other princesses and princes of Dacia are running around the world's fleshpots?'

She sent a shaft of golden fire in his direction. 'My cousin Guy is the only other one, and although he probably knows a fleshpot when he sees one, he spends most of his time looking after his business affairs,' she told him, her polite tone barely hiding her annoyance.

'Are only three of you left?'

Sunlight gleamed on her hair as she nodded. 'Quite a few of them died in various wars, but my forebears weren't prolific.'

'You said you're related to every royal family in Europe.'

Her luscious mouth curved in a humourless pretence at a smile. 'Very distantly,' she told him. 'Ah, here we are.'

Hunt leaned back while the sentries checked them through the gates. He approved the discreet surveillance as they drove through a park towards the Little Palace.

Italian in conception, the Little Palace was a large, glorious confection in stone the colour of good champagne. When the car stopped at the bottom of a magnificent flight of steps an attendant hurried to open the door and two people walked between the columns and came down towards them.

As always when she saw her cousin, Cia's heart contracted, but now she felt awkward and constrained by the presence of the man next to her. For some reason she'd be utterly humiliated if Hunter—Hunt—Radcliffe found out that she was hopelessly in love with Luka.

Alexa was looking a little tired, but she greeted them with her bright, warm smile, reaching up to kiss Hunt's cheek before introducing him to her husband. Both big men, both with indefinable charisma and authority in their different ways, they shook hands. One glance was enough to tell Cia that they liked each other.

A wave of loneliness took her by surprise, and she thought suddenly, I'll be glad to leave Dacia.

As soon as she'd realised that Luka loved Alexa she'd wanted to run as far and as fast as she could, but loyalty—

and protocol—had forced her to stay. He'd asked her to help his new wife find her way around the business of being a princess and she couldn't let Luka down—or the woman he loved.

It had been slow torture grinding away her soul, but even now, although everything was arranged and she was determined to go, the thought of only ever coming back as a guest clawed at her heart.

But Alexa had settled into island life with disarming ease and an innate dignity and discretion that would stand her in good stead. Quick-witted and sunny, she'd already captured the islanders' hearts, and court officials automatically went to their new princess.

Alexa turned to her. 'Thank you so much for collecting Hunt.'

'It was nothing,' Cia said promptly, keeping any hint of malice from her voice.

She looked up and saw Hunt watching her, his cold eyes narrowed and intent. An odd sensation in the pit of her stomach coalesced into a feverish, unknown excitement. Bestowing him a prim, cool smile, she went with them out of the sun into the elegance of the Little Palace.

Lunch was a cheerful, informal occasion. Luka had to leave early to attend another meeting, and shortly afterwards Cia excused herself on the pretext of doing some work. As she left the comfortable sitting room in the private apartments, she heard Alexa say something, followed by Hunt's deep, sexy laugh.

A familiar chill of alienation brushed Cia's spine as she walked up the stairs. Shivering, she shut the office door behind her and sat down at the desk to turn on her computer.

Some hours later she closed down the computer and got up to walk across to the window, staring down at the harmonious glory of the gardens, their classical proportions brightened by a riot of flowers from lilies to bougainvillea, glowing like stained glass amongst the soothing greenery.

Surely she'd get over this embarrassing, tormenting anguish of love? Like most women, she wanted a happy marriage, and she loved children.

Unfortunately she wanted them to be Luka's.

The sound of the door opening swivelled her around. Her heart jumped when she saw the long, lean form of her cousin.

'Hello,' she said cheerfully. 'Finished your meeting?'

'Yes.' Unsmiling, he came across the room, stopping so that he could examine her face. 'You look sad,' he said quietly. 'You looked sad before, too. What is it, Cia?'

Her mind raced, but she couldn't answer. He waited until the silence stretched too far, then said, 'You can tell me, Cia. You know that I love you, and no matter what has happened, I will support you. Is it a man?'

Oh, Luka! Emotions ran raw and angry through her. Desperately, she said, 'No, of course it's not a man. I'm feeling a bit sentimental. I've just finished the last bit of official work I had to do, and it's hitting home that in a week's time I'll have left Dacia.'

Luka was watching her closely, but at her words he relaxed and held out his hand. 'I know how to deal with that. Alexa gets homesick still.'

If she accepted the comfort he was offering she'd fling herself into his arms and bawl her eyes out. She'd kept her secret for years; she wasn't going to reveal it at the last moment.

She said, 'Once I'm away I'll enjoy myself, but at the moment I'm remembering all the things I love about Dacia and I'm in a very delicate state! I warn you, touch me, and I'll burst into tears.' Sheer inspiration produced her next words. 'And I refuse to turn up at dinner with red eyes and a red tip to my nose. Hunter Radcliffe already thinks I'm an inbred parasite with a brain the strength of soufflé and a love of the easy life. I refuse to let him think I cry.'

That convinced Luka. Laughing, he let his hand fall. 'So you like him?'

'I think he's an autocratic pig,' she returned, adding with a wicked smile, 'However, he's a very attractive, autocratic pig. Although pig is probably the wrong word too—he reminds me of something very feline, very powerful and untamed. I owe it to all princesses to keep my end up.'

Luka's brows drew together. 'I'm not sure that he's a good man to challenge.'

'Perish the thought!' She produced a wide smile. 'Pride demands that I don't let him get away with being so judgemental.' And when he continued to frown she went on, 'Luka, I'm not planning to run away with him! He has to be a reasonably decent sort or he wouldn't be a friend of Alexa's, but I don't think I like him. Of course, that might be because for some reason he thinks I'm a prissy parasite.'

'I doubt that very much,' Luka said drily, and glanced at his watch. 'I'll see you at dinner.'

When she was alone again she sagged, and her fingers came up to clutch the star on its gold chain. With a twisted grimace she let it drop.

Perhaps, to make sure neither Luka nor Alexa realised how much she was dreading her departure, she would flirt a little with Hunt Radcliffe tonight.

It would be exhilarating crossing swords with him, and not at all dangerous, because he was tough enough not to take a woman's advances seriously.

Not, she thought sadly, like poor Maxime, who had fallen headlong into love with her and when she'd tactfully turned his proposal down, had been outraged, forcing her to endure a wretched scene when he'd pleaded, then got angry and ended up calling her ugly names before storming out.

She swallowed. That final scene had been utterly distasteful, but she'd been appalled a few weeks later to read of his death. Such a waste.

Later, when the warm, lazy afternoon was on the cusp of evening, she changed into a sleek dress the colour of dark chocolate, and reapplied her make-up, sweeping her hair back from her face. Frowning, she hesitated over the star, but wore it because, she told herself, it matched the diamond stud earrings that had been an inheritance from her mother.

Normally she'd have worn plain shoes; tonight an unusual whim persuaded her to slip on a pair of high-heeled sandals.

'Well, all right, so the wretched man looms over you,' she muttered at her reflection in the long mirror. 'An extra couple of inches isn't going to make much difference.'

But she regretted that spurt of defiance when she walked out from the palace and through the parterre with its low clipped hedges. The path was level and well-rolled, but not suitable for fashionable sandals.

Halfway down the axis of the garden she looked up and saw a tall figure emerge from a walk shaded by dark, clipped conifers. Her pulse rate picked up speed when she recognised the loose, graceful stride. Austere in black and white evening clothes, Hunt overwhelmed her.

Rallying, she thought indignantly that most men his size could only aim to be rangy. However well-tailored their suits, men as tall and broad as Hunt looked either blocky and solid like bodyguards, or clumsy. Instead, he was breathtaking, the cool elegance of his clothes reinforced and strengthened by uncompromising power, both physical and mental.

Her mouth dried and she had to swallow so she'd be able to say something when she reached him.

He stopped and waited for her to come up, his lean, striking face angular in the soft dusk, unnerving her with his stillness.

The hairs on Cia's skin lifted uncomfortably. Jumpy as a cat caught in a thunderstorm, she managed, 'Good evening,' in a light, pleasant tone as she reached him.

'Good evening.' His words were abrupt and unaccompanied by anything like a smile.

Stung, she said crisply, 'Someone should have shown you where to—'

'Someone tried, but I didn't need them.' He turned to go with her down a broad flight of stairs into a lower garden. 'Am I late?'

'No, I'm early. We're dining at the summer house, so I'm just going to make sure everything's all right.'

'Summer house? That's a very English term.'

Responding to the thread of amusement in his deep voice, Cia confided in her best social tone, 'Wait until you see it! In the late nineteenth century one of the ancestors decided he wanted a summer house after a visit to England. So he built one.'

Everything about this woman set his teeth on edge; Hunt felt a slow simmer of anger at his blatant response to her. Each time he saw her—or thought of her—his testosterone levels soared off the monitor, forcing him to fight a hunger that came from a much more primal level than insipid attraction.

He wanted her, and he wanted her now, and he wanted her in all the ways a man could want a woman, including some that hadn't been invented yet. Even thinking about her stressed his self-control severely; walking beside her in the soft warmth of a Mediterranean dusk with the lazy, erotic scent of flowers floating on the air just about shattered it.

What thoughts hid behind that lovely, controlled face? That his blood was unsuitably red, not royally blue?

He hadn't got where he was by giving in to his baser desires; his hunger for Princess Lucia was purely physical, the instinctive reflex of a male animal when it encountered a receptive female ready for mating.

And as he was not an animal, he was damned well going to control it—even though he knew she was acutely aware of him. As a valet had unpacked his clothes he'd toyed with the idea of making her suffer a little for her cruel rejection of Maxime, only to dismiss it. He had no right to revenge. Besides, she was merely playing the marriage game according to the rules of her class.

Which sounded, he thought now, suspiciously as though he was making excuses for her behaviour.

One of her ridiculously high heels slid off a pebble and she faltered; his hand shot out to grasp her by the elbow. She teetered on the edge of balance and he pulled her upright, supporting her warm, curved form against his.

She froze. He looked down at her startled face, forcing himself to ignore the sudden clamour in his body. Which way would she go? If he bent his head and made himself master of that lush, sensuous mouth she'd respond—but would it be with a smile or a slap? Or both?

'Thank you—I'm fine,' she said breathlessly, stepping away and marching off down the garden without a backwards glance.

But not before Hunt had noted a blaze of colour along her cheekbones. He caught her up in a couple of strides, and fought back the uncivilised instinct to snatch her up, drag her into the shadow of the huge conifers on either side of the path, and kiss her senseless.

In a sardonic voice he observed, 'If you must wear entirely unsuitable shoes—however much they show off your magnificent legs and pretty ankles—arm yourself with a footman. Or a walking stick.'

She sent him an acid glance but didn't reply, and they walked the rest of the way in a silence thick with tension. From the corner of his eye Hunt noticed her spine, straight and true as a rod of steel, but she kept her lovely face under strict discipline.

Outside a marble fantasy that bore a strong resemblance to a Roman forum, Hunt stopped and surveyed it with slowly rising brows. 'You call this a summer house? It doesn't look like any summer house I've ever seen,' he observed drily.

Her gurgle of laughter sounded genuinely amused—and infuriatingly erotic. 'He also built a replica of a Greek temple on one of the beaches. Luka says he was obsessed by delusions of grandeur, but I think he was a raging romantic.'

'Does it run in the family?'

She walked up the marble steps and through large wooden doors studded with bosses of dark bronze. The room inside held a long table, exquisitely set with candles and flowers. Hunt, who had attended his share of banquets, deduced from the colourful china and linen that this dinner was to be informal.

'Oh, we're all very practical now,' she said flatly, casting an expert eye over the table. 'That's the thing about monarchies—the ones that don't learn to adapt lose their jobs.'

'Your family has adapted well,' he commented. 'The prince has made his mark in the cut-throat world of international banking and your cousin Guy heads one of the most innovative software firms in the world.'

'Yes,' Lucia said colourlessly. Apparently satisfied with the state of the table, she indicated the colonnade that marked the other side of the summer house. 'If you want to see why my several times great-grandfather built here, come outside.'

The columns led onto more steps, shallow and semicircular and thence to a wide, stone-flagged area where chairs and loungers had been placed to take advantage of the view. A fountain shimmered in one corner, softly caressing the air with its music.

Hunt considered himself completely blasé about the pretty things the very rich surrounded themselves with; he'd spent time in many of the world's beauty spots and lived in one of the most beautiful of all, yet something about this place stopped him in his tracks.

White-flowered vines draped the stone balustrade that seemed to project out into soft blue-hazed emptiness. When he walked beside Lucia across the terrace, a heady, far from subtle perfume surrounded them. His gaze traversed a huge lounger, plenty big enough for two.

That Victorian ancestor might have had delusions of grandeur, he thought ironically, but he'd designed this place as a seduction pad. And he'd bet his last dollar that even nowadays servants and gardeners were actively discouraged from coming here.

Lucia stopped, resting her elegant hands on the balustrade, and looked out across a great scoop of countryside, dim in the falling dusk. On the horizon the lights of Dacia's main city looped like a necklace around the harbour.

'That's the port,' she said, her voice cool and remote. 'In the daytime you can see out over farms and trees and orchards—it looks like something from a mediaeval painting.'

'My house looks out over a view like this,' Hunt told her. 'Only there's no port, no villages, no lights. And once you reach the sea, it's empty all the way to Chile apart from a few interruptions like Tahiti and Easter Island. It doesn't look at all like a mediaeval painting.'

'It sounds wonderful,' she said pleasantly. 'Like the last frontier.'

The balustrade was warm from the sun, but the heat smouldering through her was caused solely by Hunt Radcliffe. The view shimmered into a haze; she couldn't concentrate on anything but him. From the corner of her eye she saw him grip the stone edge a few inches away from her. Her heart started that crazy thudding she'd felt when he'd held her against him for those shocking, unpredictable moments.

Long-fingered, strong, his hands were those of a man who worked hard for a living. They had supported her with a confident ease that melted her bones. She tried to clear the fumes from her head by wondering what he'd done to earn the calluses; men who headed large businesses didn't usually have time—or the inclination—for vigorous manual exercise.

Hunt Radcliffe, it seemed, made his own rules.

Some elemental part of her brain manufactured an image of that strong hand against the fine-grained softness of her skin, the small roughnesses stimulating her nerves to painful intensity.

The silence seemed to whisper of forbidden hunger.

She swallowed and said in a muted voice, 'I believe New Zealand is very beautiful. I know Alexa misses it sometimes.'

'Loving Luka must make up for that.'

He had no idea how much his words hurt; loving Luka would, she thought wearily, make up for anything!

Cia hoped she hid her surprise. He didn't seem the sort of man who believed in love. In fact, a magazine had featured him as one of the most determined bachelors in the world. She remembered the parade of photographs that had accompanied the article—snaps of him with beauties of all types clinging to his arm.

'Of course,' she said without expression. 'Whereabouts in Northland do you live? Close to Auckland, I suppose.' It was logical that he'd live near the country's biggest city; he spent a lot of his time commuting around the planet.

'On a hill not far from a place called Doubtless Bay.' When he saw that she didn't recognise the name he added, 'In the far north.'

Visualising a map of New Zealand, Cia saw in her mind's eye the long, thin peninsula sticking up towards the tropics. 'Oh, a long way from Auckland.'

'About four hours' drive, or an hour's flight.'

'Not close,' she said, wondering why he'd sounded so abrupt. Had her throwaway suspicion of this morning perhaps been accurate—did he love Alexa?

She stole a glance up at him, secretly inspecting a profile etched against the soft glow the city lent to the sky. The harsh male combination of angles and lines summoned a heady rush of adrenalin. Something in him reminded her of Luka. Both were men born to rule.

If he did love Alexa, she thought sadly, he was too late, because his countrywoman truly loved her husband. It was there in her eyes every time she looked at Luka, in her smile, in her voice whenever she said his name. Nobody could mistake it.

CHAPTER THREE

MORE lights bloomed in the pavilion behind them and voices rose above the calls of the tree frogs. Relieved, her emotions too close to the surface to be comfortable, Cia swung around and said, 'Ah, here's everyone else.'

To her surprise Hunt offered his arm. 'Those shoes aren't made for climbing steps,' he said when she glanced up.

Over the years she had rested her fingers on the arms of innumerable men, yet she hesitated a fraction of a second before accepting the unspoken invitation.

His teeth flashed white in the dusk. 'Scared, your highness?' he asked in a voice that sounded like the sort of purr a lion might produce.

Sarcastic jerk! Her hand trembled on his arm. 'Terrified,' she parried. 'As you've pointed out so graphically, a woman never knows what a man might be thinking.'

He laughed, deep and low and mocking. 'I'm thinking what every other man who gets this close to you does—that you're beautiful.'

Well, she'd handed him that opportunity on a platter. The only thing to do was treat it like a real compliment. 'Thank you,' she said with false cordiality. 'And you're very good-looking too.'

'Thank *you*.' But he hadn't finished. 'I'm also wondering if you ever let the real Lucia Bagaton emerge from behind the princess mask.'

Stung, she returned, 'How sad that you're never going to find out.'

43

Hunt's eyes gleamed in the soft light. 'Now there's a challenge,' he said softly.

She stiffened and began to step away, but when Luka and Alexa came out onto the steps, a lean tanned hand covered the pale one on his black sleeve. His touch—and the very narrow, very masculine smile accompanying it—sent tiny rivulets of fire rippling through her.

'I don't do challenges,' she retorted, nerves tightening as she met his eyes.

Hunt removed his hand. 'You challenge me every time you look at me. But don't worry—I'm past the age of taking dares just for the hell of it. Nowadays I need to know that there's something in it for me.'

That final remark sounded so much like a threat that Cia retorted with a crazy lack of caution, 'Spoken like a true tycoon!'

His cold glance caught hers, refused to let it go. 'So you don't need to worry, princess,' he said obliquely. 'I'm not going to climb the tower and claim any reward.'

But the ruthless note through the words shivered down her spine, dousing her inner fire with foreboding. She couldn't think of anything to say so she settled for nothing as they climbed the steps towards Alexa and Luka.

Much later, creaming off cosmetics in front of the mirror, Cia decided ruefully that the ancestor who'd enjoyed building follies would have been happy with the evening; it could have sprung straight from his imagination.

Beautiful women in elegant clothes and jewels flirted with handsome men—some even had interesting conversations. The whole event was permeated by the smell of privilege, embellished by superb food and magnificent wines and seasoned with laughter. The croaking of tree frogs provided a suitably exotic background for those not born on Dacia, and as a final offering, a huge, wine-red Mediterranean moon, fat with promise and mystery, had risen above the edge of the sea to drench them in magic.

Of course Hunt had fitted in; he was a man who'd cope brilliantly with any situation. Millionaires usually were, she thought snidely, lowering her lashes to remove the last trace of eye-shadow.

Every time she'd looked across he'd been either talking man to man, or indulging in sophisticated banter with a woman. Her sex made much of him, the unattached ones especially; she had overheard one invitation delivered with subtlety by a Frenchwoman renowned for her beauty and her discretion.

He'd refused it with a smile in which there had appeared no hint of the cynicism he'd used on her.

Not that it mattered! She didn't give a hoot what Hunt thought of her. As for the fact that he hadn't danced with her—well, she didn't care about that either.

Not a bit.

Someone knocked on her door. Hastily she wiped the last of the cleanser from her skin and went across to open it, tightening the belt of her robe around her narrow waist.

It was Luka. Anxiously she asked, 'What is it?'

He said, 'I'd hoped you hadn't changed yet. Can I come in?'

'I—yes, of course.' Frowning, she asked, 'Is anything wrong?'

'No.' He frowned. 'How long have you known me, Cia?'

'Since I was born,' she said promptly, wondering what on earth this was all about.

'First as a cousin, and then as a kind of substitute big brother and father.' He looked around her luxurious bedroom. 'I have been very unfair to you—keeping you chained here when you should have been out enjoying life and finding yourself.'

'I've enjoyed my life very much, thank you! And I never lost myself.'

Luka stood looking at her with an expression she couldn't read, then said abruptly, 'As one adult to another, I must tell you that although—*because!*—Hunt Radcliffe is an exciting and very sophisticated man, he is not a man to fall in love with.'

'Did Alexa suggest you talk to me about this?' she asked stiffly.

His face hardened. 'No. I saw immediately that he was interested in you—and why not? You are as beautiful as a spring day. I know we joked about him being attractive, but tonight it seemed to me that perhaps you are intrigued by him.'

Cia relaxed. 'I find him interesting,' she admitted, 'but I'm not silly. I can recognise a heartbreaker when I see one.'

'I wouldn't call him that,' Luka said fairly. 'His women so far have not been the type to put their hearts in jeopardy. But you're not like them. And he has a lot more depth to him than, say, young Lorraine. I love you, and I would hate to see you hurt, little sister.'

It was unbearably painful to hear him say that, when for years she'd longed for an entirely different sort of love from him!

'I won't be hurt,' she said briskly, and summoned a slanting smile. 'Anyway, he doesn't like me. I think you could probably say that we're polite antagonists.'

The prince looked wryly at her. 'Some men find it very difficult to deal with the women who break through their shields,' he said, his voice revealing that he knew what he was talking about. 'They have always considered themselves to be strong and invincible. When they discover that one woman can shatter that belief, they—resent her.' He paused, then added with a smile that hurt her, 'For a while, anyway, until they admit that for them this is the only woman in the world.'

As Alexa was for him.

'Don't worry about me,' she said brightly. 'He's very attractive, but I meet attractive men every day. I'm not going to fall in love with him!'

He frowned at that, then said unexpectedly, 'Alexa tells me that I still think of you as the lost child who first came here. Perhaps I do.'

She had never loved him quite so much as she did that moment—and never wanted quite so hard to kick and scream and tell him that for an astute, intelligent man he could be extremely dim!

But she'd been so careful to hide her secret—how could she blame him for not noticing? Tears clogging her throat, she smiled mistily at him and said, 'Luka, you couldn't have been a kinder, more affectionate big brother. I hate to think how I would have grown up if I hadn't had you to believe in me and take care of me.'

Thoughts of her mother, dead too young from a drug overdose, of her charming, irresponsible father, hovered between them.

'You'd have managed,' he said confidently. 'You're a lot stronger than either of your parents—the Bagaton blood runs true in you. So—goodnight, then.' He dropped a kiss on her cheek and left the room.

The word that wept through her heart was goodbye. Goodbye to everything she loved, to her island home, to the man who'd made her life worthwhile.

Once the door closed behind him she sat down on the bed, looking around the room that had always been hers, at first during the school holidays, later permanently. Although

Luka's father, the old prince, had been kind enough, to him she was simply another responsibility.

Luka had filled the gap in her life; he had taken her skiing and corrected her swimming strokes, he'd taught her how to play chess and insisted she keep up her piano lessons. He'd loved her.

But not the way she wanted him to.

Slowly she got up and began to take off her robe. Leaving Dacia had been the right decision.

'Oh, admit it,' she said aloud into the silent room as she climbed into her pyjamas, 'you stayed on because you're a coward—because the thought of leaving hurt too much.' And because even the bittersweet pain of seeing Luka with Alexa was better than not being near him.

Now it was the staying that hurt too much. Cia's heart twisted; unless she could exorcise Luka, she'd be doomed to the life of good works Hunt had been so snide about.

Tears drowned her eyes. She sniffed and wiped them away with the back of her hand, but they kept coming so in the end she had to find a handkerchief.

How did you banish someone from your heart—from your life? She'd loved Luka since she was old enough to understand her own emotions.

So why, a strange voice inside her mind queried interestedly, do you shiver whenever Hunt Radcliffe touches you?

Jolted out of self-pity, Cia blew her nose with determination. Her violent response to Hunt was nothing more than an involuntary chemical reaction—neither her mind nor her emotions were involved.

It was humiliating that the real Cia, the person who lived in her head and found Hunt overbearing and arrogant and sarcastic, seemed to have no control over the body that smouldered into life when he touched her.

'It's embarrassing, but it's not fatal! It's not even important,' she muttered defensively, and finished getting ready for bed.

This brash, uncomplicated, sexual attraction was notoriously unreliable when it came to relationships. How many kings had lost their countries because they'd let themselves be carried away by passion?

'Too many to count,' she said sternly, switching off the light.

Of course she wasn't a king with a country to lose, but she'd seen enough of transient relationships to know they weren't for her. She wanted love and permanence, and judging by the gossip columnists, Hunt didn't stay faithful to a woman for more than a year or so.

She curled up in the big bed and stared out at the stars of Dacia. As her body relaxed she let her mind drift, only to shock herself by wondering whether giving in to this risky attraction—having an affair with Hunt—would finally exorcise Luka from her heart.

Smiling, she slipped into a heady fantasy where Hunt bent towards her with passion warming his midnight eyes, and she reached out and touched his beautiful mouth with trembling fingers while he murmured her name…

'No!' she exclaimed, sitting bolt upright in bed, utterly disgusted with herself for thinking about using another person, even one as arrogant as Hunt.

She'd already done that when she'd tried so hard to fall in love with Maxime. She'd liked him so much, had allowed herself to hope that their rapport was the beginning of love, only to find out she'd been completely and painfully wrong.

She wasn't going to do that again. Oh, Hunt was tough; he wouldn't look for love from her, and he certainly wouldn't be heartbroken when the affair ended, but she still couldn't do it.

She switched her light back on and picked up a book, reading with stubborn determination until she couldn't see the words on the page. Sleep claimed her like a devouring beast, but towards dawn her restless dreams were invaded by the man whose touch shortened her breath and set her heart pounding in an erotic rhythm.

In her dreams an unknown, bold Cia surrendered joyously to Hunt's touch, following recklessly where he led, her imagination supplying details of experiences she'd never had…

She woke in a dazed, blissful euphoria that rapidly diminished to hot shame. Let loose in sleep, her unconscious brain had shocked her with its explicit imagery.

In the misty light of dawn she knew that an affair with Hunt Radcliffe would be a quick path to disillusion. Sensual charisma swirled around him like a dark cloak, and he wouldn't be impressed with a lover whose experience was limited to Maxime's attempts to arouse her.

'Don't even think about it,' she adjured herself.

But a smouldering, heady anticipation infuriated her as she got out of bed.

Because Alexa and Luka both had appointments that morning she was to escort Hunt on a sightseeing tour. Her stomach tightened, and when she looked in the mirror she saw a gleam in her eyes and a wash of delicate colour along her cheekbones.

What kind of woman loved one man yet indulged in erotic fantasies about another?

'My kind, apparently,' she said grimly, and left her room.

Breakfast over, they came out of the doors of the Little Palace. Hunt looked at the chauffeur standing by the door of the car. His brows rose. 'Can't you drive?'

Cia bristled. 'Of course I can.'

'Are there security reasons that make a driver necessary?'

'Not on Dacia.'

His disciplined mouth curved into a hard smile. 'Do you feel safer with a chaperon?'

'No,' she snapped, temper flaring because somehow he'd hit the nail on the head—and she hadn't even realised what she was doing until he'd called her on it!

Reining in her unusual anger, she countermanded the order and asked for her own car to be brought around.

It amused her in an acid way to note that he watched her carefully for the first few minutes, yet she felt a swift glow of pride when he relaxed.

'You drive well,' he observed.

'Thank you. Luka taught me.'

He nodded without surprise and looked out, dark eyes sharply perceptive as she took the road up into the hills to the place where the first inhabitants of Dacia had lived. Amongst the rocks of the wall that sheltered the dark mouth of the cave, small, vivid cyclamen flowers nestled in mounds of silver-splotched leaves.

'I suppose there's a legend about this,' Hunt observed as they walked through a grove of myrtles to the entrance.

The high-pitched zither of cicadas strummed all about them, and the sun beat down on his proudly poised head, turning the mahogany highlights in his hair to fire.

He looked, Cia thought with an odd catch in her breath, like a statue newly forged as a symbol of male power and grace and beauty. A twisting, unexpected sensation arrowed down to the pit of her stomach.

'There's always a legend. The original Dacians believed their major god was born in the cave.' She swallowed an odd hoarseness to continue briskly, 'Once Christianity reached the island it became transformed into the dwelling of the hermit who is now the island's patron saint.'

He nodded. 'The usual progression.'

Cia must have shown her surprise, because his eyes glinted as he drawled, 'You've known Alexa for long enough to realise that coming from the Southern Hemisphere doesn't mean we're barely literate.'

'Most of the very rich men I've known,' she retaliated smoothly and not quite truthfully, 'are interested in very little more than making money or spending it. It's so refreshing to meet one who has a broader spread of conversational topics.'

He grinned. '*Touché!* I'm sure you feel happier now you've got that off your chest.'

Cia couldn't stop her reluctant smile as they walked around the end of the rock wall and towards the grille that barred the entrance of the cave. 'You're a maddening man,' she said. 'Does anyone ever get the better of you?'

'It happens.' He examined the padlocked door. 'Do we go inside?'

'I have a key.' She produced it from her bag.

When Hunt held out his hand she automatically gave the key to him, wondering as he opened the gate why she'd let him take over. Because he's a take-charge man, she thought. Like Luka. Setting her lips she began to walk into the darkness.

'I'll go first,' Hunt said.

She stopped. 'Why?'

'For some reason it goes against the grain to let a woman go into darkness ahead of me, so you'll have to surrender your royal prerogative just this once.'

Smarting at the jibe, yet oddly touched by his inherent sense of protectiveness, she said, 'There's nothing in there.'

'So why the grille? I wouldn't have thought you'd have much of a problem with vandals.'

'We don't. Most locals won't come anywhere near the place; the island's patron saint was not noted for his friendly temperament and he was a most determined hermit, so very few Dacians are prepared to cross him.'

Hunt set off into the dark mouth of the cave. 'In that case, why is the grille needed?'

Following him, she shrugged. 'It's a historically important site, and every so often someone—usually a tourist—decides they might find something exciting, like gold ornaments.'

The entranceway narrowed and turned abruptly away from the light. She said, 'Careful, there's another sharp turn—*oof*!'

Her last words were muffled as she collided with him. In the half-second before she leapt back she registered muscles like steel and a faint, intensely masculine scent that shivered through her like an aphrodisiac.

'I saw it,' he said drily. 'Are you all right?'

'I'm fine. You must have eyes like a cat,' she returned. 'There's a light sw—'

This time the words dried in her mouth. Wide eyes rapidly getting used to the darkness, she caught the white flash of his smile.

'Not yet.' Strong hands clamped onto her shoulders. 'Shall we get it over and done with?' he asked pleasantly.

Nerves jumping, Cia looked up into his dark face, suddenly predatory in the dim light. 'I have no idea what you're talking about,' she said with a brave attempt at her usual crispness.

'It's inevitable, and until it's happened you're going to walk around me as though I'm contagious.'

Her heart revved up, skipping beats in excited terror. 'I don't know what you mean,' she retorted breathlessly.

'This,' he said on a note of impatience, and bent his head and kissed her.

The warm, exploratory touch of his mouth against hers

surprised her with the sensuous pleasure it aroused. Once she realised he wasn't going to stick his tongue down her throat, she relaxed and kissed him back. Sharp and sexy, his natural scent echoed the man—a faint touch of salt, an edgy hint of musk—a fragrance that owed nothing to artificial means.

When he lifted his head Cia sighed silently with guilty, astonished pleasure, astonished to realise that somehow her hands had stolen around his neck and she was now pressed against him.

She could feel how much he liked it—and his obvious physical enjoyment at her closeness didn't repel her at all. Deep inside her something melted, hot and eager and ardent, both shy and avid.

'Nice,' he murmured, and kissed her again, a little less gently.

And then his mouth changed from warm and coaxing to a hard urgency that demanded infinitely more than she'd ever given any other man. An enormous, irresistible force swamped her in a tidal wave of sensation. She wanted him—she wanted everything he could give.

Here.

Now.

When his arms tightened around her, she shuddered with delight at the intensely intimate contact of her body with his big, powerful one. Hunt took instant advantage of her instinctive reaction, sending her excitement soaring to stratospheric heights as he explored her mouth with shattering expertise.

So this is what all the fuss is about.

Shocked by the violence of her hunger, she abandoned herself to the wave after heated wave of passion that clamoured through her. Her brain closed down and she surrendered wholly to the fiery, carnal possessiveness of his kiss.

Until he lifted his head and surveyed her flushed face. He couldn't hide the colour along his warrior's cheekbones or the dark glitter in his narrowed eyes, but his voice was cool and unsparing.

'There,' he said, 'now it's over and done with, you can stop peering at me every five minutes with that hunted expression.' His hands dropped and he stepped backwards.

Alone and cold, the primitive excitement that flooded her body draining away to leave her coldly disgusted with herself, Cia fought for control. Although she loved Luka, she was shaking with frustrated desire for this man—even now, if he touched her she'd follow him.

From somewhere deep inside, she summoned enough poise to say remotely, 'I'm sorry if I gave you that impression.'

'Why? In case you hadn't noticed, it's entirely mutual.'

Gritty pride tilted her chin and banished everything but brittle composure from her voice. 'I'm not hunting, Mr Radcliffe. There should be—ah, here it is.'

Although the last thing she wanted him to do was see her face, pride drove her to touch the switch. She used the sudden blare of light as an excuse to blink back meaningless tears while she stared blindly around at the rocky walls of the cave.

CHAPTER FOUR

HUNT had only kissed her! But his kisses had rocked her world. Instinct warned Cia it would be dangerous to let him know that.

She glanced at his angular face, dark and forbidding in the light of the bulbs suspended from the ceiling of the cave. The hard lines and planes revealed nothing but interest in his surroundings. Thank God he didn't seem to be thinking about her reckless response.

Of course, an experienced lover like him probably expected that sort of unleashed reaction from any woman he kissed!

When Cia regained control over her vocal cords, she indicated the area that had been dug over by archaeologists. 'It's been a couple of years since any work was done here, and as you can see, there's nothing exciting about the site. Most of the artefacts are in the museum in the port, if you're interested.' Yes, that sounded fine—entirely normal.

Hunt looked down at her. 'Oh, I'm interested,' he said silkily.

Her reply dried on her tongue and she couldn't rescue her imprisoned gaze from his. Disjointed images scurried uselessly through her brain—the cold blue gleam of moonlight on a sword blade, a warrior in full battle array mounted on a screaming war horse, a silken, perfumed, decadent pavilion in some exotic country...

Hunt finally released her by turning to survey the site. 'Does it go any further into the hill?'

Plumbing the depths of her soul, she summoned more

pride to stiffen her spine and lend some authority to her voice. 'No. This is all there is.'

She walked across to the roped-off area where the archaeologists had worked and began to tell him—in her best tourist guide's tone—of the things they'd found.

He knew enough about archaeology methods and European prehistory to keep her alert; at any other time she'd have enjoyed discussing it with him. For now, concentrating helped restore vague order to the chaos that passed for her mind, and gave her something else to think about besides her body's meltdown.

Although dank, it wasn't cold inside the cave, but it was cooler than the warm spring day outside. Not, however, cool enough for the sudden shiver that shook her.

Hunt said instantly, 'Let's go.'

He took her elbow as they walked out along the rutted path. Cia's skin tightened in a primitive, violent response. Every time he touched her she was changing, growing more and more sensitive to his touch.

Where to now? Somewhere with people, she decided, even as her mind muttered, *Coward!*

Despising herself, she said brightly, 'Luka plans to show you his reforestation schemes later in the week, so would you like to see the Old Palace now?'

Hunt's satirical smile didn't soften his striking features. 'Why not?'

'The Old Palace started out as a Greek colony before being transformed into a Roman fortress,' Cia told him, easing out of the traffic to negotiate the breach her nineteenth-century ancestor had made in the massive walls. 'After the Romans fell it suffered the usual fate—everyone who wanted to control this part of the world fought their way in here and proceeded to claim tribute and oppress the islanders.'

Hunt eyed the huge stones. 'I can see why Alexa and the prince prefer the Little Palace,' he observed. 'This looks as though it's been literally drenched in blood—and not just once, either.'

'It was never overthrown after the first Bagaton prince moved in, but you're right, it's certainly not cosy,' she said with a faint smile, nodding to a saluting sentry. 'Luka's father was the last prince to actually live in it.'

'From what I've heard, he'd have suited it.'

'He was a hard man,' she returned coolly, 'but he lived in difficult times, and everything he did was for Dacia. Given the need, Luka can be hard too.' She paused, and added with a faint note of malice, 'And that, I understand, is your reputation as well.'

'Sprung.' Lazy amusement warmed his voice. 'So a certain amount of ruthlessness is fine if it's for your country, but not for personal gain? Somehow, princess, I think you've got me positioned as one of those rich men you despise.'

He was too damned astute, and although crossing swords with him was exhilarating, she had painted herself into a corner. She drove past the huge doors to pull up outside a small entry around the corner. 'Nonsense,' she said briefly, killing the engine. 'I don't know you well enough to make any judgement.'

He laughed, low and quiet. It was stupid to read something of a threat in his words when he said, 'I'm surprised and rather disappointed; I feel I know you quite well.'

Colour sizzled along her cheekbones. 'Only by reputation,' she said, unnerved. 'And I'm sure we're both too astute to rely on newspapers and paparazzi for information!'

If she had to drive Hunt again she'd order a bigger car. He took up far too much room—and not just physical space! He crowded her. And she couldn't prise the memories of his kisses out of her mind. They replayed in endless, sexy invitation.

Nailing a smile to her lips, she got out and headed for a small side entrance where an attendant waited. 'Hello, Paolo. Happy name day for next week.'

The young man beamed at her, a beam that faded when it collided with Hunt's sardonic blue gaze. 'Thank you, your highness.'

'How is your grandmother?'

'She is improving so much after you and the Princess Alexa visited her! My mother says it has given her a new ease of life.'

'Excellent!' Cia gestured towards Hunt. 'I'm going to show Mr Radcliffe around the palace.'

He gave a little bow. 'Do you want the rooms cleared of visitors, ma'am?'

'No, it won't be necessary.'

Hunt waited until they'd reached the audience chamber before enquiring thoughtfully, 'Do you know everyone on the island?'

'I've got a good memory for names and faces—probably bred in my bones!—and it's not as though the island has a huge population.'

He surveyed the great hall; the most determined efforts of nineteenth-century princes hadn't been able to transform the huge area. It was still a grim mediaeval space.

'This looks suspiciously like the real thing,' he observed drily.

Her ripple of laughter lightened his mood. 'I think my forebears realised they weren't going to be able to civilise this part of the palace so they just replaced what decayed and left it alone. Most of the banners are reproductions— over the centuries the original ones were eaten by various insects with exotic tastes.'

Hunt ignored a woman staring blatantly at them. 'Did you visit Dacia much before you came to live here?'

'My father didn't get on with Luka's and my mother hated the place, so we only came a couple of times. After their marriage broke up, Dacia wasn't on anyone's agenda.'

Hunt heard the reservation in her voice. No doubt she knew the sordid reality of her mother's death from a drug overdose; it had been splashed over all the tabloids. Not that Princess Lucia seemed to have suffered much angst from her unconventional upbringing.

Gaze fixed on one especially large banner, dimly colourful in rich, sombre tones, she finished, 'But after my father died I spent almost every school holiday here.'

A shaft of light from a high, narrow window struck her hair, shimmering blue fire across its sleek black crown. The curve of her cheek and long, elegant line of her neck and throat stirred his hormones into sudden, inconvenient activity. Kissing her had been a supremely stupid thing to do. He could still taste her, startled at first, then sweet and soft and fiery, her body sleek and eager against his.

She looked up, and colour bloomed along those incredible cheekbones, while her lips, a little more full than they'd been before he'd kissed her, tightened.

Retiring behind a wall of aloof formality, she took him conscientiously around the old fortress, telling him of old feuds and intrigues, tragedies and battles, with the vivid realism and black humour of someone who'd learned the tales from the inside.

Normally Hunt would have found it interesting, but today the primitive desire that smouldered through his body got in the way. He found himself listening to the cadences of her voice rather than the words, and watching her with an intensity that warned him not to touch her again.

Was that how it had begun with Maxime? Torrid, uncontrollable passion a first step to the lonely road that had finally led to a miserable death from fever in a foetid tropical jungle?

Hunt stared at a sword in the armoury.

'It's a mediaeval broadsword,' Cia told him, her voice wry. 'Luka the Third demolished an invading army with it.'

Hunt's brows lifted. The blade was huge, free of any ornamentation. 'It certainly looks as though it means business, but a whole army?'

Her amber eyes gleamed with shared amusement. 'He was an excellent ruler for his time—'

'Which means he was ruthless but with huge charisma.'

'And devious and cunning,' she added with a laugh. 'Fortunately he was also intelligent, so he knew the value of a good myth. When his people attributed the victory to him alone, he accepted it.'

Hunt scrutinised the blade. A stain of some sort—not rust—ran from the tip to halfway up the blade.

Beside him Cia said lightly, 'Another myth says that that's the bloodstain from a particularly cruel pirate who tried to take over Dacia.'

'And what do you say it is?'

She shrugged. 'Nobody's ever been able to work that out.'

They moved on to examine an elaborate suit of armour. The faint, flowery scent she wore floated upwards. Hunt took a deep breath. A surge of need so intense it felt like craving made him grit his teeth.

Lucia said blandly, 'The princes were great collectors; some of it's exquisite, but more than a little is high-class trash—and some that's just spectacular.'

Hunt regarded a stuffed bear holding a tray in its forepaws, then transferred his gaze to her. 'Spectacular is the only appropriate word,' he said ironically, something in his tone making Cia uneasy.

She risked a quick glance, and caught a fleeting hint of sexual awareness. It vanished immediately from his boldly chiselled features—if it had existed. She'd probably misread his expression.

In a cool, unemotional tone she said, 'I believe this particular stuffed bear was used to collect visiting cards. The crown jewels are much more interesting.'

And more private, she hoped. Several people had been following them around, hovering close by whenever they stopped.

If they were trying to overhear their conversation they'd be disappointed; Hunt was too accustomed to the need for discretion to make any comment that couldn't have been broadcast over the island television station.

The intrusive interest, she thought as they moved into the treasury, was one thing she wouldn't miss when she left Dacia.

Ten minutes later Hunt looked up from a heavily secured case that displayed several exquisite emerald tiaras. 'Which one do you wear?'

She shrugged. 'The smallest one, thank heavens—it's the lightest of the lot.'

He examined it, then scrutinised her sleek head until she shifted a little, her skin heating. Cold amusement glimmered in his eyes, but all he said was, 'How on earth do you keep it on?'

'The more hair you have to anchor it, the easier it is. The bigger one with the pearls is Alexa's, and the solid job with rubies as well as emeralds is the royal crown. My mother used to say that while all coloured stones were vulgar, two lots in clashing colours were positively barbaric, but she was an Englishwoman with refined tastes. Luka has the confidence to carry off anything.'

She was prattling because he hadn't taken his gaze off her, and little rills of sensation were shivering through her body. *Hot* little shivers, she thought in confusion, trying to censor this primitive, runaway response.

Eyes half-closed, Hunt said, 'Cognac diamonds would suit you better. Or would your mother have thought them vulgar too?'

Her colour deepened. 'Probably, but with so many emeralds lying around unused in the vaults no sensible ruler is going to waste money on other stones.' She finished with irony, 'Anyway, these aren't meant to *suit* anyone—they're meant to strike onlookers with awe and convince them they're in the presence of someone regal and impressive.'

'These magnificent gems would do that on their own. I've heard of the Dacian emeralds, of course, but I don't think I've ever been told where they come from and how they ended up here. It looks,' he said thoughtfully, leaning forward to examine a particularly fine stone set in a ring, 'as though someone plundered an entire emerald mine.'

Cia laughed. 'Something like that. One of my raffish seventeenth-century ancestors went adventuring in South America and bought his way back into his father's good graces with the sort of treasure trove you could only find in those days. Nobody ever discovered where he got it—or how. I think he was probably a pirate who stole them off a Spanish treasure ship.'

Hunt had a buccaneer's face, dark and dangerous and intelligent; mentally clothing him in seventeenth-century clothes, she could imagine him lethally swashbuckling his way across uncharted chunks of the map to fame and fortune.

'All in a good cause, as the prince's father used them to

found the Bank of Dacia, and the island's present prosperity,' Hunt said idly. 'It's a romantic story.'

Cia gazed at the brilliant gems, their deep green facets smouldering with a dark, almost certainly bloodstained, history. 'I think there was probably more gore than romance in the story. I can't take you into the vaults—as you can imagine, security is very tight—but if you're interested in the whole collection, Luka can show you.'

His broad shoulders lifted a fraction. 'Why not?' he drawled. 'I'd like to see what a king's ransom looks like, and I don't imagine any other graduate from the New Zealand social welfare system has paid a visit to Aladdin's Cave.'

How had he got from orphan to tycoon? By being very tough and very clever and a leader of men, she reminded herself. *And this is the man you thought you might have an affair with?*

Only if she wanted a severe case of scorched fingers.

'Why can't you go into the vaults?' he asked idly, stopping to examine the sceptre.

'The emeralds belong to Dacia, not me.' And just in case there was anything the least sinister in his question, she said, 'I'm the traditional poor relation.'

His brows lifted in ironic amusement. 'So I see,' he drawled, examining her with a connoisseur's appreciation of her designer clothes and immaculate make-up.

Little prickles stabbed her skin, were transmuted into a sharp excitement that strained every nerve. 'I have a clothes allowance,' she said tightly.

'And poverty is relative.'

She shrugged, regretting her impulsive remark. 'Indeed it is.'

From her mother's estate she received just enough to keep her from starving. Once away from the security net of her job and position in Dacia, she'd have to work, because after she'd finished university she wasn't going to accept any further money from Luka.

Apart from a further hitch of his brows Hunt made no comment, but on the way back to the Little Palace he observed, 'You're very good at showing visitors around. When you leave Dacia—if you ever do—you'd be a sitter for a job in the tourist industry. The high-end market, of course.'

Something about his deliberate tone lifted the hair on the back of her neck. 'As it happens, I am leaving,' she said calmly, turning off the crowded street to dive into a narrow alley with the aplomb of years of practice. 'But I won't be going into the tourist industry.'

There was a moment's silence. 'So what will you do?'

Cia braked swiftly, stopping behind a donkey doing its best to cause a traffic jam. 'Oh, I'll find something,' she said airily.

'Join the jet set?' Scorn laced the question.

Judgemental bastard! She curled her lip. 'Some of my best friends—even the occasional relative on my mother's side—are members of what you'd call the jet set.'

A vigorous altercation broke out around them, the flower-seller whose wares were being eaten by the donkey calling on all her saints to remove the animal to its natural home in Hades.

Hunt dropped a cool, sardonic remark into a sudden silence with devastating effect. 'You could marry well. It's a traditional career path for women in your situation.'

Cia said between her teeth, *Impoverished princess newly out of a job but reasonably attractive seeks rich, aristocratic husband. Competent at organising social calendar and with suitable family contacts for any social climber?'* Her voice returned to normal. 'I don't think so.'

'Drop *aristocratic*,' he suggested cynically. 'Unless you can't conceive of marrying into the *nouveau riche*.'

Anger seethed inside her, but she responded cordially, 'If I were thinking of advertising in such a vulgar way, I probably would. I'm not a snob, and most aristocrats are finding things hard nowadays.'

'Oh, I'm sure you'd be far more subtle.' It was not a compliment.

She said between her teeth, 'As it happens, I'm going to university.'

'History of Art?' he suggested patronisingly.

'A BA,' she flung at him. 'At Oxford.'

The war outside broke out again in the sort of uproar only Dacians could produce. Lean fingers on the door handle, Hunt said, 'I'll see if I can help here.'

At that moment the donkey's owner managed to wrench the beast away from the flower-seller's blooms. It side-stepped and backed triumphantly into the car.

As the vehicle rocked, Cia commented, 'We don't have many donkeys now—most Dacians prefer motor scooters.'

'I can see why.' But he sounded amused rather than irritated.

'I like donkeys.'

This one was now braying with indignation; berating it severely and noisily, its owner finally managed to wedge it into a niche in the stone building.

Hunt observed, 'It seems that the antagonists in this interesting war of wills have just realised who you are.'

Apologising in rapid Dacian, the donkey's owner gazed around in despair before snatching a bouquet of freesias from the flower-seller.

Thrusting them through the window into Cia's face, he gabbled, 'So sorry, your highness. This spawn of the devil will be the death of me. You have no idea—'

'Not those, you fool!' the flower-seller snapped, deftly retrieving the freesias and replacing them with roses. 'Here, highness, roses to suit your beauty—and because roses are the flowers of love!'

She rolled magnificent black eyes at Hunt, who gave her a smile that made her laugh and fan her face with her hands.

With her lap full of scented roses, Cia said, 'Thank you, but—'

Hunt overrode her. 'You must let me pay for them,' he said easily.

'Ah, you must be our princess's countryman!' the flower-seller exclaimed in English, visibly impressed as she held out her hand for the money Hunt dropped into the palm. She leaned down to fix Cia with a bold gaze. 'Your highness, now that Prince Luka has taken himself a wife, isn't it time for you to find a husband? When are we going to see another royal wedding in Dacia?' Her shrewd black eyes roved from Cia's flushed face to Hunt's amused one.

Cia produced a smile. 'Unless Prince Guy has fallen in love, not for a while,' she said, then flushed as Hunt scooped the bunch of flowers from her lap. Their perfume swamped her, seductive, languorous as the smoky heat of summer, richly evocative.

His lean fingers lightly brushed her breast, sending sensation through her in a lightning assault that robbed her of her wits. Accident? It certainly appeared so.

The flower-seller laughed openly, straightening up and stepping back when Hunt turned and dropped the blooms into the back seat.

Still buzzing with a fierce, intoxicating undercurrent of arousal, Cia put the car into gear with a hand that shook too much for her comfort, waved to the small crowd that had gathered and took off too fast.

Hunt didn't say anything, although she knew he was smiling; keeping her profile stubbornly aligned at him, she debouched from the narrow maze of streets onto a wider road, grateful because the flow of traffic kept her concentrating.

She had not come out of that very well. Now rumours would be flying around the island—well, it didn't matter! By this time next week she'd have gone, without fanfare as she wanted, but for good.

Frowning into the sun, Hunt asked, 'What decided you to go to university?'

Had he picked up on her thoughts? Of course not.

'Because I want to.' She passed a truck and went on more crisply, 'I'm not necessary here any more. Alexa is already loved, but while I stay people will look to me instead of to her. They are used to me, you see. Once I go she'll take her rightful place in their lives.'

'So when is this?'

'Just after you leave.' She turned the car onto the road to the Little Palace.

He was staring straight ahead, heavy lids hiding his thoughts, but Cia had the uneasy sensation of wheels whirring in that clever, incisive brain.

Today had been a strain; tomorrow would be easier. Alexa had organised a yacht trip to an offshore island where they'd eat a barbecue lunch beside a lagoon famous for the lilies that bloomed around the silken stretch of water.

Cia looked around a beach so blazing white everyone—including the chefs at the barbecue—wore sunglasses. Another picture to warm a romantic's heart, she thought, aware of pain niggling at one temple. Men and women in designer beachwear stood or sat or swam, all chatting, all clearly having a very good time, while she seemed stuck under her own personal dark cloud.

At least with twenty people in close attendance she was

able to avoid Hunt; another restless night punctuated by luridly erotic dreams had convinced her to stay well away from him. His disturbing male magnetism was playing havoc with her sleep.

After making smiling progress along the sand, she sat down beside Alexa in the shade of the tamarisks, letting out a small sigh as the slightly cooler air caressed her hot cheeks.

'I love this place,' she said, averting her eyes from the beach. A few metres away, two gorgeous sisters in the latest bikinis were flirting with Hunt.

Alexa looked a little pale. 'So do I, although I didn't realise the scent of the lilies would be so heavy. They're not even in full bloom yet—it must be overwhelming when they're all out.'

'Is it too much for you?' Cia asked worriedly. 'We can leave—'

'And deprive Hunt of the sister act?' Alexa laughed. 'It might spoil his day. Anyway, you know we can't go. Not that I want to—I'm fine.'

'Shall I tell Luka?' Cia watched the oldest sister—by ten minutes—lift thickly curling lashes to Hunt with a pouting, provocative movement of her lips.

He gave her a wicked smile and said something that set both girls squealing with laughter.

'Don't you dare,' Alexa said swiftly, casting a smiling glance at the trio. 'I wonder what he said?'

'Who knows? He's obviously used to beautiful women,' Cia observed acidly.

'Well, yes.' Alexa sighed. 'Very rich men are, aren't they? It goes with the territory. The first time I saw Luka in the flesh, a truly stunning female was fawning all over him while she fed him oysters. He certainly seemed to be having a very good time.'

Cia forced a smile. 'But that was before he'd met you.'

The woman beside her gave a secret little smile as the prince strolled along and sat down beside her. Cia lowered her lashes; it seemed indecent to watch two people who smiled at each other like that. It's not fair, she cried in silent, bitter rebellion.

But then, who said life had to be fair?

Humiliation mixed in an intolerable fashion with a wholly unwarranted antipathy to the two girls who were flirting with Hunt.

Two men, she thought in disgust—how could she love one and shiver with debilitating anticipation when the other looked at her?

Away from both men, she might be able to sort herself out.

'I'll just make sure that everything's all right with the barbecue,' she improvised, and got to her feet.

That day set the tone for the rest of the week. Cia spent it torn by conflicting emotions, her grief at leaving Luka and Dacia somehow overshadowed by this reluctant, wildfire attraction to Hunt that seemed to grow exponentially every time she saw him.

Which wasn't often; he spent much of the time in meetings with Luka and the executives of the bank. The evenings were busy social affairs.

Some time during the middle of the week, Cia realised she was actively looking forward to seeing him at night, crossing swords with him, indulging in a subtle, edgy sort of conversation that combined flirtation and aggression.

He took care not to touch her again, for which she was supremely grateful, but she was acutely, uncomfortably, recklessly aware of him. Watching him wield that ruthless charm like a weapon, Cia wondered if her mindless surrender had satisfied that predatory instinct she sensed in him.

So, he could now claim he'd kissed a princess. Big deal; besides, she couldn't see him as a trophy hunter. He was too confident to need public validation, which meant the gossip columnists weren't going to hear about it, and it was impossible to imagine him swapping stories of conquests with friends.

But perhaps the orphan from New Zealand enjoyed the thought of kissing someone from minor royalty.

No, she thought. Not Hunt. Unlike poor Maxime Lorraine, he didn't pin his self-esteem to anyone's opinion of him.

Every year, when the gardens reached their spring glory, Luka held an informal garden party in the Little Palace grounds, followed by a private dinner and a concert in the Old Palace. It was Cia's last official event and she had expected to be wretchedly miserable at it.

Instead, as she had every time they'd been in the same area together, she was watching Hunt from beneath her lashes.

Having apparently dumped his minder, he stood talking to a superbly dressed woman in her mid-thirties, who was flirting discreetly with him from beneath the brim of her hat. Her magnificent outfit might be more suited to a race meeting, but it certainly made the most of her lush figure.

I am not jealous, Cia thought valiantly, colouring slightly as Hunt looked over the top of the woman's elegant hat and sent her a long, direct, unsmiling stare, before switching his gaze back to his companion.

Icy little thrills scudded down Cia's spine. Each time their eyes clashed, she felt that it reinforced some kind of link between them. Yet there was none. Shocked by her body's awareness, she bit her lip and looked away.

From beside her Alexa murmured, 'Notice that it's always experienced women he flirts with? He won't be leaving any broken hearts behind him.'

Cia smiled stiffly. 'A week isn't long enough to break your heart over someone, surely?'

'I suppose not.' But Alexa sounded doubtful. 'Are you looking forward to your freedom?'

'Mostly,' Cia said promptly, not exactly lying. She had reached the state where her love for Luka was like a nagging tooth; she desperately wanted it out, gone, banished so that it no longer hurt.

'And you're happy to stay in the London house?'

'Until university starts, yes.' Not after that; living with constant reminders of the past would hurt too much, so she'd be looking for a place of her own as soon as she settled.

She was grateful when Alexa said, 'Ah, afternoon tea is served,' and together with Luka they went into the huge marquee.

Much later that night, after the concert, Cia changed into a long, drifting cotton dress in her favourite shade of amber, enjoying the freedom to banish all underwear but her briefs. The garden party had only just been in time; already heat was beginning to strike the island. Soon, when summer aridity took over from spring's lush promise, Dacia would bake under a relentless sun. Holidaymakers would pour in to toast themselves on the white sand and swim in sea as blue as the sky, drink the island wine and make love.

And she wouldn't be there.

Neither would Hunt. An aching restlessness drove her, and as she slid her feet into sandals—without heels this time—and went out into the corridor she tried to convince herself that she'd be relieved when he left. He was altogether too everything. Too dominant, too hard, too formidable, too sexy, too intelligent, too rich—oh, there were a multitude of *toos* that fitted Hunt Radcliffe!

Too much man for her.

She was still smiling ironically when she opened the side door and walked out onto the terrace. It was a night for lovers, she thought wistfully; the moon had just risen, the golden globe slightly diminished from its fullness of the night Hunt arrived.

Less than a week ago! It seemed that she'd been watching him hungrily from the corner of her eye for a lifetime.

And soon he'd be gone, and she'd probably not see him for years, if ever. Just as well; she couldn't blame him for her confusion, but loving Luka yet wanting Hunt was nervous-breakdown territory, she thought, trying to be flippant in spite of the stupid, silent tears aching in her throat. She needed time to sort herself out.

Her sandals made no sound on the flagstones of the terrace. Weak tears gathered in her eyes and began to slip silently down her face. Hastily turning onto a grass path in the intense darkness beneath a row of clipped cypresses, she blinked and swallowed—and froze when she heard voices coming slowly towards her. Alexa and Luka.

Too raw to want to talk, she acted on impulse, stepping quickly and silently into the deep shade of the cypresses and stood breathless, eyes clenched shut, hoping that they'd say nothing as they passed her.

But Alexa was speaking, and her words carried too clearly on the still, warm air. '…tell Cia?' she asked, her voice worried.

'No,' Luka said instantly. 'She'll insist on staying here if you tell her.'

Breath stopping in her throat, Cia gritted her teeth, trying to block out his statement, refusing to consider its implications.

But above the roaring in her ears she heard Luka say in a voice she barely recognised, 'My heart, my dear one, my most beloved, why can't I find the words to tell you how much I love you?'

Alexa said something, and he laughed deep and slow, and then there was silence. After a long time Cia opened her eyes and saw one silhouette disentangle into two; hand in hand, they walked in the kind light of the moon up towards the palace.

Indeed, a night for lovers.

CHAPTER FIVE

LONG after Luka and Alexa disappeared, Cia stood staring blindly into the stiff shadows of the cypresses until she was certain she was alone. It hurt to breathe. It even hurt to take that first stumbling step out of the darkness into the silver brightness of the silent moon. Like a wounded animal, she sought sanctuary as far away as she could get from the Little Palace.

Down through the garden she walked swiftly and mindlessly, Luka's words playing over and over again in her brain. *She'll insist on staying if you tell her…*

Tell her what?

It didn't matter; he wanted her gone.

Blind instinct brought her to the summer house. Without turning on any lights she crossed the dining area and walked down the steps, made her way across the terrace to stop at the balustrade. Tree frogs croaked mournfully in the olive trees, and the scent of flowers hung like heavy smoke. Across the shadowy coastal plain by the port, someone was letting off fireworks.

Shivering in the warm evening air, Cia hugged herself and watched skyrockets soar into the dark sky. Each explosion into showers of glittering flowers hurt in some obscure way, yet she kept her gritty eyes fixed on each fresh golden arrow until the drifting sparks blurred and faded into nothingness.

Like stars snuffed out in the cold emptiness of space…

If only her emotions could end up as dark and dead as

the skyrockets, she might attain some peace. Unconsciously one hand went up to the pendant around her throat.

With a swift, fierce movement she whipped the chain over her head and clenched her fingers around the diamond star. Its sharp points cut into her palm. Pain and humiliation fuelled the impulse to hurl it over the balustrade. She even lifted her hand.

In the end she couldn't. Luka had given it to her with love; not the kind of love she craved from him, but love nevertheless. She couldn't throw it away.

When Luka had said, 'My heart, my dear one, my beloved,' each word had slashed through her heart like a sword, but now she knew it was time to relinquish the last, forlorn shred of hope.

But oh, it hurt so much…

She slid the pendant into her pocket and stared silently out over the plain as more skyrockets bloomed in the dark sky. She'd never wear Luka's star again.

Cia had no idea how long she stood there, dry-eyed yet aching as though she'd been physically beaten, but eventually she straightened up and dragged in a long, jagged breath. Wallowing in grief was not going to change anything. Life had to be lived, and the sooner she started, the sooner she'd be able to cope.

She swallowed the lump in her throat, then stiffened, hands gripping the balustrade. With renewed determination came something else—heightened perception that lifted the tiny hairs on the back of her neck. A panicky jolt under her ribs told her what the odd sensation between her shoulder blades had been trying to indicate for some minutes past. She wasn't alone.

One of the night-security men?

No, she thought, and slowly turned.

A tall dark shadow detached from the deeper darkness

inside the summer house, threading between the furniture with a powerful, lithe grace she recognised immediately.

'Hello, Hunt. Can't you sleep?'

'It must be the moon,' he said sardonically. 'What's your excuse?'

She sketched a brief, mirthless smile. 'Oh, I'll blame the moon too.'

Hunt stopped a pace away to look down at her, his striking face stripped to its essential strength by the hard white light of the moon. Cia's mouth dried; the elemental fire that burned in him banished her bleak chill in a surge of sensual heat. She felt dislocated, overwhelmed, her emotions jerked so swiftly from one extreme to the other that she was lost.

'The ancient Greeks had it right,' he observed, a raw edge to the words sending her heartbeat skipping. 'Their moon goddess was a chaste huntress, beautiful yet dangerous, and any man who saw her died.'

'She's long dead herself, poor Diana. You're the only hunter around tonight,' Cia countered, excitement binding her in molten chains.

'Am I?'

'My name isn't Diana,' she said unevenly. 'Lucia means light, not the moon.'

'But you're dangerous.' His smile, a masterpiece of irony, didn't quite hide the deep, abrasive note in his voice.

Every tiny hair on Cia's skin stood straight in sensual anticipation. From that first meeting this fiery anticipation had been building, building, building, until now it burned through restraint and reserve to fan her hunger into an inferno.

His smile hardened, but when she took a step towards him, tossing caution to that dangerous goddess of the night, he caught her by the wrist and held her away, scanning her face with dark intensity. 'What do you want, Lucia?'

For a moment she hesitated, torn between primitive longing and a valiant caution. Making love to Hunt would be using him…

But he wouldn't be hurt. He didn't even like her much, so it would mean nothing to him beyond easing his lust.

And oh, God, she needed warmth…

'You,' she said, the word whispering beneath the tree frogs' chorus. She wanted Hunt every bit as much as he wanted her—for different reasons, but he wasn't interested in her reasons.

'Your pulse is racing,' he said, his voice gravely neutral.

'I know.' She steepled the fingers of the hand he was holding so that she could rest the tips against his wrist. Touching him, feeling the slow regular beat begin to increase speed, gave her the same forbidden thrill as kissing him.

'So is yours,' she said on a ragged note.

'Why tonight?'

She glanced up, freezing as she braced herself for yet another rejection. But the bold features were clamped under such grim control she couldn't read his expression. In the moonlight his eyes glittered bright as diamonds, keen as the edge on a freshly honed blade.

She said briefly, 'Because it's a beautiful night.'

His mouth twisted and his voice was uncompromising. 'Tell me the truth.'

So she told him the truth—or as much of it as she was prepared to admit. 'It seems right. I want you, and I think you want me.'

After a nerve-racking silence he drawled, 'I didn't think you'd noticed, princess.'

'I'm going to stop you calling me that if it's the last thing I do,' she said between her teeth, and stepped into his arms and reached up, linking her arms around his neck.

And then her courage failed her.

His hands came up on either side of her head, holding her head still. For long moments he looked down into her questioning eyes, then lowered his head until his mouth touched hers in a kiss so gentle it seared through Cia like a laser.

She wanted heat and power and passion reckless enough to drive every thought from her brain, but Hunt gave her a cruel tenderness, exploring her face with his kisses until she groaned in supplication.

Then he laughed deep in his throat and swept her up, carrying her easily across to the biggest lounger. But before he put her down on it he asked, 'Is anyone likely to come here?'

Above the rapid, high thud of her heart she said, 'No, it's a private space.' And shivered in the crackling heat of the bridges she'd just set afire.

'I was thinking of your cousin.'

'No,' she said quietly. 'They've gone to bed for the night.'

Her voice didn't even tremble. Pain whispered below the surface, but held so close to Hunt, his faint scent mingling with the sultry perfume of the flowers, she couldn't feel anything other than urgent, primal anticipation.

'Good,' he said, the word echoing in her ears.

Still with her in his arms, he bent his head and kissed her again, and although he began with that intoxicating, dangerous tenderness, his mouth soon betrayed the urgency and raw force she needed so desperately.

Her lips softened beneath his, accepting and returning the wild heat of his kisses, so that when he at last put her on her feet she leaned against him and tried to regulate her breathing while she listened to his heart thudding in his chest.

'How does this pretty thing undo?' he asked, his amused tone not hiding the abrasive note in his deep voice.

'It doesn't.' She was nervous, but thank heavens for the training that kept her words level. 'It flips over my head.'

Expectation keen as a sword, she waited for him to strip her, but instead he kissed her again, and somehow when the kiss was over she was lying on the lounger with him—still with her clothes on.

Hunt slid an arm under her head and looked down into her face, his own cynically amused—and oddly determined. 'The moment I saw you I knew this week was going to be difficult,' he murmured, 'but it's been bloody murder. Since I lost my head and kissed you in the cave you've kept as far from me as you could, and every time I came anywhere near you, you gave me your princess smile, kind and interested and aloof. Each time I wanted to kiss that smile off your lovely face.'

Stung by his manifest unfairness, she said indignantly, 'You never came near me! You just looked at me occasionally—and you didn't smile at all.'

'Mm,' he said, kissing the corner of her mouth. 'I couldn't—I was too busy wondering if you tasted as good as I remembered...'

Hard and passionate, his mouth crushed the last sensible thought in her brain and carried her into the heart of a sun, burning away everything in a burst of need as powerful as a nova in explosion.

When he lifted his head she thought he said something against her lips, but she was too dazed to understand, and anyway, he kissed her again immediately and sweet, tantalising sensation flooded everything out of her mind. Sighing, she gave herself up to everything he demanded of her, shivering when his mouth explored pleasure points she dimly recalled reading about.

But no hearsay could have prepared her for Hunt's love-making. When he covered the throbbing pulse at the base of her throat with his mouth, it sent shudders of delight through her body, and when he nipped the lobe of her ear she almost cried out.

'Lucia,' he said deeply, and cupped her breast beneath the thin covering of lawn.

Her body tightened in delicious expectancy, arrows of pleasure shooting through her. Somewhere, she remembered, she'd read that men did what they wanted done to them, so she put her hand up and slid it through the buttons of his shirt. His skin was hot, and the soft friction of chest hair set her fingertips tingling and her heart banging against her ribs.

She looked up into smouldering, heavy-lidded eyes and saw him smile, a slow, wolfish movement of his lips that made her stomach kick in delicious panic.

'You can take it off,' he suggested.

With shaking fingers she undid the buttons and spread the thin cotton back to feast her stunned eyes on the magnificence of his torso.

He moved slightly as though she'd embarrassed him. Cia's breath sighed through her lips, and he laughed softly.

With shaking fingers she smoothed over the swell of one broad shoulder, simply enjoying the heated texture of his skin, fine-grained and flexible, beneath her palm. Hunt lay still, apparently happy to let her explore for as long as she wanted.

With renewed confidence, she remembered the exquisite pleasure of his hand against her breast; greatly daring, she progressed down towards a small dark nipple. He wasn't breathing, she realised with a sudden flare of fierce delight; this gave her the confidence to bend her head and kiss the tight, hard nubbin.

The big body beneath her lips jerked. 'Do you know what you're doing?'

She looked up, met gleaming eyes and a face set in taut, formidable lines.

'Do you like it?' she breathed, and lifted her head to trace a line of kisses across the swell of one roped muscle. It flexed beneath her lips, and she licked delicately, absorbing the salty taste of him, the clean male flavour.

'I like it.' Three guttural words, but they smashed through the last of her inhibitions.

Hunt reached up and with hands a little less deft than usual began to take the clips out of her hair. 'I've been having erotic dreams,' he said, a taut note charging his dark voice, 'of lying with your hair brushing against my skin like a cloak of silk. Trust me?'

Cia stared into eyes that were hard and hot as molten ebony. She didn't know what he wanted from her, but it was more than simple trust.

When she hesitated his eyes narrowed into fierce slits of steel. 'Don't tease the animal—it might bite. Say what you feel.'

For some reason she did trust him. She'd never have got this far if she hadn't been sure in some secret part of her mind that he wouldn't hurt her. When she nodded, the tumbling fall of her hair brushed against his skin.

'Yes.' The word fell on a soft, slumbrous cadence into silence.

He gave a low, clipped laugh and shrugged his shirt completely off his shoulders before lying back onto the lounger and examining her face, his eyes half-hidden by thick lashes. 'Just yes?'

'That's how I feel,' she said. 'One big yes.'

'Fortunately, that's exactly how I feel too.' He pulled her

down and slowly measured the length of her throat with kisses.

His skilful touch set free the wildness she'd tried so hard to contain. Bending her head, she explored his lean, powerful torso with eager mouth and questing hands, familiarising herself with his broad shoulders and rock-hard ribcage. Fascinated by the sheer male power beneath his sleek skin, the iron-hard muscles that coiled whenever he moved, she relished an odd, incongruous sense of being protected.

At last he said, 'My turn now.'

When Cia looked up, unnerved by his harsh tone, he slid her dress the length of her legs in an absorbed, intensely provocative movement, stroking skin silvered by the moon as the material moved up to reveal her legs. Sensation ran riot through her, melting her bones, pooling in her breasts and in the sensitive part between her legs.

Her breath locked in her throat; watching the lean dark hands against her skin, she had to force herself to drag air into her starving lungs.

When she swallowed, he said, 'Still yes?'

'Yes.' It was barely a sound. Everything had stopped, balanced on a knife-edge of anticipation; the owls no longer called, the tree frogs had fallen silent.

Slowly—*excruciatingly* slowly—he drew the soft thin fabric over her head. She lifted her arms and he pushed the material free of her, but instead of letting her go he held her wrists together above her head. Naked except for the narrow scrap of silk that hid her most secret parts, she felt her skin tighten, and her stomach contracted sharply as he scrutinised her body with leisurely thoroughness. Could he see her heart beating like a frenzied jungle drum? Did he understand that her breasts, soft and full and heavy, were waiting for something they'd never known…?

'I suspect that I'm going to end up like others who saw

the moon goddess,' he said deeply, moving to cradle her breast in his free hand.

The drum in her chest took over her body so that it throbbed with longing. She could feel the touch of those long fingers right down to the marrow in her bones, burning away everything but the need to experience Hunt in the most basic, intense way.

Her mouth was so dry she had to swallow hard before she could croak, 'Dead? I hope not.'

'There are different ways to die,' he murmured enigmatically, and pulled her towards him so that he could take the sensitive tip of her breast in his ravenous mouth.

This time she did cry out, transfixed by sensual pleasure so outrageously intoxicating she knew she'd never forget it.

Later, when her dazed mind went over the events of that night, she decided that Hunt was a devilish torturer—and oh, so experienced. By slow increments he led her further and further down the path of total abandonment, dazzling her with sensuous skill while he taught her eager body to accept every touch, every caress, every exquisite new sensation until, panting and desperate, she twisted in his arms, her hips rising instinctively against his big, potent body.

By then they were both naked. One long finger explored her most intimate parts; as she writhed against the voluptuous intrusion, he smiled and said softly, 'You're ready.'

She flashed, 'I've been ready for ages.'

'So it's mutual.' Smiling, he eased over her, and took her.

Cia had expected pain, but either riding horses or Hunt's meticulous preparation must have taken care of that, because he met no obstruction as he eased into her tight, slick passage. Ignoring a slight burning, a feeling of being forced to accept more of him than she had room for, she gasped, and once again her hips jerked upwards in unconscious invitation.

His face dark and intent and angular in the radiant light of the moon, he thrust home.

Her gasp turned into a kind of strangled groan, but she was beyond trying to analyse anything. A flood of strange, rich pleasure overwhelmed her, transforming her into a different woman, a woman who knew at last what her body had been made for.

Almost immediately, after a breathless moment during which her body began to adjust to the dominance of his, Hunt withdrew.

Instinctively she clung tightly, her fingers digging into his sweat-damp shoulders, and clamped her thighs together while she contracted muscles she didn't know she had, determined to keep him where he belonged, buried inside her.

He laughed deeply and lifted his hips, and she groaned again as he thrust deep, deep inside her, then withdrew again, setting up a rhythm that sent sensations bursting through her to destroy her final links to sanity.

She arched, pushing against his strength, those amazing inner muscles clamping onto him and relaxing in time with his movements.

With gritted teeth he muttered, 'No.'

Bewildered, she stared into narrowed eyes like molten ebony. 'What?'

'Next time,' he promised, each word thick and raw, 'you can do that and I'll hold out as long as I can, but right now this is going to come to an untimely end if you keep on doing that. Let's go gently.'

And that was wonderful too, until in the end the white-hot hunger inside her turned into waves that tossed her further and further towards a place she desperately longed to reach, but couldn't quite…

Hunt moved harder and faster, and she moved with him, their bodies dancing in an age-old pattern of desire and connection and offering until she convulsed in a cosmic inner explosion that flung her into an ecstasy so fantastic she thought she might die. Delight stormed her, took her prisoner, made her its own, and hurled her into a darkness where the only reality was Hunt and the response of her body to his.

Almost immediately Hunt made a deep, harsh sound in his throat. She forced up heavy eyelids to see him fling his head back.

As wonderful as her own climax was, seeing Hunt reach his drove her further up the heights of rapture until she cried out because she could bear it no longer.

And then it was receding and she was desperately trying to claw it back. Emptiness washed over her in a cold wave until Hunt's arms contracted around her, banishing that frightening sense of loss, and for the first time in her life she knew what it was like to be utterly secure.

'It's all right,' he said, kissing her forehead before smoothing back her hair. 'I'd like to lie here all night with you like this, but I suppose we can't.'

'No, it wouldn't be sensible,' she muttered, shocked by the sweet delight of this shivery aftermath, how easy it was to accept the warmth of his big body and to lie without strength against a heart that was still pounding like a piston.

He smiled, and ran his hand from her throat to her breast, smoothing the fine, damp skin in a caress that held tenderness as well as passion.

'And if we stay here for much longer,' he said, 'we're going to fall asleep. But we need to talk. Where are you going when you leave Dacia?'

'To the London house,' she told him.

He was silent for a short period. Cia didn't lift her head to look at him; it wasn't hope that struggled inside her. What they'd just shared was good sex—fantastic sex! How many women came to a climax like that the first time they made love? It was Hunt's expertise and astonishing tenderness that had done that for her, but she wasn't going to fall into the trap of thinking that sex was love—or even affection.

'Give me the address,' he said abruptly. 'I could meet you in London.'

Temptation knocked seductively on the door of her heart. He wasn't offering permanence, just a fling for a few days.

When he bent and kissed her, she shivered at the swift upsurge of desire. 'That's not fair,' she protested. 'I can't think when you do that.'

'That was the idea,' he said casually. 'You've got a couple of days to make up your mind. But just so that you don't forget—' he bent his head and girdled her waist with swift, hard kisses, taught her that her navel was another tiny erogenous zone, and then finished with a final kiss between her brows.

'Stop frowning,' he said against her skin. 'Meeting me in London is not such a big deal.'

'You can't control me with sex,' she said, although her voice wobbled.

He laughed. 'Why don't you try controlling me?' He glanced at his watch and swore under his breath. 'It's late, and tomorrow is going to be a busy day. Your cousin and I still have to hammer out the final details of our agreement. I believe we're having a quiet dinner tomorrow night.'

'Yes.' On impulse, she reached up and kissed his cheek, stimulated again by the soft abrasion of his beard beneath his skin.

'Not here at the summer house, I hope,' he said, irony hardening his voice.

Shivering, she sat up abruptly. 'No, not here.'

Hunt pulled her with him as he got up from the lounger

and tilted her chin with his thumbs so that he could see her face. 'Meet me in London,' he said quietly.

He didn't intend anything serious. For some reason that hurt, but she had to be sensible—making love to him could be addictive. However, a few wild days in London…

'All right,' she said.

His eyes gleamed in his dark face and he gave her a swift, hard kiss before letting her go. 'We'd better move.'

Cia felt awkward pulling on her dress and pants, but Hunt seemed perfectly at ease.

Naturally, she thought as she climbed into her sandals and recalled the sophisticated women he'd escorted; he was accustomed to this sort of thing.

It wasn't until she was showering back at the palace that she realised that making love to him had certainly done one thing for her—instead of breaking her heart over Luka's rejection, she was looking forward to going to London.

Which meant that her plan had worked; she had taken the first step to exorcising Luka from her heart.

She dismissed a pang of unease; OK, she'd used Hunt, but she had given him what he wanted. She was surprised that a man of his experience hadn't realised she was a virgin, but perhaps she was a better faker than she'd thought.

Now that he was coming to London, she'd have to make an appointment with the doctor. He'd used protection and she'd just had her period, so she was safe from pregnancy, but she needed back-up. She shivered, thinking of nights and days together in England.

Later, as pleasant exhaustion carried her towards sleep amidst the memories of what it had felt like to take him into her, she recalled that she'd once decided he'd make a bad enemy.

CHAPTER SIX

WHEN Cia decided to leave Dacia she'd filled her diary with appointments, leaving free only the day before her departure. Thanks to the Hunt Radcliffe effect, she thought wryly as she got ready for dinner that night, she'd spent her last busy day in a suspicious glow instead of a haze of self-pity.

As for last night—well, that morning she'd woken in a panic, wondering what on earth she'd let herself do, but she'd calmed down during the day.

Whatever the outcome, Hunt had got her through a week she'd been dreading. For that she'd always be grateful. His presence on Dacia had made her life more sharp and vivid, more challenging.

In London that rich expectation would be amply indulged, but for tonight she'd let its slow simmer wrap her in its protective cloak. Mouth curving in an ambiguous smile, she settled the waistband of her pair of velvet trousers into place, and slid into a camisole top in matching topaz silk. The sensuous textures stroked her body, setting it purring. She pressed her hands to her hot cheeks, then snatched up the brush to control the wild confusion of her hair.

This satisfaction, the general well-being of a woman who had been well and truly pleasured—to use a nice old-fashioned term—wasn't happiness, but it was the only armour she had against the pain of leaving Dacia and Luka.

And Alexa. In spite of everything she had learned to love Luka's wife.

The brush slid through her hair in slow, even strokes and

she gazed into a misty distance, snatches of the preceding night playing through her mind.

If this was physical gratification, she thought dreamily, she was glad she'd experienced it.

That was when she caught a glimpse of golden eyes, satisfied and smug as those of a well-fed cat. Hot-cheeked, she focused sharply on her reflection. Unhappiness she could conceal; her sultry expression of anticipation and secret knowledge was a dead giveaway.

'Unless you want to proclaim to the world what happened last night you'd better get that look off your face,' she told herself, and began to ruthlessly pin up her hair.

On the way to Luka and Alexa's private apartment she wondered if Hunt was feeling anything like this languorous afterglow. But then, for him any morning-after-the-night-before satisfaction would be no novelty. And why did that thought sting like a poisoned dart?

She lengthened her stride. Grow up, she commanded. Jumping from the frying pan into the fire was not a viable life plan; she wasn't going to expect anything from a man who wanted nothing more from her than her body.

Her mouth firmed. Because that was all she would get from him—his splendid body, his skill as a lover, and the exciting aura that surrounded him. Hoping for anything else was asking for trouble.

When she walked into the drawing room, the expression on Hunt's strong-boned face didn't alter, although a smile of lazy appreciation glimmered in the blue depths of his eyes when he said her name.

A piercing stab of pleasure took her by surprise. Trying to ignore it, she shored up her self-possession and embarked on a round of small talk.

With no guests it should have been a pleasant evening, free from any strain. Hunt and Luka had come to an agreement that suited them both and both men were relaxed, clearly on the way to becoming friends. Alexa was her usual bright self.

Cia did her best, but tension slowly tightened her already overstrung nerves. After dinner she would have liked to excuse herself, but Alexa looked a little tired so she stayed, listening—and taking part in—the men's wide-ranging discussion.

Would Hunt try to see her alone before he left? Her heartbeat quickened at the prospect of days—and nights—with him in London.

Some time later she looked across the room and was astonished to see that Alexa had dropped off to sleep in the most charmingly natural way, her lovely face peaceful as her head tipped sideways in her chair.

The two men were talking about some complicated business scandal, so Cia got to her feet and said quietly, 'Alexa, would you like some coffee?'

Both men fell silent when Alexa woke with a slight start and gazed around, blinking several times.

'Coffee? No, thank you,' she said with a grimace, and then laughed a little. 'Oh, dear! How shaming!'

Luka came across and helped her to her feet. 'Bed,' he said calmly. 'I'll carry you.'

'I can walk.' She looked past him to Cia and Hunt. 'Sorry,' she said simply. 'I'm pregnant, and for some reason I keep going to sleep every time I sit down.'

Pregnant? Stabbed by unbearable, shameful envy, Cia's head swam and her heart contracted in acute pain. Desperately conscious that she couldn't let them see her face, she swung around.

Above the roaring in her ears, she heard Luka's quick, concerned voice. 'Cia—what is it?'

'Nothing.' Her voice came out as a harsh whisper, so she said again, 'Nothing! I was just—'

Hunt's saturnine features came into abrupt focus. She looked imploringly at him as the last remnant of her composure shattered into splinters.

Scarcely knowing what she said, she blurted, 'I can't leave Dacia now.'

Hunt's eyes gleamed cold and hard as quartz pebbles. He looked across her head and said smoothly, 'I've asked Lucia to come to New Zealand for a holiday, but if you need her to stay, Alexa, we can postpone it until you're feeling better.'

Stunned, Cia clamped her jaws together, but she seized on his words. Trust his cold, clever brain to come up with the one thing that would ease Luka and Alexa's mind. She'd almost given herself away so she had no choice. She had to fall in with Hunt's suggestion.

Making a good effort at concealing her surprise, Alexa said briskly, 'I'm perfectly all right—pregnancy is not an illness, you know. Luka, tell Cia she's not to waste the chance of a visit to Hunt's station!'

Cold emptiness beneath her ribs, Cia darted a glance at her cousin's stern face. Part of her longed for him to insist she stay.

Of course he didn't. After a slight pause he said, 'You must do whatever you want to, Cia, but Alexa won't need you to wait on her; the doctor says this tiredness is likely to pass when she reaches the end of the first trimester.'

Cia couldn't help saying, 'I feel as though I'm abandoning you.'

'Rubbish! We're going to miss you like crazy, but you've given up enough of your life for us,' Alexa told her seriously.

That was when Cia realised that this was what she'd overheard the previous night. They must have been talking of Alexa's pregnancy; they didn't want her on Dacia. Smiling steadily, she said, 'Then I'll go, but you must promise to let me know if you need me.'

'Of course,' Luka said, his voice giving nothing away.

He bent and picked up his wife, holding her as though she was the most precious thing in his life—as she was. Luka owed Dacia his duty, but Alexa held his heart.

Cia watched the other two leave, and felt Hunt's presence behind her.

Both were silent until the door closed behind them, when Hunt said in a flat, expressionless tone, 'You might as well come with me tomorrow.'

'I thought you were going to London?' Waves of reaction stripped her strength; she wanted nothing more than to collapse in a soggy heap on the sofa, but she forced herself to stand very straight, to meet his opaque eyes and huddle the tattered shreds of her composure around her.

He drawled, 'Only because *you* were planning to go there. Do you have appointments tomorrow?'

'I—no.' She swallowed.

'I'm leaving at eleven in the morning. Can you be ready by then?' No sign of the previous night's lover—he'd reverted to type.

The arrogant alpha male, she thought bleakly.

For years she'd managed to keep her emotions under control, ignoring her knowledge of Luka's lovers with stubborn fortitude. She'd even smiled like a pro throughout his wedding, yet one night in Hunt's arms had shredded her nerves so badly she'd almost tipped over the edge. If Alexa hadn't realised before, she certainly did now—and so, she thought sickly, might Luka.

What about Hunt?

He said, 'I'm sorry it got dumped on you like this. You've

done a magnificent job here and it's understandable you'd feel supplanted when someone else comes in to take your place. Alexa's been worrying—and worrying too that the baby will push you further into the background.'

Sheer astonishment kept her silent. Did he think she was so shallow that she—?

More gently, he went on, 'She won't feel so bad if she thinks you might be trying out your own wings.'

Cia glanced down at her hands, still rigidly held at her sides. So that was it; he was doing this for Alexa.

But not last night. Last night he'd wanted her, not Alexa. She should tell him the truth, and knew she couldn't. What would he think of a woman who made love to him when she was in love with another man? Thoughts ricocheted around her brain.

Finally she said, 'I don't think going to New Zealand would be a good idea.'

He smiled at her, and the sexual tension he'd unleashed the night before exploded through her bloodstream like some acutely dangerous designer drug.

'London, New Zealand, what's the difference?' he murmured, dropping a kiss on her mouth.

Cia swayed into his arms, and as the kiss deepened her hold on reality slipped. Hunt's touch submerged the shambles of her thoughts in a driving, desperate need.

After a frustratingly short interval he broke off the kiss and set her away from him, scanning her face with a possessive keenness that took no prisoners. His narrowed, glittering scrutiny almost branded her.

Hunt saw her hesitation. Her lovely face was expressionless; last night her collected poise had shattered in his arms, but she'd rebuilt it pretty damned fast.

If he hadn't seen that moment of desperation when she'd

realised that Alexa was pregnant, he might be thinking now that the news meant nothing to her.

The pity that had knotted his gut when he'd seen her reaction to Alexa's announcement intensified. He'd had to fight to make his position in the world and she'd been born to hers, but he could imagine his own reluctance to give up everything and sink into mediocrity. A couple of weeks in New Zealand would at least give her a break.

Then her head came up and she said with the remote aloofness that irritated the hell out of him, 'All right, I'll be ready tomorrow at eleven.'

He watched her leave the room and stood for a moment gazing down at hands balled into fists. Forcibly he relaxed them, looking up as Luka came into the room.

Cia made it, but only just.

That morning when she'd gone to say goodbye to Alexa, who'd decided to stay at home instead of going to the airport to see her off, Luka had demanded, 'Are you sure you know what you are doing?'

'Absolutely sure.' Pain twisted her heart as she went on doggedly, 'I'm having a pleasant holiday in a country I've always wanted to visit.'

'And you'll love it,' Alexa said, cutting off her last chance of retreat. 'Thank you for everything you've done for me and for Luka. You've been wonderful. And when you come back, come back with a happy heart.'

She knew.

'I will,' Cia said with a quick, awkward gulp, too emotionally spent to hide behind the mask she'd manufactured over the long years of loving Luka. She hugged Alexa back before pasting a smile onto her lips. 'Luka, the Victorian papa went out with Queen Victoria! I'm going on a holiday, that's all.'

Luka inspected her face and said quietly, 'I like Hunt and respect him, but if he hurts you I'll make him sorry he ever saw you.'

Cia rolled her eyes. 'If I'm stupid enough to let him hurt me, *I'll* deal with it, dearest cousin! I'm a woman, not a child who has to be protected.'

Luka didn't look convinced, but commanded abruptly, 'Keep in touch. Regularly!'

'I won't fall off the edge of the world.' The only way she could get through this was pretend it was another royal engagement, one that had to be endured however boring it might be. She smiled at him. 'I'm taking my laptop, so we can email each other.'

His gaze rested on Alexa's bright head, kindling. 'I own a beach house on an island just north of Auckland. I'll give you the address and the caretaker's telephone number.'

Alexa looked up, her mouth trembling into a smile. As though they'd shouted it, Cia knew that they'd consummated their love in that house—and that she'd never go there. 'Fine,' she said briskly. 'Thank you.'

Now, Luka's kisses on her cheeks and his embrace still enveloping her in familiar warmth, she walked beside Hunt into the jet without a backward glance.

He looked at her with cool speculation. 'All right?'

All right didn't describe her emotions; that would need a grand opera. Over the past week her whole life had been thrown into chaos, and she didn't even know what she felt any more. She had made a decision and she just had to keep going.

'I'm fine,' she managed to say. 'I hate saying goodbye.'

Once in the luxuriously appointed plane, she settled back into the seat and closed her burning eyes. She didn't look back as Dacia fell behind them, a brightly coloured jewel in the blue, blue Mediterranean. Before long, her lashes fluttered down and she let herself drift into unconsciousness.

The long trip to New Zealand passed in a haze. As though the past months had drained every reserve of strength, Cia slept for much of the time and when she wasn't dozing or reading, she was content to watch the world slip by under their wings.

Whenever she looked for Hunt, he was working. However, he seemed to know each time she woke; he came to sit beside her and talk about nothings until she went back to sleep again. He also insisted she eat regular meals and drink plenty of water.

On the last hop she woke to find herself splayed across his chest, his arm holding her in place, his heart beating against her cheek, his subtle, sexy scent clouding her brain. For a second she froze, and wondered how on earth she could love one man and yet feel so—so safe, so secure, in the arms of another.

Nervously, she muttered, 'Sorry—I don't know—'

His broad shoulders lifted in a slight shrug. 'You were crying,' he told her. 'Bad dream?'

Her gaze collided with his, then slid sideways to the window. Biting her lip, she shook her head. 'I don't remember.'

'You looked very pathetic,' he said, a note of mockery in the deep voice. 'And I'm a sucker for tears.'

And then the simple comfort of his embrace altered in some subliminal way. Like hers, his body was reacting to hidden, involuntary signals. Desire cramped deep in the pit of her stomach, and her skin heated while the hidden places of her body prepared for him in unseen ways.

Jerking herself away, she said huskily, 'We need to talk.'

Hunt's thick lashes drooped further, unsettling what remained of her wits. 'Go ahead.' His voice was smooth.

Words tangled on her tongue. She took a deep breath and blurted, 'I don't know what you want.'

When his brows rose, she dragged in more oxygen and grabbed for the composure she'd believed had been bred in her genes. Unfortunately, now she needed it more than ever before, she could only manage a tenuous link with her usual self-assurance.

She went on baldly, 'Everything's happened so quickly. I don't—I'm not sure I want to continue the sort of relationship you might think I do.'

Oh, God, why not babble gibberish and be done with it? She started again, 'I mean—'

'I know what you mean,' he said, mercifully cutting her off before she could embarrass herself even more. 'Relax, I'm not into rape.'

'I didn't mean *that*!'

When she stared at him, great amber eyes filled with a mixture of doubt and confusion and wariness, he said less caustically, 'Don't worry, Lucia. Any decision will be yours to make.'

'Sorry,' she muttered again. 'My brain seems to have turned to custard.'

He showed his teeth in a hard smile and got to his feet. 'Perhaps you should wash your face. We're about an hour away from arrival in Auckland.'

In the bathroom Cia made running repairs, concentrating hard on reapplying cosmetics so that when she emerged into the main cabin she could meet Hunt's eyes with the confidence of having her armour fastened firmly into place.

From then on she kept a close watch through the window; as New Zealand finally began to unroll beneath the plane, she leaned forward to marvel at the vivid colour of the countryside.

A tightening of her skin warned that Hunt was taking his

place beside her. She turned. 'I'd forgotten how green a country could be.'

She flushed at his amused look and drew in a deep breath.

She needed time to herself, to find out which she really was—the woman who had loved Luka so chastely all these years, or the woman who had made passionate, ecstatic love with a man she'd known very little time at all.

The long hours of the flight had been a kind of watershed between the past and the future, but they'd convinced her that she couldn't trust herself. Erotic dreams of Hunt had plagued her sleep, and whenever he came near her body had quivered in feverish anticipation, every cell acutely poised on the edge of arousal. Waking in his arms had clinched her decision.

Staying with him would be hell. The more she gave in to this—this obsessive attraction, the less she understood herself.

Better to set her teeth and brave Luka's beach house—which didn't seem so desperately forbidding now. Distance, she thought forlornly, was working its wonders. Or perhaps she'd been fooling herself all these years, and now, literally on the other side of the world, she could see things more clearly.

In spite of the tact she'd always been rather proud of, she didn't know how to tell Hunt of her decision. In the end she said bluntly, 'I don't think it would be a good idea to stay with you.'

Black brows lifting, he looked at her. 'No?' he said after a moment that drummed with tension. 'Why not?'

Because I want you so much my mouth dries whenever I see you, and every time you come into the room it feels as though you've sucked all the oxygen out of the air.

Of course she didn't say it; he'd think she was mad. And he might take advantage of her admission. In his world, sex was common currency; it meant little beyond satisfying a hunger.

Cia could read nothing but dispassionate interest in his angular, forceful face, and hesitated a moment before saying sturdily, 'I just don't think it would be a good idea. I'll stay at Luka's beach house.'

'When did you work this out?'

She flushed, but met his eyes, cold and blue as a polar sky. 'Somewhere between Dacia and here.'

'No.' The word was said without expression, yet its impact made her flinch.

'I'm afraid you don't have the right to forbid it,' she pointed out with a smile she suspected ended up more placating than determined.

Hunt in a temper was intimidating.

He leaned back into the seat and said calmly, 'I promised your cousin I'd take care of you while you were in New Zealand. I have no intention of letting you swan off on your own. If you go off to the beach house I'll feel obliged to let Luka know, and I imagine he'll wonder why.'

Cia sat up very straight and said between her teeth, 'Why should you? He offered me the beach house when I told him I was coming here, so it will be all right—'

'It is not all right.' He frowned, a muscle jerking in his jaw. 'You have no idea how life functions outside the protected little enclave you've inhabited all your life.'

She flushed. 'Oh, for heaven's sake, what on earth could happen to me? I've always heard that New Zealand was safe.'

'It's safer than most countries, but I'm not thinking about home invasions or robberies.'

'Then what?'

'Paparazzi. They're already here *en masse* for Pagan

Russell's latest film, which is being shot about half an hour by water away from Luka's beach house.'

Cia recognised the name of a Hollywood star whose name had been linked with Hunt's the previous year. Pagan Russell was a glorious redhead with porcelain skin and eyes that exuded sensuous knowledge. She was also a brilliant actress.

I am not jealous, Cia thought sternly. Jealousy is an ignoble emotion and I won't give in to it.

Hunt pointed out with infuriating logic, 'The Ice Princess would be a titillating contrast to the Queen of Sex. I'd give you—oh, two hours—before the bay is filled with photographers.'

'But no one will know I'm there,' she retorted robustly.

He shrugged. 'I know what this is, of course.'

'What?' Cia asked, anger frosting her tone.

'You're afraid,' he said coolly.

Cia lifted her brows in delicate scorn. 'Afraid of what?'

He sent her a slanted look. 'Of yourself, I suspect,' he said. 'Life in a golden tower has kept you nicely insulated from all the temptations that assail the rest of us. But when I touch you—'

Cia jumped as a lean forefinger came to rest on the middle of her bottom lip. Sharp points of desire arrowed through her, drowning out everything but the remorseless goad of passion. When her eyelids sank down she had to force them up so she could glare at him.

Only to fall headlong into icy hunger, into a darkness that threatened everything she was…

'Don't,' she said hoarsely, her mouth so parched she could barely get the word out.

'When I touch you,' he said with ruthless honesty, 'or come near you, or even walk into the same room, you realise that you're not able to control me. Or yourself.' He smiled and removed that taunting finger to lean back into his seat, all aloof, maddening authority. 'And as you're a control freak, it scares you.'

'Lust happens,' she returned, trying hard to sound frivolous.

Hunt's narrowed eyes—crystalline jewels in his lean, dark face—glinted with cold scorn. 'It's a normal reaction between normal people,' he said, turning his head so that all she saw was his profile, hawk-angled against the bright sun of New Zealand. 'But you'll be quite safe at Hinekura. I'll give you a key so you don't have to spend nights waiting for my footsteps at your door.'

She said stiffly, 'I'm not afraid of that. Or of you.' He wanted her, but he wasn't like her, tangled in a net of passion. He could control it.

'And you'll be quite safe from yourself,' he promised, his voice lazily amused. 'As safe as you want to be.'

'That is such a big deal,' she said venomously.

He laughed. 'Relax. You're a grown woman, not a blushing virgin.'

No longer. Stung, and hugely embarrassed, Cia leaned back in her seat and watched with blind absorption the vibrant green countryside of New Zealand slip silently beneath.

Of course he couldn't force her to go with him. If he tried she'd simply go to the nearest security person at the airport and ask for protection. Plutocrats shared with royalty a hatred of the wrong sort of publicity. Once Hunt realised that she wasn't going with him, he'd give up.

He'd have to.

But another glance at that strong profile ate into her confidence.

After clearing Immigration and Customs they were met by a young man with red hair and a respectful smile.

'Airport security suggests you leave by a private exit, Mr Radcliffe,' he said, indicating a door. 'There are photographers lying in wait.'

Without breaking stride Hunt took Cia's elbow and steered her through the door and down a corridor. 'For us?' he asked.

His aide said smoothly, 'They know the princess is accompanying you, sir. I've taken the precaution of having a limo lurk inconspicuously around the corner as a decoy, and the chopper's geared up and ready to go.'

When he turned to speak to the security man, Cia said something under her breath.

'Exactly.' Hunt's voice was crisp and unemotional.

She risked a swift upward glance. 'You don't speak Dacian.'

'I understand swearing when I hear it in any language,' he said with a slashing white grin.

Unwillingly she smiled back. 'I gather this isn't your usual welcome when you come home?'

'No.'

Cia frowned. 'I wonder how they found out I was coming to New Zealand with you.'

'There are probably tabloid stringers on Dacia. It wouldn't have been difficult to find out that you were leaving with me.'

'No one on Dacia would do that,' she said indignantly.

Hunt's beautiful mouth compressed into an uncompromising line. 'Welcome to the real world, princess. Tabloids pay good money for information. There's a huge, high-paying market for pictures of royalty—especially young, beautiful princesses on holiday with men who are neither brothers nor fiancés. Your cousin controls the situation in Dacia, but once you stepped off the island you moved out of his sphere of influence.'

She retorted tartly, 'And your highly publicised affair with Pagan Russell last year would have set them quivering with anticipation. Where are we going?'

Hunt shrugged. 'We're taking the helicopter to another airport where we'll go straight to my plane. Once we're at Hinekura no one will bother us.'

'Why not?' Only when the words had left her lips did Cia realise she'd tacitly accepted his right to hijack her.

'We don't cater to prying photographers in the far north.'

The note of cold determination in his voice sent a shiver across the sensitive spot between her shoulder blades. Staring straight ahead, she said, 'How do you manage that?'

'The road is fifteen kilometres away through my land. And I don't like trespassers.'

She said, 'How long is Pagan Russell going to be here?'

'I have no idea.'

Chilled, she ploughed on, 'I'll go to the beach house once things settle down.'

Hunt released her elbow as they came through the door into the sunlight. 'OK, here's the helicopter. Get in.'

While Cia scrambled into the back seat he and the aide and the security man heaved their luggage into the boot, then Hunt slid in beside her and the chopper immediately pulled away.

CHAPTER SEVEN

SETTLING back into the helicopter seat—too small to be comfortable, as they all were—Hunt regarded Lucia's classical profile, his loins stirring at the silken glory of her skin and the elegant curves of that sultry mouth. Was she as naïve as she seemed to be?

Probably. Her cousin's protectiveness and the Dacians' affection had sheltered her from the worst excesses of the gutter Press; here she'd be a spicy sitting duck.

He assessed the slight tinge of pink along those stunning cheekbones. She knew he was watching her. The lush mouth compressed and she turned her head away so that all he could see was the curve of her cheek and her ear. A small diamond stud winked in the lobe.

A swift surge of passion infuriated him. How the hell had he managed to get himself into this situation? If he'd had any sense he'd let her go to Luka's beach house. Hell, if he'd had any sense he wouldn't have slept with her in the first place, and he certainly wouldn't have allowed himself to invite her back home.

He'd always been careful not to involve himself in messy situations with the women in his life, yet his stupid, reckless impulse, prompted by her reaction to Alexa's bombshell, had led to her presence in his house for at least a week.

He noted the black hair primly smoothed back from her serene features. The night they'd made love he'd pulled it from its knot, and let it tumble in a silken flood across his chest…

Ruthlessly he yanked his mind above his belt. Apart from

that, he knew very little about Lucia Bagaton. She was intelligent; she had all the qualities she needed for the position she'd inherited.

And one second of shock had told him how she felt about being relegated to the background. Apart from that, her regal air of composure was seamless—except in his arms.

Since the age of sixteen he'd had no problems attracting the opposite sex. In fact, while he was still at high school a woman of thirty had taught him how to play the stock market. That wasn't all she'd taught him, but it had laid the foundation for his future. He'd learned how women thought, and how they felt. Was that why he was so attracted to a woman who gave nothing away?

Think of it as a new experience, he advised himself cynically.

He glanced down as the chopper started to lose height. He knew one other thing about her; in spite of her antagonism, she wanted him every bit as he wanted her. And he'd never asked any more of a woman than that.

So why the desire to throttle her?

No paparazzi lay in wait for them at the much smaller airport. As they walked from the chopper towards the private plane that waited for them, Lucia asked suddenly, 'What does the name of your farm—station—mean? Hinekura?'

'Excellent pronunciation,' he drawled.

She shrugged. 'The vowel sounds are the same as Italian.'

'It's made up of two words—*hine*, meaning woman or girl, and *kura*, meaning beautiful. In other words, beautiful woman.'

'Is there a story?'

He repeated the words she'd used to him when they'd gone to the cave, the first time he'd kissed her. 'There's always a story. It was once the home of a woman of such exquisite beauty that she caused a vast amount of trouble. Neighbouring chiefs fought over her, and even when she married, men tried to abduct her. In the end she caused such turmoil that her husband, clearly a pragmatist, killed her.'

Cia's stomach contracted. 'A much grimmer story than the one I told you,' she said politely, then added, 'Hunt, I don't want you to think that I'm ungrateful when I say I'd rather go to the beach house.'

She wondered why he was scrutinising her face, his long lashes hiding everything of his eyes but a narrow, lethal line of steel.

But when he spoke his voice was negligent. 'It's not a good option. You're too exposed at the beach.'

Stupid colour stung her cheeks. 'Exposed?'

'Too easy to get at. Paparazzi are noted for their ingenuity, and New Zealand's small enough for someone to let slip that you're in residence. They could land from the sea, and in New Zealand it's perfectly legal to walk below the high-tide mark. I doubt if you'd enjoy having them camped out on the beach with telephoto lenses.'

Frustrated and uneasy, she bit her lip. 'Of course I wouldn't. But I won't impose on you for very long.'

They stopped beside the plane. In ten minutes Cia was staring out of the window at Auckland's twin harbours. Hunt sat in the front, talking to the pilot as the plane flew high above the long northern peninsula, and eventually her lashes fluttered down and she drifted off into a kind of half-waking, half-sleeping trance.

An alteration to the engine noise stirred her, as did the bump of their landing, but she found it almost impossible to lift her lashes. A kind of fearful excitement possessed her; she felt that when she opened her eyes and saw Hunt's home everything would change, as though she'd crossed some forbidden border into dangerous, unknown territory. Once she'd arrived, she'd be unable to go back.

'Lucia, we're here,' Hunt said quietly into the sudden silence when the engines were cut.

Eyes still shut, she yawned and nodded.

He laughed. 'I'll carry you.'

The same words Luka had used—how long ago? She couldn't recall. Delivered without Luka's love for Alexa and in Hunt's deep, cool voice, they chilled her.

Cia forced up her eyelids to say with dignity, 'I'm not usually such a sleepyhead; I can walk, thank you.'

To prove it she unclipped her seat belt and got up, only to stagger slightly. Hunt's arms came around her in support, and she looked up into hooded eyes, glittering in his tanned face.

Her bones melted, and in the silence of the plane she heard her heart thud rapidly in her ears.

Then she was free. Her lips felt stiff as she said, 'Thank you.'

He stood back. 'My pleasure.' The deep voice was level and completely without emotion.

As warily as a cat, Cia climbed down the steps onto the airstrip, a mown stretch of grass running gently up to the crest of a hill; waiting a short distance away was a four-wheel-drive vehicle spattered with red mud. As she watched, it backed up to the plane.

The driver was a woman a few years older than Cia. She greeted Hunt with every appearance of pleasure and sent a swift smile Cia's way before seizing a small package from the pilot and loading it into the back of the vehicle.

Too late, Cia realised that she should have offered to help, but between the pilot, Hunt and the woman, it was clearly a well-rehearsed procedure; the woman dealt with the smaller parcels while men carried the heavy stuff.

Oppressed by a chill of alienation, Cia looked past the half-round hangar made of corrugated iron. The hill sloped gently towards the east before falling away sharply to a coastal plain, now gathering a blue-grey cloak as twilight swept across it. Sunlight still gleamed on the sea, turning it to a slab of polished silver under a cloudy sky. Green, lushly beautiful, Hinekura was as different from Dacia as any place could be. A great, shivering wave of homesickness rolled over her.

'Hop into the Range Rover,' Hunt said. When she stared at him he picked her up and dumped her into the back seat.

Feeling like a recalcitrant child, she sat up very straight and watched as he and the woman got into the front, Hunt behind the wheel. He turned slightly and said, 'Lucia, this is Sheree Anderson, who runs my office for me.'

After a quick exchange of greetings he switched on the engine, frowning as the woman began to talk.

Cia heard a few words—'can't be helped,' and 'I'm so sorry, Hunt, but there's nothing else I can do,' and 'tomorrow.'

She looked away as Hunt spoke swiftly and decisively. The road wound down a steep hillside, a narrow red-brown gash between dense, heavily leafed trees that looked like jungle. Great Catherine wheels of delicate fern fronds sprang from rough black trunks, and in the dimness beneath the trees more growth pushed towards the light, eager and fecund and riotous.

The woman in front nodded, and the vehicle burst out onto a wide rolling area covered in bright grass. Huge, stolid red cattle lifted their heads to watch the vehicle go past. In the distance Cia caught glimpses of houses sheltered by trees, and other buildings.

Another wave of homesickness drenched her. It looked

wild and different and exotic—in truth, a world away from all she knew and loved.

She sat up straight. OK, so she'd clutched at Hunt's offer of sanctuary without thinking past her need to convince Luka—and Alexa—that she wasn't pining. Coming here had been risky, but she trusted Hunt to keep his promise.

Making love to him had been crazy; she didn't regret it, but repeating it would be rushing rashly into a situation she couldn't control. Ignoring the swift thud of her pulses in her ears, she forced herself to gaze around at the empty land and the strong lines of the hills, so utterly different from Dacia and England, so alien...

Hunt drew up outside a high hedge of trees cut by a long metal gate; without killing the engine, he said, 'All right, see what you can do, Sheree, and let me know as soon as you can. If you need any help, tell me.'

'I should be able to give you a straight answer tonight,' the woman said, flashed a smile at Cia, and left them, running through the gate between big, fat drops of rain from a dark cloud overhead.

Hunt glanced in the rear-vision mirror. 'All right?'

Something sharp and barbed pierced Cia's heart. 'Fine, thank you,' she said prosaically.

He put the vehicle in gear and drove along the narrow road towards a collection of buildings. As the rain stopped he turned off onto a long drive beneath a tunnel of trees.

When they left the shelter of the avenue the house swung into view. Eyes widening, Cia stared and leaned forward.

'It's beautiful,' she breathed. 'Like a miracle.'

Hunt had excellent hearing. 'What's miraculous about it?'

'Finding a house like this here in the wilderness.'

'New Zealand does a much better wilderness than this,' he said coolly.

Cia sat back and admired the gardens as the Range Rover

climbed a low rise between lawns gleaming silver with rain.
And such a house! Mediterranean in style, but she glimpsed
huge walls of glass, and was sure she saw a long deck or
terrace. Cia drew in a sharp breath and looked down as the
noise of the wheels changed.

They were crossing a bridge over a narrow, rock-bound
stream; judging by its direction, the stream passed very close
to the house. Trees followed its banks, and exotic plants
sheltered between the huge rocks. She saw familiar ones—
the long, scented trumpets of datura, and the sensuous splash
of hibiscuses.

The drive led past a big front door, but the Range Rover
swept onto a gravel courtyard behind the house bordered by
a high wall and a large garage.

'Home,' Hunt said laconically as he killed the engine. 'I'll
take you straight in—you're whacked.'

It was true. 'Why aren't you?' she asked crossly, undoing
her seat belt and clambering out.

'I'm used to air travel, but even so, jet lag is insidious. I
didn't pilot the plane up because I don't trust myself after
a long flight.' He looked at her. 'Can you walk?'

'Of course I can,' she said with dignity, demonstrating by
taking a few steps away from the vehicle.

Hunt escorted her along a covered walkway and through
a door in the wall into a large courtyard. A flash of green
proclaimed a swimming pool; Cia noted roses and dahlias
and the vivid blossoms of bougainvillea, the familiar flowers
and scents easing some of her loneliness.

They were met halfway by a large, stately woman with
keen dark eyes and a pleasant smile.

He introduced her as Marty, the housekeeper. She smiled
at Cia and said, 'Welcome to Hinekura.' The name ran off
her tongue like liquid silver, smooth and rhythmic. 'I hope
you had a good journey.'

'Thank you, I did.' But by now tension was clutching her in a grip of iron.

Inside the house, she relaxed a little. Airy and modern, it achieved both warmth and grace. And it fitted its formidable owner; yes, she thought, taking in a superb abstract picture on one wall, this belongs here, with Hunt.

It looked as different from Dacia as anything could be.

'What a lovely house,' she said brightly and inanely, all her glib small talk left behind in Dacia.

From behind Hunt said, 'I'll tell the architect and designer you liked it.'

He sounded fed up. She bit her lip but persevered, 'How long have you lived here?'

'Six years.' He turned to the housekeeper. 'I'll take Lucia up to her room.'

At the top of the stairs he opened a door. 'In here.'

Cia walked in and after a quick glance around said even more brightly, 'Thank you.'

'Your bags will be up shortly. Marty will unpack for you—'

'Oh, there's no need for that,' she said, smiling dangerously. 'I know how to unlock my bags and I can see a door over there that must lead to a wardrobe. Possibly even a bathroom? Hanging things up won't tax my strength too much, I'm sure.'

Blue fire glinted in his eyes above a smile that mocked her combativeness. 'I'd suggest a shower and a nap if you feel like it. Dinner is at seven, but for the next couple of hours I'm going to be busy in the office. If you're hungry, Marty will get you something to drink and eat.'

'I don't—'

'I'd suggest that you at least drink some water to rehydrate. If you'd like to, I can take you out to see the horses before dinner,' he finished smoothly.

Her hand sought reassurance from the diamond star, but dropped when she remembered it was now hidden in her luggage, never to be worn again. Meeting his hard eyes with a lift of her chin, she said, 'You've got horses here? I thought all farms in New Zealand were completely mechanised.'

'You have done your homework,' he said admiringly. 'This is a hill station. We use quad bikes where we can, but a lot of the land is too rugged for them, so horses are necessary. I'll see you later.'

She waited until the door closed behind him before exhaling forcefully. For a few seconds there she'd felt a chilling draught, like a blast from the north pole. In this hemisphere it would be the south pole, she corrected herself, and went across the room to the door on the far side. It led to a big, airy wardrobe with a bathroom next door.

A bathroom made for luxury. Cia examined the smooth, flowing lines of the fixtures, the soft rose and cream marble, thick towels, deliciously scented soaps, a vase of flowers picked from the garden.

Entirely suitable for a self-made millionaire, she told herself, angry at the snide comment the minute it had formed in her brain. Hunt had taken what he was born with and transformed his life; she doubted very much whether he cared much about his surroundings, although she liked the restrained luxury she'd seen so far.

Sudden tears blinded her. She wiped her eyes and blew her nose, and told herself that she was embarking on a new stage of her life. Surely once the turmoil inside her had settled she'd be whole again.

In the meantime, she wanted nothing more than a long, hot shower and a complete change of clothes.

A knock on the outer door heralded the arrival of her

cases. 'You must be Peter,' she said as she let in the man who carried them. 'Thanks so much.'

He was stocky and middle-aged, his muscles rippling when he put the cases on the floor at the foot of the huge bed.

'I'm Peter,' he agreed cheerfully. 'Marty said to tell you that if you need anything, just call on the phone and she'll be up straight away.'

'I'm sure she's too busy to be climbing the stairs,' Cia said. 'I can come down if I need anything.'

He grinned. 'There's a lift,' he confided. 'Don't worry about Marty—she'll tell you if she's too busy.'

When Cia laughed his grin widened. 'See you later,' he said cheerfully, and left her.

A couple of hours later Cia had unpacked, ironed the creases from her clothes, and indulged in a long, long shower. Although Luka had modernised the island's water supplies, living on Dacia meant embracing the saving of water as an art form. Here there might be greater leeway. She glanced out of the window as more rain, heavier this time, shadowed the garden and dashed drops against the windows.

'We don't encourage anyone to waste water, but we don't have a shortage. We have bores,' Hunt told her later that night in the dining room.

Cia laughed. 'So does every place, alas. What do bores have to do with the water supply?'

'We bore down into an underground spring or stream and pump the water into tanks for filtering. Also, we collect rainwater from the roofs of the buildings.' Wind pounced on the house again, hurling a stinging fusillade across the windows. Hunt added drily, 'As you may have noticed, it rains a lot here.'

'It's very different from Dacia,' she said, swirling the last of a glass of water in the bottom of her goblet. For some reason she hadn't wanted wine tonight, but Hunt had drunk a glass of red with his meal. 'Our rain comes in winter, with very little for the rest of the year.'

'We do have droughts, but not often, not in the north.' His tone was aloof and she glanced up.

The candles in the centre of the table guttered a little, and the flickering light played over his face, highlighting the magnificent bone structure that would make him a striking man all his life. She remembered how he had looked the night they made love, and sensation collected in a pool of sensuous heat at the base of her spine.

All evening she'd been fighting a rising tide of excitement. This was the first time she'd eaten a meal alone with him—almost the first time they'd been alone together except for that night.

She'd tried to push the memory away, but it came back to torment her, vagrant images suddenly blazing like beacons, dissolving her brain into a loose collection of desires driven by compelling hunger.

'Such a temperate climate must make farming as easy as it gets,' she said, aware of a slight roughening in her voice.

'In many ways. We fight diseases, of course, and idiots who try to bring in food and other stuffs made from animals without declaring them. New Zealand is finding that although it is so far from the rest of the world it can't hold everything bad in it at bay.' He looked directly at her and said softly, 'But that's not a particularly interesting subject.'

'I find it very interesting,' she said indignantly. 'Luka—'

She stopped, because his raised brows and half-closed eyes sent a chill through her.

'Luka?' he said politely, and finished the rest of his wine in one swallow, setting the glass down with a slight clink against his dinner plate.

'Luka discussed such things with me,' she said with cool detachment, wishing she could retire behind the temporary, cowardly shield of a wine glass. Instead, she lifted her chin and met his gaze steadily.

'And now,' he said blandly, 'he discusses them with Alexa.'

'Yes.'

Humiliation gripped her, hollowing out her stomach until all she could feel was cold shame. However, it was none of Hunt's business who she loved. Unlike poor Maxime, he hadn't asked for anything more than a night of passion.

And he'd got that, she thought, all the fire suddenly quenched.

If his ego needed stroking, her response surely had been enough.

She bit her lip as it occurred to her that part of the reason for her turmoil was exactly that—he'd wanted nothing more from her than the temporary loan of her body and its responses. She hated herself for her hypocrisy; she was in love with Luka, yet she wanted Hunt to feel more for her than lust.

He said, 'I'm sorry we missed out on visiting the horses this afternoon. My secretary has had health problems, so I had to do some catching up. And although I'm reasonably fast on the computer, I'm not as good as she is.'

Impetuously Cia said, 'Can I do something? I'm excellent on a computer.'

He regarded her with a twisted smile. 'Are you?' he said. 'This is a little different from keeping a social diary and writing the occasional letter for your cousin to sign.'

Cia bristled. 'Oh, I can do a little more than that,' she said sweetly.

The minute she'd said she might be able to help she'd regretted such rashness—after all, she'd planned to head off to Luka's beach house as soon as it was safe. However, in the face of that patronising comment she'd show him.

'We can give it a try to see how it goes,' he said slowly.

'Certainly. You must tell me if I'm hopeless,' she returned, and only then wondered if she'd been manipulated into this offer.

A glance at Hunt dampened that idea. He planned to give her a chance to show how far out of her depth she was, and then no doubt he'd summon one of a hoard of secretaries or personal assistants or aides he had at his fingertips.

'Done,' he said, and held out a hand.

Cia extended her own, shocked when he lifted it to his mouth. Warm, persuasive, his lips touched the soft skin on the back of her hand in a formal European salute, then, setting her heart pounding madly, he turned it over and kissed the palm, folding her fingers over the spot.

'Thank you,' he said as she retrieved it. He looked up and said, 'Ah, here comes Marty.'

Intensely grateful for the housekeeper's entrance, Cia folded her hands in her lap, but those kisses burned in her mind long after she'd sampled the splendid cheeses and fruit that finished the meal.

And that night Hunt invaded her dreams again until she woke, panting with erotic need, her whole body screaming with frustration when she opened her eyes into the cold, lonely darkness.

Eventually she went back to sleep, but was pulled out of her dreams by sunlight on the curtains and the enthusiastic song of birds. She lay listening to one that sounded like a peal of bells, then got out and padded across to the window, pushing back the curtains to peer out.

She didn't catch sight of the bird that sounded like a carillon, but across a splendid sweep of lawn and a dense border of trees, where raindrops refracted the sun's light into diamond points, she saw a man on a horse.

Hunt. How on earth did he learn to ride like that? Her breath came shortly through her lips and she leaned out into air so clear and fresh it was like diving into the sea on a hot day. He was riding a horse the same rich mahogany as his hair, either a stallion or a gelding.

Cia had been around horses since she was a child, but except in competitions she'd rarely seen anyone so powerfully attuned to his mount. Together they looked like a centaur, the mythic man-horse of ancient Mediterranean legend.

'Perhaps it's in the genes?' she asked him over breakfast.

He shrugged. 'I doubt it, although I learned to ride before I could walk. As you probably know, my father was a trainer, so I grew up around horses and stables.'

'Life must have been difficult with both parents gone.'

'I never knew my mother.'

'I'm sorry,' she said inadequately. Introduced to drugs by a lover after her marriage broke up, her own mother had been pretty useless, but Cia had always known that she loved her.

His glance was keen. 'Apparently she had an affair with my father then disappeared, only to reappear nine months later with me. My father didn't know whether or not I was his child, but he accepted responsibility. I think he loved her.'

'I'd have liked to meet your father,' Cia said calmly, above a seething outrage that anyone could do that to a child they'd borne. 'He sounds a gallant gentleman.'

He gave a cool smile. 'You'd have had nothing in common. He was tough and foul-mouthed and he was a gambler—although always within limits. He loved horses and me in that order, but he did his best for me.'

'I'll bet he was proud of the son he raised,' she said firmly, pouring very rich milk into her tea.

'He'd have certainly approved of the way I got my start,' he said sardonically.

She laughed. 'Trading in penny dreadfuls? You really have to know what you're doing.'

Hunt's brows shot up. 'You did some in-depth research,' he said softly.

Her smile congealed. 'Research is a necessary part of modern business.'

'Modern business, yes, but we have no business together. Did you want to find out if I knew which fork to use?'

Coolly, denying his right to demand an answer, she said, 'I did a lot of Luka's research. And no, the question of forks never came up.'

An odd little silence—tense with unspoken emotions—prickled between them. He broke it. 'I'm not ashamed of getting my start that way, but moving in and out of the sharemarket day by day, buying cheap shares low and selling them a little higher, comes very close to gambling.'

Cia nodded. 'But like your father you knew when to stop.'

He drank some coffee, watching her as he did so. When he'd set down the cup he said, 'Like you, I did a lot of research. What else did you learn about me?'

Well, the names of his mistresses and the duration of each one's stay in his bed, for one. She said evenly, 'Don't worry, I only used reputable sources.'

The smile curving his mouth came close to a taunt. 'Ever diplomatic. I dislike appearing in the Press so I take care not to give them too much fodder for speculation.' He glanced at his watch and got to his feet, towering over the table in instant, automatic domination. 'I'll see you in the office in an hour.'

CHAPTER EIGHT

'AN HOUR? Of course.' Cia got up from the table and walked across to a wall of glass that opened onto a wide terrace. 'Whose idea was it to build on the edge of the stream?'

Hunt rose to accompany her out into the warm sunlight. 'Mine.'

Cia wasn't surprised. The architect who'd designed the house had been brilliant, but the house showed signs of constant input from the client. Every picture she saw, every colour and pattern and arrangement of furniture reinforced Hunt's personality, brushing against her nerves like an invisible velvet cloak—tactile, potent, seductive.

She walked across to the railing and looked down. Immediately below, the little rushing brook found its way between smooth, rounded boulders, its music a jingling counterpoint to the song of birds.

She sighed. 'It smells so fresh here—like a new day. I love the way the house is surrounded by forest, and yet the sun pours in. And those tree-ferns are truly spectacular.'

He was watching her; even with her back to him she could feel his attention. In fact, she thought, looking into the green depths of the trees, she felt new-born herself, as though she'd shed a skin and been transformed. Her tiredness had dropped away, leaving her senses singing.

From behind Hunt said, 'Later you might like to swim. The pool is kept at a constant temperature.'

'That would be lovely,' she returned politely, and smiled over her shoulder.

Blue-sheened eyes held hers. Often enough, Cia had heard people say that the world stood still; she took it for a tired old cliché, but now she knew what it meant. Everything froze; she heard nothing but the beating of her own heart, felt nothing but the impact of Hunt's gaze, and saw nothing but the hard, striking face with its fierce cheek-bones and the mouth that took her to ecstasy.

'Lucia, stop it,' he said harshly.

The world began to move again; birds sang above the sound of water, a slight breeze caressed her bare arms, her insides reassembled themselves into a functioning body. She shook her head numbly, tensing as he came up to her.

'I don't know whether you're a tease or just incredibly naïve,' he said beneath his breath, and bent his head and kissed her as though driven by an imperative desire beyond his control.

After a shocked moment, Cia's mouth softened under his. This was what she'd been waiting for since the night they'd made love, she realised dazedly. Her arms stole up around his neck and she responded with a desire that matched his, lost to everything but the taste of him and the texture of his body against hers, his arms around her, his hair against her fingertips.

He lifted his head and asked harshly, 'Which are you, Lucia? Temptress or innocent?'

'You know I'm not an innocent,' she whispered, skin burning at memories of the night she'd spent in his arms. Her body ached with feverish hunger and it took every bit of composure she possessed to allow her to say, 'But I don't think I'm a temptress, either. Do I have to be one or the other?'

He kissed her again—lightly, with tantalising expertise this time—and then stepped back, a humourless smile bracketing his beautiful mouth. 'You'd better go for that walk,' he said quietly, 'before I carry you up to my bedroom.'

He'd reimposed control so easily; it took Cia half an hour of exploring the magnificent grounds to put a fragile leash on her emotions. She felt as though she was on the verge of some magnificent discovery—as though life had suddenly given her a rare and precious gift, and she needed only to accept it to find herself.

'In other words,' she told herself severely as she checked out a tennis court hidden behind a tangle of profuse growth, 'you're letting yourself get carried away by a man who only has to kiss your hand to get your blood pressure steaming out of your ears! He might make love like—well, like one of the old gods, but he changes lovers every year or so.'

She stopped, and smelt a late rose, realising with stark insight how close she'd come to admitting that she wanted more from Hunt than sex.

It would be so easy to just drift along and let this overwhelming passion take her where it wanted, she thought longingly. But it would be dangerously reckless.

She had a life to make, things to do, a career to plan, and it wasn't Hunt's fault that these seemed suddenly hollow ambitions. Because she'd first experienced sex with him, she'd always remember him as the man who had shown her a whole new other side of herself.

But it had been nothing more than a temporary aberration.

A pale smile tugged at her lips. *Aberration?* Now that was a stiff word for mind-blowing eroticism!

It was the truth, though, and she had to face it. In his arms she'd tasted heaven, but he'd said nothing about any future for them.

And she was beginning to want one. If she stayed around too long, she might commit another unforgivably stupid act and become addicted to him.

Firming her mouth, she glanced at her watch and turned back to the house.

Hunt's office was exactly that—a large room holding everything the modern tycoon needed to run a world-spanning empire. Although Luka had insisted on the most modern equipment, and using Guy's software had given her the knowledge to hold up her end in conversations about information technology, Cia was impressed.

When she commented on it, Hunt said casually, 'I choose to live in New Zealand, so I make sure I have everything I—and my employees—need to keep in the closest contact. I've left letters for you to type on the dictaphone.'

Very cool, very businesslike.

So? she thought, seating herself at an ergonomically-designed desk and a chair that looked as though the user needed a pilot's licence to run it. You offered to do this, and you'd hate it if he treated you like a piece of fluff.

She began to type, glad now that after leaving school she'd insisted on doing a secretarial course at a high-powered technical academy.

For ten minutes or so Hunt kept a close watch on her, only relaxing when he saw that she knew how to use a computer. However, he couldn't concentrate on the papers that needed his attention. Every movement she made, every sound from her, sent signals to his libido.

So now you know why you've never had a lover share your office before, he thought irritably. Forget about long, sleek legs and that passionate mouth—and forget that she's also sharing your house, and would share your bed if you wooed her.

What did she want—the man or the position? It had never mattered before. He'd never brought a lover here before, either. Now he realised that he'd wanted to find out how she dealt with surroundings so different from the ones she was used to.

In other words, he thought, dragging his eyes back from her profile, you're testing her. Why?

Half an hour later he looked up from his desk and frowned. She hadn't adjusted the chair, and Sheree was at least four inches taller.

'You're going to get a stiff neck,' he said, getting to his feet before he could stop himself. Angry at his inability to keep his distance, he came over and bent to twist a knob.

Her faint, sensuous perfume drifted into his brain, clouding it and opening the door to a rush of memories. His body hardened. Just as well he was standing slightly behind her. 'Tell me when it feels comfortable,' he said shortly.

She answered equally abruptly. 'Just show me which levers do what and I'll get it right.'

But a note in her voice and a rush of colour along the vulnerable back of her neck told him she was as aware of him as he was of her. A rush of sheer male possessiveness drove through him, shredding his will.

Straightening up, he stepped backwards. 'That knob adjusts for your back—yes, that's it. Now for your neck—no, not there.' He reached for the knob at the same time as she did, and their hands collided.

Damn, he should have let her fix the chair by herself. Unable to resist, Hunt turned the chair so that he could scan her face. Satisfaction geared up a notch as he read in her gold, tiger-coloured eyes a hunger as devouring and mindless as his. For three heartbeats his will held, but then he said something—her name, he thought—and drew her fragrant slenderness out of the chair before he took her soft, parted lips.

He broke off the kiss when his legs threatened to give way, but he couldn't let her go. Lucia looked as dazed as he felt, as lost to the heady, mind-altering power of their desire. If he had any sense he'd send her straight off to the beach house—but for the first time ever he was a prisoner of a passion he couldn't master.

With a muffled curse, he took that soft, inviting mouth again.

Cia shuddered; the craving to touch him, feel him, taste him again had been building for too long. She opened her mouth beneath his, recklessly surrendering to the skilful, devouring exploration that stoked her passionate hunger to a dangerous inferno.

She burned where his hand slid beneath the tail of her shirt, stroking across the skin at her waist, long fingers playing delicately on the vertebrae of her spine and sending sensuous shivers its length.

Deep in the spell of his kisses, she mimicked his action, but pushed her hands up beneath his shirt to splay across his shoulders, relishing the way the powerful muscles shifted beneath the sleek, hot skin. She thought dazedly that he was all around her, all power and grace and glory...

His mouth drifted down until it found the vulnerable hollow of her throat, and his hand drifted up, but only as far as her breast, shaping it with infinite care. The small nipple budded sharply, sending a shaft of exquisite fire to the pit of her stomach. Tempted beyond endurance, she fought to retrieve a sliver of control.

Every part of her resisted the cold voice of common sense, but eventually she managed to mutter hoarsely, 'Hunt, no—'

It sounded like a plea. He lifted his head and she almost forgot whatever she'd planned to say in the glittering intensity of his gaze.

'What is it?' His voice was as guttural as hers, stripped of everything but the need to drive headlong to satisfaction.

'I don't think this is a good idea,' she said forlornly, knowing how silly it sounded, knowing that if he kissed her again she would give in and do whatever he wanted wherever he wanted—here on the desk if that was what he wanted.

Every muscle in his big body went rock-solid for a fraction of a second before he dropped his arms to his sides and stepped back. 'It seems a damned good idea to me,' he said lethally.

'Now, perhaps, but you swore just before you kissed me—and I know exactly how you feel.'

The dangerous, leaping lights in his eyes turned wry. His smile turned from feral to real, if reluctant, humour. 'Like being hit by a runaway bus,' he said. 'Only good.'

Although it was perilously sweet to share a moment of amusement with him, she struggled for the words to tell him it mustn't happen again. Finally she said, 'It scares me.'

He frowned. 'Why?'

'I'm not scared of you,' she said quickly. 'I know you wouldn't hurt me.'

But she couldn't go on and tell him that she was terrified of her own response and total lack of will-power where he was concerned. One touch, and she threw everything she'd ever learned out of the window and surrendered to this fiercely carnal longing.

He surveyed her with narrowed eyes until she could bear it no longer and turned away. Then he strode across to the window and looked out of it for long moments.

'All right,' he said curtly without facing her. 'Just keep out of my way from now on.'

'If you'll keep out of mine,' she retorted.

He shrugged. 'We'll adopt a policy of non-contact, and no, we won't shake on it.'

Relieved, yet unaccountably depressed, Cia went back to

setting the chair for her own comfort. For the rest of the morning they worked in silence, a silence that buzzed with dangerous tension.

When a clock chimed midday she glanced at her watch with surprise. A swift glance revealed Hunt leaning back in his chair, rubbing a long-fingered hand across his eyes as he stared at the screen of his own computer. An odd pang—surely not of tenderness?—shot through her, so strong she had to stop herself from getting up and bending to kiss the lines away.

'Lunch time,' he said, looking up as though her thought had been communicated to him. His mouth hardened and he got up, long body moving with the elegant economy of a predator. 'Marty gets uptight if we don't eat on time, so you'd better back up and close down now.'

More worried by that stray pang of tenderness than by her blatant physical response, Cia went through the process of backing up and shut down her computer.

When she stood up tiredness caught her unexpectedly, and she staggered.

Frowning, he ordered, 'Make sure you stand up and move around every half hour or so.'

'Yes,' she said quietly, and escaped to wash her hands.

It wasn't the work that tired her, she thought in the exquisite little powder room, it was the strain of being in the same room as Hunt. Had he felt it? It didn't seem so; she'd sneaked the occasional glance at him and felt piqued when each time he'd clearly been totally concentrating on whatever he was doing.

Whereas she, idiot that she was, registered every movement, every time he shuffled papers, every time he got to his feet to consult a file or a book, her body responding with a helpless, mindless intensity that made a mockery of her trademark composure.

Drying her hands, she thought mordantly that it was just as well he was too far away across the office for her to hear his breathing, or she'd have been obsessing about that too.

She covered a yawn and stared at her face for a second. Her restless night had painted shadows under her eyes, but she still felt that alert, vital rush of expectancy. Both shadows and weariness would disappear after another night's sleep.

After a delicious lunch Hunt said, 'Would you like to ride? It's a glorious day, and I'd like to see you on a horse.'

Perhaps some of the fresh, crisp air would clear her head. 'Love to,' she said.

'Put on a windcheater, or a jersey; there's often a wind up here. And a hat of some sort, because although you're used to putting sunscreen on in Dacia, New Zealand is directly under the hole in the ozone layer.'

Coins of colour burned along her cheekbones. He was remembering his comments just before she'd flippantly told him that sunscreen was the predominant scent in Dacia.

Skin the colour and texture of pale gold satin, and eyes like hot amber...

And afterwards he'd said, *As for your skin—don't tell me you don't know that every man who sees it wonders how it would look against his...*

Well, now she knew how it looked against his—gold against bronze—and the memory wrenched her heart and sent complex, tantalising shudders of sensation through her. Without looking at him she said lightly, 'Yes, of course.'

'Have you got boots?'

She nodded. 'Not riding boots, but something that will do.'

'I'll see you in half an hour.'

Brows rising, she looked at him. 'If you're giving me half

an hour to get ready,' she returned with delicate precision, 'I can be down in ten minutes.'

His brows rose. 'Fifteen.'

Suddenly light-hearted, she said, 'Done!'

They walked down to a large barn that held a tack room, and while Cia looked with interest at various items there Hunt took down two bridles and saddles. 'I'll carry something.' She held out a hand.

He hesitated and she said crisply, 'I'm not made of sugar, Hunt!'

Smiling, he handed over the bridles. 'Take those.'

Four horses and a large sheep grazed in a paddock close by; as Hunt and Cia came up the wire they all lifted their heads curiously and came ambling across.

'Feed the sheep first,' Hunt advised. 'Otherwise he's a damned nuisance.'

Cia held out her hand and let the sheep take several nuts from her palm. It removed them quickly and efficiently, its lips tickling her skin. 'What's the sheep doing in the horse paddock?'

'He used to be a pet lamb, so he doesn't think of himself as a sheep. He and Mike became best mates, and the others tolerate him.'

'Mike?'

Hunt held out his hand to the big stallion, the superb beast she'd see Hunt on from her bedroom window. It crunched the small treat it had taken from Hunt's palm and then stood patiently while he slipped on the bridle. 'This is Mike,' he informed her.

'That's a very prosaic name for a gorgeous beast like that.'

'His official name is Lucifer, but he's far too sweet-tempered to be lumbered with that.'

A black mare shooed the sheep off and demanded her

share. Laughing, Cia held out her hand and while the mare chomped the nuts she stroked her nose and said, 'I've heard of cats and dogs living together happily, but I don't think I've ever come across horses and sheep.'

'It happens reasonably frequently here. Horses and goats often do well together, and my father once trained a gelding that refused to be parted from his best friend, a donkey.' Hunt hefted the saddle onto his mount and bent to fasten it.

'That's Rio,' he said, watching as the mare tried to coax more treats from Cia. 'Do you want to ride her?'

'Yes, please.'

He bridled the mare, pandering to her flirtatious overtures with a gentle stroke to her nose, before leading both mare and stallion through the gate.

He watched as Cia saddled her, then nodded. 'Need a hand up?'

'No, thanks.' Expertly she stepped into the stirrup and up and into the saddle in one lithe movement. The mare jibbed a bit, but Cia settled her with a competent hand and watched Hunt. Like her, he lifted himself easily into the saddle, then nudged his mount towards her. The combination of the big bay's height and Hunt's meant he towered over her.

Pertly, she said, 'I do know what I'm doing.'

'And now I know it too,' he shot back. 'Let's go.'

Hunt's station was beautiful, a massive chunk of land extending from the hills to the sea.

Gazing out from the edge of the escarpment that dropped down to the coastal plain, Cia looked her fill, finally sighing and turning to the man who watched her. 'You're wrong.'

Hunt's brows lifted. 'On occasion,' he said drily. 'What are you referring to?'

'You said that this didn't look like a Renaissance painting; it does. It's like the landscapes the Old Masters painted—it has an untamed air.'

'I'm surprised you remember.'

Cia suspected she remembered everything he had said to her.

After a moment he went on, 'The light's different, of course. In summer it hazes over, but the autumn rains always wash it clean.'

'It's so—empty,' she said quietly. 'Fresh and new and green. I can't even see a road—oh, yes, I can.'

'Those are farm races,' he told her. He sat back on the stallion and examined the land below him with keen eyes.

'It didn't occur to you to build on the coast?'

'Too inaccessible. The main road goes up the centre of the island.' He turned inland and pointed to a range of blue-purple hills. 'But one of these days I plan to build a new beach house—to replace the old shack at the bay.'

When he had children? Cia wondered, and was surprised at the complex mix of emotions that thought brought with it.

He looked entirely suited to this, sitting so easily on his horse, looking out over his land. 'Lord of all he surveyed,' she said unevenly.

He lifted an eyebrow. 'No, that's your cousin,' he said. 'Literally. But Hinekura is not as big as Dacia.'

'Dacia doesn't belong to Luka. It's a democratic monarchy, not a dictatorship,' she said defensively, shocked because it was the first time she'd thought of her cousin all morning.

In a piercing moment of understanding she realised that her love for Luka had faded like the memory of stars on a sunny day. For the first time since she'd been an adolescent, she felt whole again.

And naked. Loving Luka had been her safe harbour, she

thought desperately, gazing at the clumps of trees that dotted the grassy slopes below, the forested gullies and the straight lines of fences. But it had never been real love; just moon-beams and star-shine, lacking the tangible intensity of Hunt's touch on her skin.

And what she felt for Hunt wasn't love either. She glanced sideways, transfixed by the familiar shock of plea-sure. Everything about him stimulated her, from his strong profile to his lithe, casual grace, but it was a purely physical response, the earthy attraction missing from her feelings for Luka.

Perhaps one day she'd find a man who combined both tenderness and passion. But when she tried to imagine it, she could only see Hunt's face, superimposed over every-thing else as though his potent magnetism had stamped itself onto her innermost being.

With words like *dangerous* and *reckless* and *heady* flash-ing around her brain, she went on, 'Which reminds me—I forgot to email Luka and Alexa last night—I'd better do it when I get back. Can I just hook into your phone line, or will I need a special cord?'

Hunt's mount fidgeted as though an unwary hand had tightened the reins. 'I'll check it when I get back, but I imagine it will need a special cord. New Zealand is a long way from Dacia; we do things differently here.'

An odd tension pulled between her shoulder blades.

Then Hunt wheeled the big bay and said laconically, 'Time to go back.'

A warm wind, heavy with moisture, whipped across her cheeks as she followed suit. When the stallion lengthened stride into a gallop she let the mare follow, relishing the opportunity to satisfy some hidden, inner wildness with vi-olent action.

CHAPTER NINE

BACK at the house Cia went up the stairs feeling a pleasant ache in her thighs and calves. It had been too long since she'd ridden—and it would be too easy to fall in love with this beautiful place.

After showering off the scent of horse, she changed into a pair of slim-fitting trousers and a shirt. The residual energy from the ride had leached away under the warm spray; yawning, she slipped on her watch, then looked at Luka's star, glimmering in the depths of her jewel sack. She almost put it on, using it as a talisman against something she didn't dare identify.

But it was ridiculously superstitious to think that Luka's gift could protect her from…

From what? In the mirror her mouth tightened into a straight line and her eyes slid sideways, lashes drooping to hide her thoughts.

She wasn't falling in love with Hunt. Oh, she was attracted to him—

'You want him,' she said brutally, watching the words form on her mouth, the way her lips suddenly looked full and provocative and eager. 'You're an idiot because you want him so much you can't think straight. He's invaded your mind, and when he touches you it's like being struck by lightning.'

And it was the same for him. Inexperienced she might be, but she recognised the very sensual challenge in his eyes. Trying to ignore the heat kindling in the pit of her stomach, she combed back her hair and picked up the drier.

133

'So what are you going to do about it?' she asked the woman in the mirror as she went through the routine of drying her hair. 'Run away? Or give in and get him out of your system?'

If she stayed at Hinekura she'd end up making love with him. It was as inevitable as the setting of the sun and the rising of the moon.

Which did she fear most—sating this fierce hunger of the senses, or starving it? Of course running away could pitch her into the middle of a media frenzy.

Her teeth savaged her lip until another yawn took her by surprise. Wistfully eyeing the elegant, comfortable daybed, she chose a book from the bookcase—one with coloured photographs of Northland—and stubbornly sat down in an armchair. She'd give herself ten minutes of calm repose, and then she'd go down.

But she woke to a darkening sky and the pricking of faint stars through the fabric of twilight. Stunned, she shot to her feet, then had to grab the back of the chair as her head pounded.

Five minutes later, after splashing her face vigorously with cold water, she opened her door to see Hunt coming towards her, lithe and silent in the rapidly darkening passage.

'Are you all right?' he asked abruptly.

'I seem to have a lingering case of mild jet lag,' she told him with a wry smile that hid, she fervently hoped, her shivering pleasure at the sight of him. 'Another night's sleep will cure it, but I'm surprised. I've never had jet lag before.'

'You've never flown to the other side of the world before.' Frowning, he examined her face, a merciless scrutiny that made her feel as though she'd been caught out in a lie. 'It's a natural response to having your internal clock thoroughly disorganised.'

'I'm sorry to be such a boring guest,' she said with dignity.

His eyes kindled. 'Boring? Far from it, princess.'

'Don't call me that,' she said between her teeth.

His eyes challenged her. 'What would you like me to call you?'

Darling, hope whispered wickedly. *Dearest one, my heart...*

'I've got a perfectly good name,' she retorted.

He gestured for her to walk with him. 'You've got a formal name, Princess Lucia, and a family name, Cia. I'm not family and I'm a New Zealander, which means I don't go for formality, so I'll call you princess. Would you like a drink before dinner?'

'Orange juice would be lovely,' she said stiffly, her throat dry.

Hunt put her into a chair on the terrace overlooking the stream, beneath one of the big market umbrellas that sheltered the outdoor furniture from both the heat of the sun and evening's softly drifting dew. The little stream chuckled by as small birds with bright beady eyes and tails like fans whisked silently around her, catching invisible insects in the soft, scented air. On the other side of the stream soft lights bloomed amongst the rocks, highlighting ferns and water plants.

'I'm surprised you don't have mosquitoes here,' she commented, accepting the long glass of juice Hunt handed her.

'Mosquitoes prefer stagnant water, and any that manage to make it get eaten by the fantails.' The lights picked out the arrogant blade of Hunt's nose, glowed warmly over the brutal sweep of his cheekbones and the determined jaw.

A fierce pang of need tore through her. Hastily she drank some juice and said the first thing that came into her mind.

'This is delicious—so sweet, with just a faint note of acid to give it zing.'

Heavens, she was babbling!

He directed a sardonic look her way, a look that tingled through her. 'It's a local product. Northland produces a lot of citrus—mandarins and oranges as well as limes and lemonade fruit and lemons. Tangelos too.'

'Lemonade fruit? What are they?'

As she settled back in her chair to listen to his brief rundown of the local delicacies, a deep, aching contentment seeped through her. It didn't banish the tension; in an odd way it added to it. Desire she could understand; this sweet feeling of rightness was new, and, she suspected, even more dangerous.

But for those quiet minutes when the dusk fell silently around them, she listened to Hunt's deep voice with its excitingly raw undernote and pretended that she hadn't made love with him, that he didn't despise her, that they were two people who'd just met.

Later that night while she slept, she finally let her longheld love for Luka slip away like a skein of silk, waking in the morning to memories free of pain.

Bewildered, bereft, she lay still in the big bed, listening to the dawn chorus. How had it happened? Until yesterday morning she'd been utterly convinced she loved Luka, yet this morning it had gone, as though one night had cut the past cleanly off from the present.

Not one night, she thought with a flash of apprehension. Hunt. Like a conqueror he had moved in and taken over, sweeping away everything but her response to his powerful presence.

But he's far too dangerous to love, she thought, and firmly squelched the little thrills of anticipation that chased each other down her spine.

She had believed that once she was able to escape her unrequited feelings for Luka, she could be happy. Instead, as she got ready for the day, she was torn between apprehension and a smouldering excitement.

So she should have been relieved when Hunt told her over breakfast, 'I have to go to Perth in Australia for a few days.' He sounded curt and businesslike.

Cia fought back a corroding sense of loss. 'When do you leave?'

'In half an hour.' He glanced at her, eyes cool and opaque as lapis lazuli. 'There's some work you could do if you want to, but don't feel obliged. It's not very important, and you don't look as though you've got rid of that jet lag yet.' He drained his coffee and stood up. 'Don't ride until I come back.'

Tilting her chin, she replied with syrupy sweetness, 'Would you like me to get Marty to do lifeguard duty whenever I swim?'

'A good idea,' he tossed back succinctly. 'Did you hear from Dacia overnight?'

Irritated, she picked up a piece of toast. 'Yes. They're fine, and Alexa sends her love.'

He nodded and looked at her. 'Goodbye. Don't come out,' he said, and left the room.

Offhand described him exactly, she thought, wondering why she was so angry.

She forced food down her throat, drank a cup of tea, and stubbornly stayed in the breakfast room. She heard him call out to Marty, the slam of the door, and then the sound of the Range Rover. Stupid tears clogged her eyes as she sat in the sunny room and waited until the noise of the plane engine coming towards the house brought her to her feet.

She shot out onto the terrace and waved crazily, laughing

when the pilot waggled the wings on the turn south to Auckland.

Marty came in as she walked back through the doors. 'So the house loses its heart,' the older woman said with a smile. 'You haven't had enough to eat, surely?'

'I'm fine, thank you,' Cia told her brightly, and went into the office to type the few letters Hunt had left for her.

Although she missed him so acutely it felt as though she'd lost a limb, she settled into life on the station with real pleasure. She walked around the homestead area, acquiring a follower in the shape of an alert, half-grown farm dog called Bonzo who took a fancy to her. She waved to men on horseback or driving tractors, stopped and talked to children on their way home from school, and helped women hang out the family wash on the clotheslines.

They were friendly and not in the least awed by her. It was a huge change from the constant attention in Dacia, and she revelled in it.

Yet each night in her lonely bed she knew she was spending each day listening for Hunt's plane to return.

'You're looking shadowy under the eyes again,' Marty said sternly on the third day. 'Go up and have a nap.'

Cia glanced out at the sunny day, but the tiredness that had bedevilled her since she'd landed in New Zealand dragged her down. 'This wretched jet lag,' she complained cheerfully. 'Next time I cross the world I'm going to do it in stages.'

'Might be an idea,' the older woman agreed noncommittally.

An hour later when Cia woke, she felt the difference in the house immediately. In fact, she thought, bouncing off the bed, she'd probably heard the plane arrive in her sleep, because it was impossible for the atmosphere to change, yet she knew that Hunt was home.

A powerful cocktail of emotions fizzed inside her—eagerness, joy, excitement and something else she had no intention of examining. Humming a pop tune, she got into a pair of sleek trousers and a silk shirt, both the soft burnished topaz that went so well with her eyes and skin.

But when she came out of her room she was assailed by a piercing shyness. Her breath locked in her throat, she walked down the stairs and through the silent house. Hunt wasn't in the office; he wasn't on the terrace overlooking the little stream.

After a short hesitation she walked around under the wide overhang towards the courtyard with the swimming pool.

And there he was. Her heart contracted painfully.

From the shadow of the overhang she watched his strong arms cut through the water with such force it made her feel weak. The sun burned his bare shoulders copper, and the water darkened his hair into a slash of black as he swam length after length. There was something hypnotic about the powerful rhythm of his strokes, the relentless pushing of his body that shivered through her.

Her heart jumped when he finally stopped and climbed out of the pool in one strong, practised heave. Water streamed from him, outlining with loving precision his sleek, strong body as he dragged a towel off the back of one of the steamer chairs.

Only then did he look at her. Transfixed by his unsmiling scrutiny, she forced a smile and said lightly, 'Hello. How did the trip go?'

'Fine.' He rough-dried his head and shoulders, then dropped the towel. 'But I'm glad I'm home.'

He stooped and kissed her, and this time there was no holding back for either of them.

But Hunt lifted his head too soon, metallic blue eyes burning into hers. 'Made up your mind?'

Somehow all her cowardly caveats didn't seem important now that he was back. And her kiss had already answered him in the most basic way.

'Yes,' she said simply, reaching up to cover his heart with the palm of her hand. Its beat drove into the soft skin, heavy, regular, emphatic.

Hunt smiled, the intent, hungry smile of a lover close to triumph, but his voice was amused. 'Marty's in the house, so we'd better not startle her by heading up to a bedroom now.'

When Cia flushed he laughed quietly in his throat. 'But she'll be gone by six o'clock—it's her choir-practice night.'

Excitement rode her hard. 'Have you got any correspondence you want done?' she asked, adding demurely, 'To fill in time.'

Hunt covered the hand on his chest with his, pressing down so that the intoxicating rhythm of his heart mingled with the beat of her quickening pulses. 'No. Let's ride until she goes. It will help me to keep my hands off you.'

It did, but although they were careful not to touch each other, their eyes exchanged messages that wound the tension between them tighter and tighter until Cia thought she might explode with frustrated need.

Marty left them a superb dinner, which neither did justice to. After they'd stacked the dishes in the kitchen Hunt said starkly, 'I'd like to do this the romantic way and carry you up the stairs, but I don't dare touch you.'

Cia's smile trembled on her lips. 'I don't dare touch you, either, and although I'm sure love in the kitchen is incredibly wonderful, Marty might not approve.'

So they walked up the stairs side by side, tension smoking between them—a wild clamour of desire and certainty. This, Cia thought, was why she had stayed at Hinekura. She was free now, and this time there would be no regrets.

She'd spent the past few days—no, every second since they'd made love in the summer house in Dacia—craving Hunt. Her heart and mind had tried to lock him out, but her body had known better; with simple, primal insistence, it recognised its mate.

But once in her bedroom, she didn't know what to do. Bracing herself, she turned to glance up at him through her lashes. What she saw in his face made her drag in a jagged breath.

'Don't look so scared,' he said harshly. 'Somehow you've got under my skin and into my blood. I spent these last three days in a constant state of arousal, missing you, stopping myself from ringing you every ten minutes just so that I could hear your voice.'

It wasn't a declaration of love, but it would do for now. Beggars, she thought painfully, can't be choosers.

'At least you knew where I was,' she said.

He made a soft guttural noise in his throat and reached for her, crushing her mouth beneath his with passion enough to burn through her resistance and carry her defences by storm.

Shaking, so caught up in the moment that she couldn't think, Cia surrendered utterly to the demands of her own body.

'Hunt...' His name tapered away into a soft moan when he pushed away the silk of her shirt and kissed her breasts.

Sensation roared through in an all-consuming flood and she was lost; this time they came together with an untamed ferocity that shocked and excited her.

The first time they'd made love he'd led her by slow, sensuous increments to ecstasy. This time it was fast and fierce, a swift shedding of clothes, an eager, savage possession for both of them—her fingernails tearing into his shoulders, his arms fastening around her like iron bands, the bold masculine power of his big body as he drove into her, her urgent demands for satisfaction, until rapture rolled over them like a tidal wave, hurling them up on some unknown shore where the only thing that mattered was their mutual pleasure…

With the tremors from their explosive climax still shuddering through them, Hunt lifted himself onto his elbows and stared into her eyes as though he was trying to read her soul.

She met his gaze fearlessly. 'Did you prove whatever it was you were proving?' she asked in a voice husky with residual heat.

His mouth twisted. 'No,' he said. Then, 'Yes.'

'No and yes?'

'That you want me as much as I want you.'

She moistened her lips. A slow, sweet shudder of renewed energy ran through her when she saw the fire the tiny movement kindled in his eyes. 'And the negative?'

His eyes went dark. 'That you're no more able to resist it than I am.'

Was that what he'd meant to say? His kiss, tender and sweet, silenced the little doubter in her brain.

He said, 'I don't want to share you with anyone—we can take a few days off. Pack some clothes and we'll go down to the bach.'

She hesitated, then laughter swelled inside her. 'The shack you're going to tear down?'

'It's primitive but comfortable—nothing like the summer house in Dacia.'

A flicker of something in his midnight-blue eyes made her wonder if he was testing her. It didn't matter; sooner or later he'd realise that she didn't insist on luxury.

'I like the sound of comfort, and just you and me,' she

purred, and bit his shoulder in a thoughtful way. 'How long are we going to stay there?'

'Pack for several days.'

Joy burst inside her like a skyrocket. 'I'll be ready in twenty minutes.'

He stretched, a magnificent sight, and grinned. 'Is there a princess school where you learn to get ready in half the time of most women?'

Cia refused to acknowledge the slight chill his words produced. Of course he was accustomed to this. He knew how long it took a woman to get ready. 'I've always been like it.'

The bach was tiny and old, and primitive described it fairly well, but it was clean and the bed was huge and exceedingly comfortable.

This was important, because for the next four days they didn't move far from that bed. Each morning and night Hunt checked in with the homestead, but apart from that they spent all their time on or very near the small, white curve of sand with its huge overhanging trees whose name took her some time to learn to pronounce.

Hunt took her fishing; she teased him unmercifully when she caught one bigger than his, but he got his own back when she had to admit that she didn't know how to cook them. They swam. They talked, they discussed the elderly books that lived in a makeshift bookcase, and other books they'd read, and they found they could sit in silent companionship.

But mostly they made love.

Cia had never thought of herself as a passionate woman; her love for Luka had been almost entirely without any sexual feeling, but Hunt showed her how sensual she could be. In a continual glow of excitement, her system became sensitised to him until he had only to look at her in a certain way, gleaming eyes narrowed, a half-smile on his lips, and she was ready for him.

One night, lying near to sleep in his arms, she thought a little sadly that he was so *good* at this. He'd taught her the earthy delights of foreplay, the languid eroticism of afterglow, the screaming ecstasy of white-hot speed and power, and the simmering, unbearable pleasure of making love with slow tenderness. He was an expert.

As though he sensed the bleak way her thoughts were heading, he nuzzled her ear and murmured, 'I have this fantasy of making love to you when you're wearing nothing but jewels.'

'I don't have many jewels,' she said, laughing a little. 'If we were in Dacia we could borrow some emeralds, but not here.'

He laughed too, and kissed a certain intensely excitable spot below her ear. 'How about the diamond star?'

She froze, and he lifted himself on his elbow, looking down at her with lazily amused eyes. 'No?'

'No,' she said, adding with a different little laugh this time, one that was brittle and artificial, 'Luka gave it to me. I'd feel embarrassed—a bit like having a photograph of your mother on the bedside table.'

He laughed at that and eased her on top of him. 'I see.'

Thoughts roared through her head, but she couldn't stop any for long enough to catch one. In that frozen moment she realised that she had made the unforgivable mistake; she'd fallen in love with him.

And as his hand stroked the length of her spine from her neck to the dip at her waist, and the familiar craving smouldered into life, she understood that she'd never really loved Luka.

He was the past; Hunt was the present. She refused to speculate about the future.

Tomorrow they were going back to the homestead after the most wonderful four days of her life. Cia didn't want to leave; if they stayed there in the bach, in this precious limbo, nothing could harm them or the fragile relationship they'd forged.

Of course they couldn't; Hunt had a series of meetings in Auckland. He'd asked her if she wanted to go with him, but she'd said no. She didn't want the world intruding on their idyll.

But she was bright and cheerful when they went back to the homestead, and she waved him goodbye with a smile.

And then she waited for him to come back, sleeping long hours to catch up on the sleep she'd lost in his arms.

He came back five days later. Cia was swimming when she heard the plane come in low overhead, and such joy tore through her that she sank to the bottom of the pool. She burst out into the sunlight to the sound of the engine changing as it touched down. Excited and euphoric, she hauled herself out of the water and dashed into the cabana to shower and pull on her clothes.

'You're too late to go up to the airstrip with Ben,' Marty called out as Cia ran into the house.

'I know. I was swimming.'

The housekeeper appeared at the door. 'He'll be glad to be back. That trip to New Caledonia to see an old friend came out of the blue.'

'Mm.' She was radiant, so glad that Hunt was back she suspected she might not be able to hide her delight.

Humming, she ran up the stairs and leaned out so that she could see the Rover come up the drive.

Hunt looked a bit drawn, the angular features more sharply defined than usual, and after greeting her he apologised briefly for having to work until dinner. Disappointed,

Cia read and walked in the garden, eagerly looking forward to the night.

Long before the evening ended her delight had dwindled into foreboding. She couldn't put her finger on any change in Hunt, but the lovely closeness they had achieved at the bach had gone, evaporated like morning dew. When he looked at her it was with burnished, unreadable eyes, his control very evident.

Had he met someone else?

Painfully she hid behind her princess mask, produced small talk, discussed the news and told him small events that had taken place while he was gone.

Eventually he said, 'You're looking a little tired, so perhaps you'd like to go to bed now.'

'I would,' she said politely, and got to her feet. 'Goodnight.'

Ten minutes after she'd closed her bedroom door behind her someone knocked on it. She shrugged her dressing gown on over her slim cotton pyjamas and went across. Hope burst into bloom again; Hunt was standing there with a small parcel in his hand.

'Yes?' she said remotely.

'I need to talk to you.'

She stood back to let him, watching uneasily as he walked over to the bed and dropped the parcel on the coverlet. Long and slim, it looked—it looked like a jewellery box. A cold stone lodged just under her breastbone.

Then he turned and faced her, his face dark and austere. 'The friend I went to see in New Caledonia,' he said deliberately, 'was Édouard Lorraine.'

Cold with foreboding, Cia repeated the name in a flat voice as though she'd never heard it before.

'Maxime Lorraine's father,' he said.

'I know.' She swallowed and said, 'How—how is he?'

Hunt shrugged. 'He's married again. I went to his wedding.'

She stared at him and he sketched a brief, cold smile. 'He's a pragmatic Frenchman; he wants someone to leave his money to. And Maxime is dead. He's married a woman young enough to bear him children.' He paused. 'So tell me about Maxime Lorraine.'

Panic kicked beneath her ribs. 'I don't know what you mean.'

'Was he your lover?' He examined her face with the scalpel sharpness of a scientist checking out a hypothesis.

Cia's legs threatened to fold underneath her, but self-preservation stiffened them. He was too tall—darkly intimidating, he towered over her. 'We were not lovers, and why do you want to know about him?' she asked distantly.

A black brow lifted in silent disbelief. Ignoring her question, he said, 'So what did you feel for him?'

Cia told him the truth. 'I liked him.'

'*Liked* him? Poor bastard.' When she didn't answer he didn't attempt to hide his disbelief. 'Why did he think you were going to marry him?'

Talking to him was like climbing an icy, implacable wall. Her hands clenched at her sides. 'He—I hoped...' Her tongue seemed too big for her mouth and she didn't know what to say. Stiffly, she stated, 'You have no right to cross-question me.'

'You hoped that he'd be a good husband? A good lover? That he'd keep you in the style to which you've become accustomed? That he'd be so delighted to have snared a princess for a wife that he'd be complaisant when you sought out other men to slake that hunger of yours?'

The swift, cruel accusations cut her pride to shreds, but she kept her head high. 'I hoped that I'd learn to love him,' she said remotely, the words an admission of culpability.

'But it didn't happen. And his proposal came as a surprise—we weren't close enough for that.'

'If that's true, why was he so shattered by your rejection that he went off on some stupid expedition to the Congo?'

Cia's head came up proudly. 'My rejection had nothing to do with that—he planned to join the expedition whatever happened.'

'Not according to his father.' His eyes blazed with coldly furious fire.

It seemed treachery to be talking like this of poor dead Maxime. He'd fretted because his father didn't treat him as an adult, as a leader of men. The expedition had been his chance to prove that he could meet his father's expectations.

'He and his father loved each other, but I gathered they weren't close,' she said quietly. 'Perhaps you'd like to tell me exactly what this has to do with you.'

'Why didn't you fall in love with him?'

'Nobody can fall in love to order!' she shot back.

'Especially not if they're in love with someone else—someone out of reach,' he said with merciless scorn. 'You loved Luka when you caught Maxime in that sensuous snare you weave so well, and you loved him when you made love with me. You're in love with him now.'

Her skin went hot, then chilled as a cold sweat broke out on her brow. She thought she might be going to be sick, but she fought the sensation and said proudly, 'I'm not. Even if I was when I met Maxime, what does that have to do with you?'

'Just this,' he said between his teeth. 'I don't like standing in for another man. In fact, I can think of nothing more humiliating than to realise that the woman I'm in bed with is imagining another man in my place.'

CHAPTER TEN

'No!' THE word burst from Cia. She finished fiercely, 'It wasn't like that.'

Equally fast was Hunt's brutal rejoinder. 'But you're in love with him. No wonder you stopped wearing his star when you decided to make love to me.'

She made a weary gesture, and said, 'I thought I was in love with him. I know now that I wasn't.'

'Why? Because you came to orgasm in my arms?' he demanded contemptuously.

Cia had no answer. To try and convince him would only mean revealing how she felt about him—and pride forbade that. Nausea gripping her stomach, she said woodenly, 'All I can say is that when we make love I didn't then and don't now imagine anyone else. Of course I can't prove it. And who told you that I was in love with Luka?'

'Édouard again,' he said crisply. 'Apparently Maxime worked it out from something another woman said when he was in Dacia. Although Édouard believed that who you love is your business, when he realised you were living here with me he decided to make sure I knew what I was up against.' He smiled with a merciless lack of humour. 'He thought I might be in love with you.'

His tone told her just how ludicrous he found that. Pale and shaken, Cia said quietly, 'Will you go now, please?'

'Not before you've opened your present,' he said, indicating the package he'd dropped on the bed.

'I don't want it. Please take it and go.'

'It's yours,' he said negligently. 'I'd hate you to leave

149

this place feeling that you'd wasted your time.' He picked up the package and stripped the wrapping from it. It was a jeweller's box; he flicked it open and drew out a rivulet of golden flames and ice, a chain set with diamonds and an exquisite pendant.

He held it out. 'These are Australian diamonds—better suited to your colouring than emeralds, or the stones your cousin gave you. Consider it payment for services rendered.'

Cia's stomach lurched. She flung him a desperate look, then turned and raced into the bathroom, only just getting there in time. A few seconds later in the midst of her misery, she heard him follow her in. Wretched as much with humiliation as the misery of being sick, she closed her eyes.

When the paroxysm had passed, leaving her white and shivering, Hunt sat her down with alarming gentleness and wiped her face with a damp, warm cloth, waited while she cleaned her teeth, and then picked her up and carried her back to the bed, already pulled back.

The diamond chain, she was thankful to see, had gone.

'Stay there,' he said. 'I'll get you something to drink.'

'I don't want anything,' she whispered.

But he brought a jug of water and a glass, only leaving when she'd sipped some of it.

Exhausted, Cia slept as though she'd been slugged with an iron bar, waking to another bout of nausea. Tension—or a stomach bug? At least while she was throwing up, she thought with black humour as she showered, she wasn't grieving over the shattered remains of her affair with Hunt.

But when she came back into the bedroom he was halfway across her room, frowning and angry. He stopped and watched her cross to the bed, his eyes keenly watchful.

Once she'd pulled the blanket up he said quite pleasantly, 'Do you have anything to tell me?'

Cia croaked, 'Like what?'

'Marty says you're still sleeping a lot of the time.'

Anger and a bitter premonition licked through her. 'I didn't realise she was a spy.'

'She's concerned about you.' His casual tone was countermanded by the keen intensity of his gaze.

'I've obviously been incubating this bug,' she said uncertainly. 'I'll get over it.'

'You're not drinking coffee or wine.'

Cia shrugged. 'More grilling, Hunt? When I'm by myself I don't drink alcohol.'

'But you usually drink coffee. You haven't since you've been here.'

She shrugged a little more deeply. 'For some reason the smell has made me feel a bit queasy, so I've been drinking tea. What has that got to do with anything?'

'For some women, it has quite a lot to do with being pregnant.'

Shock hit her like a blow to the heart. She stared at him, saw icy anger in his eyes and groped for composure, but could only stutter, 'P-p-pregnant?'

'Sleepiness and an aversion to caffeine are common indications. Were you on the Pill when we made love that first time?'

The colour drained from her skin. 'No, but you used protection—'

'They've been known to fail,' he said lethally. 'I assumed you'd be sensible enough not to make love unless there was no chance of conception.'

Sensible? At that time all thoughts in her head had been swamped by desire.

He went on, 'However, I'm not blaming you—I should damned well have known better.'

Cia had thought the long-drawn-out agony of loving Luka

had inured her to pain; now she discovered that she hadn't known anything about it at all.

A cold, still pride came to her aid. She said woodenly, 'This is pure supposition. I don't feel—'

'If it's mine, you can't be much more than a fortnight pregnant, so I don't suppose you *feel* anything. I suggest you find out.' Contempt hardened his voice.

She had once thought he'd make a bad enemy. She'd been right. Squaring her shoulders, she said icily, 'If—and that's a huge if—I am pregnant, believe me, it's yours!'

His face closed down. 'Rest here for the time being. Once the shops are open I'll send Marty into town to collect a pregnancy kit.'

Heat flamed across her skin. She said angrily, 'You don't need to involve her in this. She's done enough, surely, by telling you of her suspicions. I'll get one myself—'

'And run the risk of someone recognising you?'

'No one knows who I am,' she returned, head held high.

His face didn't relax. 'How do you know?'

'I've been walking around here talking to your people, and no one's said a word.'

'They know,' he said shortly. 'New Zealanders tend not to make a big fuss of visiting notabilities.' He forestalled her next objection. 'And anyone in town will certainly know who I am. Marty is utterly trustworthy. Once we know, we can take it from there.'

With the taste of ashes clogging her mouth, Cia leaned back into the pillows and closed her eyes.

'Are you all right?'

'No,' she muttered, opening her eyes to glare at him. 'Will you please get out of here and *leave me alone*?'

He said, 'I'll get Marty to bring you up some dry toast.'

'I don't want anything, thank you.'

But Marty brought up the toast anyway, with tea and

some orange juice. 'Hunt said you like it,' she said calmly, putting the tray on Cia's lap. She straightened up. 'I'll be up in an hour or so.'

By then the stone in Cia's stomach had assumed giant proportions, but she forced herself to drink the tea and some of the juice and nibbled at the toast.

Hunt was right; it did make her feel better, so much so that an hour or so later she got up and dressed. Going downstairs wasn't an option; unable to order her thoughts or emotions, she paced the floor of the room, her mind racing as futilely as a trapped animal.

After an hour or so of merciless worrying, another knock on the door heralded Hunt again, big and aloof and determined.

'Yes?' she asked stonily.

He handed her a paper bag. 'And I want to see the results.'

Humiliation burned like a hot brand through her. Her chin came up and she looked at him unwaveringly. 'Go to hell,' she said pleasantly. 'If I'm pregnant it's none of your business.'

'If you're carrying my child,' he bit out, 'it's definitely my business. Now get into the bathroom before I forget the deference due to a princess.'

So angry she couldn't articulate any of the words that burned her lips, Cia shut the door in his face.

For long moments she stood just inside, hands clenched at her sides while she thought vengefully of all the things she'd like to do to Hunt Bloody Radcliffe.

But eventually she walked into the bathroom, staring with acute distaste at the package. Eventually she forced herself to open it and read the instructions, noting bleakly that the makers promised accuracy even if the pregnancy had been established only a couple of weeks.

If she was pregnant, she vowed, she'd go back to Dacia and have her baby there. The chilling distaste in Hunt's tone still rang in her ears. Eating her heart out for Luka had been much safer than this foray into the wilder regions of love.

Slowly she followed the instructions and waited, staring at the stick until it changed colour. Her hand touched her waist, and she looked up to meet Hunt's eyes in the mirror, chips of ice in a face so angular that it could have been carved from stone.

She demanded harshly, 'What do you think you're doing?'

'I'm making sure you're all right,' he said, clipping each cold, terse word. 'Tell me the truth—whose child is it?'

'Yours,' she said, white-lipped and shaking.

'How do you know?'

Goaded into fury, she spun on her heel and threw at him, 'Because until I slept with you I was a virgin!'

'Not according to Maxime,' he said.

'Then Maxime lied. I don't care what he told you, or his father, or whoever he told all this to; I did not make love with him,' she said unevenly, fighting raw desolation. 'Now, let me past. I need to start organising things.'

'What things?' he asked dangerously, stepping back.

'I'm going back to Dacia.' With chin angled high she looked him straight in the eyes, her own blazing. 'You can forget about me—if I am pregnant, I won't tell anyone that you are the father. I can look after my child myself. It won't ever be alone.'

He followed her into the bedroom. 'You're damned right it won't,' he said grimly, 'because you and I are getting married.'

For a split-second hope burst into glory in her heart, but one glance at his face killed it. It tore her to shreds to refuse him when she so passionately wanted to accept everything he offered, but she couldn't marry a man who despised her. 'No.'

'Yes,' he said.

Cia saw his complete determination, and her heart quailed. She said quietly, 'Why would you marry me if you don't believe the child is yours?'

'I do believe it's mine,' he said quietly.

Her skin tightened. 'You won't believe anything else I say—why would you believe this?'

'Because if you were a virgin when we first made love, it has to be mine.'

She met his sceptical scrutiny with as much composure as she could. Time seemed to stretch as she lost herself in the frigid depths of his eyes. A bird called outside, a wistful little trill that ached through her.

He said curtly, 'The evidence backs it up.'

'What evidence?'

'Your passion seemed to surprise you, and you showed a charming, and very appealing lack of experience. I was pretty sure you were a virgin until you climaxed.'

Colour stung her skin.

He said with dry irony, 'I'm sure I don't have to tell you that a woman rarely comes to orgasm her first time, so I dismissed my suspicion for a more likely scenario—that you were relatively inexperienced, but I'd given you your first orgasm.'

'I see,' she said tonelessly. 'In other words, the evidence of your own eyes. But you have no evidence that I led Maxime on then dumped him when I realised his father was in financial trouble.'

'I have pretty good evidence.' He shrugged. 'You, to start off with. I've been fairly constantly in your company over the past couple of weeks—enough to know that you understand business. Wedding or not, you'd have known about

Lorraine's situation—and it was pretty grim for a week or so. But Édouard Lorraine wouldn't lie to me, and he told me what Maxime had told him.'

She stared at him, a cold knot of angry fear contracting in her stomach. Only the composure of long practice enabled her to say without expression, 'And you believe that Maxime wouldn't lie to his father.'

He was watching her with the flinty ruthlessness of a man who had fought his way to the top. 'Once Édouard told me that you are in love with Luka, it all made sense. You realised that it was no use hoping for Luka to wake up and see that he had the perfect wife in you, so you decided to cut your losses and do what any sensible, penniless princess would do. You looked around for a husband to keep you in the manner to which you've been accustomed.'

Stiff-lipped, her heart frozen and dead in her chest, she said, 'And when it looked as though Maxime wouldn't be able to keep me in luxury, I got rid of him? It does make sense—if you're a cynic.' Another thought struck her. 'Tell me, Hunt, do you think that I was actively trawling for another rich man to *keep* me? Do you think I decided you'd do as well as Maxime?'

He shrugged. 'It doesn't matter now. What matters is that you are pregnant with my child, so you're going to marry me.'

'Just like that?' she asked dangerously. 'You'd marry a woman you believe to be a fortune-hunter, a woman in love with another man?'

He came across the room in a silent lunge, all primitive hunter. Cia flinched, but stood firm when he said in a silky voice that lifted the hairs on her skin, 'I can deal with your childish crush on Luka. I'll make sure that you don't miss him too much.'

She opened her mouth to insist that she no longer loved

Luka, but primitive self-preservation closed her lips without letting a word escape. Once he knew she loved him, he'd take advantage of it. Later, when this icy serenity had shattered, she'd feel pain, but at the moment she was in control.

His eyes narrowed. 'You were going to say?' he prompted, his voice a rough purr.

'Nothing.'

He lifted her chin and subjected her to another probing examination. 'And I'll make sure you don't want for anything,' he said deliberately.

'That's an inducement?' she asked, white with temper.

'Most people,' he said with insulting confidence, 'would agree that my money in return for your title and social position is a fair exchange.'

'Do you believe that?'

This time the silence rang with unbearable intensity. Hunt didn't move when he said, 'Do you?'

'No, but don't worry.' The words rocketed out like bullets. 'I can introduce you to several very eligible princesses—and quite a few of the lesser ranks—who'd be happy to marry you on that basis.'

Sickened, she picked up the diamond chain she'd found in the drawer of the bedside table. She turned and in a spasm of rage and grief, hurled it at him. He made no attempt to catch it, so the exquisite insult dropped onto the carpet.

Each painful word ringing with conviction, she said, 'I'm not going to marry you. You don't trust me enough to believe me—why should I believe that you'd be a good husband to me and a good father to a child? If there is one.' She angled her chin in a movement as unconscious as it was defiant and walked towards the bathroom.

He stopped her easily, big hands holding her until she gave up the struggle and settled for glaring at him.

He said, 'I'm sure you have a list of princesses a mile

long, but none of them have tiger eyes and skin as cool and fragile as silk—until it heats under my touch—and none of them make me laugh and infuriate me. And no other woman has ever got between me and my work.'

'And no other woman has let herself get pregnant by you,' she said wearily.

'Don't cry.' He kissed her eyes, closing them on the tears aching behind them, and then kissed her mouth and the point of her chin, and her temples.

It took every ounce of will-power she possessed to stay wooden in his grip. When he let her go she said rigidly, 'You can make me want you, but I'm not going to marry you.'

His eyes were as lethal as the blue sheen on a gun barrel. 'You'll marry me,' he said in soft intimidation. 'You'll marry me if I have to force you to. I know what it's like to grow up a bastard; the innuendoes still turn up now and then in the gossip columns. I'm not going to put any child of mine through that.'

Ghost-white, she turned towards the daybed. Hunt saw her falter and took the three steps to catch her, holding her slender, rigid body close. In spite of everything, his hormones roared into life, primitively possessive, fiercely determined to protect her even when she didn't want it.

And she didn't want it. Her eyes glittered like the golden gems she'd flung at him, but at least colour had returned to her skin.

'I am not going to faint,' she said between her teeth. 'I have never fainted in my life, and your baby—if there *is* a baby—isn't going to make me start.'

Although his grin was reluctant, it was definite, a flash of white teeth in his tanned face, an unwilling glint of admiration in the blue eyes. He tightened his arms around her, bringing her closer.

Temptation hammered at the bars of her will, already weakened by his admission that he'd been hurt by his situation as a child. Resisting it, she said abruptly, 'Let me go.'

But the words emerged only a few decibels above a whisper. She repeated them, more strongly this time.

'All right,' he said, and lifted her to her feet, carrying her effortlessly to the bed.

Eyes enormous, she stared at him. He looked down at her, and the anger in both pairs of clashing eyes faded, to be replaced by something far more dangerous. Cia felt the soft rasp of her breath in her lungs, and the swift tattoo of her pulses as frustrated sexual tension brought with it a surge of passion.

She repeated desperately, 'I'm not going to marry you.'

'So what will you do? Run back to Dacia and steal Alexa's thunder in a storm of gossip?' he returned, setting her on her feet.

Cia bit her lip, stopping only when she saw his gaze rest on her maltreated mouth. 'I haven't yet decided,' she said reluctantly, adding, 'And this—possible pregnancy—might just be a false alarm.'

'It's certain enough for me,' he said caustically. 'I don't know how you feel about it, but the last thing I want for any child of mine is for it to grow up in a fanfare of controversy and media speculation.'

Hunt watched the colour drain from her lovely face, leaving stark cheekbones and trembling lips. He'd deliberately chosen to remind her of the media frenzy that had followed her mother's death. Ignoring a twinge of sympathy, he pressed her further. 'If we're going to put a stop to that, we need to get married fast.'

She shook her head. 'I'll go to Dacia.'

Hunt had had enough. Coldly furious, he said roughly,

'The international gossip circuit will go crazy about the fall of the Ice Princess—especially as Alexa is also pregnant. You can never go back.'

He was right, damn him. She couldn't do that to Luka and Alexa. Steadying her voice with an effort, she said, 'Hunt, you can't force me into this or persuade me, or run roughshod over me. I need to think, and you're stopping me.'

The anger he'd been keeping under control threatened to break free. When she blocked him out by closing her eyes, he said fiercely, 'Look at me.'

She shook her head, but her eyes flew open when he sat down on the bed.

With sombre forcefulness he said, 'We have several things going for us, princess—passion, and a certain compatibility of mind.' He touched her waist lightly, then withdrew his hand. 'And a child.'

Oh, he knew how to persuade!

When she stayed silent he went on uncompromisingly, 'If we don't get married soon, the world will know that we conceived the baby before our marriage. Because of who you are—who I am—there will always be gossip.'

She hesitated, then gave a reluctant nod.

He said explosively, 'I wish to God we were just a couple of ordinary people off the street, able to live ordinary lives.'

'No you don't,' she said, shaking her head. 'You could have chosen a life like that, but you wanted more.'

The flicker of emotion in his expression was swiftly concealed by his frown. 'Ordinary or not, I'd still want you,' he said and stood up, towering over the bed. His deep voice hardened. 'And I'd want my child to grow up confident that its parents cared enough for it and each other to marry, to give it roots.'

Cia's heart twisted at the thought of the boy who'd never

known his mother, wasn't even sure that the man he called father was the man whose genes made him what he was.

She said crisply, 'I've got more than roots—I've got a whole blasted tree stretching back a couple of thousand years. It means nothing. My father used his title and his charm to con my mother into marrying him. Her pedigree was almost as long as his, but when the marriage disintegrated she used drugs to stop the pain, and eventually killed herself with them. You don't need roots, you need good basic foundations; the important thing is the person you turn out to be. Your father taught you well, but he had excellent material to work with.'

'My child isn't going to grow up not knowing who it is,' he said impatiently. He turned and looked at her and smiled—pure devilry, both calculating and sexy as hell. It set her heart flipping. 'Fortunately I have the weapons to make sure that you'll enjoy being my wife.'

When she didn't answer he bent, and as her eyes widened and she said sharply, 'No!' he traced a snaking line from the corner of her mouth to the centre of one expectant breast.

His touch was so light that Cia glanced down, thinking dazedly that flames should be licking along the path his finger took.

Dry-mouthed, her body craving more, she managed to say, 'And I'm not going to be seduced into this, either. It's not just you and me—if I am pregnant, we have to think of the child. An unhappy marriage is sheer hell for children—trust me, I know.'

'Then we'll have to make sure it's not unhappy,' he said coolly. 'Has it ever occurred to you that falling in love with your cousin was an attempt at replacing your own useless father with one who loved you?'

Startled, she looked up into a face both angular and controlled. 'It could have been,' she admitted, wondering what other thoughts were circulating in the clever, analytical mind behind his angular features.

'And Maxime Lorraine?'

Her teeth clamped on her lip. 'I did use Maxime,' she said, low-voiced. 'I liked him so much—and it's no excuse, but I was vulnerable and unhappy.'

Knowing she wouldn't make a difference, she tried to make Hunt understand. 'I hoped—I thought I could will myself into loving him. But I didn't feel—when he tried to make love, I realised I couldn't. So I told him it wasn't—that I was sorry.'

Hunt got up and walked across to the window. 'What sticks in my craw,' he said with cutting contempt, 'is the cold deliberateness of your behaviour.'

That hurt, but he was right. 'You can't make me feel worse than I already do about it,' she said wearily.

'And your timing.' He laid out his objections with the merciless dispassion of a judge. 'How could you have been unaware of his father's business problems? Lorraine's is one of the biggest conglomerates in France.'

'I told you, Alexa and I were organising a wedding,' she flared, indignation driving her. 'It was a madhouse, and I simply didn't have time to read the papers and watch television.' She paused, then said bluntly, 'I can't prove I didn't know, just as I can't prove that I was a virgin.'

Silence spun a web of tension between them. Hunt didn't move; he didn't believe her.

Shrivelling inside, she added, 'But it wasn't my refusal that drove him to Africa; he had every intention of going on that expedition. He knew his father wouldn't approve, but he was excited about it; he thought it would prove once and for all that he was his father's son.' Poor Maxime.

Hunt was staring out of the window, broad back and shoulders making a perfect male triangle above his narrow hips and long, muscled legs. Every waiting nerve strung taut, Cia took in several deep breaths and tried to regulate her pounding heartbeat.

She didn't ask for love from Hunt, but if he didn't believe her, she couldn't marry him. Trust was imperative in any relationship. Especially marriage, she thought wretchedly.

'None of that matters now,' he said indifferently, turning to look at her with burnished blue eyes, emotionless and fully in control. 'I'll make an appointment for you to see my doctor as soon as possible. But even if there's only a fifty per cent chance that you might be pregnant, you're marrying me.'

Under the shower a few minutes later, Cia let the hot water play over her shivering body. He meant it.

For a weak, stupid few moments she let herself fantasise that she could be content with crumbs rather than the feast. Better a loveless, practical union than never seeing him again.

After all, plenty of her ancestors had coped with an arranged marriage. The sex would be fabulous, and in time he might learn to trust her.

Colour heated her skin and with a short, vicious twist of her wrist she turned the water on to cold and endured it for several depressing moments until she flicked it off and got out.

'Is that a pig I see flying above the trees?' she wondered aloud, rubbing her hair.

And then she wept a little into the soft towel, because she'd made a terrible mess of everything.

She'd just emerged from the shower when someone knocked on the bedroom door. Nausea roiled in her stomach. Now that the adrenalin surge of quarrelling with Hunt had faded she was exhausted and ominously weepy.

After more deep breaths she went across and opened the door. Without preamble, Hunt said, 'I have to leave. There's been a forestry fire in Sarawak with deaths—I need to be there.'

'How many deaths?' she asked quickly.

'About ten so far.' His hard features clamped into a harsh mask. 'This is a joint venture with several villages—if I'm on the spot I can see what's needed, and I have the power to get equipment into the area. Cia, I need your promise that you'll do nothing about this situation until I come back.'

'You have no right to ask that of me,' she said quietly, hurting.

He hesitated, then asked with rough insistence, 'Please.'

One of the disadvantages of loving someone, she discovered, was the desire for them to be happy. With a touch of bitterness, she said, 'I'll stay.'

He nodded and looked at her, and then reached for and kissed her, a hard, swift kiss that frightened her with its savage intensity. 'I'll see you when I get back,' he promised, and left her.

Half an hour later she waved at the plane from the terrace with an inward shiver.

The fire—a huge jungle fire set by subsistence farmers—made the following night's news, as did Hunt's arrival with specialist firefighters and aid. Cia watched greedily, then went to bed with that dart of fear working itself further into her heart.

The next day she decided she needed to go into the nearest town to buy a few odds and ends. When she told Marty, the housekeeper looked surprised.

'Make a list out,' she suggested, 'and I'll order them for you.'

Cia said pleasantly, 'I'd rather get them for myself, thank

you. I could take the Range Rover—I have an international driver's licence.'

Marty gave her a wary glance. 'I don't think Hunt would approve of that,' she said quickly. 'Our roads are pretty bad. I'll go in with you.' She glanced at the clock in the huge kitchen. 'Give me half an hour.'

Not only did she drive Cia in, she stayed with her while she did her shopping. Cia realised with a sick fury that Hunt had given orders for her not to be given a chance to leave.

It reinforced every fear she had about the marriage; Hunt's lack of trust chilled her. It was bleakly ironic, she thought when they'd arrived back home, that she had gone from not being able to have the man she wanted, to an offer of marriage from the man she loved—one she didn't dare accept.

Hunt came back four days later, after the fire had been doused with no further loss of life. Cia was cutting flowers for a vase when she heard the sound of the plane. Her heart lifted in sudden, fierce joy.

The plane came in from the sea and swung over the house. As it disappeared below the bush to land, she heard an alteration in the sound of the engines.

Her heart stopped. And then she heard the crash.

CHAPTER ELEVEN

AFTERWARDS she could never remember what she did between hearing the rending, tearing groan as metal tore into the grassy paddock, and finding herself in the Range Rover with white-lipped Marty and Ben.

Marty said harshly, 'They'll be all right. They're both brilliant pilots.'

No one answered. The vehicle shot out from under the trees and up towards the airstrip. Well before they reached it they could see the plane, lying on its side in the grass with one wing torn free. Several people were clambering around it.

'Landing gear failed,' Ben muttered. 'At least it didn't flip. They should be all right—they'll have been wearing seat belts.'

Cia didn't dare let hope grow to more than a tiny flicker in case he was wrong.

As soon as the Rover stopped she forced open the door and jumped out. Snatches of images flashed across her brain as she ran towards the crippled plane—one of the shepherds talking into a mobile phone, a man racing back towards her, a woman standing with her hands pressed to her mouth.

When Cia had almost reached the plane she was grabbed and held. 'Let me go,' she panted, struggling with her captor.

'Miss, I can't. There's avgas leaking—you mustn't go any closer.'

Her heart stopped and for a second the bright grass and the wrecked plane whirled in hideous confusion. Ferocious blinking stopped the rotation. 'You can let me go,' she told him, swallowing hard. 'I'll stay here.'

He released her with alacrity, stepping back as Ben came to stand beside her. Gruffly he said, 'You can't do anything until they've got them out of the plane.'

She stared at the fuselage with straining eyes, searching for signs of movement. 'Are they—are they all right?' she croaked.

'They're both alive,' the man who had stopped her said, his voice sympathetic, 'but Hunt's in and out of consciousness. The ambulance is on the way, but they have to get them out of the plane as quickly as they can.'

He didn't say why, but she knew. The stench of leaking avgas was thick in her nostrils. She clamped down on rising hysteria and began to pray.

Ben said soothingly, 'If it had been going to burn it would have happened as soon as they crashed.'

Hunt, she thought painfully, willing him to be all right, to be barely hurt. Oh, God, please…

She spared a moment's prayer for the pilot, but her mind immediately jumped back to Hunt. A man roared up in a van and others dragged out poles that they assembled into a stretcher.

The pilot emerged first, shaken but conscious. It took them much longer to get Hunt out, but eventually he was flat on the stretcher. Men grabbed the poles and carried him across the strip, Marty jogging beside with a medical kit.

Rigid with anxiety, Cia made her way through the small group of people and stopped beside the stretcher, looking down at Hunt, lying strapped in. Blood streamed across his face from a wound on his forehead and beneath the deep tan, his skin was pale.

'It looks worse than it is,' Marty told her bracingly. 'He can feel his toes so it's pretty unlikely that he's got anything wrong with his spine, but the straps are just in case. Don't worry; he's as tough as old boots.'

'I know.' Cia's voice was low and bleak; the thought of all that splendid strength crushed and confined to a wheelchair made her feel sick.

Hunt opened his eyes and looked straight at her. The quiet hum of the onlookers faded; Cia smiled down at him and said, 'Well, you certainly know how to make an entrance. Next time, a little less drama, OK?'

Someone laughed, and Hunt lifted a hand. She knelt beside the stretcher and took it in both of hers. 'You've probably got a beastly headache; don't talk,' she said, and held his hand to her cheek.

She stayed like that until the ambulance arrived, only moving away to let the nurse stabilise him. A short distance away the pilot sat wrapped in a silver survival blanket. Pale and sweating, still in shock, he managed an awkward smile when she came across.

'How is Hunt?' he asked.

'He's going to be fine,' Cia said, desperately hoping she was right. 'How are you?'

'All right—I didn't hit my head.' He shrugged. 'I'm trying to work out what went wrong.'

'Don't worry about it—you got both of you down more or less undamaged.'

'Yeah, I suppose, your maj—highness?' He looked embarrassed.

Smiling, Cia said, 'My name is Lucia.'

He lifted his head and listened, then said with relief, 'Here comes the chopper.'

It came in with noisy brashness, disgorging people who went about their business in a kind of organised rush.

When Ben came across Cia asked in a thin voice, 'What's happening?'

'They'll take them to the hospital to check them over,' Ben said.

'I'm going too.' Cia ran across towards the big chopper, determined to stay with Hunt.

A pleasant woman barred the way. 'I'm sorry, but—'

'I want to be with Hunt,' Cia said fiercely. 'I'm his fiancée.'

From behind Marty said, 'I'll drive down with some clothes and your bag—you might need to stay the night if he's got concussion.'

'Thank you.' Cia ducked. Wind from the big rotors whipped around her as she ran across and scrambled into the helicopter.

Hunt still lay with his eyes closed, the cut above his eye bruising fast. Cia knelt and breathed his name, and to his astonishment his eyes opened. His lips formed her name and her tears started to fall softly and silently.

Carefully, she laid her head down against his and whispered, 'It's all right. Everything's going to be all right.'

'Can you hold her hand?' the woman who'd tried to stop her asked Hunt.

He lifted his and clasped Cia's, and the woman laughed. 'And you can wiggle your toes so there's not much wrong with you,' she said. 'But we'll make sure everything's in good shape before we send you home.'

Cia held his hand all the way down to the hospital. Once there she huddled in a waiting room while he went through interminable procedures, grateful when Marty and Ben arrived because talking to them took her mind off the appalling things that could have happened.

When at last she was allowed into Hunt's room, he turned his head to watch her come in.

'How are you?' she asked, suddenly shy.

'According to the medics, I'm fine. Slightly bruised, but not anything to worry about. How are you?'

Her lips trembled. 'All right now you're all right.' She blinked back tears. 'You look very interesting. That bandage across your head is an improvement. Did you have stitches?'

'Only those butterfly sutures.' He swallowed and she found a glass of water and held it to his lips.

After he'd sipped some he said ironically, 'Not the way I'd planned to return.'

'No. Don't ever do it again.'

A minor stir at the door heralded a doctor, who introduced himself and then said, 'Well, you and the pilot were pretty fortunate. We're keeping you both for observation tonight, but there's nothing wrong with either of you. If you have a good night your fiancée can take you home tomorrow morning.'

When he'd gone, Hunt said, 'Fiancée?'

Colour streaking her cheeks, she muttered, 'They weren't going to let me on the helicopter.'

'Ah, I see.' He was silent, and then he opened his eyes again. 'You're crying.'

'I'm allowed to be a bit emotional,' she said inadequately. 'I love you.'

He was silent for a long time, then said, 'A fine time to tell me.'

'It doesn't matter. Go to sleep.'

His head must have been throbbing because he closed his eyes again and drifted off. Cia allowed Marty and Ben to take her to a motel, where she spent much of the long night wondering what had possessed her to blurt out her greatest secret.

Hunt, sporting a rakish patch on his forehead and a formidable air of self-possession, was ready to head home when they arrived at the hospital the following morning. With Marty and Ben in the car as well, Cia didn't expect him to refer to her confession of the night before, but as he sat silent and aloof beside her on the drive back to Hinekura, the joyous expectancy she'd woken with faded.

She wanted him to go to bed when they got home, but he refused. 'I'm fine,' he told her, brows drawing together. 'You, however, look a bit pale. Why don't you rest?'

'I might do that,' Cia said. Clearly he was in no mood to talk.

In her room she stood by the window and looked out across the garden she'd come to love. Once again she felt torn, but this time between a tremulous hope and a cold dread.

She'd nailed her colours to the mast; there was no going back for her. Hunt knew she loved him.

The rest of the day passed uneasily; the media had got wind of the crash, so Marty spent a lot of time fending off telephone calls. An insurance agent came and went, and an inspector of aviation accidents flew in by helicopter to check the plane. The farm manager was closeted with Hunt for most of the afternoon; during dinner he spoke firmly of nothings, and went to bed early.

At breakfast the next morning he said, 'Would you like to go to the beach today?'

Cia looked up. 'The beach?'

Was he going to tell her that he didn't want to marry her after all? A sensible marriage was one thing; marrying a woman who'd admitted she loved you was a much more complex situation.

'We'll take the Range Rover and some lunch and spend the day there.'

Apprehension churned her stomach. 'It would be lovely,' she said sedately. 'I'll drive, though.'

This produced the first smile she'd seen since he'd come back from hospital. 'Fine. You might as well learn how to drive on the left.'

Once she got behind the wheel, Hunt explained the gears and gave her directions, his cool pragmatism easing the spiky tension between them. While she was concentrating on negotiating farm roads, she could banish the thoughts that chased fruitlessly through her brain.

It took almost an hour to get there, and as she braked to a stop outside the little bach she remembered with aching clarity the days—and nights—they'd spent there.

'You're a good driver,' Hunt told her.

Smiling, she switched off the engine. 'Thank you. Still no headache?'

He gave her a quizzical glance. 'Not today.'

Still formal, still somewhat detached, as though warding off any intimate conversation, yet his eyes kindled whenever he looked at her.

Because the simple pleasure of being alone with him was enough, she forced herself to relax in the warmth of the sun, to walk along the warm sand beside him and breathe in the sharp tang of salt and talk inconsequentially.

Back by the car they spread out a rug and sat down on it. And Hunt said quietly, 'When did you realise that you were no longer in love with Luka?'

Cia had been picking out the pattern on the rug with a stem of dry grass. It wavered in her hand, but she said steadily, 'I wasn't ever *in* love with him. I know that now. Love killed my mother, so I chose someone unattainable.'

'Safe,' he said.

Yes, he understood. She nodded. 'I always knew that he'd never love me as a man loves the woman he wants.'

'But when he married Alexa you were desolate.'

She flushed. 'I wasn't ready to admit that I was too scared to trust any man enough to fall in love with him!'

'So you chose Maxime, whom you didn't love, because he was safe too.'

'At least I didn't go through with it—I'd have made him utterly wretched.' Cia glanced at him, and then glanced away again. 'I pray he didn't let himself die because he was unhappy—'

'Very few young men in the prime of life allow themselves to die of a broken heart,' Hunt said brusquely. 'The expedition wasn't well organised. When it ran into trouble they had very little medication left—not enough to get him through a bout of fever.'

'Did his father tell you that too?'

'Yes. I dropped in to see him on my way back from Sarawak. While he was dealing with Maxime's estate he discovered that Maxime funded the expedition, so he'd contacted an expedition member, who was much more forthcoming than the official account had been.'

She should have felt relieved that she'd been vindicated, but she still grieved for the laughing young man who had been such fun. Over the lump in her throat, she said, 'His death was such a waste.'

'But not your fault.' He waited then said with an abrupt change of subject, 'I'm sorry for putting you through that scene.'

She moved uncomfortably. 'I understand why you were so angry.'

'Nevertheless, I had no right to subject you to such a confrontation. And not realising that you were pregnant is no excuse.' Leaning back on his elbows, he watched her from hooded eyes. 'You didn't go to bed with him; why did you go to bed with me?'

'Because I couldn't stop myself,' she said honestly. She

flushed, but met his eyes. 'I despised myself because I was convinced that Luka was the love of my life, yet I wanted you desperately.'

Eyes intent, Hunt said, 'That's sex, not love. The two are not necessarily connected.'

Cia's heart contracted. Somehow she had to convince him that as well as wanting him she loved him.

'I know the difference,' she said, dropping the grass stem to loop her hands round her knees. 'Meeting you—making love with you—made me realise that what I felt for Luka was a child's hero-worship. I didn't *want* to accept that because I felt such an idiot for suffering all those years for some unrealistic dream. Of course I love him—but not the way I love you.'

'You think you love me because I gave you your first experience of sex. It's good—hell, with you it's bloody fantastic!—but don't fool yourself that it's love,' he said indifferently.

His cool, judicial words stripped the last, hidden, shameful thread of hope from her. This, she thought desperately, is the most important conversation I've ever had. She paused, searching for words to explain how she felt. 'I know the difference. I wanted you before I loved you. That might make me a freak, but it doesn't make me stupid.'

'You're not a freak,' he said bluntly. 'You're an intensely passionate woman with a thing about control.'

'Listen to who's talking!' she returned childishly.

He was watching her with hooded eyes that concealed everything but glittering blue sparks.

Controlling a kick of panic beneath her ribs, she said, 'When you were on Dacia you took over my mind; I couldn't think of anything but you, where you were, what you were doing—I was so aware of you my skin hurt and my brain buzzed! I really enjoyed being with you, I loved the way we talked, and I felt renewed, a different person.'

She got to her feet and walked across to the nearest pohutukawa, tracing its furrowed bark with her forefinger. 'As for confusing sex with love—the day before yesterday when we drove up to the airstrip thinking you'd been killed, I wasn't worrying about how much I'd miss the sex!'

Hunt was silent, and she thought bleakly, *He doesn't believe me. He'll never believe me.*

And she knew that marrying him would kill some essential part of her. She said quietly, 'Hunt, it's no good. I saw what an unequal marriage did to my mother; I'm not going to let it happen to me.'

From behind her Hunt drawled, 'You're stronger than your mother ever was. And in this, princess, you have no choice. If you don't agree to marry me I'll contact the first tabloid I can and feed them details of our relationship—including the fact that you spent so many years in love with your cousin.'

She froze. 'You wouldn't.'

'I don't imagine either Alexa or your cousin would enjoy the resultant uproar,' he said implacably. 'Nor would the baby when it's old enough to realise what happened.'

Cia knew he was tough, had accepted that he was formidable and determined, but his ruthlessness appalled her. She remembered the horror of her mother's death, the avid interest, the mobs of journalists yelling her name and the flash of cameras. To her horror tears gathered in her eyes and began to spill over onto her cheeks.

'Why won't you believe me?' she blurted as she scrabbled for her handkerchief, so angry she could barely speak. 'What makes you so smugly sure that you can read my mind and my emotions? What do you want me to do to prove it to you—give you my heart's blood? I refuse to be black-mailed into marriage.'

She scrubbed her eyes and gulped, hauling up the last remnants of self-control.

Apparently unmoved, he said, 'When did you fall in love with me?'

The sound of the tiny waves sweeping the beach provided a peaceful background to the conversation, a bitter contrast to the turmoil that fogged her brain and clogged her thought processes.

'You walked through the gate at the airport and started being snide and sarcastic and I thought, Who does he think he is? I don't believe in love at first sight, but I was running scared from that moment, because my world changed when you walked into it.'

'I know the feeling,' he said harshly. 'I saw the woman who'd driven Maxime Lorraine to his death, and my first thought scared the hell out of me. I wondered if I was rich enough to have a chance. I've never felt such abject need, and I resisted it with everything I had.'

'There is nothing abject about you!' she snapped.

'Cia, what I'm trying to tell you—and making a pig's breakfast of it—is that all this angst isn't necessary.'

She didn't hear him move, but his arms around her were hard and purposeful, and the heat of his body surrounded her, sapping her strength and fogging her brain. He didn't try to turn her, but kissed the tingling back of her neck and murmured, 'Love, sex, whatever—we have more than that to forge a relationship from. If we don't set our sights too high, we can make a decent marriage.'

Shaken and desperate because she wasn't getting through to him, Cia felt something inside her snap. 'I've little taste for ritual humiliation,' she said in a low, passionate voice.

'I'm sorry you think that marriage to me will be humil-

iating, but you'll do it just the same, if I have to drag you
to the altar,' he promised, his level voice utterly convincing.
'That's a given, princess. So is the fact that I'll be faithful,
and the best husband and father I can be. Why is it so
important that I believe you love me?'

'I don't know! Pride, I suppose—and because I'm not a
child. I know how I feel.' In frustrated impotence, she
clenched her fist and punched the trunk of the ancient tree.

Hunt moved like a hunting leopard, snatching her hand
and cradling it in his own. 'Stop that!' he commanded, and
as though driven, lifted it and kissed the reddening skin.

Cia's eyes filled with tears again. 'I don't usually bawl
all the time,' she wept.

On a goaded note, Hunt said, 'It's all right. Don't cry—
don't cry, damn you.'

His arms tightened around her and although the temptation to lean against his big body and accept his support was
almost overwhelming, she resisted.

'You make me so angry!' she snarled into his shoulder.

'I can see that.' His voice sounded shaken. 'No, don't hit
me.'

'I wasn't going to!' She gulped again, and this time gave
in, surrendering to the strong haven of his arms with a sense
of such profound homecoming that she knew she'd never
be free of him.

He said in a wry voice, 'Right from the beginning, I was
sure that hiding under that cool, very English, very royal
princess there was a volatile Latin.'

And he lifted her, carrying her back to the rug. Still holding her, he sat down, and tucked her comfortably against
him.

Tears drying miraculously, Cia glowered at him. 'So
every chance you got you tried to dig her out.'

Hunt acknowledged the accusation with a sardonic smile.

'Only to find that your patrician self-control seems pretty damned shatterproof except when we make love.'

Heat arrowed through Cia, tempting, hugely seductive. I'm going to give in, she thought fatalistically.

He paused and when he spoke she sensed that he was picking his words carefully. 'This has all happened far too quickly. We've known each other less than a month, and neither of us have been thinking straight, but when that plane came down I could only think, *I'll never see her again.* And I knew I'd go down into death in rage and desperation.'

Tears ached at the back of her throat.

'Stop fighting,' he murmured, his mouth tracking across her forehead. 'We'll make a good marriage—I want you and our baby to be happy.'

When she opened her mouth to speak he kissed her parted lips, and as the sweet, familiar hunger burst into flames inside her she surrendered, as she would always surrender to Hunt because she loved him.

Although they made love with a powerful energy fuelled by the adrenalin left over from their quarrel, Hunt was infinitely tender, until she tantalised him into taking her without finesse, his raw sexual drive sending her into that welcome place that was theirs alone.

Much later he smoothed a long tress of tangled hair back from her face. 'We need to get married as soon as possible.'

She hesitated, then accepted her destiny with a faint, bitter regret that she had better get used to, because it would be with her for the rest of her life. 'But first we should make sure that I am pregnant.'

'Even without the test, I'd know you're pregnant.'

'How?'

'There's a glow about you, a softer kind of radiance,' he said with calm certainty. He pressed a line of kisses across her waist. 'And once I'd got rid of the idea of jet lag, your sleeping habits are a giveaway.'

Lifting her with him, he sat up and cuddled her against him, resting his cheek on her hair. 'I suggest we marry in Dacia. That way Luka can make sure it's not a media circus. Here, if news gets out, we might not be able to stop helicopters from buzzing the ceremony.'

Her cheek warm against the hard muscles of his chest, Cia shuddered. 'I'd like to be married there. And I think it should be private.'

He kissed her eyelids closed. 'I'll marry you in the biggest, most elaborate wedding you can organise, if that's what you want.'

'No thanks,' she said smartly. 'I've discovered the values of privacy while I've been in New Zealand. But if we are married in Dacia, Alexa's pregnancy means nobody would be surprised at a small wedding.'

'I don't care if the whole world knows you're pregnant,' he said, the words deep and quiet in his throat. 'In fact, some primitive male part of me feels like shouting it out to everyone at the top of my voice. I want you and our child safe and secure and with me.'

Eyes brimming with tears again, she touched his face. 'You'll be a wonderful father. I hope I'm not going to sob my way through this entire pregnancy!'

'Hormones,' he said with a laugh. 'Come on, let's get back to the homestead and finalise some plans.'

That night, just before she went to sleep in his arms, Cia wondered again if she'd sold her soul to the future. As sleep pulled her under, she decided that it was done; there could be no going back. Hunt might not love her, but he wanted her and the child she was now sure rested under her heart, and she had time on her side. He wouldn't abandon them as her father had abandoned her and her mother; his word was his bond.

Three weeks later they were married in the small chapel at the Old Palace. Luka gave her away, and Alexa made a charming matron of honour; the only other people in the chapel were friends and the closest members of her family.

Afterwards they drove through streets filled with cheering, petal-throwing Dacians to the Little Palace, where they held a reception for local worthies followed by an informal lunch.

Alexa went up with Cia to help her change and said when they were alone, 'I don't need to ask if you're happy— you're positively shining with it.'

'I feel great.' Cia removed the small emerald tiara from her head. She'd never wear it again; it belonged to the women of the Dacian royal family, and she was now Mrs Hunter Radcliffe.

Her heart sang.

Alexa laughed. 'I notice you no longer seem to mind the way Hunt calls you princess,' she said slyly.

'I rather like it,' Cia admitted.

'I imagine you would, the way he says it! It's terrific that our babies will be so close in age,' Alexa remarked, skilfully removing the exquisite lace train that fell gracefully from the back of Cia's silk chiffon dress, cut in neoclassical lines.

Cia froze. 'Oh,' she said. And then guiltily, 'I was going to tell you soon.'

Alexa hugged her. 'Luka and I guessed the minute we saw you. Luka's delighted, and so am I. Right from the start I was pretty sure that you and Hunt were meant for each other.'

Astonished, Cia said, 'Why? We have nothing in common!'

'This sounds hugely silly, but you look right together,' Alexa told her seriously. 'Like a really good photograph—something just fits.' She grinned. 'And of course we'd have had to be blind and deaf and stupid not to register the bolts of lightning between you! I'm so glad I convinced Luka not to object when you went to New Zealand with Hunt—he was all set to come over patriarchal and insist you go to England.'

Cia looked at her. 'Are you a witch?'

'I just want everyone to be as happy as I am. What are you going to do about your plans for university?'

'Hunt tells me that New Zealand has an excellent system for students who can't attend lectures,' Cia said. 'I'll use that.'

'Good for you.' Alexa kissed Cia's cheek. 'You deserve every happiness. Now, let me help you into that lovely suit.'

Cia nodded, but as she changed into her going-away outfit, she wondered if she was crazy to want more, when most other women would envy her.

She had made her bed; she had to lie in it.

The loud clatter of a helicopter coming in low overhead brought Cia to her feet. She walked across to the window of her office and looked out over a scene of seeming confusion. A quick glance reassured her that everything was going to plan; the marquee was up and although people were moving around, there was purpose in their actions. She examined the sky with narrowed eyes, but so far the forecasters had been spot-on; it wouldn't rain on the day of the annual Hinekura stud-bull sale.

Smiling, she went back to her lists.

A little later, a knock on the door whirled her around. 'Come in.'

It was Hunt, and as ever, her heart skipped a beat. 'I

thought it would be you,' she said, going swiftly towards him. 'Good trip?'

'Not too bad, but I'm damned glad to be home.' He held her close, his smile both tender and fierce. 'How are you both?'

'The baby and I are fine,' she said demurely, and pressed his hand against her thickening waist. 'Very active—she's heard your voice and is glad you're back.'

'Are you glad too?' Hunt tipped her chin so that he could see her face.

She nodded. 'Of course.'

'I love you, Lucia.'

In the five months of their marriage Cia had been happier than ever before. But now, with his eyes burning into hers and his hand on her waist as their child kicked with vigour, she rejoiced as the last citadel fell and Hunt let her see his real emotions.

'I love you too,' she said quietly.

He kissed her as though she was something rare and precious. 'I don't know why it took me so long to admit it. My father's experience with love didn't help; he loved my mother until the day he died—but even when I found that the more I have of you, the more I want, I wouldn't accept that it was anything more than a passionate friendship.'

Cia knew him much better than she had when they married. 'You said once that I had a problem with control,' she reminded him. 'You do too.'

'And once you admit you love someone, you hand over control to them.' He looked down at her face, his own stark with purpose. 'Every second of every day I spend with you tightens the chains. I want more from you than the rapturous welcome of your body and your quick, clever brain, your tact and discretion and brilliant organisation.'

She touched his cheek gently, the canary diamond of her

engagement ring flashing in the low winter sunlight. 'You've got it,' she told him, her voice soft. 'You've got everything.'

His arms tightened around her. With his cheek on her hair he said harshly, 'I love you so much, my darling, my dearest girl, my princess. You've warmed my cold heart and my life. Each morning I wake up and I think, She's here and we have the rest of our lives together, but I've never told you because it gave you such power.'

'What made you decide to do it today?' She was so happy she could barely articulate the words.

'I missed you so much, and I thought about the crash, and I knew I was just being a coward. You had the guts to tell me you loved me; I wanted you to know.' Eyes gleaming, he looked down at her. 'So, my heart's delight, will you forgive me for being so damned stubborn?'

'You ask that of a woman who convinced herself she was in love with a man for about ten years and never once asked herself why she didn't want to make love to him?' She laughed. 'Forgiveness isn't necessary. Just don't ever stop loving me.'

'I swear.'

He kissed her, and then she said, 'Oh! I forgot to tell you—Alexa had her baby this morning. A big, bonny boy, and they're both well. Luka was over the moon.'

The telephone rang and she said something crisp in Dacian beneath her breath, disentangled herself and answered it.

Hunt watched her, amazed at the freedom finally saying those three words had given him. She was beginning to round out deliciously, and their baby was making her presence felt. He laughed out loud, thinking he could take on the world and conquer it for his princess. She looked up and the golden glow in her eyes filled his life.

Smiling, she hung up and came across, and he said deep in his throat, 'When I hold you, I hold all that's important in my life.'

'Ditto.'

Their child kicked her vigorously again, and they both laughed, and went out into their future together.

PREGNANT: FATHER NEEDED

by

Barbara McMahon

Barbara McMahon was born and raised in the American South but settled in California after spending a year flying around the world for an international airline. After settling down to raise a family and wok for a computer firm, she began writing when her children started school. Now, feeling fortunate in being able to realise a long-held dream of quitting her 'day job' and writing full-time, she and her husband have moved to the Sierra Nevada mountains of California, where she finds her desire to write is stronger than ever. With the beauty of the mountains visible from her windows, and the pace of life slower than the hectic San Francisco Bay Area where they previously resided, she finds more time than ever to think up stories and characters and share them with others through writing. Barbara loves to hear from readers. You can reach her at PO Box 977, Pioneer, CA 95666-0977, USA. Readers can also contact Barbara at her website: www.barbaramcmahon.com

Don't miss Barbara McMahon's exciting new novel, *Greek Boss, Dream Proposal*, available in August 2009 from Mills & Boon® Romance.

FDNY – We'll Always Remember

Thanks to the men and woman of the United States
Armed Forces – Thank you. May you all return
home to live long and prosper.

PROLOGUE

AMBER WOODWORTH sat in the front of the small church, trying her best to ignore the words the minister spoke. Her gaze was fixed on the flag-draped coffin at the front. Her husband of less than three months was inside. She still couldn't believe it. How could Jimmy have been talking on the phone with her one day and dead three days later? Their marriage hadn't really started. Now it would never unfold as they once dreamed.

Tears threatened again. She took a deep breath. If she could just hold on a little longer, she could escape to the sanctuary of her apartment and fall into tiny pieces.

Her mother reached out and squeezed her hand. Amber tried to smile at her, but it was too hard. Her mother and new stepfather, Matt, had been so supportive these last few days. Amber didn't know what she would have done without them. She knew she could depend on them to help her in every way possible. But it would never change the fact she had to go on alone.

No, not quite alone.

She hugged her secret. Her mother knew, and Matt. But no one else. She hadn't even had a chance to tell Jimmy.

Now he would never know he would have become a father in November.

She glanced at her mother. She was also pregnant—with Matt's child. How odd to be pregnant the same time as her mother. Her friend Kathy from high school was pregnant, but that was normal. Not that her mother was so old, but Amber still felt it peculiar to know she and her mother would have their babies practically at the same time. Would she ever think of that child as a brother or sister? She'd literally be old enough to be its mother.

The minister finished his eulogy and the last hymn was sung. On her left, Jimmy's mother sobbed. Amber knew Virginia Woodworth would grieve her son's passing the rest of her life. She had doted on him. Maybe too much.

Amber remembered how uncomfortable she'd been with Virginia interfering in their brief marriage. The woman had stopped by the apartment almost every day. Amber sometimes thought Jimmy stayed at the Army Base to avoid his mother.

That was unkind. He had been involved in his job. But she'd resented the time he'd spent at work or staying overnight at the Base when he could have been with her. If they'd known he had such a short time remaining, would it have made a difference?

The trip to the cemetery passed in a blur. As did the short graveside service. When Taps sounded, Amber let the tears fall. She would never see Jimmy again. Never laugh with him, or plan a wonderful future together. She'd loved him since age fifteen. Almost five years. She had always thought they'd spend the rest of their lives together.

The military honor guard folded the flag, and handed it to the lieutenant. He stepped to her and offered it.

"On behalf of a grateful nation," he said solemnly.

She took it, hugging it to her breasts, looking through her tears at the polished casket. She would be twenty next month, and she was already a widow. How could she go on without the man she'd planned to spend her life with?

"It should have been mine," Virginia wailed. "He was my son for longer than he was her husband. It should have come to me."

Her husband tried to hush her, drawing her into his arms, but her cries grew louder. The others stared at her.

Amber was startled. She looked at her mother.

"Do I give it to her?" Amber asked.

Sara shook her head and spoke softly for only Amber. "It's yours. Save it for his child."

CHAPTER ONE

JULY was really a lovely month in San Francisco, Amber thought as she sat on the park bench and studied the ocean she could glimpse in the distance. A steady breeze blew from the west, keeping the temperatures cool. She felt as if she were awakening from hibernation. Which, in a way she was. Jimmy's death had been so unexpected, she'd seemed to view everything through a fog. But lately, she'd started to notice things.

Like the jogger who ran into view from her left. The park had an exercise course along the jogging track. Those who wished could stop and do the exercises in the fresh air and sunshine. The station opposite the bench consisted of iron bars at various heights for chin-ups.

She'd seen the man before. He came as regular as clockwork every other day at this time. Amber wondered if she'd decided to take a break at this particular moment because of that fact. Or could she convince herself her being here was purely coincidental?

She watched him as he stopped at the bars and began a series of chin-ups. His arms were muscular and he seemed to do the pull-ups without any effort. His back and shoulder muscles rippled and moved as he pulled himself up over and over. His T-shirt was tucked into the back of the waistband of his jogging shorts leaving that golden expanse of chest and back bare. Long, muscular legs ended in running shoes.

A light sheen of perspiration coated his tanned skin. She watched as he pulled himself up at least two dozen times. When he was finished, he glanced at her. Raising his hand in silent salute, he began jogging again, soon lost from sight.

She let out a breath she hadn't known she'd held.

Wow. He could be a calendar model with those shoulders and that muscular body. She had told her friend Bets about him. She'd wanted to come to see for herself, but Amber guarded this time. She didn't want to share.

Guilt assailed her. She couldn't be interested in another man, she'd just lost her husband.

Though, she argued, she was not really *interested,* it was more of an observation of a male physique.

All right, with a quick fluttering of interest—just to prove life goes on, as her mother had said.

Ten minutes later, enough time to make sure he'd passed the next station and was well beyond sight, she rose to head for home. Her finals were finished, her second year of college completed last month. She needed to sort through her papers and toss those she'd never need again. Then she had to clean out the flat and decide what to do about living arrangements in the future. A studio flat near the university wouldn't do when the baby arrived. She knew that. But she had delayed making any decisions until school ended.

She wasn't interested in moving in with her mother and stepfather, though they had both urged her to do so. Sara and Matt had married after her own wedding to Jimmy.

Amber considered them still newlyweds. She didn't want to intrude.

Besides, she was uncomfortable around them. They were so obviously in love. She envied her mother the lavish attention she received from her new husband. Amber hadn't had that during the few months she and Jimmy had been married. He'd been too caught up in his work. And in taking her for granted.

Crossing the street from the park, she turned toward the apartment building. She'd been coming to the park since the good weather arrived. She wasn't sure when she began noticing her jogger. A couple of weeks ago maybe? Now she waited each day to see him and wonder about him. Was he also a student that he could take time to jog in the middle of the afternoon? He seemed older than most students she knew.

Maybe he had a night job and exercised before heading off to work.

Not that she should be speculating at all, she chided herself as she opened the large glass door that led to the small lobby of the building. Her husband hadn't even been dead five months. Wasn't there supposed to be a year of mourning?

Her phone was ringing when she reached her apartment and she hurried inside to answer it.

"Amber?" It was Virginia Woodworth, her mother-in-law.

"Yes, Virginia." She sank on the sofa and leaned back. Another wave of guilt swept through her. She had not yet told Virginia and James that they would be grandparents before Christmas. They would be thrilled to know there was a baby of Jimmy's on the way. She was already starting to show. So why hadn't she told them?

"Where were you? I tried calling three times. James and I want you to come to dinner tonight. James wants to discuss dismantling Jimmy's room. I think it's too soon. What do you think?"

"When the time is right, you'll know it," Amber said. Virginia asked her this question at least once a week. Amber had been spared that kind of decision in her own home. She and Jimmy had never really lived together during their brief marriage.

What kind of marriage was that?

"It's not as if we need the room for anything else. I think we should leave it the way he had it."

"He's never coming back, Virginia," she said softly.

"I know that!" Virginia's voice cracked. "I can't believe my baby's gone."

Amber heard the tears and blinked back her own. She, too, had difficulty believing she'd never see him again. During the last two years, she'd only seen him a few weeks.

And he'd changed. She'd changed.

For the first time she wondered if they had married too quickly. Her mother had said so before the wedding. Amber remembered she'd urged them to wait until Jimmy finished his tour of duty. How different would things be if they had waited?

"I can't come for dinner tonight," Amber said. "I have plans. But I suggest you wait a little longer on the room." She didn't want to get in the middle of an argument between James and Virginia. Most of the time she sided with her father-in-law, which upset Virginia. But he took a much more pragmatic view of things, which Amber liked.

"What plans?" the older woman asked quickly.

Amber sighed softly. Lately Virginia had grown more

and more demanding. She wanted to spend time with Amber—to talk about Jimmy. She resented Amber's study time and school work. When courses ended for the summer, Virginia wanted to spend even more time with Amber.

Virginia seemed to have stopped on the day Jimmy died. And she expected Amber to stop everything as well.

Amber was trying her best to move forward.

Would knowing about the baby help or not?

"Virginia, I'd like to come to dinner on Saturday. Will that work for you and James?"

She'd tell them then. She had kept it a secret long enough. She had an appointment with her obstetrician on Friday, so she'd have the latest update to share. Maybe knowing about the baby would help Virginia move on. With a new baby to plan for, she could slowly let go of her son.

"Yes. Any time, you know that Amber. We'll look for you at six on Saturday."

Amber hung up the phone and looked at the photograph of Jimmy on the table.

"Your mother is driving me crazy," she said.

There was no response.

Guilt seemed to be a constant companion lately. Amber should be grieving as hard as Virginia, but she wasn't. She felt as if she were in limbo. She missed Jimmy, no denying that. But they hadn't been as inseparable in the last year or so as they had while in high school. She had her life and he had not fit into it. He'd been in the Army, and she certainly had not tried to fit in there.

She patted her stomach, wishing her baby could have known his father. Amber's own father had deserted them when she'd been three months old. She knew how much she'd missed having a father around while growing up. But there was nothing she could do about that. At least the baby would have Matt and James. Amber hadn't even had grandparents in her life.

Rising, she went to the kitchen to get a drink of lemonade. She would have to rely on friends and her stepfather to give her baby a male role model. She didn't think she was up to getting married again any time soon. If she ever did, it would be to a man with a safe occupation like an accountant or mechanic, not someone in a dangerous field like the armed forces!

Adam Carruthers pushed himself to finish the course. The highlight of his run had been the high bars—where the pretty blonde sat on the nearby bench. He'd first noticed her a few weeks ago. She seemed to visit the park every afternoon at the same time. And he'd made sure he was at the park the same time every afternoon he could make it.

Once finished with the bars, he began to lose interest in the exercise course. He remembered her smile the first time he'd waved. He kept trying to come up with a way to meet her, but not when he was wearing jogging shorts and sweating up a storm. Twice he'd returned to that area to see if he could strike up a conversation, but she'd been gone.

She must live near the park to come so frequently. He himself had an apartment in an older building only a couple of blocks away. It was close enough to the fire station he could walk to his shifts, and inexpensive due to its proximity to the University. Several of the other tenants were students. Not that he knew many of his neighbors; he'd only moved in a few weeks earlier when he'd been transferred from the Hunter's Point station.

He retraced his steps, noting the empty bench when he passed. Maybe Friday he'd forget working out and come to meet her.

Friday Amber caught the bus to her mother's new apartment in the Marina District. Matt opened the door when she rang the bell and gave her a quick hug.

"How are you doing?" he asked.

"Fine. How's Mom?"

"Also fine. She has more energy now that she's into the next trimester."

Amber smiled. Matt was thrilled about the new baby he and her mother were expecting. He would accompany them to the doctor's. She and her mother had decided to use the same obstetrician and had moved into a schedule that let them make their checkups at the same time. Matt often accompanied Sara, which had Amber feeling left out. But she still liked going with them. If Sara had the first appointment, sometimes Matt left afterward and Sara came in with Amber.

"Hi, honey," her mother said, joining them. She gave her a hug and kiss on the cheek.

"I hope I didn't keep you waiting long," Sara said, giving her husband a private smile.

Amber looked away. She had a good idea what they'd been doing to keep her mother so long. Envy struck again. She was delighted for her mother. It was way past time for her to find happiness with someone. Amber just wished she could have had that, too. She felt as if she hadn't been part of a couple in a long time. The short honeymoon and few weeks Jimmy had been on temporary duty stateside didn't count.

"We want to go to lunch afterward, is that okay with you?" Sara asked.

"I'll head for home, if it's all the same. Time's a little tight." Lunch would put her back too late to see her jogger today. And if he kept to the schedule, it would be Sunday before she saw him again.

"We'll run you home afterward," Matt said. "Save you riding the bus."

"Okay." She'd keep track of the time and make sure she was back early enough.

For a moment it struck her as funny she made such a big deal out of seeing a stranger from a distance for about ten minutes. But it had been so long since she wanted to do much of anything, she hoped this was a good sign.

She'd have to ask Bets. She wasn't sure she wanted her mother to know she was ogling strange men.

"I'm planning to tell Virginia and James about the baby tomorrow night," Amber said a short time later from the back seat of the new minivan Matt had bought for her mother. His sports car would not be suitable for a family, he'd declared. After a quick lunch, Matt would then drive her to her apartment.

"They'll be thrilled," Sara said, looking over her shoulder at her daughter. "Of course Virginia will want to know why you didn't tell her earlier. But James will simply be happy to hear the news."

"I'm hoping it'll give Virginia something to think about beside Jimmy. It's hard dealing with her, Mom. All she wants to do is look at old photographs, and talk about every aspect of his life. I know how well he did in school, what sports he played, who his friends were. I was there. But sometimes I think she doesn't remember that."

"It's hard for her, Amber. She's trying to hold on as best

she knows how. Time will help. And the news about the baby," Sara said gently.

"Want to go shopping with us tomorrow?" Matt asked. "We're going to check out cribs, changers, rocking chairs and other paraphernalia your mother assures me a newborn needs."

Amber smiled and shook her head. "I'll probably be getting my things from the secondhand store. But not yet. I have nowhere to store anything in my apartment. I have to move. Now that school is out, I need to concentrate on finding another place. Thank goodness Jimmy's insurance covers everything for a while. I don't know what kind of job I'd be able to get five months pregnant."

"You're not getting anything in a secondhand store," Matt said. "Doting grandparents to the forefront." He smiled at Sara. "We want to buy the baby's furnishings."

"I can't let you do that," Amber said.

"Sure you can, sweetie," her mother replied, reaching out to touch Matt's hand. "We want to. There's no reason to say no. You just have to pick out what you want."

Amber was overwhelmed by their generosity. She blinked back tears. "Let me get an apartment first."

"I still have the one we lived in. You could move there," Sara suggested tentatively.

"Mom, you moved out of it a couple of months ago. Why are you still holding on to that place?"

Sara was silent for a moment, then looked at Amber. "Because of rent control, and how long we lived there, the rates are low. I wondered if you'd like to move in after I heard about Jimmy. I didn't want to pressure you in any way, but it does have two bedrooms, it's on the bus line, and you know where everything is. It's a nice neighborhood. Still no pressure, but think about it."

"I will." She swallowed the lump in her throat. Her mother had always taken such great care of her. Would she be able to take such good care of her baby? Her mother had been left alone with her newborn when her husband abandoned them. Her parents had never helped. Amber was far better off with her mother and Matt to offer support. And she knew Virginia and James would help out for Jimmy's sake.

She could do this. She'd love her child and raise him or her to be the best person possible. And tell them stories of their father. Jimmy would have loved children.

Amber made sure she was at the park early. The doctor's appointment had reassured her everything was progressing normally. She'd taken a battery of tests, normal procedures these days. She was scheduled for another sonogram in a few weeks. So far she'd held off finding out the gender of her baby. She had until then to decide if she wanted to wait until it was born.

She was showing, but not a lot. Her appetite hadn't been that robust after hearing about Jimmy. The doctor had said everything was fine. She could still wear some of her clothes, but soon would be forced into maternity attire.

Sitting on the park bench, she leaned back, letting the hot sun shine on her face. She felt happier than she had since she'd received the news about Jimmy. In only a few months she'd have a new baby to love and raise, and a new brother or sister to get to know. And if her baby was born first, it would be older than its aunt or uncle. How weird was that?

She waited. Time moved slowly. She looked down the path. No jogger.

A young mother pushed a toddler in a stroller. Birds sang in the trees. The breeze was missing today, it was hotter than it had been earlier in the week.

Still Amber waited. She checked her watch. He hadn't come earlier, had he? She thought she'd been here with time to spare. But as the minutes slowly ticked by, she knew she wasn't going to see the man today.

The disappointment was surprising. She didn't even know his name. She knew nothing about him. Yet, she waited with anticipation each day to see him.

A half hour later she gave up. Would he come tomorrow instead? She'd be here just in case. She had time before her dinner engagement with the Woodworths.

CHAPTER TWO

AMBER was feeling almost sick by the time she arrived at the Woodworths' home Saturday afternoon. She'd been lucky to miss the morning sickness that her mother experienced from time to time. She hadn't gained much weight. Even the tiredness her mother felt wasn't a problem.

But telling Jimmy's parents had her so nervous she was stressed to the max.

Virginia greeted her sadly, hugging her for a long moment, as if capturing some of her son through Amber.

James waited for his hug, then ushered her into the living room.

"At loose ends now that summer is half over?" he asked when they were seated. Virginia hovered about, pouring iced tea.

"Not really. I have a lot to plan for," Amber said.

"School starts up again in September, what will you do until then?" Virginia asked.

"Sit down, please, Virginia, I have something to tell you," Amber said. She had rehearsed what she'd say over and over. Why was she feeling so defensive? They would be delighted with the news.

Virginia perched on the edge of the sofa beside her husband, looking worried. "What is it?"

"I'm pregnant. I'm going to have a baby in November. You two will be grandparents," Amber said quickly.

The older couple stared at her.

"Pregnant?" James said.

"With Jimmy's baby?" Virginia asked, a spark of enthusiasm showing for the first time in months. "Why didn't you tell us before? How long have you known? How are you feeling? Oh, James. We are going to be grandparents. I never expected this when we heard the terrible news."

James hugged his wife and smiled at Amber.

"That is wonderful, honey."

"Why didn't you tell us sooner?" Virginia asked, struggling to free herself from her husband's embrace. "You must have known before today. Did Jimmy know?"

Amber shook her head. "I didn't know the last time I spoke with him. I never had a chance to tell him."

"But you had a chance to tell us before now," Virginia said waspishly. "Why haven't you told us before today?"

"Dear, the important thing is we know now," James said, a hint of warning in his tone.

"When is it due? We have such plans to make. You should move in with us, dear, rather than stay in that poky little apartment where you're living. There's lots of room here. You have no room for a baby in your place. You can have the guest room and the baby can have Jimmy's room."

"Thank you, Virginia. I appreciate the offer, but I do have options. My mother and Matt have invited me to live with them—"

"Ridiculous. Your mother is expecting a new baby herself. She'll have enough to deal with without a second infant. I insist."

"Actually, I also have another choice. For the time being, I'm thinking of moving back into our old apartment. It has two bedrooms, one for me and one for the baby when it comes. And it'll be close to both you and Mom."

"I won't hear of it. I insist you move in with us. Do you know if it's a boy or girl yet? We'll have to get new furniture, we didn't keep Jimmy's baby things, did we, James?" Virginia jumped up, a list of things she wanted to do tumbling forth.

Amber watched, bemused. She had hoped for some enthusiasm, some indication Virginia could move on, but this was getting out of hand. She had no intention of living with Jimmy's parents. And despite the plans Virginia was making, Amber was the mother of the baby. She would decide where she lived and the furniture she wanted.

James picked up on Amber's silence. "Virginia, let's discuss this further over dinner. I think we are all hungry."

"How can you think about food? James—we're going to be grandparents!"

"But not tonight. We invited Amber for dinner, let's feed the girl."

Amber tuned Virginia out through much of the meal. The older woman needed no response to her verbal list-making. She would have the child's life planned through college, if Amber allowed it. Let the woman dream. It was better than more recent thoughts. Time enough for Amber to let Virginia know what she would be doing. Nothing had to be decided tonight.

She wondered how Jimmy would have viewed a baby. They had not discussed children. He had been focused on his work in the Army. When they married, she'd wanted to finish college and begin teaching before starting a family. Would he have been happy to have a baby so early?

Not that it would have had the impact on his life it did on hers.

If she budgeted carefully, could she still take classes? Maybe her mother or Virginia would watch the baby while she finished school. Long before the child was ready for kindergarten, she'd have her degree and be ready to teach.

Amber came back to the present when Virginia's voice stopped. She looked at her.

"Did you hear a word I said?" Virginia asked, with a trace of frustration.

"I'm afraid I was thinking about the future. I hope I can get my teaching credentials by the time the baby is ready for school. It would be the perfect job. I'll be home summers and holidays and not need childcare except for a few hours a day."

"Nonsense. You have no need to work. We can take care of you and Jimmy's child."

"I don't plan to be a stay-at-home mother," Amber said, remembering her own mother had worked. They had always been close despite the hours apart. And Amber thought she had a pretty terrific childhood to remember.

"Maybe you should consider letting us raise the child," Virginia said slowly. "You're young, have your whole life ahead of you. We can raise him. Tell him about his daddy. You go get your job."

Amber shook her head. "I'll raise my own child. But I do hope his grandparents will be an integral part of his or her life."

Amber left as soon as she felt she could politely do

so once dinner was finished. She didn't want to rock the boat with her relations with the Woodworths, but she was tired of Virginia's assumption she'd play a major role in her child's future. She would be one of two grandmothers. And of the two, Amber would count on her own mother more.

She called her friend Bets when she got home.

"How'd it go?" Bets asked when she heard Amber's voice.

"Virginia is obsessing on the baby now. She even asked me to let her raise the baby."

"She misses Jimmy. Stand tough."

"I plan to."

"So, did you see your friend?"

"What friend?" Amber suspected she knew who Bets meant, but she played dumb.

"Oh yeah, like you have a lot of secret friends."

"I don't even know the man."

"So take him some water. It's got to be hot work showing off to the ladies, offer him some next time."

Amber laughed. Never in a million years could she envision herself doing such a thing.

"Bets, I'm not looking to meet him. I just enjoy looking at him."

"Hon, you didn't die when Jimmy did. You need to find yourself another hunk and move on."

"He hasn't been dead that long."

"But he's been gone forever. I never even met the man and we've been friends for almost two years."

Amber acknowledged the fact. When Jimmy had flown home for a few weeks' temporary duty in San Francisco, they'd rushed to get married. Bets had been invited to the wedding, but had been unable to attend. The few times

Jimmy was available after that, Amber had selfishly wanted his attention, not to share him with friends.

"I'm not looking to become part of a couple again any time soon," Amber said.

"Fine. Give it a little longer. But don't shut yourself away just because Jimmy died. It's the pits, don't get me wrong. But you're too young to stay a widow the rest of your life. Want to go to the show tomorrow afternoon?"

Amber was tempted. But Sunday was a jogging day.

"Maybe later in the week."

They chatted for a little longer, then Amber said goodbye. She couldn't believe she was turning down a guaranteed fun afternoon with her friend on the off chance she'd get to briefly glimpse a man she didn't even know.

The next afternoon Amber went to the park early. She hoped her jogger showed today. She wanted something to take her mind off the confrontation with her mother-in-law. Virginia had already called once today, suggesting Amber come over to discuss things. The baby wasn't due for another four months, but Virginia was anxious to make plans.

Once again her jogger didn't appear. Had he stopped exercising? Maybe he had worked a night shift and his hours had been changed. Or maybe he was a student and had gone home for part of the summer.

Whatever the reason, Amber was disappointed that she hadn't seen him.

Instead of craving ice cream and pickles while pregnant, was she getting fixated on a stranger? She wanted her fix of seeing the man, admiring his body as he exercised, maybe even fantasizing about meeting him one day.

Like he'd be at all interested in a pregnant woman who,

if her mother was to be believed, would soon look and feel like a walrus.

Not that she wanted someone interested in her. Not exactly. But she was lonely. Had been for more than a year. Brief e-mails from Jimmy hadn't done much to alleviate that feeling when he'd been alive. Now she didn't even have that.

After three more visits to the park, Amber was ready to give up her quest. The man was obviously not running in the early afternoons anymore. She had to find something else to do at one.

Saturday afternoon was a busy time at the park. There were little children chasing each other around. More people used the jogging path and exercise equipment. An elderly couple strolled along the grassy edge, talking quietly.

She watched as squirrels ran up the trees. The sun was too hot to sit in for long. Maybe she'd take a walk along the path for some mild exercise. She had only packing to look forward to when she returned to her apartment.

"Hi."

She looked up, and blinked in surprise. Her jogger was standing right in front of her, fully clothed, with his arm in a sling.

"Hi. I missed you, were you in an accident?" she asked, taking in the cast on his arm, and burns along his neck and cheek.

He sat beside her. "Slight altercation with a recalcitrant fire. Can't run for a while."

Amber felt fluttery as he leaned against the wooden back. She'd never even waved to him when he waved to her. Now she'd told him she missed him. How dumb was that? But embarrassment didn't explain the tingling feeling that swept through her. He sat too close, taking up her space. She was more aware of him than she'd ever been when he'd been wearing jogging shorts. How had he managed to steal the very air she was trying to breathe?

"I'm sorry," she said. The burns didn't look too bad, but were still red and blistered. "What happened to your arm?"

Keep it friendly and normal, she thought. Her gaze was drawn to his mouth. To lips that were firmly shaped and moved enticingly as he talked.

"Broke it when I fell through a floor. I'll be good to go in a few weeks. Until then, no chin-ups." He nodded toward the bars.

"Or jogging, either, I expect," she said, smiling at him. A warm glow began to replace the flutters. *He'd stopped to talk to her.*

"I'm Adam Carruthers," he said, offering a hand.

"Amber Woodworth," she said, taking it. "Was it your house that burned?" She withdrew her hand, clenching it into a fist. His palm had been warm, hard, as if callused. His dark eyes looked directly into hers. Somewhere she heard the background noise of the children, but she felt detached—cocooned alone with Adam Carruthers.

"Not mine. I'm a firefighter. We were trying to save an old building off Masonic. The fire had too much of a hold on it. We lost it."

"Oh. That's a dangerous field. I'm glad you weren't badly injured." A firefighter—that would explain his ability to exercise in midafternoon. Didn't they work alternating days?

"Do you come to the park often?" he asked.

"Almost every day. I'm going to miss it." Miss you.

"But I'm moving soon. There isn't a park near my new place," she said. Time to end this. There was no future in a friendship. Before long, she'd be back at the apartment across town she and her mother had shared. Adam would still be living in this section of the city. It was unlikely they'd have any reason to run into each other.

She'd miss watching him, though.

She rose. "I'm glad you're going to be all right."

He stood beside her. "When are you moving?"

"End of the month, or early next. My lease is up the end of August and I'm not renewing. I've got to go now. Goodbye." She had to leave before she thought up a bunch of reasons to stay in touch, to return to the park in the afternoons and watch as he ran past showing more skin than was good for her equilibrium.

"I'll walk with you," he said, falling into step.

"My apartment isn't far. I don't need an escort. Goodbye."

"Goodbye, Amber Woodworth."

She turned and walked out of the park. Waiting at the traffic light, she noticed he'd followed her and was standing a couple of paces behind her. When the signal turned, she hurried across the street and turned toward her place. She could hear his footsteps behind her.

Turning, she stopped and put her hands on her hips. "Are you following me?"

"Now that sort of depends on your point of view," he said, stopping a few yards away. Even from that distance, Amber could see the mocking amusement in his eyes.

"What does that mean?" she asked suspiciously.

"You're going in the direction I'm headed, so if my walking behind you is following you, then, yes I am. On the other hand, if you turn off before I do, and I keep going, then no, I'm not following you."

"You go first," she said. He didn't look dangerous, but one never knew. Though she didn't feel threatened by a man with a broken arm. Or one who seemed to be laughing at her.

The amusement in his eyes irritated her. She waited for him to walk past, then began following him. At the next intersection, he turned onto her street. How had he known where she lived?

He glanced back when he was partway down and when she turned onto the street, he called, "Are you following me?"

At least she lived in a secure building. He couldn't get inside unless she let him in.

"No, I live in that building." She pointed to one ahead of them.

He looked at it, then back at her. "I live there, top floor, right side."

That information startled her. Was it true?

"Are you a student?" he asked.

She nodded.

"Figures. There are a lot of students in the building. Pleased to meet you, neighbor." He turned and headed to the building. When he drew near the bank of mailboxes, he pointed to one. She stepped closer and read the name: A. Carruthers.

He moved his finger along the names and stopped by hers, A. Woodworth. Then he opened the lobby door with his key, holding it for her.

Amber stepped by him to enter, smelling a woodsy scent as she passed. Her heart raced. Her mind wanted to explore this connection just a little more. What could it hurt? She wasn't moving away for a couple of weeks. To be friends with someone didn't mean a lifelong connection.

"Thank you," she said and walked to the small elevator. He stayed by the door, watching her with those amused eyes. "Is it following you if I ride up the elevator in the same car?"

"A woman can't be too careful," she said primly. Wouldn't her mother be proud of her?

The amusement left. "You're absolutely right. If I make you uncomfortable, ride up alone. I'll wait."

"Don't be silly. Come on. I'm on the fourth floor, left side in a studio."

Amber wondered if she'd made a mistake when the elevator doors slid shut. Adam seemed to fill the space in the small car. She tried to ignore the sensations that began to clamor inside, the fluttery feeling had returned. She wanted to check her hair, make sure her lipstick was still on. The loose top she wore camouflaged her blossoming figure. Would he have noticed? She noticed every thing about him, from the crinkles near his eyes, to the over six foot height, to the trimmed dark hair, worn longer than Army regulations.

She was more conscious of him beside her than she expected. Bets would say something, do something to end the awkwardness. But Amber remained tongue-tied.

Fortunately the elevator lumbered to her floor and stopped. When the doors opened, Adam reached out to hold them from closing as she stepped out.

"Want to meet on the roof for a drink later?" he asked.

The building had a flat roof, a portion of which had been covered with wooden decking and a railing. The landlord allowed tenants to bring their own chairs and tables and use it as a private garden area. Amber had loved that feature when she rented the apartment last summer.

"Amber, where have you been?" Virginia came down the hall. "I've been waiting more than twenty minutes. I didn't expect you to be away from home." Virginia gave Adam a sharp look.

"Who is this?"

"This is Adam Carruthers—a neighbor. Adam, Virginia Woodworth."

"Her mother-in-law," Virginia said quickly. "Come along, Amber, I have some catalogs to show you."

Adam watched as Amber turned to walk away with the harridan who had accosted them. Feeling poleaxed, he stepped back inside the elevator and pushed the button for his floor.

He hadn't known she was married! He tried to remember if there was a ring on her finger. Surely he would have noticed.

Even if he hadn't, what was she doing flirting with strange men when she had a husband?

He was disappointed in the fact she was unavailable. Not that he was looking for a lifelong commitment, just a friendly neighbor to hang out with from time to time.

And if he'd wanted to explore where this sexual awareness might lead, well, that was normal. But not if she was married. He didn't mess with other men's wives.

He let himself into his apartment. So much for trying to find out more about the lady who seemed mesmerized by his body. He'd been deluding himself. Or maybe he'd totally misread the situation. For all he knew, she'd hadn't been watching him but mentally compiling a grocery list. Laughing wryly, he headed for the kitchen.

He'd get a cold soda and head for the roof. Nothing else to do. They'd released him from the hospital yesterday. He was on medical leave from the department until he got an okay from the doctor. Which would be in about six weeks when his arm healed and he could pass the physical.

So what was he going to do for that long?

"Where were you?" Virginia persisted as Amber unlocked her door.

"I went for a walk to the park. As I do most days," she said. "What are you doing here?"

"I came to see you. Can't a woman visit her daughter-in-law?" Virginia said defensively.

"Of course. I didn't expect you, however. Otherwise I would have stayed home until you arrived. Have a seat. Would you like something to drink?" If Virginia hadn't been here, would Amber now be on the roof with Adam sharing a cold drink?

"I'll take iced tea if you have it. Who was that man?"

"A neighbor. He lives on one of the upper floors." Amber quickly prepared the beverage for Virginia. She took some water for herself and went to sit beside the older woman.

"What did you bring?" She stifled a sigh. She hoped Virginia wasn't going to prove difficult. She wanted to decide for herself what she and her baby would be doing, not fall into Virginia's wishes without comment.

Virginia pulled a catalog from her purse, opening it to a double page spread of baby furniture. "I got this from the baby store. They have lots of furniture on display, but this gives the full range. I thought that was nice," she said, pointing to a fancy French provincial baby set.

Amber closed the catalog and handed it to Virginia. "I

told you, my mother and Matt are buying the baby's bedroom furnishings."

"We're the baby's grandparents, too. I want to do something. Your mother doesn't need to do this. She has her own
baby coming. I have no one. I'm buying the crib."

How did Amber handle this? She didn't want to hurt
Jimmy's mother. But the woman was driving her crazy.

"Virginia, we don't need to do anything today. I've got
to move and get settled before I'll be ready to think about
acquiring more furniture. We'll have time to discuss all this
after I've moved."

"I don't see anything to discuss," Virginia said in a huff.

"There'll be lots of things to talk about. But not today."

"Amber, you are just putting off the inevitable. Time
goes by so quickly. Before you know it, you'll have the
baby here and not be ready. I say get prepared early."

"I will, I promise. Where is James today?"

"He went to play golf."

"Maybe you should take up the game."

"I hardly think so," Virginia said, not at all mollified by
Amber's attempts to defuse the situation.

What her mother-in-law needed was a hobby, Amber
thought. Something to take her mind off her lost son, and
the coming baby. She had never worked outside the home,
though Amber thought she was a member of some wom-
en's club.

"Did that man know you were married?" Virginia asked
suddenly.

Amber looked at her. It struck her—

"Technically, I am not married, Virginia," she said
slowly. She had never really felt married. They'd had a
lovely honeymoon the week after the wedding, then five

other nights scattered across several weeks before Jimmy had left. They had never gone grocery shopping together, argued over which television show to watch, or had friends to dinner.

"What do you mean? Of course you're married." Virginia looked shocked.

"Actually, the vows were until death parted us," Amber said gently.

"So you're dating again?" Her shocked tone couldn't have been worse.

"I am not! Virginia, the man rode up in the elevator with me. He's a neighbor, nothing more."

"He asked you for a drink, I heard him."

"A neighbor being friendly. You're making too much of this."

"Come stay with James and me. Your mother is busy, school is finished for the year. You don't need either apartment. We have plenty of room."

"I'm not going to move in with you, Virginia. Thank you for the offer, but I moved out from Mom's when I went to college. I'm grown up now and I like being on my own. Please stop pressuring me about this." Amber wasn't sure what she had to do to keep Virginia from trying to take over her life, but she'd do whatever it took.

"Well, if offering you a home is pressure, I'm sure I didn't mean it." She rose and snatched up the catalog. "I'll see myself out."

Which didn't mean much, Amber thought with a hint of amusement. The apartment was a single large room, with an area for a kitchen and a private bath.

She felt bad for Virginia, but knew she needed to stand firm or the woman would take over her life.

"She needs a hobby," Amber said to herself once Virginia had gone. "What would fill her need to be needed?" Something beside her grandchild!

A half hour later, Amber rode the elevator to the roof. She stepped out onto the decking, looking around. There was no one else in sight. She refused to admit she was disappointed.

She walked to one of the chairs she'd left up here and sat down. She'd miss this feature when she moved back to the apartment she'd grown up in. There was no park nearby, nor a rooftop garden.

The sun was still warm, but there was more of a breeze. The bright sparkling water of the Pacific could be seen. She loved this feature about the apartment building.

But she wouldn't be far from the marina and the wharf or Fort Mason in the other flat, so there'd be plenty of places to walk.

Only none would have Adam Carruthers.

She remembered the amusement in his eyes when he looked at her. Slowly she smiled. He was a good-looking man, even when he wore clothes. Had it been hard to get dressed one-handed? It was probably difficult to prepare food.

Maybe, as a good neighborly gesture, she should prepare dinner for him tonight. She could make something easy to eat one-handed, and take it up around six. No one could find fault with that, could they? It was a neighborly thing to do.

CHAPTER THREE

EXACTLY at six o'clock, Amber rang the bell for apartment 5C. The shepherd's pie had turned out perfectly. It was an easy meal to prepare, and easy to eat without needing to use a knife.

Adam opened the door, obviously surprised to see her.

"I thought it might be difficult to cook, so I made you this," she said brightly, holding out the covered plate.

He looked at the plate then at her for a long moment.

"Thank you, that's kind of you."

He stood aside and gestured for her to enter.

Amber stepped inside the apartment and looked around. It was sparsely furnished, with few pictures on the walls. Those that had been hung were photographs of white water rivers and soaring mountains. She liked the bold, clean lines of the room.

He pointed to the dining table near the window. "I usually eat there. Is it hot, or do I need to warm it up?"

"Do you have a microwave?"

He nodded.

"You might wish to put it in for a couple of minutes. I just dished it up, but it cooled coming up here."

"Nice of you to take the time. I'd invite you to stay, but I guess your husband will expect you right back."

She looked at him. "My husband was killed several months ago, overseas. He was in the Army."

"God, I'm sorry. I didn't know that. From what that woman said earlier, I expected him to be waiting in the apartment."

"A studio would be cramped quarters for two," she said. Turning she reached for the doorknob. "I hope you enjoy the meal."

"Wait." He reached the door at the same time and held it shut. "Join me, unless you have other plans. Is your mother-in-law still downstairs?"

"She left shortly after she arrived." Amber hesitated. She hadn't expected an invitation. Yet, why not? He was alone, so was she. A meal together would be a change from the lonely meals she'd eaten during the last months.

"Okay. I'll run down and get my plate and be right back."

Adam waited by the door. He felt like he was on a roller coaster. First he thought she was single, then learned she was married. Only she wasn't still married, she was a widow. She couldn't be more than twenty or twenty-one. Hell of a deal to be widowed so young.

He was sorry for the husband. But he was not sorry she was single again. How long ago had the husband died? Was she starting to date again? He wanted to be first in line if that was the case.

Glancing at the cast, he shook his head. Who would have thought being laid up was a way to get attention?

She was back in only a moment, smiling shyly. Reminding himself they'd just met and she hadn't a clue to the fantasies he'd woven starring the two of them, he vowed to take things slowly.

The meal was delicious. And so he told her.

"I'm glad you like it," she replied. "Can you cook?"

"Enough to get by, but not with this," he said, raising the cast. "Maybe in another week or two, but right now my arm aches too much to use it. I was planning to order in."

"That's fun, once in a while."

"Not as good as home cooking," he agreed. "So what course work are you taking at the University?"

"I want to be a primary school teacher. I've just finished my second year, so I still have a long way to go."

"Good job choice. Teachers are underrated, I've always thought."

She smiled at him, and Adam felt a spark of awareness shoot right to the center. She should smile more often; she was beautiful when she did.

"I think so, too. And they can make such a difference at the early stages of education. I want all my students to love to learn, and achieve great things."

And everyone would probably do his or her best if they received a smile from the teacher. He would, for sure.

"Just as I want that for my baby," she finished.

Adam stared at her. "You're pregnant?" He looked at her. She didn't look pregnant. Maybe a little pudgy around the waist, but he'd been more interested in her blue eyes and bright smile than taking inventory of her figure.

"Yes, I'm almost five months along. Which makes it doubly hard not to have a husband and father for the baby. I wish that was different."

Being pregnant was worse than being married. Married,

she was off limits. Being pregnant and a widow, she suddenly took on a new look. Did her comment mean she would welcome a new husband and father for her baby? Was she on the prowl for a man?

"I don't do happy ever after," he blurted out.

"Pardon me?" She stared at him in surprise.

"I'm not looking for any kind of long-term relationship." Might as well be upfront about everything.

"Neither am I," Amber said, pushing back her chair. "Did you think I was coming on to you? I was just making a neighborly gesture bringing supper, not looking for some kind of relationship. I lost my husband only a few months ago. What kind of person do you think I am? I'm not looking for some substitute for Jimmy. And even if I were, the last person I'd choose would be another man in a dangerous occupation. If I ever get married again, which I doubt, it'll be to some nice guy who's an accountant or salesman where the most dangerous thing he does is drive to work each day!"

"Hey, you said you wished that was different. What would any man think?" he protested.

"That a neighbor offered to help him out when he hurt his arm," she retorted, rising and taking her plate, and reaching over for his. She looked into his eyes, fire sparking from her own. "I didn't realize your ego was so monumental you'd misinterpret an act of kindness for a come-on. But thank you for expanding my education. I'm always ready for that. I won't make such a gesture again any time soon."

He hadn't finished the meal, but she snatched up the plate and headed for the door.

"Wait."

But this time Amber Woodworth didn't wait a heartbeat. One moment she was storming away, the next gone.

Adam groaned aloud. He'd made a total mess of the evening. She'd been kind enough to bring him dinner and he acted like she had been hunting him down. He was an idiot. He rubbed his face with his good hand, wincing when he touched the burned skin.

He hated relationships. He could certainly understand her reluctance to get involved with anyone doing what he did. Casual dating was all he was good for. And after this fiasco, he wasn't sure he was even good for that.

He'd been so surprised to learn she was pregnant. Not that that excused his outburst. She had never given him a sign she was interested in him in any special way. Was his ego as inflated as she said that he expected every woman to have her own private get-Adam-married agenda?

Now he had to do the apology bit—and he hated that.

But he couldn't let her leave without some explanation. The irony of it all struck him as he headed downstairs. He hoped she'd listen to his apology.

Amber was so angry she'd like to spit. How dare that arrogant male think she had some designs on him when she was only trying to be helpful? As she scraped the remnants of dinner from their plates, she thought of a half dozen other scathing comments she should have blasted him with.

When she heard the bell ring, she paused. If it was Virginia again, she didn't know if she'd be able to keep a civil facade. She was angry and not in any hurry to get over it. Woe to anyone crossing her now.

Opening the door, she saw Adam. She slammed it

shut—only, quick reflexes prevailed and he caught it with his good hand, pushing it open.

"I'm sorry," he said.

The simple words dissipated some of the anger. He looked contrite. And good enough to eat.

That she'd even think that for a second spiked her anger again—this time toward herself.

"Fine. Goodbye." She pushed against the door.

He held it open.

"Let me explain. I know I came across sounding like a first-class jerk."

"You did." She crossed her arms, resigned to listening to some half-baked excuse for his acting the way he did. Was she supposed to forgive all and fall into his arms when he was done? Not likely! Her anger grew when she realized she was fighting the notion. Did she really want to fall into his arms?

"No one ever says anything, but I can see for myself what people do. My mother did."

"Your mother did what?"

"Tried to find a husband. My father abandoned her, she had me to raise. She wanted help. A natural enough desire. I think two parents are needed to raise a child."

"There are a lot of single parents, men and women, raising children just fine, thank you." She would not hear a word against her own mother.

"I know. But there are some who could do a whole lot better with a mate to share the responsibilities. So my immediate reaction to hearing you were pregnant was that you were on a husband hunt."

"I had a husband. He died. I don't need another."

"Amber, you're young. You'll change your mind."

She shrugged. "So you're sorry you leaped to conclusions based on your mother's husband hunt. Fine. Apology accepted. Shut the door behind you."

She returned to the kitchenette, struck by the similarities between Adam and her. Both had been raised by single mothers. But hers had not been out husband hunting. Sara had gotten an education, went to work and provided Amber with a terrific childhood. They might not have had a lot of material things, but they'd had what counted—love.

"So do we have a truce?" Adam asked.

She spun around. "I thought you left."

"You said close the door behind me, didn't say which side I should be on. No wonder you're moving, this place is small, especially if you're having a baby. I'm amazed you could cook for two. You should see the size of my kitchen in comparison. I'll never complain about it again."

"Why are you still here? You gave your apology, I accepted. End of discussion."

"Is it? Don't women usually harp on things long after they've passed?"

"More of your mother?"

"Girlfriends over the years."

"I'm not your girlfriend, not do I plan to be." She didn't want anything more to do with the man. How dare he think she was on some kind of husband hunt just because she cooked him a meal?

"Great. I'm not in the running for being a husband."

Amber stared at him suspiciously. "So that's settled. You can leave now."

"Fine. Thanks again for dinner. Maybe I'll run into you on the roof one day."

His tone suggested if he did, he'd probably push her off.

"Maybe. I go there sometimes. I need to take advantage of it since I won't have a rooftop garden at my new place." He couldn't scare her away from the roof just because he would be there.

"When are you moving? Maybe I can help."

"I have my own help."

"Just trying to be neighborly," he said.

"Right, or trying to get rid of me sooner. I'm here for another couple of weeks." She tilted her chin, glaring at him. She couldn't believe he'd thought she was chasing after him. With his attitude, no wonder he wasn't married. Who would have him?

He turned and went to the door, pausing as he opened it. "Thanks for dinner. I enjoyed what I had of it."

She raised her finger and shook it in front of him. "Don't blame me for that. If you hadn't come out with that totally inappropriate comment, you could have finished the meal. Remember that next time."

"You'll make a terrific teacher, you already have the finger down pat."

He gave her a two-finger salute and left.

Amber stood bemused. Her anger had fled. She almost laughed at his last comment.

Once she finished cleaning the kitchen, Amber went to call her mother.

"What's up?" Sara asked when she heard her daughter's voice.

"Nothing much. I wanted to go look at the old apartment tomorrow, if that's okay. You took most of the furnishings, right? What do I need to get?"

"We'll meet you there in the afternoon and go over things," Sara suggested. "Virginia called."

Amber sat on the sofa and leaned back, gazing at the ceiling. "About me living with them?" she guessed.

"She said it would be the best solution."

"We don't have a problem needing a solution. I'm all set. I did think to ask her to watch the baby some when I'm back in school, but now I don't know. Mom, she said she wanted to raise the baby herself, as if I want to go off somewhere and not be bothered. I love this baby. I haven't even held it yet, but know I'll love it forever. I'm not giving it up even to its grandparents."

"Give her some time."

"Like I have a choice. She's always coming over. When I move back to the other apartment, she'll only be a few blocks away. Maybe I should tell her I'm dating again," she grumbled.

"What's that? Dating?"

"She saw me with a neighbor and leaped to conclusions. If only she'd seen Adam tonight, all her fears would have been dispelled. The man thinks the world revolves around him and that every female in creation wants to marry him," she grumbled.

Her mother was silent.

"Mom?"

"Who is Adam?"

"A neighbor, he lives upstairs somewhere. I just met him at the park today." No need to burden her mother with the weeks of watching him. She had only met him today.

"Young and single?"

"Of course. And I have it on good authority he plans to stay that way. He thought just because I made dinner that I was after him. Especially after he learned I was pregnant."

Sara insisted on hearing the full story. Amber had trouble relating everything without giving away her trips to the park to watch him when he exercised. That part sounded too needy.

"Do you think I should stay home and not go anywhere for a while?" she asked. "I mean, I'm not mourning Jimmy like maybe I should."

"As to that, people mourn differently. I'm not sure there is a single correct way to mourn. Or a single time span that encompasses everything."

"Did you mourn my father's leaving?" Amber asked.

"In a way. But I think I was so angry at him, and so scared, the mourning was more for the way of life I had thought we'd share than anything else."

"That's the way I feel sometimes. That we never even had a start on a life together. We went steady in high school, then he left for the Army. He wasn't the same when he was here in February."

"As people mature, they do so at different rates. Maybe he went one way and you another."

"You've said we should have waited."

"Maybe. Maybe not. No one expected him to be killed. I think you have to decide how you want to face the future and not waste time lamenting the past," Sara said. "And that will include dating and possibly falling for some other guy."

"And if I ever do, he'll have a safe job where I won't have to worry he'll go off and get himself killed," Amber said with spirit.

"Um, sounds like a plan. What does your neighbor do?"

"He's a firefighter. He broke his arm fighting a fire last week, and it's in a cast."

"So he's not in the running."

"Mom, I'm not looking for anyone right now. I have enough with the baby and school and all."

"We'll meet you at the apartment tomorrow afternoon and decide what you need to get going. Still want to go shopping for baby things next week?"

"I'd like to see what's out there. But don't tell Virginia, she wants to buy everything. I know she's a grandmother, but she's never been close with me and I don't see this as a bonding time."

"Just be patient. You're her last link to Jimmy until the baby comes."

"I guess. What are you and Matt doing tonight?"

"We're getting ready to eat dinner, then, gee, I don't know. I'm sure we'll find something to do," Sara said vaguely.

Amber laughed. "You go, Mom! But don't tell me everything. I'm still the child."

"Honey, you've grown up fast. But some X-rated things are still too much for my baby girl's ears."

Amber hung up a few minutes later, glad for the happiness in her mother's voice. But once the connection was broken, she was enveloped by a wave of loneliness. There was no one special for her anymore.

She had friends she could call, but it wasn't the same. Kathy was pregnant, but happily married. Bets was great, but not suffering from loneliness or a lack of dates.

Was she the only person in the city home alone tonight?

No, there was at least one other—the insufferable man in 5C who did not want to be married.

Cheered by the thought, she headed for the bathroom. A long soak in a hot tub would be just the way to get relaxed before bed.

* * *

Sunday Amber spent the early part of the afternoon with her mother at their old apartment. They planned the furniture she wanted for the baby, and one or two other things she would need to get to furnish the rest of the apartment.

"So have you thought of baby names yet?" Sara asked as they measured some of the windows for which Amber wanted new curtains.

"No. I thought I should check with Virginia to see if there are any family names or something. If it's a boy, I could call him James after his father and grandfather."

"Have you decided whether or not to find out the sex of the baby at our next appointment?" Sara asked.

"Have you?"

She nodded. "We've discussed it endlessly. Matt really wants to know. I guess it'll be fun to know ahead of time. We can decorate accordingly, and not be stuck with yellow or green. I didn't know with you. You were a surprise."

"I'm sort of hoping for a girl," Amber said. "It would be easier on a girl not having a father than a little boy."

"Oh, honey, you'll be a wonderful mother. Boy or girl, they'll never want for anything."

"I know. Still, it would be nice to have a father for my baby." For a moment Adam's face flashed into her mind. Amber shook her head as if to knock the image away. He had made it perfectly clear he was not interested in any pregnant woman. He probably hated children. And she was not interested in hooking up with any man at this point. She had lots more to do before she wanted to risk her heart again.

"Matt will be in high heaven if he gets to act as father to your baby. He can hardly wait for ours," Sara said.

"What a turnaround. You were afraid a few weeks ago

he'd leave when he learned you were pregnant. Now he's curtailed his traveling and knows more about babies than I do
from all the books he's reading," Amber said in amazement.

"Once the idea took hold, he ran with it," Sara said, smiling serenely. "He's excited about the baby. I'm so glad."
She jotted down the last measurement and looked up.

"Want to go out for something to eat? I'm craving a hot
fudge sundae."

"I'll have one with you, then head home."

"No cravings?" Sara asked as they left the apartment.

Just seeing Adam run by and stop at the exercise bar,
Amber thought, though she shook her head at her mother's question. She frowned. She was over that craving,
after having met the man. At least she hoped she was.

When Amber returned to her apartment later, she spotted
Virginia's car parked at the curb. Sighing, she entered the
building. What did she have to do to have some privacy?
This made the fifth day in a row Virginia had come by. She
was no longer content with telephone calls.

Stepping into the elevator, Amber hesitated a moment,
then in a gesture of rebellion, pressed the button for the
rooftop. She'd sit on the deck a while and hope Virginia
would get tired of waiting and leave.

Amber scanned the garden area when she arrived at the
roof. There was that couple from the second floor. A student she recognized from campus looked asleep on a
lounge chair. And Adam Carruthers, sitting near the edge,
looking toward the ocean.

She walked over and sat in the chaise next to him. He
glanced up, frowned and looked back to the ocean.

"How are you feeling today?" she asked.

"Hungry," he said.

She smiled. Maybe next time he'd learn not to snap at the hand that fed him. Though he'd had plenty of time to eat since dinner last night.

"So order in," she said, leaning back and gazing in the same direction. Sunshine sparkled on the water. The rays felt warm against her skin and she began to relax as she let the soft breeze cool her skin. Too bad there wasn't a larger apartment in her price range in this building. Then she wouldn't have to move.

"Mothers should be more compassionate," he mumbled halfheartedly. He was leaning back in the chair, his eyes narrowed against the sun's glare.

"I will be to my child," she replied. "But I'll also teach him to be polite so when someone feeds him he gets to finish the meal."

"How was I to know you're so touchy?"

"You could ask, how was I to know you would immediately leap to stupid conclusions."

He glanced at her. "You always bring your purse up to the roof?"

"No. My mother-in-law's car is out front. I thought I'd stop here first. Don't get me wrong, she's a lovely lady. But she's driving me crazy. First because of Jimmy, now because of the baby."

"Jimmy?"

"My husband." Amber felt Jimmy slipping further and further from her memory every day. She had pictures of him in the apartment, but when closing her eyes, she had trouble visualizing him. No trouble in remembering things they had done in high school or the plans they'd made. Just difficulty in remembering how his hair fell and the way his eyes looked into hers.

"You must really miss him."

"Not really." She opened her eyes and stared at him in dismay. "That didn't come out right. I do miss him. I can't believe I won't ever see him again. But for the last couple of years, he was stationed overseas, so we didn't have much to do with each other except e-mail. Then he was home for a few weeks, and now he's gone forever. It's so weird."

"Tell me about him," Adam suggested.

"Why?"

He shrugged. "Give you something to talk about and me something to listen to. I tried going to the fire station today, but the watch commander booted me out and told me not to show up again until I was ready to work. He means well, I know, but I'm bored with my own company."

"So hearing about a stranger you'll never meet is better than nothing?" she asked.

"Listening to your voice is what I'm after," he said.

"I'll read you a book." Amber was flattered by his implication.

"Tell me about Jimmy instead."

She complied, starting when they first met, what fun they'd had in high school, and how bummed she'd been when he enlisted.

"Sounds to me like he had some growing up to do."

"He was grown up. He was twenty-one."

"A great age."

"How old are you?"

"Twenty-seven. And from here twenty-one looks young."

"I'm only twenty."

"A baby," he teased.

She glared at him. "Not. I'm grown up. Soon I'll be a mother."

"Do you and the kid a favor. Give him up for adoption."

"What? Give up my baby? Are you nuts?"

"It's a hard life for a single parent. Much better for both of you to avoid the pitfalls before you become attached."

"Just because your childhood wasn't so great doesn't mean every child with a single parent can't have a terrific life. My mother was single almost my entire life. She went to school and raised me before getting a job. We had a great life."

"Where is she now?"

"Here in the city. She got married shortly after Jimmy and I married. I'm happy for her, but she wasn't searching for some man to take care of her like you said your mother was."

"My mother was the neediest woman I ever saw. She didn't seem to think she could do anything on her own, so she didn't. She complained about my father the entire time I was growing up. And tried to find a new father for me. Only it was really about someone for her. She was scared to be on her own."

"That's sad. I bet she did fine."

He was silent for a couple of moments. "You're right," he said with some surprise. "We had a clean apartment, never went hungry. It wasn't the life she wanted, though, and she never accepted what she had. She was always searching."

"Where is she now?"

"She died a couple of years ago."

"I'm sorry."

"Yeah, me, too."

"No siblings?" Amber asked.

He shook his head. "You?"

"I'm going to have a baby brother or sister in November."

"What?"

She nodded. "My mother is pregnant. She and Matt are thrilled. And her baby and mine are due practically the same day."

"You and your mother are pregnant? At the same time? How old is she?"

"She's thirty-eight. Matt's a few years younger. They're thrilled."

"What happened to your father?"

"He left when I was a baby. What happened to yours?"

"Same. Not named Carruthers, was he?"

"Nope, Simpson."

Adam fell silent, letting the quiet grow. Amber relaxed against the chair, almost dozing in the sun's warmth. She could stay up here the rest of the afternoon. And would, if Virginia didn't leave. When she had a bit more energy, she'd go to the railing to see if she could spot the car. Surely Virginia would get tired of waiting in the hall and leave.

"Want to get a pizza later?" Adam asked.

Amber was almost asleep. She rolled her head along the back of the chaise and looked at him through narrowed eyes. "I guess."

"I'll buy and we'll eat at my place. Then if you get in a snit, you can leave without finishing the meal."

She smiled sleepily and closed her eyes. "Sounds like a plan."

CHAPTER FOUR

ADAM looked at her. She was asleep. He glanced at her skin. It was not turning pink, but he'd keep an eye on the time. She didn't need to get sunburned.

He leaned back and tried to let go of the feeling he'd just done something stupid. How could he push her away with one hand and invite her to dinner with the other?

Looking at her again, as if unable to help himself, he knew the answer. She was better company than a rerun on television.

Heck, she was actually fun to be around. Prickly as all get out, maybe, but then he hadn't been at his best since accusing her of trying to trap him in marriage. At least he'd cleared that up. She wasn't looking for a man and he wasn't looking for a woman. Maybe they could muddle through until she moved. It beat being alone.

He didn't like to think how much of his life was wrapped up in his work. But being banned from the station sure made an impact. He'd call some of the guys tomorrow and see if they wanted to hang out on their day off. Three of the men on his shift were also single, though Bart had a steady girl. The other men and women were married, and always talking about family outings and obligations.

He liked being single. Being responsible for someone else's happiness seemed a burden too big to be borne. No wonder his father had left. Had Amber's father felt the same? Adam had more integrity than to desert someone who depended on him. Much better never to get entangled than to have to make a decision like that.

He nudged Amber's shoulder a little later. He was getting hot and wanted to get out of the sun. "I'm going inside. I think you should, too."

"Not if Virginia is still here," she mumbled.

"I'll check if you like."

She nodded sleepily.

He headed for the elevator. No one was left on the deck but Amber. The sun was low, but there were still several hours of daylight left. He'd make sure the way was clear and then see about ordering pizza.

The hall on her floor was empty. Did the older woman hound her? Maybe Amber should take a stronger stance and make sure Virginia got the message. He shook his head. From what he'd seen so far, Amber was too kind for her own good.

Reaching the rooftop in short order, he called across the expanse. "Coast clear."

She waved a hand but didn't sit up.

"You need to get out of the sun," Adam said, crossing the deck.

"I need to take a nap," she said grumpily.

"Downstairs, then." He pulled her up onto her feet almost laughing at the cranky look she gave him.

"Not if Virginia calls to see if I'm home."

"Nap on my bed, then. She can't call my place."

"Um."

Amber stumbled when she took a step. Adam put his un-injured arm around her waist and pulled her close against him. "No falling," he instructed.

Less than five minutes later he was in his apartment, a pretty blonde in his bed. Adam sat in the living room wondering what had possessed him to invite her to his bed. Now he would have a hard time not seeing her there when he went and used it himself.

He switched on the television, surfing until he found an old war movie. Not the greatest thing on the tube, but it was something to pass the time until his guest woke up and they could eat.

Amber awoke, disoriented as to where she was. The bed was huge, much bigger than her own single. The room was dark, shades pulled. The duvet on which she lay was as soft as a cloud. She ran her fingertips over the velvet cover. She remembered Adam letting her use his room so she didn't have to go home and be awakened by the phone if Virginia called.

Slowly she sat up. How late was it?

She went to the bathroom and splashed water on her face. She felt better for the nap. Heading to the living room, she stopped when she saw him sprawled on the sofa in the midst of some gun battle on TV.

"Sorry I slept so long," she said.

He looked over at her. "You obviously needed the rest."

She nodded. "I don't always sleep through the night. What are you watching?"

"It's almost over." He clicked it off. "A World War Two flick. I know how it ends."

She laughed.

"Ready for pizza? What do you want on it?"

They agreed on a pizza with everything and Adam called in the order. He poured them each a soda and sat beside Amber on the sofa.

She felt awkward. What would they talk about? Maybe eating dinner together was a bad idea. Yet she didn't want to return to her empty apartment. Pictures were already off the walls. Boxes had been packed and stacked near the door. The place looked bare and uninviting. Maybe she should begin moving her things into the other apartment. There was no reason to remain in this one until the end of her lease. She could move any time.

Looking at Adam, however, she decided there was no rush.

"If your mother-in-law is harassing you, maybe you need some deterrents," Adam said as he sipped his cola.

"She's not really harassing me," Amber said. Though when she thought about it for a moment, it almost seemed like it. "She's so excited about the baby. Jimmy was her only child, so she's latched on to the fact I'm having her grandchild. Learning that I was pregnant actually perked her up. She's been so depressed."

She wished she'd felt more depressed. She couldn't tell anyone except Bets how she felt. Her mother and Virginia would think she was crazy not to be grieving for months and months. But the truth was, she hadn't seen much of Jimmy since he'd graduated from high school two years earlier, and it was hard to miss someone who had been gone that long. Unless she thought about it, she could almost imagine he was still overseas.

"She needs something to take her mind off Jimmy and the new baby. If I let her, she'd have me moving into her home and letting her take over completely," Amber said.

"So tell her to bug off."

"I can't tell her that," she replied, horrified. "She's my mother-in-law."

"I'm not up on all the technicalities, but I think once your husband died, the relationships changed," Adam said.

"Still, she'll be one of the grandmothers of my child. I need to keep good relations going."

"I'm not saying cut her off at the pass, just set some boundaries. Otherwise, you're going to have to deal with this for a long time."

Amber didn't think she could set boundaries Virginia would accept. To the older woman, Amber was still that high-school girl who dated her son.

"What would you suggest?" she asked.

"Tell her not to call so often, not to show up unexpected. That's not asking too much," Adam said. He placed his glass on the table.

Amber held hers out to him. It was cold and she wasn't going to drink any more until the pizza arrived. His fingers brushed hers when he took it. She watched as he placed it on the coffee table beside his. The warmth from his touch seemed to linger. Maybe her hand had been colder than she thought. She felt that fluttery sensation in her stomach. She looked at him, swallowing hard as she tried to remember what they'd been talking about.

"I'll tell her, but she won't listen."

"Then you aren't being forceful enough. Tell her like you expect her to respect your wishes."

"You think I'm a wimp?" Amber suspected he was right, but it stung.

"Not necessarily. I hardly know you. But you seem nice to me. Maybe too nice."

Why was it *nice* seemed almost like an insult when Adam said it? She bristled. "I'm not too nice. There's nothing wrong in being kind to people who are hurting."

"But there is something wrong when you're sacrificing your own rights for someone else. If you don't want her to call, tell her."

"Great idea." She jumped to her feet.

"Where are you going?"

"To my place to tell Virginia not to call. And for practice, I'll tell you not to bother me again!"

She turned to leave but Adam caught her arm. Rising, he towered over her. Amber glared up at him. "Don't touch me!" she said.

Slowly his fingers released her, trailing over her skin as he held her gaze.

"I didn't mean now. Pizza's coming."

"Eat it all. I'm not hungry."

"Liar."

Her temper flared. "You don't know me. Leave me alone."

He held his hands out as if in surrender.

"I was offering some advice. Take what you paid for."

"Which was nothing."

"Then ignore it."

She turned and walked to the door. Adam followed her. When she tried the handle, he placed his hand against the door and held it closed.

"Let me out," she said softly.

"Don't go," he replied.

She looked up. His eyes searched hers. Then he leaned forward and kissed her.

Amber stood stock-still in shock. His lips were warm

and firm, moving against hers in invitation. He didn't touch her anywhere except on the mouth, which was more than enough. She felt lightheaded. Slowly she leaned into the kiss, savoring the sensations that spread through her like melted butter. He made no further demands, didn't push for more, just let his lips caress hers while she thought she would float away in delight.

Her heart was pounding when he ended the kiss. He stayed close, his breath soughing across her cheeks. Slowly Amber opened her eyes.

"You can't kiss me," she said, trying to sound forceful. That wispy voice couldn't be hers. "I'm a widow."

"Which means you're free and available again."

"No it doesn't. I'm still mourning Jimmy."

"Doesn't matter. You're still free and available."

She stepped back, frowning. She had to get her thoughts under control, not fantasize about another kiss.

"I'm not free and available and even if I were, you are not someone I want to take up with."

"What's wrong with me?" Adam asked in surprise.

"First of all, you have a dangerous job. If I ever think about getting involved again, it won't be with someone who puts his life on the line every day."

"Every other day. I have alternate days off," he said smoothly, his eyes dancing in amusement.

"And I don't like arrogant men."

He raised an eyebrow.

"And I'm not interested in some man who doesn't want to commit."

The amusement left his face. He pushed back away from the door and headed for the center of the room. "So go."

Amber watched him close down. It was like seeing him

don a cloak or something. One minute he was warm and friendly, almost laughing at her, the next he was cold and remote—a different man.

She slipped out of the apartment and headed for her place feeling as if she'd had a lucky escape.

Reaching her door, she stopped. She'd left her purse in Adam's apartment. She was not going back up there!

But how to get inside her own place? She had given her key to one of her neighbors shortly after moving in—for emergencies. Crossing to the opposite door, she knocked, hoping they were home.

They were and in only moments, Amber was safely inside her own apartment.

The answering machine was blinking furiously when she looked at it. Reluctantly she played the messages.

The first two were from Virginia. Bets had called. Then Virginia again, growing more demanding in each message. Then her mother left a message.

"Amber? Virginia has been calling here all afternoon. When you get home, give her a call, will you? She's driving us crazy."

"Try being me, Mom," Amber said, erasing the message. Bets called again and yet another one from Virginia—this one almost hysterical.

Sighing softly, Amber dialed the number. Maybe she was too nice and let Virginia walk all over her, but she could understand the woman's grief, even if she didn't share the depth.

Maybe it was guilt that had her bending over backward to make things all right. She felt more guilt than grief. How dumb was that?

"Where have you been?" Virginia demanded when she

recognized Amber's voice. "We've been worried sick. I called, I stopped by. Really, Amber, I've been frantic. Your mother said you'd been over there earlier, but even she didn't know where you were."

"Virginia, I'm a grown woman. I don't have to answer to my mother or to you. I have a life, you know. What I do and with whom I do it are my own business, not yours or my mother's." Amber was surprised at her own words.

"I was worried about you," Virginia said stiffly.

"I appreciate that, but I'm fine. If anything awful happens, Mom is listed as the person to notify, so she would have known immediately. I really need to have some space. If you want to get together occasionally, let me know and we can work something out. But please don't keep stopping by."

"It's that man, isn't it?" Virginia said. "You're dating again."

"What man?" Amber said, trying to play dumb. Virginia wouldn't like hearing about Adam's role in Amber's sudden rebellion. Amber was surprised herself. Was this all in reaction to the word *nice*?

"The one you say is a neighbor."

"Adam? I'm not dating him or anyone else," Amber said firmly.

"Then I don't see why there is any problem."

"Nor do I, as long as we continue to respect each other's right to privacy. I don't drop by your place uninvited, and I would appreciate it if you would reciprocate."

"You are always welcome here," Virginia said.

"Thank you. Once I'm in my new apartment, I'll invite you and James for dinner."

"When are you moving? I thought it wasn't until the end of the month."

"That's right."

"So you don't want anything to do with me before then?" She sounded horrified.

"How about we talk on the phone a couple of times a week," Amber said, getting tired of holding firm. It would be easier to just give in and deal with her annoyance when Virginia pushed.

"Jimmy would be appalled at your attitude," Virginia said.

Amber wondered what Jimmy would have thought. He'd avoided both Amber and Virginia as much as possible when he'd last been home, in her opinion. The man could have done more to spend time with his mother, and her.

"Maybe, or maybe not. But that's the way I want it right now," Amber said, proud of the firm note in her voice.

"Hormones," Virginia said wisely.

"What?"

"Hormones affect pregnant women in various ways. You're going through a bad patch right now. I understand. I'll wait. Call me tomorrow."

She hung up before Amber could reply. Good grief, was it hormones? Was her every move and thought now influenced by the changes in her body with the baby?

A knock sounded on her door.

It couldn't be Virginia, she'd just hung up from talking with her. She crossed the room to open it. Adam stood there, her purse hanging from the hand that held the flat pizza box.

"Dinner," he said, stepping inside.

Immediately Amber felt as if the space had shrunk. Her apartment wasn't as large as his, but she'd never felt so crowded as she did now.

"I'm not hungry."

"Too bad, I ordered enough for two. You have to help

me eat it." He marched over to the small table that served as study center and dining area, and slipped the box onto the surface. He dangled her purse on his fingers.

"You forgot this."

She took the purse and tossed it on a nearby chair. The sooner he was fed, the sooner he'd leave. The aroma from the pizza box had her mouth watering. She loved pizza and it had been ages since she'd had one.

She drew out two soft drinks, glasses and two plates, then headed for the small table.

He held her chair for her and Amber felt that fluttery sensation again. Good manners were something her mother would love.

When they each had a slice of pizza, Amber began to eat hers without looking at him.

"Should I take my slices and head for home?" he asked a couple of minutes later.

She met his eyes. "Stay, you're already here."

"Rousing invitation. Maybe I'll take a page from Virginia's book."

"I spoke to her when I got home."

"A gazillion messages on the answering machine?" he guessed.

"A few. Anyway, I made it clear I didn't want her dropping by uninvited."

He looked around the apartment. "Working so far, I see."

Amber smiled. "So far."

The lighthearted comment defused the tension and Amber began to relax.

"You look ready to move," Adam said noting the boxes.

"I just about am. There's still all the kitchen stuff to pack up, but I don't have a lot, so I can just pack as I go."

"End of the month?"

"Maybe earlier if I can get the guys at my stepdad's work to help. They moved my mom and stepdad and it went great. Plus it was a lot of fun."

"If not, I can get some of the guys from the station to help out. We can do it on a weekday, when the traffic is less."

"Can't wait to get rid of me?" she asked, feeling just a twinge of disappointment at his offer.

"Not that. Just want to make sure I know where you're moving."

"I could give you an address."

He nodded.

The pizza was finished in short order. They lingered over the soft drinks, talking about many things.

When the rap came on the door, Amber looked up in surprise.

"Virginia," Adam guessed.

She groaned softly. "I told her not to come unless invited. I said I'd be in touch soon. Does she have to show up all the time?" She rose and headed for the door, the light of battle in her eye.

"Mom, Matt. I didn't expect you." Amber was startled to see her folks.

"Hi, honey," Sara said, stepping inside. "Virginia is in a hissy fit about you and we went out for ice cream and so..." She trailed off as she noticed Adam.

He'd risen when the Tuckers entered the apartment.

Sara glanced at the table with dinner clearly in evidence, back to Adam, then to Amber. "Are we interrupting?"

"Mom, Matt, this is Adam Carruthers. He has an apartment on the fifth floor. We were just sharing a pizza. Adam, this is my mother Sara and my new dad, Matt Tucker."

Adam shook hands with Matt. He smiled at Sara. "Nice to meet you."

"Nice to meet you," she replied with a quick glance at her daughter. "We won't stay. I just wanted to make sure Amber was okay."

"I'm fine. Come in and sit down. Did you get ice cream?"

"Your mother had a double hot fudge sundae. We can't keep the ingredients in the house, or she'd eat them three times a day," Matt said, teasing Sara.

"Or more. You're so lucky, you don't have any cravings," Sara said, sitting on the sofa.

Adam smiled and took a step toward the door. "I'll leave you all to visit," he said.

"Oh, no, you don't," Amber said, stepping between him and the door. "You can stay and visit. They said they wouldn't be here long."

"If we're intruding—" Matt said.

"No," Amber and Adam chorused together.

"How did you break your arm?" Sara asked when they were all seated.

If Amber had thought the apartment small when Adam arrived, it was positively minuscule now that she had another large male and her mother. At least the apartment she was moving to was big enough to have a few friends over at once without feeling they were stepping on each other's toes.

Adam had brought the chair from the dining table. Amber was perched on the edge of the end table while Sara and Matt shared the sofa. She hoped her mother wouldn't be staying long. But it would be too much to hope there wouldn't be questions soon as she got home.

"On the job. I'm a firefighter. Had a floor collapse on me a week or so ago and this is the result," Adam said, holding up his arm.

"A firefighter?" Sara asked. "That has to be one of the most dangerous jobs going."

"Not if you're trained for it. I've had excellent training."

"Still, the unexpected happens," Amber said, looking at his arm. She hadn't known the man for long, and wasn't even sure she liked him very much. But the thought of him plunging into a burning building sent shivers down her spine.

"Occasionally, but not as often as you might think. I've been doing this for seven years and this is the first major problem."

"You could have been killed."

"But I wasn't," Adam said gently.

She looked away.

Sara smiled brightly. "I have news," she said.

"What?"

"Matt and I are leaving for Athens next week!"

"Wow, Mom, that's fabulous. How long will you be gone?"

"A week at least," Matt said. He looked at Adam. "I'm a troubleshooter for my company, and we have a major problem with some clients in Athens. I've curtailed a lot of travel until after the baby is old enough to go with us, but when I mentioned this, Sara decided she was up for a week in Greece."

"I would be, too," Amber said.

"Do you travel a lot?" Adam asked.

"I used to. Now I'm home most of the time," Matt said.

"Only until the baby comes and gets old enough to

travel," Sara said, squeezing Matt's hand. "In the meantime, we do want to take a few trips."

"And you can, now that you finally quit your job," he said.

Amber felt a pang at the happiness the two of them shared. They complemented each other in ways she would never have expected. She was glad her mother had found happiness with a great guy like Matt. But deep down inside she was envious. She didn't have that special connection with anyone, not even with Jimmy when he'd been alive. She wished she could find that special something that made a couple perfect for one another.

"I was thinking of moving in a few days," Amber said. "Guess you two lucked out and won't have to help."

"Put it off until we return," Sara suggested.

"I'll see when the guys at work are available," Matt said.

"Actually Adam said he and some of his friends would help me," Amber said. "I think he wants to get rid of me."

CHAPTER FIVE

ADAM wanted to deny Amber's statement, but knew it would only add fuel to the speculative fire already burning in her mother. He rose and nodded to Amber.

"I'll be heading home. Let me know how soon I can get rid of you."

She jumped up and followed him to the door, and outside into the hallway, pulling the door almost shut behind her.

"Thank you for dinner," she said politely.

"Thanks for letting me in when I brought it down," he said gravely, wanting to laugh at her prim attitude. Instead, he did what he'd been wanting since about three hours ago, leaned over and kissed her again.

This one was not nearly as satisfying. It was too brief and too soon over. But he knew her parents were just on the other side of the door, and he didn't want to give rise to further speculation.

"I know," he said, tapping her chin with his finger, before she could say a word. "Don't do that, you're a widow. Ever hear of the merry widows, darling?"

With that he turned and headed for the stairs, not wanting to wait for the elevator.

He entered his apartment thinking about Amber. He felt

a touch of pride in her for standing up to her mother-in-law. Would she be able to hold to her edict?

Not that it mattered to him. She was just a soon-to-be-moving neighbor. They'd shared a pizza, no big deal.

But the kisses had been a big deal, he thought, flinging himself down on the sofa and switching on the television. He didn't watch it, however, his mind a million miles away, or one floor down.

Was her mother as pushy as Virginia? Would she demand answers Amber didn't want to give? Maybe he should have stayed longer, out-sat the parents and stayed by her until they'd gone.

That was a hell of an idea.

It was better to cool things. They'd eaten a couple of meals together. She'd be moving soon. He still had his bachelor life intact. No danger of falling for a pretty girl, especially one who was pregnant and had a mother-in-law who barged in at her own convenience. If she didn't cool things off, Amber would never find a man willing to marry her and take care of her and the baby.

Thinking about his own mother always made Adam feel helpless. He shook off the mood and began to channel-surf. There was bound to be something on that would take his mind off his pretty neighbor with the soft, warm lips.

"Well, that went well," Amber said to the empty room when her parents left. Sara had refrained from making a big to-do over Adam's being here. Matt had eyes only for Sara, so Amber didn't have to worry about him cross-examining her. But she waited for the other shoe to drop. Surely she wasn't going to be able to go to bed and get some rest without something else happening.

Sure enough, a half hour later the phone rang.

"Hey, girlfriend, what's up?" It was Bets. Amber clutched the phone with relief.

"I'm so glad it's you," she said.

"Who else would call you this late?" Bets asked.

"Virginia, my mother, who knows. Anyway, can you talk until midnight, I'm sure they'll all be in bed by then."

Bets laughed. "What's got the older generation in an uproar?"

"Adam."

"Whoa, who is Adam? Oh, wait, is he Adam of the body to die for that exercises in front of you every other day of the week?"

"He's a neighbor."

"What?"

Amber explained what had been happening over the last couple of days. Had it been such a short time since she found out Adam lived upstairs? She'd already shared two meals with him. And two kisses.

When she casually mentioned them, she thought Bets would come through the phone line.

"Tell all. I can't believe you've kissed the man. I thought you'd be a nun the rest of your life."

"Give me a break, Bets, Jimmy's only been dead a few months. I'm horrified."

"Honey, you are alive. It was only a kiss. What's the big deal?"

Amber didn't want to talk about it, didn't even want to think about what the big deal was. The fact she reacted to Adam's kisses more deeply than she had Jimmy's worried her. She and Jimmy had been high school sweethearts. She'd known she wanted to spend her life with him since she was sixteen. How could she even think about another man?

"Amber, you still there?" Bets asked.

"Yes. It isn't such a big deal, I guess."

"Unless you want more," Bets guessed.

"Of course not. A friendly kiss between neighbors, that's all it was. He offered to help me move. Obviously he can't wait to get rid of me."

"Hmm. When are you moving?"

"Soon."

"Include me in. I want to meet this Adam. Unless you want to have me over and invite him to dinner."

"Not likely. Let's change the subject. What have you been up to?"

Bets regaled her with tales of her weekend, which had been full of activities, and men. Amber didn't know how her friend had so many dates, and never seemed to settle on one particular man. Of course, that was a safe way to have fun and not get involved. No commitment for Bets until she had her degree! She'd said that more than once.

Amber had made her commitment—to Jimmy.

Until death do you part. The familiar condition echoed in her mind. Her commitment to Jimmy had been severed. As Adam said, she was free. But she was not available!

After Bets hung up, Amber was restless. She prepared some hot chamomile tea, and wandered around her small one-room apartment. Soon she'd be back in the place she'd called home most of her life. Things would settle down into some kind of routine. She planned to start school again in the fall, hoping she could work something out with her professors to take a leave for when the baby was born.

She had a lot to do before the child arrived. But she couldn't make up lists like Virginia liked to do. She didn't want to go shopping like her mother wanted.

She didn't know what she wanted.

Finally the soothing tea calmed her enough she could get to sleep.

The next few days Amber did her best to ignore her upstairs neighbor. She finished packing everything she didn't need on a daily basis. The boxes were stacked near the door. It wouldn't take much to move her across town—with a little help.

She ventured forth to the park a couple of times, making sure she chose a different time from the one Adam had normally used when exercising. She saw him one afternoon when she returned home. He was heading out and already greeting a friend who waited in a car.

Despite her best efforts to remain aloof, Amber strained to see who was driving. Some other guy. The relief startled her. She had no claim on Adam. If he wanted to date every day and twice on Sunday, fine with her.

He waved before climbing into the car. She lifted her hand, wishing wistfully that he was going to spend the afternoon with her.

When she reached her apartment, she called her mother.

"How are you doing?" Amber asked when Sara answered.

"I'm frantic with packing and trying to make sure all the deliveries will be covered and rescheduling appointments. I thought going to Greece was a good idea, but now I'm wondering."

"I can be at your place for deliveries, if you like," Amber offered. "Why didn't you ask me?"

"I know you're busy."

"Not really. In fact, I feel at loose ends."

"Oh, honey. Want to go with us?"

"No, Mom, I definitely do not want to go to Greece with you and Matt."

"Why not?"

"Talk about a fifth wheel. You know Matt hardly notices the rest of the world when you're around. You two go and have a great time. Let me know when I need to be at your place and I'll open the door for whoever."

"We're having the baby furniture delivered on Friday. We'll assemble the bed and all when we get back. If you wouldn't mind letting in the deliverymen."

"Of course not. What else?"

Amber jotted notes on things her mother was worried about, glad to have something to occupy herself in the next few days. Maybe she should take Adam up on his offer to help her move and get it over with. She could spend the time setting up her new apartment.

"That's everything," Sara said. "You'll be all right?"

"Of course. You two have a great time."

"How's Virginia?"

"So far, so good. She's called once a day, but hasn't come by. She blames my attitude on hormones."

Sara laughed.

"Who cares what she blames it on as long as she gives you some peace. You still seeing Adam?" she asked casually.

"I'm not *seeing* him. He's a neighbor. I saw him today as he was going out with a friend."

"I liked him."

"I like him, too. But it's too early to think about dating again," Amber said quickly. Was it because sometimes she did think about it?

"Not necessarily. Jimmy wouldn't want you to stay single."

"I guess. But I have so much going on with the baby and all, I don't have time to get interested in a new relationship. And how many men want to take on a ready-made family?"

"Lots of men, especially if it includes my wonderful daughter."

Amber shook her head, smiling. "Mom, you're prejudiced."

"Not about my kids. Wow, isn't that cool, kids? I can't wait!"

"Neither can I," Amber said. The reality felt strange, but she wanted to see her new brother or sister. Wanted to hold her own baby in her arms.

"Got to go. Thanks, sweetie, for taking care of everything for me."

"Just have fun," Amber said. She slowly hung up the phone, feeling a wave of sadness sweep over her.

Her mother sounded so happy. She had Matt, the exciting life they'd planned and soon a beloved child would complete their family. Amber knew she'd always be a part of her mother's life, but it wouldn't be the same anymore. Sara and Matt would have their own family. There was every likelihood her mother would have more than one baby. Amber would never live with her siblings, never get to know them on a day-to-day basis. She'd be more like an aunt.

Unexpectedly she burst into tears. She missed Jimmy.

Missed the life she had counted on sharing with him. She was afraid of having a baby all by herself. How would she manage? Should she consider Virginia's offer to raise her child?

She didn't want to do that. She wanted to love her baby, care for it and help it grow into a wonderful adult. She had so much she could share with a child. She'd tell him about his daddy every day.

Her tears came harder. How could Jimmy have died! It was so unfair. He'd been too young, he'd had a life to live, not to be cut short in some foreign country by some soldier he never even saw. She wanted her baby to know its daddy, to learn of that family and feel connected and whole. Not like a piece was missing—the way she felt not having any relatives beside her mother.

She didn't begrudge her mother her happiness, but it pointed out how alone Amber was, how lonely she'd be in the days and years to come.

Amber didn't know how long she cried. Her heart felt as if it were breaking. She struggled for composure, only to sob even harder. She had cried for days when she'd first learned of Jimmy's death. She should be beyond this. Yet, it wasn't only for Jimmy that she cried. She wept for herself.

"Amber?" A loud knock sounded on the door.

She sat up, holding her breath. She didn't want to see anyone. Especially Adam.

"Amber, open up. I can hear you in there. What's wrong?"

"Nothing. Go away."

"No." He knocked again. "Open up. I'm not going away."

She rose, blowing her nose and blotting her eyes once more. She opened the door and looked out at Adam.

"I'm fine. Go away."

He pushed the door open and stepped inside the apartment, reaching out to draw her into his arms.

"What's the matter, honey?" His voice was so warm and compassionate, she burst into tears again. It felt like heaven to be held against him, his good hand rubbing her back gently. She heard the door click shut but it didn't stop the crying. His voice was like a lifeline as she burrowed into his chest, trying to escape the sadness and hurt. He didn't say much, but the tone was reassuring, the words comforting.

Finally she felt spent. She rested her cheek against his chest, hearing the strong steady beat of his heart. His warmth surrounded her, his comforting touch eased the distress.

"What happened?" Adam asked.

"Nothing." She didn't want to raise her face, didn't want to have to look at him. She felt like an idiot. And was exhausted to boot. "It just caught up with me, I guess."

"What?"

"Being alone, having to raise this baby without its father. How happy my mother is."

"Isn't that a good thing?"

"Yes it is. I'm happy for her. But it does point out how unhappy I am."

"I didn't pick up on that," he said. He put his hands on her shoulders and gently pushed her away, bending down a little to look into her face. "You seem happy and doing great. I know you must miss your husband, but you've started to move on. Just take one day at a time."

She nodded.

"Go splash on some cold water and we'll go for a walk. Fresh air will do wonders," he said, gently pushing her toward the bathroom.

"You don't need to stay, I'm fine."

"I like someone with me on walks."

"You don't," she argued. "You exercised every day without anyone."

"That's different."

"I've been to the park today."

"Let's go to the beach."

Amber went to rinse her face in cool water, appalled at the blotchy skin, the swollen eyes. It was amazing Adam hadn't run like crazy after taking one look at her. Instead, he'd invited her to take a walk along the beach.

Ten minutes later she climbed into a small sports car, the top already down.

"My stepfather has a convertible sports car. I think my mom likes it better than Matt does," Amber said, fastening her seat belt. The sunshine was almost too bright to stand. She put on her dark glasses and watched as Adam backed the car from the narrow garage and headed the short distance to the edge of the Pacific.

They parked in a lot that held only a few other cars. Weekdays the beaches weren't crowded.

The breeze blew steadily off the water, fresh and cool. Crunching along on the sand, they headed for the damp area near the water. The breakers splashed up, near them, but they stayed just out of range of the surging water. When it receded, the damp sand glittered in the sun.

They walked in silence. The sound of the surf and the crying gulls made the perfect background. Amber began to relax, to feel rejuvenated being by the ocean. A few daring souls were swimming in the cold water, their shrieks and laughter carrying on the wind.

She stumbled and Adam's hand shot out, grasping her arm so she didn't fall. He slid his hand down to hold hers.

Amber felt his touch to her toes. Her heart slammed against her ribs, the tingling awareness that she always had around him notched up and filled her. She slipped her hand free. Too dangerous with the mood she was in.

"This is nice," she said, sidestepping just a bit to put some distance between them. "I love the ocean. My mother brought me often when I was a child."

"I like it, too. First time I came was when I moved to San Francisco about seven years ago. I spent my second day in the city walking along the beach, intrigued with all the water. Sometimes I wish we could harness it better to quench fires."

"A large hose directly from the sea," Amber said.

"Yeah, that'd be a hell of a way to put out flames."

"Your work is so dangerous," she said slowly, watching the waves break, relishing the feel of the fresh breeze.

"There is some danger, but it's dangerous to drive on the freeways. I've been trained, and I practice when the department does drills."

Amber shivered.

"Are you cold?" Adam asked, putting his arm around her shoulders.

"No. Just thinking we never know when life will end."

"Or begin. You and your mother are both on the brink of something exciting. Seems odd to know two generations will be doing the same thing, but your mother is young. And you'll have someone to share the ups and downs with."

Amber nodded, extremely conscious of his arm across her shoulders. For a moment she imagined they were lovers, strolling along the edge of the sea, sharing time and life together.

But they weren't lovers. And she didn't want to even think about such a thing. She needed to remember Jimmy. And remember, if she ever did fall in love again, she wanted her husband to have a safe job, not something dangerous like fighting fires.

"Do you ever fight the forest fires California has every year?"

"I went to the big one in L.A. a couple of years back. Normally our units aren't called."

"Walls of flames a hundred feet high," she quoted.

"I stayed clear of those."

Amber stopped and turned to face him, dislodging his arm. "Aren't you ever afraid?"

He shrugged slowly. "There's no time to be afraid when we are doing our job. Sometimes when it's all over, I think about what could have happened. But it didn't. We usually have a debriefing to go over what we did right, what went wrong, and how to combat such fires again. Keeps us on our toes, and our edge sharp."

"You weren't sharp enough to keep from falling through that floor and breaking your arm," she argued.

"The unexpected does happen. It's still the greatest job going."

"Are you an E.M.T.?" she asked, referring to the special Emergency Medical Technician training which went beyond mere first aid.

"I qualified a couple of years back," he said.

"But you still fight fires."

"If one of the regular E.M.T.s is out, I fill in. But, yeah, I'm usually fighting the fires."

She nodded and turned to start walking. She was clear in her mind. Even if she was interested in the man, there was no way she would risk her heart a second time with some man who flirted with danger on a daily basis. She'd move to her new apartment and forget all about Adam Carruthers.

Adam walked beside her, about a half step behind. He watched her, almost seeing the wheels turn in her mind. She didn't like his job. That was clear as glass. He felt defensive. It was a great job, one he was good at and liked. He was in line for a promotion soon. With any luck, in a few years, he'd be chief of a small station. Or he could join the arson squad, or move into full-time E.M.T. work. He had options and opportunities. But for the moment, he liked exactly what he did.

He hadn't considered how someone else would view his job. His mother had been more concerned that he make enough money to support himself. She had never voiced any concern about his safety. He always thought it was because she knew he'd been trained enough to stay as safe as anyone could. Or was it she hadn't thought it through, hadn't considered how dangerous it could be?

Glancing at Amber again, he wondered how to breach that wall. He wanted to see more of her. Since neither of them was in the market for a long-term relationship, what could it hurt to spend some time together?

"Given any thought to moving?" he asked. That didn't sound like spending time together. Dumb question.

"I'm ready to go, actually. If your offer is still good, I'd like some help. There's really no reason to stay where I am—except for the roof garden. I'll just have to get used to doing without."

"I'll ask some of the guys. Friday suit you?"

"Not Friday. I'll be at my mother's. They're expecting

the baby furniture to be delivered and I said I'd be there to let them in since they'll be in Athens."

"That's right, they're off to Greece."

Amber nodded, looking out across the expansive Pacific. She looked at her watch. "They're at the airport now. My mother loves to travel. Thanks to Matt's job, I bet she gets to see the entire world before long."

"How about you? Do you long to travel as well?" he asked.

Amber shook her head. "I might like to see some places sometime, but I'm happy staying right here. I've seen the snow in the Sierra in winter. Been to the hot southern California beaches. But mostly, I like staying close to home."

Adam shared her feelings, now that home was San Francisco. He had no burning urge to return to Fresno, where he'd been born and grew up. He loved the City by the Bay, however. When he first arrived, he'd explored all the various sections, from the Wharf to Chinatown, Japan Town and the Avenues. As a firefighter, he knew all the streets, and the quickest way to get from point A to point B. For relaxation, there were a plethora of activities, from swimming and surfing, to clubs and bars, to dancing or attending a rodeo.

Though he could relate to her loneliness. Sometimes it was hard to find someone to do things with. The guys were great, but most women he dated seemed to see it as a prelude to a deeper relationship. Those not husband hunting were few and far between.

They sat at one of the benches that faced the ocean.

"Thanks for suggesting we do this," Amber said.

He smiled but remained silent. She was always so polite. She'd make a good mother for her baby. It was a tough break that her husband died, but she had lots of support. Too bad his mother hadn't had it as well.

She cleared her throat. Adam glanced at her. Often that presaged an announcement that wouldn't be well received.

"I think we shouldn't see each other anymore, after I move. In fact," Amber continued, "you may not wish to help me move, if that's the case."

CHAPTER SIX

ADAM was caught by surprise. It was the last thing he'd expected to hear.

"The move comes with no strings," he said, touched a little by anger. "I'm not pushing this arrangement, though I did think we made the perfect couple. Neither is looking for a deep involvement, neither wants to marry. Who better to pal around with than someone who shares the same views?"

"I'm not palling around with anyone," she said stiffly.

"Figure of speech. Maybe not now, but in the future you might need an escort, or want to do something that would be more fun with two. If so, you can give me a call." Fine by him if she didn't want to hang around. He'd help her move to her new apartment, then let her make the next overture. If she really didn't want anything to do with him, so be it.

He rose. "Ready to head back? I don't want to impose my company on you any longer than necessary."

"Sit down," she said, looking up and reaching out to tug on his arm. "I didn't mean it like that. I just feel, I don't know, guilty, I guess. I shouldn't be going out with such a sexy guy when my own husband hasn't even been dead a year."

He sat. "A year? Is that the magic formula?"

"Usually people mourn for a year or longer."

"Usually?"

"I'm still mourning Jimmy. I wish he hadn't died."

"I wish the same thing and I never even knew the guy. To die so young is awful, no matter what the circumstances. But you didn't die with him. From what you said earlier, he's really been gone a lot longer than the few months he's been dead."

"Sometimes it feels as if I never knew him. He was so different when he was here in February."

"He wasn't part of your day-to-day life. There's not a wrenching hole he filled that is now empty. I bet you can still imagine him elsewhere in the world."

She looked at him in surprise. Adam wanted to wrap her in his arms and hold her. But he took a deep breath instead.

"That's exactly how I feel. How did you know?"

"That's how I felt when I heard my Mom had died. I was shocked, sad she was gone. But after the funeral and her affairs were settled, it didn't seem real. She lived in Fresno, I live here. I only saw her at Christmas, so her dying didn't change my day-to-day life significantly. Don't get me wrong. I loved her. I miss her. But sometimes I almost think she's at our place in Fresno, doing whatever it was she did after I moved out."

"So you don't think I'm too awful to feel that way?"

"I'd say it's perfectly normal."

She leaned back against the bench and seemed to relax.

Adam wished they taught grief counseling at the station. He didn't know much about it, except what he'd experienced when his mother died. In his book, Amber's feelings were expected. The guy hadn't been around, how could she grieve now when their parting had really taken place long before?

Amber wasn't sure how long they sat on the bench. She replayed the discussion, feeling relieved Adam didn't think badly of her because she wasn't as grief-stricken as Virginia was. Although her crying bout this afternoon had been due to grief. And fear. She would take one day at a time, as he said. Some days she'd be fine. On those when she couldn't hold it in, well, a good cry never hurt anyone.

"Want to go?" he asked.

"Yes. This has been great."

They headed back to the parking lot.

"Can we take a drive down the coast for a little way?" Amber asked when they reached the convertible. "Unless you have to get back for something."

"I'm not going back for anything. Tim took me shopping for lots of TV dinners that I can heat and eat."

"I'll cook dinner tonight, if you like. To say thanks for the beach trip," Amber said. Dinner wasn't seeing someone. It was just a way to say thank you for getting her out of the apartment and in a better frame of mind.

"You don't owe me anything," Adam said gruffly as he started the engine.

"I know, but I like to cook. And it'll save one of your dinners for later."

He gunned the engine and the car shot out of the parking lot like a bullet. They sped along The Great Highway, the Pacific on their right, houses flashing by on the left.

Amber loved it. The wind whipped through her hair, blowing it every which way, until she reached up to hold it away from her face. It was exhilarating! If she ever bought a car, she'd make sure it was a convertible. She felt carefree and happy as they drove miles down the coast.

An hour later they returned to Amber's apartment. She quickly washed up, pleased to see color in her cheeks, and that her eyes had lost the swelling.

"How about spaghetti," she asked when she came out to the kitchenette. "I can make garlic bread and a salad."

"Whatever, I like everything."

He sat at the small table and watched her as she went about preparing the meal. He offered to help, but she said no. With his arm, he should take things easy. Besides, Amber liked cooking, especially when it was for more than one.

"Do you cook?" she asked.

"As rarely as possible," Adam said.

"So you eat out all the time?"

"Not all the time. But more than you do, I bet."

"So learn to cook."

"Maybe I need a teacher."

She looked at him, a smile hovering around her mouth. "Is that a challenge?"

"Not if you don't plan to see me after you move."

The smile faded. "I think that's best."

"Why?"

She couldn't tell him it was to safeguard her heart. That she was attracted to him and didn't like the position that put her in. He'd probably laugh his head off after his comments earlier about neither of them being interested in an involved relationship. And how could she be interested and not want to see where it would lead?

She was better off sticking with her plan to cut him right out of her life.

"If you don't have a reason, then it's a dumb idea," Adam said.

"What?"

"I asked you why you didn't want to see me after your move and you don't have a single reason."

Caught. There was no way to explain.

The phone rang.

"Saved by the bell," he murmured.

She wrinkled her nose at him as she passed to pick up the phone.

"Amber?"

Her heart sank. It was Virginia.

"Hello, Virginia. What's up?"

"I'm calling to see how you're feeling. Better?"

Amber took a deep breath, trying to quell the instant annoyance she felt whenever she was around Virginia. "I'm feeling fine, Virginia. I'm not sick, I'm pregnant."

"I know, but hormones can wreak havoc with a woman's system. James and I want you to come for dinner Friday night. In fact, since your mother is out of town, maybe you should plan to stay the weekend with us. We can shop for some baby things."

"I have plans," Amber said desperately.

"What plans?"

Quickly she tried to think of something she could do that would satisfy the other woman. "My friend Bets and I are going to the show," she said.

"When?"

Amber's mind went blank. She looked at Adam. He was leaning back in the chair, balancing on the back two legs, watching her with that amusement that drove her crazy.

"Saturday. I'm not sure what time. Maybe afternoon, or evening."

"Well you can still come over afterward and stay the night. We can have a nice brunch on Sunday."

"On Sunday I'm... I'm..." Her look conveyed desperation.

Adam held up his arm and mouthed, *Visiting a sick friend.*

"...visiting a sick friend. Really, Virginia, I don't need to come to your house to stay for any length of time. It's not like I live that far away. Maybe you and I can have lunch one day next week."

"What day?"

"Tuesday," Amber said. "We'll meet at that place on Sansome that you like, at eleven."

The water was boiling, steam rising from the stove. Amber pointed to it. Adam looked over and rose, peering into the pan. He turned around and raised his shoulders.

Amber covered the receiver with her hand. "Put the spaghetti noodles into the pan, turn it down a bit and time it."

"Amber?" Virginia asked.

"Yes."

"Is someone there?"

"I have a friend over for dinner and I need to go. Dinner is almost ready."

"Who?" The sharpness in her tone once again annoyed Amber. She wasn't sure how she was going to handle Virginia over the next few years.

"A friend. I have to go. I'll see you on Tuesday."

Amber hung up even though she heard Virginia talking.

"You held tough," Adam said with admiration.

Amber went to check on the sauce. "It's hard, though. Virginia can be so needy."

"She has to find her own way. I know it's tough to lose a family member—I don't have anyone. But that doesn't make you hers."

"I know. She means well. I think she needs a new hobby. She was involved in some women's club, but when I asked her the other day about it, she blew it off. Doesn't have the same appeal, she said. She doesn't like to garden, to sew or anything as far as I can see."

"She'll dote on your child," Adam said.

"I hope not. I want a healthy relationship with the baby's grandparents, but not to be at their beck and call forever."

"She's scared," he said. "Once you marry someone else, she's afraid you'll forget about the baby's grandparents."

"I wouldn't."

"No, I don't think you would. But she does."

Amber hadn't thought about that. She frowned.

"I told you I didn't think I would get married again any time soon. Maybe never."

"Maybe, or maybe when the right guy comes along, you'll fall hard and fast."

She laughed. "Don't see it. How about you?"

"Never marrying."

"Unless the right woman comes along and you fall hard and fast," she repeated.

"I'm having too much fun now," he said, leaning over to kiss her.

Steam filled the small kitchenette area. The soft bubbling of the water provided a soothing background noise. Amber felt Adam's touch to her toes. She leaned against him, savoring the feeling of his arms coming around her, holding her, sheltering her. His mouth wrought miracles. Her being focused on the sensations that coursed through her as he moved his lips against hers, drawing a response she was more than happy to give. Endless moments drifted by until the sound of water splashing on the stove burner penetrated.

She pulled away. The spaghetti water was bubbling over the edge of the pot.

She quickly turned down the heat and pulled the pan away. In a moment, she slipped it back onto the burner. "Glad it was only water," she said, keeping her gaze firmly on the food cooking on the stove. "If the sauce had bubbled over, it would take me forever to get it cleaned up."

He moved away, giving her much-needed breathing space. Her heart pounded. Her mouth still craved his touch. She wasn't interested in eating dinner, she wanted to feel his arms around her again, savor the taste and touch of him.

"Dinner is almost ready," she said.

Adam didn't care a fig for dinner. He studied Amber. She avoided looking at him. He didn't blame her. She probably wanted him to leave and was too polite to say anything. He had no business kissing her. She was vulnerable. He should stand her friend, or get out. Not latch on to her like she was the best thing that ever happened to him.

He scowled and walked the few steps to the center of her small apartment. He couldn't even work up a good pacing here. Not that he needed to pace. They'd eat dinner, behave civilly and then he'd leave.

Only—he glanced out the window, almost afraid to give thought to his feelings—only he didn't want to leave. He wanted to spend some more time with Amber. Find out more about her. Learn what she liked to do when she wasn't studying to be a schoolteacher.

Discover how she planned to make room in her life for a baby and keep to her goal of becoming a teacher.

"It's ready," she said.

Adam turned and went to the table. She'd already served their plates, and placed the salad and hot garlic bread in the center. He held her chair. She smiled at him over her shoulder. At least his mother had taught him manners. Which Amber seemed to like.

Seated a moment later, he was pleased to note she met his look full on, no averting her eyes.

The first bite exploded with flavor. "This is terrific," he said. "You said you liked to cook. If I could cook like this every day, I'd like to cook, too."

She smiled at his compliment. "Thanks. I don't cook like this for one. Usually I eat my main meal at lunch, on campus. Then just have sandwiches or soup for dinner. I thought firefighters took turns preparing meals."

"We do. But the crew made sure I only get lunch—which is sandwiches. I guess they figure I can't mess up on those too much."

The tension from the kiss seemed to have dissipated. Gradually he relaxed and enjoyed the meal.

Despite wanting to stay, once the dishes were washed and put away, Adam announced his departure.

Amber didn't try to change his mind.

"Thanks for taking me to the beach," she said, walking him to the door. "I'm sorry I cried all over you."

"Any time." He stopped at the door feeling like an uncertain teenager again. Did he kiss her, or just pat her shoulder and leave? Would she let him kiss her again? Or had she had it with him trying to come on to her? She was so into that widow role, he wasn't sure he wasn't pushing just to get a reaction.

Wrong. He was pushing because he wanted her.

"Good night," Amber said, holding the door open.

He pushed it shut and drew her into his arms. Her eyes widened slightly, but he was sure he saw a spark of happiness before she closed them to his kiss.

Adam was going crazy with boredom. His arm was feeling better. It no longer ached all the time. He hoped it was healing fast so he could get back to work. This forced inactivity was driving him nuts.

It had been two days since he'd seen Amber. He wanted to call her, but didn't have her number. He'd checked the listings in the phone book, but there was no A. or Amber Woodworth. He couldn't remember her maiden name, which was probably what the phone was listed under.

He'd walked downstairs twice but didn't stop, turning around and retracing his steps. She knew where he lived. She could make some effort if she wanted to see him.

That was the kicker. He didn't think she did. Not as much as he wanted to see her.

Thursday he spent the day cleaning the apartment, doing laundry, stopping at her floor on his way down and back to the laundry room. Never saw another soul.

Friday Adam decided enough was enough. He'd risk another visit to the station to do something, if only to sit and watch while the on-duty crew washed the rig.

He was almost ready to leave when his phone rang.

"Adam, I'm running so late. I overslept. Can you possibly give me a ride to my mom's apartment?" Amber's frantic voice came through almost in a jumble, she was talking so fast. "I'm supposed to be there when they deliver the baby furniture this morning and I can't make it on time going on the bus."

"Calm down. Of course I can give you a ride. Are you ready?"

"I will be in five minutes. Thank you, I owe you." She hung up.

He smiled. He liked the thought of her owing him. What would equal a ride to her mom's place? Dinner every night for a week? The thought had possibilities.

Amber gave him directions when they were in his car a few minutes later.

"Sorry if I'm keeping you from something," she said, almost straining against the seat belt in her effort to go faster.

"Nothing important. Relax. We'll get there when we get there."

"I know." She checked her watch. "It's not quite nine. They said they'd be there between nine and noon."

"I've never known delivery people to show up until the last moment. Which always makes me wonder how many people they really have deliveries for. Somewhere in the scheme of things, I should be first on the delivery list, wouldn't you think?"

Amber laughed. Adam caught his breath. He loved hearing her laugh. He chanced a glance and had a hard time returning his gaze to the road. She was beautiful when she laughed. He wished he could hear it every day.

"It's on this street, up about three blocks," Amber said when he turned onto the street near the marina. "Oh, look, the truck is in front. Quick, don't let them drive away."

Adam saw a man walking up the three stairs to the lobby when he pulled in behind the double-parked truck. If traffic had to go around the truck, it could go around him.

Amber scrambled out and hurried to the man on the stairs. Adam watched as they talked for a moment, then Amber nodded. She came back to the car.

"They just got here. Thank you for the ride. I made it!"

"I'll park and come help. Then I can give you a ride home," he said.

"You don't need to," she said. "I know you have things to do."

"It'll keep. I'll be back as soon as I find a parking place."

Fortune favors the few, he thought a moment later as he turned the corner and saw an empty parking place at the curb. He slid in, amazed at how easy it was. In only seconds he was back at the apartment building. The lobby door had been propped open so he stepped inside. He hadn't a clue where Amber's mother and stepfather lived. He'd have to wait for the delivery men.

He rode up with them on their next load, following them into the large apartment which overlooked the Bay. The living room was about the size of his entire apartment. The floor to ceiling windows had minimal coverings, framing the spectacular view.

Pausing only a moment, he continued down a short hall to the bedroom designated for the new baby. A new changing/dresser was against one wall. Several large boxes were leaning against another wall. A border of bunnies and teddy bears had been placed at shoulder level around the room. Curtains on the windows matched.

"That's it, sign here," one of the men was saying, holding out a clipboard with papers for Amber's signature.

Amber signed and thanked the men. When they'd left, she looked at the boxes.

"I thought all the furniture would come assembled."

"Too bulky that way," Adam said. "Want to assemble the pieces for your mother?"

Amber couldn't believe Adam had offered to assemble the crib and rocker. Didn't he have something else to do today besides help with another family's furniture?

Yet, how cool to have it all set up when her mother returned. She knew where the crib sheets and blankets were already stored.

"If you wouldn't mind, that would be great. Then when they get home, the room will practically be complete."

"I don't mind. I have some tools in my trunk, unless you know where Matt keeps his."

"I don't. And I'd feel a bit funny going through all their things looking for them. It was one thing when Mom and I lived in our apartment. I grew up there, I already knew where everything was. But this—it's not really my home anymore."

"I'll get what I need and be right back."

Less than a half hour later, the parts of the crib were spread over the floor in the baby's room and Amber was handing pieces to Adam when he requested them. He studied the directions for assembly for a moment, then put the paper aside. From there on, it seemed as if he knew instinctively how to put together a crib.

She watched fascinated as the bed took shape. Even the cast on his arm didn't hinder his efficiency.

"Have you done this before?" she asked.

He looked up. "What, put together a crib?"

"Yes."

"Maybe once. But I've done other projects. We do work in various communities as part of our outreach at the fire station. Once on vacation, I went on a Habitat for Humanity project in Arizona. Hot as could be, but rewarding work. Especially when the family saw their new home for the first time."

"Tell me," she said, sitting beside him on the rug. There was more to this man than she suspected. She'd known him for weeks, and yet hardly knew him at all.

As the morning progressed, Adam regaled her with his forays into construction and assembling toys for children at Christmas as he assembled first the crib, then the glider-rocker her mother had ordered. His funny stories didn't jive with the efficient, knowledgeable manner in which he assembled the furnishings. She suspected he was elaborating for her enjoyment. And she was enjoying herself.

Twice she laughed aloud at his tales.

"You're outrageous, that couldn't have happened," she said at one point.

He looked up, the familiar amusement dancing in his dark eyes. "I said so, didn't I?"

It was after noon when he gave the glider-rocker a push. "Try it," he suggested.

Amber sat in the chair, moving gently, as if rocking. "This is great. I guess I'll get one after all. I thought I wanted a traditional rocking chair, but this is so smooth and easy to rock on."

He pushed the crib against the long wall. "I don't know where they want everything," he said, gathering up his tools.

"Me, either. It looks good there. Wait a minute. I want

to make the bed and put in a couple of the stuffed animals they've acquired."

In moments the bedroom looked ready for its new occupant.

Amber stood in the doorway and looked at it all. Would her own baby's room be as nice? Probably, since her mom and Matt were insisting on buying the furnishings. Of course, that second bedroom at the old apartment wasn't as large as this one. But she did cozy just fine.

Adam put his arm around her shoulder and looked at the room.

"It's nice, isn't it?" she asked, leaning slightly against him. For a split second she could almost imagine Adam was the father of her baby, and they were admiring the room they'd prepared for their child.

Quickly she moved away. Foolishness, nothing more.

"Thank you for doing all this." She waved her hand indicating the room. "It'll be a great surprise when they come home."

"I enjoyed it. Let's get rid of all the boxes and then we'll be ready for lunch."

"Oh, um, I, uh, have plans," Amber said, caught by surprise.

"What?" he asked, looking directly at her. "Can't be visiting your sick friend, that's on Sunday."

She felt the heat rise in her face. She didn't lie worth beans.

"I'm happy to take you to lunch if you like," she said. The wiser move would be to flee from the attraction that plagued her whenever she was around Adam, or thought about him, or dreamed about him. But she did owe him for the ride, and for helping her assemble everything.

"I thought we could eat lunch at Embarcadero Center,

then go over to the baby store and check out your own furniture. Unless you already know what you want," he said.

Amber's heart sped up again. He was willing to go *baby
shopping*?

"I haven't decided. But Mom and I measured the space a
little while ago, so I know what I can and can't get. My baby's
room won't be this large," she said, glancing around again.

"Babies aren't too big, they don't need a lot of room,"
he said. "Lunch?"

"Fine, thank you. But I'll treat, I owe you."

He lifted the tool box and a couple of the larger folded
cardboard pieces and headed for the front door. "I'll treat.
I'd rather you cook me a few more meals before you leave,
if you really feel you owe me."

"That's too easy," she said, picking up several pieces and
following him.

They locked the apartment, deposited the cardboard in
the apartment Dumpster and headed for his car, lunch and
shopping.

Amber was tired when they reached home. And feeling
fairly guilty once again. She wondered if that would be a
constant feeling. Guilt that she was alive and Jimmy was
dead. Guilt she enjoyed herself today, instead of being in
tears as she had been earlier in the week. Guilt she shared
her choice of furniture first with Adam instead of her mother
or Virginia. Guilt they'd bought the baby's first teddy bear
together. Along with a few other items. She protested she'd
only have to move everything, but Adam insisted.

Guilt was something she was getting used to, she thought
as they waited for the elevator. Would it fade? Or was it
something that would be with her for as long as she lived?

The elevator stopped on her floor and they both stepped out.

"Where have you been?" Virginia asked.

CHAPTER SEVEN

AMBER tried to smile politely, but a spurt of anger flared instead. "What are you doing here?" she asked. She'd told Virginia they'd get together next week. The woman had no business showing up unannounced. Hadn't Amber made that clear yet?

Virginia stared at Adam. "He's the reason you don't want me over here. What is going on? Jimmy would be horrified. What are you doing? You forget him so quickly, on to the next man?"

Amber was so surprised by her words she couldn't respond. Was that what everyone would think? That she didn't care Jimmy was gone? That she couldn't wait to get back on the dating scene again? It wasn't true!

"I don't believe we've been introduced," Adam said, filling in the gaping silence. "I'm Adam Carruthers, a neighbor from upstairs." He held up the bags from the baby store. "I was helping Amber carry up the bags."

It could sound as if he'd just met her in the lobby, Amber thought. Not that she was trying to hide anything.

Virginia didn't look mollified.

Amber stepped around her and unlocked her door. Thank goodness she'd never given Virginia or James a key.

She didn't know what had happened to Jimmy's, but at least his mother didn't have it.

Adam handed the bags to Virginia and left. Amber was torn between wishing he'd stood by her, and feeling glad he'd gone in case his presence agitated her former mother-in-law.

Amber waited until Virginia came inside the apartment and closed the door before speaking.

"I am so angry I can hardly stand it. I asked you not to come over here unless invited. You've embarrassed me in front of a neighbor, and you are driving me crazy. Virginia, I do not want you hounding me like this! I have my own life to lead and I need my space to do that."

"You're Jimmy's wife, the mother of my grandchild—" she started.

"I'm now Jimmy's widow. You will always be the grandmother of my baby, but the baby isn't born yet. I am in perfect health, so there is no need to worry on that account."

"You are all the family we have left," Virginia said.

Amber's heart ached for the woman. Her baby hadn't even been born, yet she was bonding with the child that grew beneath her heart. How would a mother stand losing her precious child? She sympathized with Jimmy's mother. But she couldn't let that sympathy establish patterns that were driving her crazy.

"I will always hold you and James in the highest regard," she said slowly. She gave the woman a hug, wondering if she'd made a mistake when Virginia clung.

"But I am not your child. Jimmy was. I have a mother and now a new stepfather. Virginia, I can't be your daughter. I can't take Jimmy's place," Amber said firmly.

The older woman released her and went to sit on the

sofa. She had tears in her eyes. "I only want what's best for you and Jimmy's baby."

"I know you do. I appreciate—"

A knock sounded on the door. Amber spun around and went to see who was there, wondering if Adam had come back to offer moral support.

A young man in a crisp Army uniform stood at attention before her.

"Mrs. James Woodworth?" he asked, not making eye contact.

"Yes?"

He relaxed a smidgeon and looked at her. "Jimmy's wife?" She nodded.

"I'm Lance Corporal William Collins. I was with Jimmy when he died. He asked me to give you a message."

"Come in." Amber held the door wide, her heart racing. This man had been with Jimmy at the end. She had been told there had been only one survivor from the attack. When he stepped inside, she made the introductions. "Do have a seat," she urged.

He sat stiffly on a chair while Amber sat beside Virginia on the sofa.

"You were with Jimmy at the end?" she prompted.

He nodded. "Sorry to be so long in getting here, but I just got out of the hospital in Bethesda yesterday."

"You were injured in the attack," she guessed.

"Yes, ma'am. I was the only survivor."

"How fortunate you were. I'm sorry you were in the hospital for so long. Are you all right now?" Amber stared at him, seeing some of the man Jimmy had been when she'd last seen him. Young, full of pride in the work he did. A little distant and focused on other matters.

"I'm on my way home for convalescent leave. I hope to rejoin my unit in a few weeks," he said.

She took a deep breath. This young man had escaped death when all the others in the vehicle had been killed. Yet he was planning to jump back into the fray at the first opportunity. She didn't understand men at all.

"Jimmy was my son," Virginia said needlessly. Amber had introduced her as Jimmy's mother.

"Yes, ma'am." He looked at Amber. "He didn't suffer. We were hit without warning. The driver and Gary, the other man riding on the left side, were killed instantly. Jimmy and I were thrown from the vehicle, landing a few feet from each other. I crawled over to try to help. There wasn't anything I could do."

He seemed as distressed as Amber felt. Her heart went out to him. He would have to live with that regret forever.

"I'm sure you did your best, thank you," she said gently.

Virginia gave a small sob.

"He wasn't in any pain, ma'am. He said he felt numb from the neck down. He didn't live for long, but he wasn't in any pain."

Amber nodded, wishing she could have been there with Jimmy. Knowing this man had tried to help made all the difference in the world. She knew nothing could have saved her husband, but it was comforting to hear he had not suffered, nor been alone at the end.

"His last words were about you. He told me to tell you. Made me promise. I would have come anyway. But I gave my word."

Amber nodded, feeling the overwhelming sadness take hold.

"He said, 'I wish I could see her smile again. She has the best smile in the whole world. It lights up her whole face. Or hear her laugh. It's magical, making everyone smile who hears it.'"

Amber blinked back tears, almost hearing Jimmy's voice.

The young soldier cleared his throat, and glanced down at the beret he was twisting in his hands. "He said he wished he could kiss you just one more time."

The tears welled.

"Then he said, tell her I love her best." He looked at her, then at Virginia.

Virginia was in tears as well.

Amber tried to stem the tears, but they kept falling. "That was a joke between us. One of us would tell the other we loved them, then the other would say, I love you more. We went back and forth until finally one of us would say, I love you best. Then we'd kiss."

She'd never again be able to tell Jimmy how much she loved him. She would never again have another one of his kisses, laugh with him in the sunshine. He had had the last word.

The young man cleared his throat again. "Then he said, 'Tell her to find a great guy and have a huge family and name one of the kids for me. I want her to be happy, not be tied up with old memories. Tell her to live long, live happy and think of me once in a while.' Then he died."

Amber burst into tears, trying to stop crying, but feeling the ache in her heart as never before. Even when dying, Jimmy had thought about her. And about her future. He'd given her his blessing on whatever she decided to do.

A weight lifted from her shoulders. The sadness would

pass in time. And she would go on, with their child. She wished he'd known he was going to leave a child behind.

"Thank you for coming," Amber said, wiping the tears from her cheeks, wishing she had a tissue or something. "Thank you for being with him when he died so he didn't die alone."

"I wouldn't have left him, ma'am."

"I know you wouldn't. How long before help arrived?" she asked.

"A couple of hours later," he said, looking down at his hands, still gripping his beret.

Her heart ached anew. He must have been so scared, wondering if help would come in time for him with all his comrades dead around him.

"I'm glad you're all right," she said gently.

Virginia had found a handkerchief in her pocketbook and was dabbing her own cheeks. "I second that," she said. "I'm glad to know he didn't suffer and wasn't alone at the end."

"He's buried in Colma, in the National Cemetery there," Amber said.

"Good to know. I'd like to visit the grave my next trip here. But not this time."

"I understand." She brushed the tears away again. Sometimes she felt as if she'd spent the last several months of her life crying. Yet Jimmy's final words opened the gates to the future. He had wanted her to move on. She would do so without the guilt that has so plagued her.

"Anything else I could tell you?" Will asked.

"Don't go just yet," Amber said. "I'll fix us something to drink and you can tell us about Jimmy and his work over there—what you can, of course. Was he happy for the most part?"

"He loved working in communications. We have the latest in satellite uplinks, in observance equipment and telecommunications. He learned a lot, was up for promotion after that assignment. He and I worked together for several months." Will seemed relieved to have fulfilled his promise. He relaxed and began to tell Amber and Virginia about life on the Army post overseas.

Lance Corporal William Collins stayed for more than an hour, sharing stories about their adventures in Europe, and then the temporary assignment in a dangerous spot that ended so tragically.

He left when time grew short for his flight to Seattle. Virginia left a few moments later.

Amber cleaned the cups and put them away, thinking about all Will had told them. Jimmy's words echoed over and over in her head. She wished so much things had been different, but they were as they were. He'd known the end was near, and had given her his blessing to move on.

Maybe he had loved her best.

Saturday morning Amber slept in late, having the first good night's rest in a long time. Bets was due to arrive at eleven. They were going to lunch and the cinema just as she'd told Virginia. Amber couldn't wait to tell her friend what had happened.

She wanted to tell Adam, too, but hesitated. Theirs was a tenuous relationship. Both said they didn't want a relationship, yet she was growing involved. Look at her inclination to immediately share the information Will had given.

For a moment, she wondered if Adam would see her telling him as a subtle hint to let him know she was ready to find a new relationship and become a couple again. He'd feel threatened, she knew.

Maybe she shouldn't tell him. Maybe she should move to the old apartment, and ease off any contact with the man. He didn't want a future together.

But she was beginning to have doubts about her own protestations.

She liked being with him. He made her feel safe and cherished. She knew he was a man to depend upon. Too bad he had such a dangerous job, not to mention such a biased view toward pregnant widows.

Better she continue as they had been.

"Hey, girlfriend," Bets said breezily when she sailed into the apartment right at eleven. She gave Amber a quick hug and then studied her for a moment.

"Looking bigger than the last time I saw you. Clothes getting a bit snug?"

"I'm into elastic waist pants now, can't close my jeans. But I like my bigger breasts, I actually have a cleavage. Not that anyone's seeing it to be impressed."

Bets laughed. "Let's pick up a couple of low cut tops and see if cleavage has any effect on your neighbor. Will he be dropping by sometime?" she asked.

"Not likely. You ready to go? I don't want too big a lunch, I like popcorn at the movies."

The two young women left, talking and laughing. They took the bus to the mall where there were shops, fast-food restaurants, and a multiscreen theater. On the ride, Amber told Bets about Will Collins' visit.

"Wow, that's so cool. He came all the way to give you Jimmy's last words. Wish I could have met him."

"You want to meet every male in sight," Amber said.

"No, really, he sounds special. That was really a great thing he did. Right out of the hospital, too. How do you feel about it? I mean, it had to be tough hearing Jimmy's last words, but don't you think he gave you his blessing to go forward?"

"It sounded like it to me. But not yet, I'm sure."

"Oh, he had a date tagged on? I hope you have a happy life starting in four years, seven months and thirteen days, or something?"

Amber smiled and shook her head. "No dates attached. But I'm not ready."

"What about Adam Carruthers?"

"He's just a neighbor. Besides he's a firefighter. The last thing I'd want to do is fall for some guy who has a dangerous job. What if after a month of marriage, he got killed? I don't think that's a pattern I want repeated."

"I don't know, there are a lot of older firefighters. Plus they move up in the ranks and have easier jobs than the front line."

"Still, I think I want another teacher, or an insurance agent or something."

"*Boooorrrring*," Bets said. "I want someone with dash and flair."

Amber knew Adam would fit that bill. She should introduce the two of them.

The thought didn't sit well.

Maybe later, after she moved, she'd see about introducing them.

The day spent with her friend was fun. Bets had an irreverent way of looking at things. Her upbeat optimistic personality seemed contagious and by the time Amber returned home in the early evening, she was feeling better than she had in months. She hadn't laughed so much in ages. They agreed to get together more often over the remainder of the summer, and talk every few days on the phone. Bets worked full-time during the summer to afford school. But there were plenty of weekends and evenings.

Amber felt restless when she was alone. She went up on the rooftop deck to sit and watch the sunset. The couple from the third floor was there, with eyes only for each other. She wanted to tell them to cherish every moment together, but no one felt life would end soon, and they'd probably think she was crazy.

She pulled a chair near the rail and sat. Putting up her feet, she rested her hands on her tummy. She could feel the baby move from time to time, like a little flutter of a butterfly. She and her mother had discussed the changes, and how they felt about carrying new life—awestruck and humble, and thrilled beyond belief. Amber loved this child. How blessed she was to have it.

"Care for company?" Adam asked, standing near her.

"Sure do." She flashed him a smile, wondering if he thought it lit her face like Jimmy had.

"What did you do all day?" he asked after he dragged another chair over and sat. They were far enough from the other couple their conversation wouldn't be overheard.

"Went to the show with my friend Bets. We saw a comedy and laughed ourselves silly."

"Your mother-in-law okay?" he asked.

She nodded and looked at him speculatively.

"What? Do I have mustard on my chin or something?"

Amber laughed. "No, I was just thinking about something. After you left yesterday, I had a visitor." She proceeded to tell him about Lance Corporal William Collins, and the message he delivered. Adam listened attentively.

"How did you feel, hearing from your husband after so long?" he asked.

"It felt totally strange. And sad. And yet, I'm so glad to know he wasn't alone, that he didn't suffer pain. I felt sorry for Will. Imagine how he must have felt after Jimmy died."

Adam nodded and gazed out toward the ocean. "Tough position to be in. Nice of him to come by."

"It wouldn't have been the same in a letter, he said."

"Probably not."

Amber wasn't sure what she expected, but it was not this seeming disinterest. Not knowing what to say, she kept silent.

The sun was low on the horizon. Before long it would slip beneath the edge and darkness would fall. If he didn't say something by then, she'd get up and leave.

Adam looked at her again. "You okay with all this?"

"I'm fine. Why wouldn't I be?"

"Seems to me it brings it all back, like it just happened, instead of happening several months ago."

Amber nodded. "In a way. But the best part was where he said go on. That's what I heard. And Virginia heard it, too. So when the time is right, I know I can do it and not worry about being true to Jimmy or something."

"So now you're looking to move on?"

"I've been trying to do that for the last few months." Amber narrowed her eyes. "Or do you mean, now am I on the prowl for another guy?" She jumped up. "I should have known you'd think that way."

"Why else tell me?"

"I thought you'd be interested in something that happened to me. I should have known better." She headed for the door that led to the elevators.

"Wait." Adam rose and followed her.

"I don't think so," she said, continuing. Unfortunately, the elevator didn't immediately respond when she pressed the down button. He caught up with her easily.

"I didn't mean you were out trying to snag some guy. I meant, now you can move on without feeling guilty about everything."

"How did you know I feel guilty about everything?" she asked, startled. No one else had picked up on that.

He gave a half smile. "Honey, your emotions show clearly in your face, from happy to sad to guilty. Plus I know something of what you're going through, remember? My mom died. The first time I laughed after her death, I felt like the worst guy in the world. How could I laugh when my mother was dead?"

"Exactly," she said. "Or like kissing someone else when my husband of only a few months was dead."

"Oh." Adam looked flummoxed by that comment.

The elevator arrived, the door sliding slowly open.

She stepped inside. He followed. When the door closed, he pressed the button for her floor.

"Coming to visit?" she asked. She felt daring tonight. Hearing Jimmy's last words, being with Bets all day, had freed her. Maybe she'd explore this friendship and see where it led.

"I wanted to talk to you about moving," he said. "I was at the station today and four other guys have agreed to help. We can go as early as Tuesday, if that works for you."

So much for being daring, Amber thought. He couldn't wait to get rid of her.

"I was having lunch with Virginia on Tuesday, but I'll postpone that. Don't want to waste manpower when it's available."

"Want to go out to dinner?" Adam asked when the elevator reached her floor.

"What? Wouldn't that seem like I was pursuing you?"

"Cut it out, Amber. I didn't mean that. You know my position, I know yours. We both have to eat. Why not together?"

"Dinner out on a Saturday night sounds too much like a date," she said slowly.

They walked to her apartment and she opened the door. Adam followed her in. He looked around, as if judging the number of boxes and how long it would take him and his friends to move them.

"Not a date. You don't date, you're a widow, remember?" he teased.

She threw him a dark look and went to get her purse. It was after six. By the time they got anywhere, it would be time to eat.

"Where to?" she asked.

"What do you like?"

"My favorite is Chinese."

"Then Chinatown it is."

Amber relished soaring up San Francisco's steep hills, and down. The wind blew her hair in the open car. She almost laughed with joy. The baby kicked and rolled, as if enjoying the sensations as well.

Before long they were in the narrow streets of Chinatown. Adam parked in a city lot and took her hand to join the throng that crowded the sidewalk. A favorite tourist attraction, Chinatown was crowded with natives and visitors alike. He led her to a small establishment off

Grant Avenue. Entering, they had to walk up a flight of stairs to reach the restaurant. By the time they were seated, Amber noted they were the only Caucasians in the crowd.

"Must be good," she murmured.

"I think so. What would you like?"

After they ordered, he asked about Corporal Collins' visit. She told him some of the stories Will had shared. "I think I understand a little better why Jimmy liked his job so much, and preferred to spend time on the Army base rather than with me."

Adam shook his head.

"What?"

"Maybe you understand it, but I don't. Why wouldn't he want to spend every minute he could with you?"

She smiled at the compliment. Looking at Adam, Amber realized she didn't know as much about the man as she'd like. Even just friends shared more.

"So tell me about your work, about why you became a firefighter. Did you always want to be a fireman when you were growing up?"

He shook his head. "At one point I wanted to be an astronaut. Another time I thought I'd like to be some gazillionaire. But a neighboring apartment building in Fresno burned when I was fourteen. Two people lost their lives, several families lost all they had in the world. I'll never forget the work the firefighters did to try to save everything—possessions and people alike. The feeling they must have had when they succeeded in saving two-thirds of the building and apartments had to be great. That was when I thought I'd like to do that—help people, make a difference."

"And have you?" She still couldn't understand men and women risking their lives in such a dangerous pursuit.

Granted, saving lives was worthwhile, but to her, all the possessions in the world didn't equal the risk of one person's life.

"A few times. Once I received my E.M.T. certificate, I started going on patrols once every few months to keep current. I've delivered a baby. What a high that was."

She smiled. "Tell me."

Dinner passed swiftly as Adam regaled her with the adventures of his world. She marveled at the things he'd done from delivering the baby, to saving two lives, one a heart-attack victim and another who was choking. She wondered if he glossed over the dangers when he told her about some of the fires they fought. He already knew she thought his job was highly dangerous. Maybe he sugarcoated things to make it seem not so.

Adam knew he was bragging, but he wanted Amber to be impressed. And to understand why he liked his work, felt compelled to do only this job. If she could understand, maybe she wouldn't be so worried about the dangers. He tried to explain how their training was ongoing. How the buddy system had everyone watching out for each other. How the captain would never deliberately put his crew into a situation beyond what they could handle.

And if she saw how much good they did, it had to outweigh the danger.

Dinner was long finished when he slowed down.

"I've probably bored you to tears," he said, noting the time.

"Not at all, and you know it. I'm fascinated. Horrified a time or two, I have to admit. I can't decide whether to admire you to death, or be fearful the next time I hear a siren. Don't you worry the next call will be your last?"

"Amber, most firefighters retire from their jobs, not die in the field."

She shivered. "That may be true, but it doesn't stop all the deaths that happen in spite of all the precautions you talked about."

He didn't want her to focus on that. He wanted her more open about his job.

"Ready to go?" he asked.

She nodded.

He quickly settled the bill, and took her hand as they exited the restaurant. The lights from all the shops on Grant Avenue made the street almost as bright as day.

"Want to walk a bit?"

"Sure."

Adam was pleased she wasn't in a hurry to return home. He wanted her to enjoy the evening, not just have dinner and return to their separate flats.

For the first time ever, he considered asking a woman to move in with him. Without his job to go to, he was lonely. Amber met a need he didn't know he'd had. Different from the camaraderie at the station. A longing rose that was hard to define. Lust? Desire?

Or the yearning for permanency?

CHAPTER EIGHT

TUESDAY morning Bets arrived before eight.

"What are you doing here?" Amber asked, greeting her friend.

"I took a day off to help with the move."

"Oh, no you didn't. You wanted to see Adam," Amber said, laughing. She hugged her friend. "But whatever the reason, I'm glad to see you."

"Here, bagels and lattes," Bets said, holding out a white bag. The hot drinks were balanced on a cardboard tray. "We can eat and then I'll have enough strength to help however you can use me."

"We just might have time to eat. Adam and his friends will be here at nine."

Bets surveyed the stacked boxes, the bed already stripped of its linens.

"You seem ready."

"As ever. By the time my folks get home tomorrow, I'll be only a few blocks from their place, and settled in. I will still need more furniture, and all the baby stuff."

"Does it seem strange going back to where you grew up?"

"Yes, especially since the things I remember won't be there. Mom got rid of a lot of the furniture when she and

Matt bought new things together. But I have my furnishings, and a couple of items I liked from our place. Think how spacious it'll feel without a lot of stuff."

Promptly at nine, Amber heard a knock at the door. She and Bets had eaten, then begun putting the kitchenette items into boxes and bags.

Adam grinned at her when she opened the door and her heart tripped into double time. His eyes seemed to stare right down into her soul. That smile had every fiber of her being focused on him.

"Ready to rock and roll?" he asked.

She glanced behind him where several tall, muscular men filled the hall.

"Come in. I'm as ready as I'll ever be."

The next few moments were taken up with introductions. Amber was bemused by the tiny apartment full of robust, healthy young men. They all resembled Adam in their size and fitness. Bart was tall and dark. Jed was blond, and so tanned Amber knew he had to spend his off time at the beach. He looked like a surfer. Trevor and Brandon were almost interchangeable with their short brown hair and infectious grins. Trevor's wife Jill was also introduced.

"I thought you might need some balance to the testosterone overload," she said with a laugh. "These guys can be intimidating if you don't know them."

Bets was introduced and flattered by some of the compliments she heard from the men. She, Jill and Amber hit it off perfectly and were soon laughing together as if they'd all been friends for years.

Adam took charge, despite some teasing from the other men. In short order, the pile of boxes disappeared.

"You're riding with me," he said to Amber when the last

box left in Bart's strong arms. "You'll have to show us how to get to the apartment and let us in."

"I'm ready," she said.

"We'll keep packing the kitchen stuff," Bets said as she and Jill worked together.

"Then we'll move to the bathroom. The rest is gone, right?" Jill asked.

"Except for the furniture. Wow, I can't believe I'll be all moved before dinner."

"Oh, yeah," Jill said. "That way we get to all go out together and have fun."

Amber smiled and followed Adam. They led the small caravan through the city streets. Bart, Trevor and Brandon all had pickup trucks they'd volunteered. Each was packed high with boxes, tied down for safety.

Of course there was no parking in front of the apartment, one reason Amber had never longed for a car. But there was a loading zone, so two of the pickups swooped into the space. Brandon double-parked. When Adam dropped Amber off, he told her to let Brandon know as soon as he parked, he'd be back to stay with the truck while Brandon helped the others unload. His frustration at limited mobility due to his arm was evident. Amber patted his shoulder and smiled.

"I'm sure you'll have many chances to help out. Let your friends do it today," she said.

He scowled at her. She laughed and headed off to unlock the apartment.

Two more trips and her entire household was moved. The men set up the furniture exactly where she wanted it. Jill and Bets helped her unpack the kitchen and bath. Both were huge in comparison to the ones in her studio apart-

ment. She felt like she'd won the jackpot with the spacious-
ness of the apartment and so many people helping.

It was only late afternoon when everyone finished, but
when Brandon asked if they were ready for dinner, everyone yelled yes.

"Where do we go?" Trevor asked.

Jill rolled her eyes and smiled at Amber. "Wait for it."

"Tony's!" the men yelled.

"Tony's?" Amber asked.

"Home away from home," Bart said.

"Pizza," Adam explained. "A place near the station.
Best pizza in the city."

"I'll treat," Amber said. She was quickly outvoted when
the men said no way would they let her pay. They were
glad for the exercise. And for a chance to meet Adam's
new girl.

She looked at him, hoping the panic that hit didn't show.

He shrugged, amusement evident. Leaning close, he
brushed back her hair and whispered in her ear, "Let them
think what they want, we know the truth."

"Hey, none of that. Wait until you're alone," Jed said,
nudging Adam. "Let's go eat, I'm starving."

The firefighters laughed. Apparently Jed was perpetu-
ally hungry.

Tony's was a typical pizza parlor with large tables, a juke-
box playing popular tunes, and lots of noise. They comman-
deered a large round table near the back. Pitchers of soft
drinks soon appeared, and orders were placed for several
large pizzas with the works. Bets sat between Jed and Bart,
Jill between Trevor and Brandon, with Amber beside
Brandon and Adam on the other side. Before the pizza arrived,
however, Jill switched with Brandon and sat beside Amber.

"It's hard to have a normal conversation when these guys are celebrating," Jill said.

"Celebrating my move." Amber shook her head. "What else do they celebrate?"

"You name it and they find a cause to celebrate." Jill looked at them all for a few moments, then at Amber. "They're tight, you know? Have to be, doing the kind of work they do. I think it's amazing how fast Adam fit in. He's only been at this station since May. The others have been here for years."

"Scary job," Amber murmured, studying the men. They were confident, bordering on arrogant. Maybe they had the right. They faced death daily, and won. She shivered.

"Maybe, but they're trained for it. And better they do what they love than be stuck in some job they'd hate. Life wouldn't hold much meaning then, would it?" Jill said.

"Don't you worry about Trevor?"

"Every day. But he wouldn't be who he was if he didn't do what he loved," she said. "I wouldn't want to change him. I love him just as he is."

Amber kept her eyes from Adam. She would not look at him, though the urge to do so was strong. She did not love him. She would not love him. He was merely a neighbor who helped her out. After dinner, she'd go back to her apartment near Van Ness, and he'd return to the one near the University and they'd probably not see each other again.

The thought almost stole her appetite.

Despite working hard all day, no one was in a hurry to end the evening. The tall tales and jokes the men told entertained them all. Bets was in heaven, throwing out jokes and telling funny stories about her own work and efforts to get a college education.

Amber had the best time she'd ever had, sitting back and enjoying the fun that swirled around. She and Jill made plans to get together for lunch before the group finally broke up at almost midnight.

"I can't believe it's so late," she said when the others had said goodbye and left her and Adam on the sidewalk in front of the restaurant. He was driving her home.

"Time flies when you're having fun," Adam said, slinging his good arm around her shoulders as they walked to his car.

Amber leaned against him a little, feeling safe and secure. She was tired, but in a pleasant way.

"Thank you again for all your help."

"If you say that one more time tonight, I swear I'll do something drastic," he said.

"Like what?"

"Like this." He stopped, turned to face her and took her into his arms, kissing her long and deep.

"Oh," she said endless moments later when he raised his head.

"You've thanked us enough times. It was our pleasure to help you out."

"The others didn't even know me."

"They still like helping out. And now they know you. So if you need help in the future, don't hesitate to call."

Amber doubted she'd need their services for anything ever again. But it felt nice to have Adam say they'd come if she called.

The entire evening had been special—because of Adam. He'd made sure she was included. Laughed when she'd told a funny story, and just been beside her the entire time. Occasionally he'd touched her, brushing against her arm when reaching for more drinks, or linking fingers with hers on the bench after they'd finished eating.

Amber was afraid she was falling for the man, and she couldn't let that happen. Ever. She couldn't go through losing a special person in her life again. Not any time soon at least. Maybe when she was eighty.

When they reached the apartment, she was reluctant to go inside. But there was no handy parking place, and who knew how far away they'd find one.

"I'll say good-night here and run on up," she said when he pulled into the loading zone.

"I can park here long enough to see you to your door." He climbed out and went to her door, opening it and reaching for her hand.

Amber didn't want him to go, but it was late. Despite his cast, he'd done a lot in the move. She knew he had to be tired. She was.

"Good night, Amber," he said at the door, kissing her again.

Wednesday Amber finished putting things to suit herself. It was her apartment now, not her mother's. Though by the end of the day, it resembled the home she'd known as a child. Which wasn't all bad; at least she knew where everything was.

She called Virginia to let her know she had moved in, arranging to have lunch on Friday after her appointment with the doctor. She left a message at her mother's to let her know she'd moved.

Then, at loose ends, Amber went for a walk, to refamiliarize herself with the neighborhood.

It was a short walk to Fort Mason and the Bay. She sat

on steps overlooking the water and remembered the roof garden in her old apartment house. Would Adam be up there now, staring out to the ocean?

Maybe she should call him to thank him again for his help yesterday. She laughed. "Right, like he didn't make it clear last night I'd said thank you enough." Thinking about his kiss had her yearning for more.

Sighing, she rose and began to walk. Exercise was good for her and the baby. She wanted to be the best mother in the world. Or second best, after her own.

The next afternoon her mother called to let her know they were home, and to invite her to dinner to tell her about their fabulous trip to Greece.

Amber gladly accepted. She was frankly bored and wanted some company.

Her mother looked radiant when she greeted Amber that evening.

"The baby's bedroom looks wonderful. How did you ever get it all set up yourself?"

"I had help," Amber said, returning her hug.

"Oh?" Sara asked, looking at Matt. "Did someone from Matt's work come over? Dex, maybe?"

"No, it was Adam Carruthers. My neighbor." Amber went to sit down.

"Oh, that was nice." Sara seemed at a loss.

"We appreciate both of you taking care of that. The room is all ready now for the baby," Matt said, filling the awkward silence.

"So tell me all about your trip," Amber said, hoping to change the subject.

"You have got to go to Greece. It's the most wonderful

place on the earth," said Sara, her whole face alight with enthusiasm. "The beaches are incredible, the people so warm and friendly, and the food is delicious. The hotel was exotic. Our room was fantastic."

Amber laughed.

"So you liked it, huh?"

"I did. So did Matt, right?" Sara asked, slanting her husband a sexy look.

"Yes, but I suggest you not give her a play by play recap of everything we did."

Sara blushed and shook her head. "Just the touristy things," she teased.

Amber smiled, enjoying the interaction between her parents.

Her parents. Matt was now her stepfather. She wasn't sure how to react to him sometimes. He was only fourteen years older than she was, but a world of experience separated them. He was perfect for her mother—who had never looked so happy. Once again Amber was struck by envy. She wished she had a special someone who would look at her as if she was the greatest thing on the face of the earth.

"Sara told me you've already moved. How did you manage that?" Matt asked.

"Adam rounded up some of his friends from the fire station and between us all, we moved in no time."

"Adam, again," Sara said.

"He's just a neighbor, Mom."

"Not anymore."

Amber nodded.

When they sat down for dinner, after hearing about Sara and Matt's trip to Greece, Amber told them about her visit from Corporal Collins. And about Virginia driving her crazy.

"She needs a hobby," Amber grumbled.

"So suggest one," Sara said. "You know some of her friends, don't you? Ask them to invite her to lunch or something. Sometimes it's hard to get back into the swing of things after being out of touch for a while."

"Maybe, but I still wish I could find something for her to do that would focus some of her attention away from me," Amber said.

They arranged to meet the next morning at the doctor's office. Amber said she had errands to run so would meet them there, rather than have Matt pick her up as he'd offered.

"Going to let them tell you the sex of the baby?" Sara asked as Amber was leaving.

"Yes. I think I will."

"Me, too. Tomorrow we'll know!"

There was a message from Virginia on her answering machine when she returned to her apartment. Amber had hoped maybe Adam would have called to see how she was doing. But he hadn't. She couldn't think up a good reason to call him. They had exchanged phone numbers on Tuesday. Maybe she should have withheld that as a reason to call.

Once she found out what gender her baby would be, she'd call him and tell him. He'd want to know, wouldn't he? On impulse, Amber invited Virginia to join her at the doctor's the next morning. They could go to lunch together after the visit, since their Tuesday lunch had been canceled.

"I was sure it would be a boy," Virginia said when they sat down to lunch at the Tea Garden Restaurant on Van Ness shortly after one o'clock the next afternoon.

"Are you disappointed?" Amber asked, thrilled to know

her daughter would be born before Thanksgiving, if the doctor was right.

"I guess not." Virginia tried to put on a brighter face. "I just never thought about a girl. I thought it'd be a boy, like Jimmy."

"But this isn't Jimmy." Amber wondered if Virginia had thought the baby would be just like her son—a replacement almost. "It's part of Jimmy, but part of me and my family as well. It might be better to have a girl, we won't be looking for her to be so much like he was."

Virginia nodded. "Sometimes, Amber, you are wise beyond your years. I think I'll just have a light meal today. I want to get home to James."

"Call him, tell him the news if you like. Lunch can wait."

"No, I'll tell him when I get home."

"So do you want to come to the hospital with me when I go for the tour?" Amber asked, trying to make up for the other woman's obvious disappointment. Amber was delighted with whatever the baby would be, and it had been a lovely surprise when the doctor told her this morning the baby was female. She mainly wanted a healthy baby.

But for a split second, she'd wished for a rowdy little boy, getting in and out of trouble. Would she find someone one day to marry and have a family with? Would she get her little boy with dark eyes and dark hair?

Adam immediately came to mind. She pushed the image away. She hadn't seen nor heard from him since Tuesday night. Now that they were no longer neighbors, she didn't expect to hear from him often.

Who was she kidding? She wanted to hear from him every day. Suddenly she looked at Virginia and realized she wanted what this woman had, a loving husband and devoted father. She wanted the closeness her mother and Matt shared. She wanted someone to love and to be loved by.

And she wished with all her heart it was Adam Carruthers.

"No," she said involuntarily.

"What?" Virginia looked up from the menu.

"I mean, no fattening stuff for me. I'll join you and have a salad as well."

"I thought you'd take the hospital tour with your mother," Virginia said after they'd placed their orders.

"She'll be going with Matt. I'd like someone to go with me," Amber said.

"I'd be delighted. Thank you for asking me," Virginia said rather formally.

"I'll call you as soon as I make the appointment. What day works best for you?"

They discussed the tour, the news about the baby being a girl, and argued slightly over the furnishings yet again.

"Tell you what, why don't you work with Kathy and Bets on the baby shower? They're throwing one for me in late September at Kathy's place. You remember Kathy, don't you? She went to school with Jimmy and me."

"The red-haired girl with a million freckles?" Virginia guessed.

"Right. She's pregnant, too. Her baby is due any day. She said she'd be ready to give the shower easily by the time the date arrives, but I'm sure there are things that need to be done beforehand."

"I'd love to," Virginia said.

Amber breathed a sigh of relief. Maybe she could find other things for Virginia to do that would help her occupy her and leave less time for dwelling on Amber and the coming grandchild.

When Amber returned home it was late afternoon. She called Adam, anxious to speak with him. His answering machine picked up. Slowly Amber hung up. She wanted to talk to him, not leave some message. She'd try later.

Amber tried three more times before going to bed that night. She didn't leave any messages. She'd rather catch him than wait or look needy by calling after she left the message.

Saturday morning Amber was busy vacuuming the empty bedroom in preparation for getting the furniture. She had bought some curtains she liked, and bedding to go with them. Her plans today included shopping for furniture, and a few things like diapers and bibs. She wanted to wait until after her friends threw her a baby shower to see what she got there that she wouldn't need to buy herself. Money wasn't that lavish that she could duplicate things.

When she heard the knock on the door, she thought her mother had dropped by. She hoped it was that, and not Virginia.

Adam stood in the doorway when she opened the door.

"Hi," he said, stepping inside. "Busy?"

"Hi yourself," Amber said, shutting the door and looking at him. She could study him all day. He looked fit and even darker tanned than the last time she'd seen him. His cast was still in evidence, but otherwise he looked as fit as ever.

"What are you doing here?" she asked.

"Came to see if you wanted to do something today."

"I was thinking of going shopping for baby things," she said, ready to cancel at a moment's notice if Adam wanted to do something. Being with him would be more fun.

"I guess you need to get things going with that," he said.

"I guess. It's not like I can change my mind or anything. Besides, I can't wait to see my daughter."

"It's a girl?" he asked.

"I found out yesterday," she said.

"You should have called me," he said.

Amber cleared her throat nervously. "Actually I did."

"I wasn't home. You could have left a message."

"I guess. Where were you?"

"Went to the station. They're shorthanded on the ambulance crew, so I helped out with paperwork. Never the fun part of the job, but it got me out of the house."

"Getting cabin fever?" she teased.

"You know it. Can't wait to get back to work." He held up his arm. "It's healing good, the doctor said. I saw him on Thursday. Might get a limited release in the next week or two—for light work, not normal activities. But heck, something is better than nothing."

"I wouldn't be so impatient to get back into your line of work."

He ruffled her hair. "You worry too much. I'll be fine."

"Maybe, or maybe not. Isn't there something else you could do that wouldn't be so dangerous?"

"Like what? Be a dispatcher?" His demeanor changed. The amusement that usually lurked in his eyes was missing. He didn't like talking about changing jobs, she could tell that instantly.

"Not a dispatcher. What about—" Amber's mind went blank. She couldn't picture Adam in a suit and tie in some dull job in the city. Maybe a construction worker. Until she pictured him climbing up the high-rise buildings that were going up around the city. That didn't seem any safer.

"Never mind. Want to come shopping with me?"

"What do I know about baby furniture?"

"Probably as much as I do. But you might have pointers from things you've seen on the job that I wouldn't think of."

He seemed to weigh the pros and cons of her invitation then slowly smiled. Amber felt her insides turn over.

"I'll come shopping if we finish by noon. Then we can take a ride up the coast, and be back in time for dinner at Trevor's. Jill wanted me to bring you over."

It was just after nine o'clock in the morning. Adam wanted to spend the entire day with her—including dinner?

"Let me change quickly and I'll be ready," she said.

Adam thought she looked fine just the way she was, but he realized women had different outlooks on things. He wandered around the living room. She'd hung pictures on the walls, better seen in this room than in the studio she'd had before. Or maybe the pictures hadn't been in the old apartment. He didn't remember them.

He looked into the kitchen. It was larger than his. Perhaps he could get her to offer to cook a couple of meals for him. It didn't take as long as he'd thought it would to get from his apartment to hers. Not as convenient as running down a flight of stairs, however.

He went to the window and looked out over the busy street. He'd missed her. Clenching a fist, he raised his arm and rested it against the window edge, staring out, seeing nothing. He hadn't expected to miss her so much when she moved. It had been all he could do to keep from calling her every day this week. She'd only been gone four days. He couldn't believe the hole she'd left.

It wasn't as if they were dating or anything. Or had even known each other for that long, come to that.

But there was something about Amber that had gotten beneath his skin, and he wasn't sure that was going away.

She was meant for love and family and babies. A home full of laughter and commotion and activities that revolved around family.

He'd been alone a long time, even before his mother died.

"Ready," she said.

He turned slowly and looked at her. She was beautiful. Obviously pregnant, but not huge yet, she had the glow that he'd heard pregnant women got. Her smile was infectious, and he felt the kick of attraction deep inside. He wanted her. He wished he could see that blond hair spread on his pillow with her eyes shining up at him. He'd love to touch and taste that satiny skin, run his fingers through her silky hair, and lock the world outside, making a place for only the two of them.

He shook his head slowly. He was losing his mind.

"Something wrong?" Amber asked.

"Not a thing. Baby store here we come."

Adam couldn't believe he'd said that. He knew nothing about babies, or children in general. He'd never expected to have any, since usually a wife was first required. He could change that, by staying in touch with Amber. She'd invite him over to see her new daughter, and he would go, to see the mother.

He felt like he was playing with fire—exposing himself to the flames, dancing away when he felt himself drawn too close. Would he get singed? Or worse, hurt her in some way?

CHAPTER NINE

ADAM felt like a bull in a china shop in the baby store. It was huge, with everything imaginable for babies, from car seats to cribs to toys and clothing.

"Big business," he murmured following Amber to the furniture section.

"People always have families," she said. "First-time parents especially want everything for their new baby. I was going to get some secondhand things, but Matt insisted on paying for new."

He looked at some of the tiny clothes hanging from racks as they passed by. Did babies really come that small? They looked as if they'd fit dolls.

Amber seemed to know exactly what she wanted for her baby, and was soon discussing pros and cons with the salesclerk, glancing at Adam once in a while. "What do you think?" she asked.

"Whatever you want," he said.

The clerk beamed. Undoubtedly the man thought Adam was a doting husband and father-to-be. He had an urge to set him straight, but hesitated. It didn't matter. He'd never see the guy again after today. Why make things awkward?

"Is that everything?" the salesclerk said, checking his list.

"I want a glider rocker like my mother got here recently," Amber said, walking over to a row of rockers. She sat in one and moved back and forth, then rose and tried another.

Adam watched her. For a moment when she pretended she was holding a baby to test the armrests, he pictured her with a child of his. Dark hair and eyes, lusty cry, fretful until his mother soothed him and fed him.

He looked away and scowled. He was not going down that road. What if the worst did happen and he was killed at his job? Did he want some woman to be left alone with kids, struggling to make it, like his mother had been? Like Amber was since Jimmy died?

Only, Amber wasn't struggling. She had herself together, had set goals, and had a loving support network surrounding her. She was stronger at this young age than his mother had ever been.

The salesclerk finished writing up the order and discussing delivery dates with Amber.

"Make it next Tuesday and I'll be there to set it up," he said, stepping into the conversation. He didn't like the way the man was looking at Amber. Couldn't he see she was pregnant? Didn't seem to matter, he was definitely interested in her. Time Adam let him know she was not available.

"Of course, sir," the clerk said, stepping back hastily. He looked at Adam and immediately stepped back another foot. "I just need an address and contact phone, in case the delivery runs late."

Amber took Adam's arm as the clerk left to confirm the order. "What's the matter with you? You looked as if you wanted to chew him up and spit him out."

"He was flirting with you."

"He was not."

"Yes, he was."

Amber frowned. "He was? He couldn't be, I'm pregnant."

"So? You're still a beautiful woman."

"You're nuts. Wait another month or two and say that."

"I probably will," he muttered.

They took his car and drove north on Highway One, heading for the redwoods. Amber loved driving with the top down. She had lots to think about as Adam competently handled the convertible through the twists and turns in the road. He'd called her beautiful. And actually thought a stranger would flirt with her. How cool was that? Not that she wanted anyone to flirt with her. But the mere thought she wasn't invisible any longer intrigued her.

Did Adam want to flirt with her?

She looked at him. Did she want to flirt with him?

Jimmy had been gone longer than the few months since his death. She was young, healthy and falling for the man next to her. Could she make him change his mind about his job?

She turned to watch the trees whiz by. No, she couldn't move Adam from his chosen path. That wouldn't make a good relationship. If he did that, in time he'd come to resent her. And she wasn't sure she wanted a long-term relationship with a man who would give in to her every whim. Not that she didn't like getting her own way in things, but she didn't need it all the time.

Could she bear to have him leave each day and be scared all the time he wouldn't come home? She had had that basic trust shattered by Jimmy's death. It wasn't something she'd regain soon.

When they arrived at Muir Woods, Amber looked at him.

"We're going hiking?"

"After we eat. They have a nice deli here that serves terrific sandwiches. Then I thought we could take one of the walks. They're easy—even for a pregnant woman."

"I love it here," Amber said. "I've only been a couple of times, but it seems a world away from San Francisco."

"It's one of my favorite places," Adam said, getting out of the car.

Muir Woods was an old-growth forest of Coast Redwoods. The climate was a microcosm away from San Francisco's, and usually cooler than the surrounding countryside.

The tall redwoods towered above them, shading everything, allowing dappled sunlight to spot the forest floor.

Lunch was quick and before long Amber walked along the level wide path of beaten dirt, lined on both sides by split rail fencing. Adam reached for her hand.

"You're not too cold are you?" he asked. "It's cooler here than in the city."

"I'm fine." With his hand wrapped around hers, she was toasty warm. And her heart was beating fast enough to keep her blood warm all day. She tried to enjoy the walk. Her awareness of Adam escalated. As if the mere thought of a kiss conjured up the notion in his head, he stopped on a deserted spot of the trail and leaned over to kiss her.

Amber wished the quick brush of lips had evolved into more, but they were in a public venue and other visitors to the park could come by at any moment.

She had never come with Jimmy, only with her mother. Adam's bringing her was special. And she vowed to enjoy every moment of the experience.

By the time they drove back to the city heading for Trevor and Jill's, Amber was growing tired. She'd already had a full day, and the further along she got in her pregnancy, the more quickly she became fatigued. Yet she never suggested that Adam call and cancel. She looked forward to seeing Jill again, and seeing the interaction between Adam and his friends.

It gave her greater insight into the man himself, though she was playing with fire learning more about him. So far it had all been to the good. He would make a wonderful partner, and, she suspected, a wonderful father. But she needed to keep things in perspective. He was not interested in a relationship, and certainly not marriage. She wasn't either, so friends it was.

Trevor and Jill greeted her warmly. Jill invited her into the kitchen while she finished preparing the meal, while the men stayed in the living room.

"So, are you all settled in the new apartment?" Jill asked.

"Pretty much," Amber said, sitting on the high stool indicated at the breakfast bar, watching Jill whip around her kitchen. "Can I help?"

"Nope, but I do like the company."

"We went shopping for baby furniture today," Amber said.

"We?"

"Adam and I."

Jill smiled. "Good. I was hoping you two were hitting it off. He's a great guy and needs someone special."

Amber was startled at the comment.

"We're just friends."

"Best kind of marriages are between friends who are also lovers, don't you think?" Jill asked.

"Marriage? There's no talk of that between us. I hardly know the man. And there are complications."

Jill looked up. "Oh, I'm so sorry. I almost forgot about your husband. Of course it's too soon, and all. I'm not saying you two will rush off to Tahoe and get married right away."

Amber thought about the last time she ran off to Tahoe to get married. She and Jimmy had rushed through a wedding, but never really built a marriage. If she ever took the plunge again, it would definitely not include a Lake Tahoe wedding.

"Adam doesn't want to get married."

Jill shrugged.

"And I don't want to marry a firefighter," Amber said firmly.

The other woman looked up at that.

"Why ever not? They're terrific. And really hot lovers." She laughed at her joke.

"Don't you worry every day when Trevor leaves that he may not come back?" Amber asked.

Jill shook her head. "Not really. I trust things will be fine. But if not, what am I supposed to do, live in fear for a future that might never come? I want to enjoy life to the fullest right now. I have a great husband, a good job, and if fate is kind, I'll have it all until I'm an old, old woman."

"But what if you don't?"

"Then I don't. But should I miss the love of my life out of worry about what might never happen?" Jill countered.

Love of her life. Amber had at one time thought Jimmy the love of her life. But that had been back when they were in school. Lately, however, she was changing her mind about things. She wondered, if Jimmy had returned, if they would have rediscovered that special spark that had once blazed between them.

"It's hard to lose someone you love," Amber said slowly.

"I bet it is. I haven't had that experience yet," Jill said.

"My grandparents and parents and all are still around. But a person can't just shut down after someone dies, either. It's a normal part of life. Here, help me carry the food in and we'll call the men."

Amber carried the platter of roast beef, went back for vegetables. Jill carried in the potatoes and rolls. When she called Trevor and Adam, they quickly joined them.

Amber thought there was enough food to feed a small army, but with the two men it quickly disappeared.

Jill and Trevor kept her entertained. Trevor loved to tell stories about the fire station. Adam didn't play a part in most of them, he'd transferred recently to this station so was still considered the new kid on the block. He'd act defensive sometimes, but by the twinkle in his eye, Amber knew he was just playing along with Trevor.

It was late by the time Adam suggested they leave. Amber had been tired earlier, but had found her second wind, and thoroughly enjoyed the evening.

"They are so fun to be with," she said when Adam pulled away from the curb, driving toward her place.

"I know. Trevor is funny at work, too. Keeps things from getting too serious at times."

"Are all the men like that? You seem to keep a bright outlook on life."

"It's a great life, why wouldn't I? There are as many different personalities as there are men and women working at the station. Most are optimistic, I think. Aren't you?"

Amber felt her usual outlook was definitely more positive than negative. Though she'd lost some of that over the last months. "I think so. Even when I get knocked down, I come back." She was surprised to realize she had come back. She still mourned Jimmy's passing, and as her mother said, would probably always miss him. But she was looking to the future, to the birth of her daughter, and getting her teaching credential.

"Thank you for a wonderful time," she said when Adam pulled into the loading zone before her apartment.

"I'll be back on Tuesday to set up the furniture," he said.

"You don't have to," she said.

"Yes, I do." He brushed back her hair, threading his fingers into the softness and pulled her closer. His kiss was gentle, sweet and far too short.

Tuesday morning Adam woke with a feeling of anticipation. He hadn't seen Amber in three days. And as far as he was concerned, that was three days too long. He wished she hadn't moved across town. It was one thing to run into her in the same apartment, or even at the park, something else again to run into her across town. She'd know he'd come just to see her.

"Is that so wrong?" he asked as he shaved. Being with her made him happier.

He stared at his reflection. Was that what love was about? Not making someone else happy, but finding happiness in their company? Was he falling in love with a widow who never wanted to marry again?

He swished the razor in the water and applied himself to shaving. Philosophy so early in the morning wasn't his thing. Yet the more he thought about it, the more he wondered if he could convince her to take a chance—at least let them explore their friendship to see where it would lead.

He had never planned to marry, himself, but if Amber changed his mind, maybe he could change hers.

He banged the cast against the doorjamb in his hurry to get dressed. It didn't even hurt. He flexed his fingers, tightened them into as much of a fist as he could with the plaster covering his palm. A mild ache was all. He was definitely healing.

It wouldn't come fast enough. He was bored with his own company and lack of activity. He would never take perfect health for granted again.

Grabbing a bite to eat, he quickly headed for Amber's place. He couldn't wait to see her again.

When she opened the door a half hour later, Adam felt the punch of seeing her clear through. Her eyes widened when they saw him. He would swear he'd seen a glimmer of happiness. She swept her arm to the side inviting him into the apartment.

"What are you doing here so early?" she asked.

She was dressed. The shorts revealed long slender legs. Her loose top couldn't completely camouflage the growing mound of her stomach. Except for that distinctive bulge, she was still slender.

Her hair was shining, hanging down to her shoulders. He wanted to wrap it around his hands, let the strands flow through his fingers. If he leaned closer, he'd smell that special scent that was Amber's alone. He leaned forward a bit, and she came to meet him, raising her face to his, letting her eyes drift close.

Adam kissed her, stepping in closer, drawing her into his arms. She was so sweet and warm. He wanted to lose himself in her embrace and spend the next millennium without moving.

A short jab to his abdomen had him jerk back.

"What was that?"

Amber giggled, taking his hand and putting it on her stomach.

"Little missy is up and about," she said, holding it on one part. In only seconds, Adam felt the definite movement, and another jab. Awe filled him. This was her baby, moving in the womb, making her presence known. He'd never felt an unborn child before. His eyes locked with hers as they shared the moment. He could feel a poke again, and this time he tried to figure out the shape—a foot maybe.

"Does it hurt?"

"No. Sometimes it's a little uncomfortable, and I expect as she grows and the space becomes tighter, it'll be even more, but it doesn't hurt. I think it's cool."

"I do, too."

A few minutes later all activity ceased.

"Over for now, I think," Amber said.

Slowly Adam raised his hands to cup her face. He kissed her, in longing and in gratitude for sharing.

He was breathing hard when he pulled back. This wasn't the time or the place to follow through. She was still hurting from her husband's death, and the deliverymen could show up at any moment.

"Want some coffee?" she asked.

Adam was pleased to note she was breathing as hard as he was. Her mouth was rosy from his kiss, and her eyes still held the mysterious look women got when they were caught in the moment.

He didn't want coffee, he wanted her. Or a cold shower.

"Fine," he said, walking across the living room to the small hallway and into the baby's room. The curtains were on the windows. Otherwise it was empty. Soon to be filled with the furniture they'd selected last weekend.

He wanted to do more than set up the furniture. He wanted to make a contribution for the baby. But her parents had bought about all she needed. At least he could put it together.

"I can't believe soon I'll have a little girl sleeping in here," she said from the doorway, holding out a mug of hot coffee.

He took it and nodded, thinking she looked too young to be a mother.

"You going to be able to manage school in the fall?"

"I think so. I might have to take delayed finals, but I'm hoping I can keep up. If not, then I'll just take the course work over in the spring. It'll set back my graduation, but I can handle that."

"Who will watch the baby?"

She turned and led the way back into the living room. "That's still open for discussion. Virginia wanted to raise the baby altogether. Or at least she did before she found out it was a girl."

"What does that mean?"

"I think she thought it'd be a little boy just like Jimmy. That she could relive his childhood through his son."

"It wouldn't be the same."

"I know that. I think she does, too, now. So she's a possible."

"And your mother?"

"Until they start traveling. She's really got a case of wanderlust. Whatever happens, I'm sure I'll find someone."

For one startling moment, Adam thought he'd volunteer. He'd love to watch Amber's child. He could take her to the fire station and show her off. Take her to the beach and watch as the baby stared at the ocean with wide eyes, or followed a seagull as it soared above them.

He looked away. He was losing it. Too much inactivity had atrophied his brain. He wasn't a baby person. He was a firefighter. A lone wolf who liked the status quo just fine.

He sat on the sofa and sipped the hot coffee. The sooner the furniture arrived, the sooner he'd have something to do besides give way to flights of fantasy.

Amber brought out some cinnamon rolls and sat in the chair near the sofa.

It was midmorning when the furniture was delivered. Because Amber had chosen a simpler style than her mother, the bed and rocker were quickly assembled. Adam tightened every bolt securely, made sure the sides moved smoothly, and tested the rocker. If it would hold him, it would hold Amber.

"How is it?" she asked as he was rocking. She brought sheets from her room and was making up the bed.

"Works fine."

"I know I'll have to wash these again by the time she's born, but I think it makes the room look finished," she said, smoothing the cotton over the small mattress.

Adam watched her as she worked, his temporary respite from wanting over. When she leaned over, he wanted to cup her bottom and feel the firm curves. When she straightened, and arched back a bit, his palms itched to hold her breasts in them, to caress the skin he knew had to be as soft as down.

He stood abruptly, this was driving him crazy. Either get on with it, or walk away.

"Are you hungry?" Amber asked. "I could fix us lunch."

He gathered up the cardboard, bending the larger pieces. "I'm hungry, but let's go out and get something. Save you the work."

"I don't mind."

"Still, let's go." Outside where there were other people, where he could concentrate on other things besides Amber and how delectable she looked.

"Okay, let me wash up."

"I'll take this to your trash area if you tell me where, then come back and wash—" Adam began. The knock on the door interrupted him.

He finished gathering up the trash when she went to open the door. When he heard Virginia Woodworth's voice, he wasn't surprised. Amber had the patience of a saint to put up with the woman.

How would she react to seeing him here? No time like the present to find out.

He lifted all the large pieces, scooping up a couple of the smaller ones as well. Balanced perfectly, he headed out.

"So I said to James..." Virginia's voice trailed off when she spotted Adam.

He almost smiled. He could have orchestrated her reaction.

"What is he doing here?" she asked.

"Adam, you remember Virginia Woodworth, don't you?" Amber said calmly. "Virginia, Adam was helping me put together the baby furniture. Do come and see what I've picked out. I still need more things, but I'll wait a while longer."

Virginia glared at him before following Amber.

Someone could have gotten the door before they left, he thought, trying to find the knob beneath all the folded cardboard. If he didn't keep a grip on it, the pile would fall every which way.

Five minutes later he headed back to the apartment. He'd left the door unlatched, so he could let himself in. He could hear the voices from the baby's room. Bypassing the opportunity to visit more with Virginia, he went to the bathroom to wash his hands.

Girly things were everywhere. He smiled at the pink razor, the bottles of lotions and creams. Did Amber really use everything in sight? Or were all the primping things there for special occasions?

He'd like to see her all dressed up. Maybe he could take her out to celebrate the new furniture. They could go to dinner, then dancing. Maybe head back to his place for a nightcap—and he'd bring her home first thing in the morning.

He splashed cold water on his face, hoping to knock some sense into his head. Amber wasn't the kind of girl who would sleep casually with whoever asked. She was going to be a mother, for heaven's sake. Even if she wasn't, she was the type to expect commitment and a ring.

She had seemed happy to see him this morning, but was that just her polite facade? How could anyone be expected to keep another person happy for a lifetime? Whoever thought up marriage hadn't thought it all through. Too many pitfalls.

But for one instant, Adam almost wished he dare try.

Amber took a breath and tried to hold on to her temper. If Virginia said another word about Adam's being here, she would scream.

"He is a friend who came to assemble the baby's furniture," Amber explained again.

The edge in her voice must have penetrated. Virginia looked at her sharply.

"So you said. James could have done this. Or your new stepfather."

"Matt is busy. I know James could have helped, but Adam volunteered. Firefighters spend their off-hours helping people. He has experience in this kind of thing." If nothing else, he'd practiced on her mother's new furniture.

"It just doesn't look right. People will talk."

Amber almost laughed. "What people?" she asked. It wasn't as if she were some big public figure that everyone clamored to learn more about. As to the people who counted, so far no one seemed to find anything out of the usual. Except Virginia.

"Jimmy's not even been dead for a year."

"I know how long he's been dead. And how long he's been gone. Two different things."

"What do you mean?"

Amber really didn't want to have this talk with Virginia. But maybe she could make her understand a little better if she cleared things up. "Virginia, he left town almost two years ago. Except for a week's leave a year ago, and when we got married in February, I hadn't seen him in all that time. I feel he left then, not when he died."

Virginia looked shocked. "He was just away, not dead."

"I know. But in a way, things all changed when he left. I started college, he embraced his military career. We didn't have the same things in common anymore."

"And you and this Adam have things in common, I suppose," Virginia said.

"Not so much. We are not involved, no matter what you think."

"Not that I wouldn't like us to be," Adam said from the doorway.

CHAPTER TEN

AMBER turned abruptly. "What did you say?"

"When the time's right, maybe we will become more involved." He looked at Virginia as if in challenge. "You don't expect Amber to mourn her husband the rest of her life, do you? She's only twenty. She has a lifetime ahead of her."

"She has a baby to think about now," Virginia said, outraged.

"And the baby will need a father," Adam said gently.

Virginia looked at Amber in horror. "Is that your plan, rush right out and find some other man to be father to Jimmy's child?"

"I don't have any plans right now except to have a healthy baby. As to getting married again, I don't know about that. I'm still grieving for my husband. I don't know if I'll ever risk falling in love again. What if something happens to that man? I don't think I can stand losing someone dear to me again." She looked at them both. "You've each lost someone, but not at my age. Not at my stage in life. It hurts. My entire world has been rocked."

"We all die in the end," Adam said.

"Most of us die when we're old, not before we've had

a chance to live," she retorted. "Anyway, you're a great one to talk. Look at what you do for a living—daring death every day. I don't want to discuss this. Thank you for your help. Goodbye."

Adam didn't move.

"Virginia, I asked you not to badger me so much. We're scheduled for the hospital tour next week, I'll see you then." Amber spun around and pushed past Adam to go to her room. She shut the door and leaned against it. Wasn't Jimmy's death enough to deal with without all the stress of his mother pushing into her life? And what had Adam been thinking when he made that comment—that he wanted to become more involved? Was he deliberately provoking Virginia? Or had he meant it?

She felt almost giddy with the thought. Just how much more involved did he want to be? Not that there'd be any long-term future together. They both had issues that precluded that.

Adam had stood up for her, though. That was something she hadn't expected. Could she get him to change his job to something safer?

Unlikely. He loved his work. She couldn't imagine anyone trying to talk her out of teaching. What if someone suggested she become an accountant or something? She'd hate that.

Pushing away from the door, she went to lie down on her bed, her thoughts jumbled.

"He's right," she said softly, rubbing her stomach. "One day I might consider getting married again."

And if so, she'd like the man to be just like Adam—only with a safe job.

"Except—it's scary falling in love."

There would be the excitement of being with a man she loved. The commitment to share lives and futures. She'd have to make sure. She knew in her mind she didn't want a man with a dangerous profession. Yet her heart yearned for Adam.

"No!" she said aloud. It was too soon to be thinking about marriage again. Yet she couldn't help think how awestruck Adam had been when he felt the baby move. How kind he'd been to help her set up the nursery. How interested he always was when she spoke of her plans, or what she wanted to do for the baby.

He had other friends. But he chose to spend a lot of his time with her. And she relished every moment they had together.

Maybe, just maybe, she was falling for him. She liked spending time with him. Looked forward to the hours they shared. He made her laugh, and made her angry sometimes. But overall, there was a blossom of happiness surrounding her as fragile as gossamer.

Panic clicked in. She couldn't love Adam. She couldn't love anyone. She needed stability, safety. She wanted the quiet ache in her heart to fade completely, not to miss Jimmy so much. To get to the stage where she only remembered the fun they'd had.

She was also making memories with Adam. Would she remember him fondly as the years went by? What if his life was cut tragically short? How could she deal with that?

She missed him already. A phone call would have him back in no time. The better plan, however, was to curtail her time with him. Once his arm was healed and he was back at work, he'd be too busy to spend much time with her.

The apartment was quiet. Sighing, Amber rose. She was hungry. Food would give her the energy to face facts. She wished they'd gone out to lunch as planned. But after her curt goodbye, she'd be lucky if Adam spoke to her again.

She stopped at the edge of the living room in surprise. Adam sat on the sofa, leafing through a magazine. If the surprise hadn't been so great, she might have laughed to see such a macho male studying a woman's magazine with every appearance of fascinated interest.

"I thought you left," she said.

He lifted his head. "I'm not Virginia. She left. We were going to lunch, remember?"

She nodded. "I still thought you left. What if I took your attention for more than you mean? What if I wanted to pursue you, as you are so afraid of?"

He laughed, rose and came toward her. "Pursue away." He pulled her into his arms and kissed her.

Time seemed suspended. The room spun around, and Amber caught hold of the only solid anchor, Adam. Her arms tightened as she pressed herself against him, feeling desire rise, sensations sweep through and ecstasy blossom.

His hands pulled her against him, rubbing her back, setting every cell ablaze. She put her fingers in his hair, feeling the warmth, the thick texture, reveling in the intimacy between them.

When he moved his mouth to trail kisses across her cheek, to her jaw, to that pulse point at the base of her throat, Amber gave herself up to the delights only Adam brought. His muscles were strong; she could feel them moving as his arms moved. His chest was solid, and she relished the strength.

Even the baby seemed to enjoy the man's touch. She was as still as could be as if not to interrupt this special embrace.

Endless moments of delight cascaded, one after the

other. Amber savored every second, relishing the feeling of being alive to Adam's touch as the blood that pounded through her veins affirmed life and love.

The knowledge shot through her—she loved Adam Carruthers, as she'd never loved another, not even Jimmy.

Shocked, Amber pulled away, fear crowding in.

"Stop. We can't do this." She was breathing as hard as if she'd run up the stairs from the street. She couldn't be in love with this man. It was too dangerous, too risky.

Adam just looked at her.

"It's too soon. Too much. We can't get involved. I don't want to be involved."

"Honey, we are involved, and your denying it or my denying it doesn't change it."

"But you don't like the situation," she guessed.

He shrugged. "I told you about my mother. I never want to be responsible for another person's happiness."

"You aren't responsible for anyone but yourself," Amber shot back.

"Unless I get hooked up with some woman who expects me to make her happy."

"Won't you expect her to make you happy in return?" Amber asked.

Adam hesitated a moment, gave it some thought. "I make myself happy. Though I find happiness in unexpected places and with unexpected people."

"Maybe your mother was needier than most. Was she so happy with your father?" She didn't really care, but couldn't deal with their own situation. She wanted to think about something else, anything else.

"I don't know. She remembers being happy with him. But they weren't together that long."

"Maybe she remembered happier days. But she had the ability to find her own happiness. She chose not to."

"And I can choose whichever way I want?" he asked.

"You already have."

"What if I say I'm happy around you?"

"What if I say you're happy around Trevor as well."

He almost smiled at that. "Yeah, Trevor can make me laugh. But you bring happiness."

Amber felt a glow at his compliment. But she didn't want that. She wanted them to go back to being mere acquaintances, without kisses and shared experiences or any attraction. Without these feelings that were filling every inch of her.

"Just being with you, doing mundane things, and I'm happy," he said.

"You look surprised," she commented, feeling that fluttering feeling again. She didn't want this.

"I am. For years I've thought my mother's view of things was the right way. Now I'm not so sure. Ready for lunch?"

Amber was confused at his quick change of subject. But she was relieved to get off the personal and back to the more general. She couldn't be in love with him. It was just infatuation, or hormones. Yes, that was it. Hormones, as Virginia had said a while back. They'd go to lunch, spend another couple of hours together and say goodbye.

Adam did not allude to their relationship over lunch, keeping the conversation safely impersonal. Amber had a harder time turning off her thoughts. Or her feelings.

When he invited her out the following evening, she refused, despite his urging. She was feeling more and more panicked at the feelings that kept surfacing. She needed to back away before she got hurt again. The fun wasn't worth the pain of loss.

She called her mother when she got home.

"Hi, sweetie, what's up?" Sara asked when she recognized her daughter's voice.

"Come see my baby's furniture. Adam set it up today. It looks great."

"I'll be over soon. Is Adam still there?"

"No. We went to lunch, then he took off. Virginia was here earlier."

"I bet that went well if Adam was there."

"She asked me what people would think."

"About?"

"About my seeing someone else so soon after Jimmy's death, of course. Bets thinks I shouldn't act like a nun all my life. Kathy wants to meet him to make sure he's good enough for me. What do you think?"

"Is this Adam important to you?"

Amber closed her eyes, wishing she could say a resounding No! But she was fearful she was in over her head and whichever way she chose would cause heartache—either now or later.

"I don't want him to be," she said at last.

"Why?"

"He's a firefighter. He was hurt in the last fire he worked, he could be killed in the next one. Or the one after that."

"And?"

"I can't go through losing someone I love again. It hurts too much."

Sara was silent for a moment. "We don't always get to choose," she said at last. "And as one who thought my life was set when I was eighteen, and found it completely turned around without any warning, I'd say consider carefully before you make any long-lasting decision. Do remember that not everyone has the chance to fall in love with a wonderful man who will share life's journey with you. Don't throw away something precious."

"I can't do it again, Mom. I can't risk it. You saw me when I learned about Jimmy. I was a wreck. I can't bear that pain again." And she feared it would be worse with Adam. She hadn't known him nearly as long, but her feelings seemed more intense, more mature. She couldn't imagine a world without him in it. How would she ever live through his death?

"Then you have your answer. Do you still want me to come over?"

"Yes. Bring Matt."

"Of course. Where I go, he goes," Sara said. "And hopefully soon where he goes, the baby and I'll go. See you in a few minutes."

Amber hung up. She had her answer. She would call Adam tonight and tell him she didn't wish to see him again.

No, he deserved to have her tell him face-to-face. She wouldn't hide behind a phone that could be quickly hung up. She owed him more than that. It would be the last time she'd see him.

Just the thought was painfully sad. But better sad now than risk devastation later. It wasn't as if he'd been a big part of her life for long. She'd only known him for a few weeks. It wouldn't take long to get over this infatuation.

School would soon be starting. That would take care of the immediate future. Then she had the baby to plan for. If she kept focused on what was important, things would come round. She'd keep her equilibrium and find contentment with her work and her child.

* * *

Afraid she'd chicken out if she called ahead, Amber took a chance he'd be home and went to Adam's apartment the next afternoon. Taking a deep breath when she stood before his door, she tried to quell the butterflies kickboxing in her stomach. She was doing what was right for her. She repeated the words like a mantra.

She knocked.

He opened the door a moment later and she almost forgot why she'd come. He looked wonderful. His shirt was unbuttoned, his sleeves rolled back over his arms, the cast still dominating one. His jeans were fitted, soft from wear and molding his long legs. His hair needed a trim but he still looked terrific. Her heart sped up.

"Amber, I didn't expect you," he said, opening the door wide. "Come in." Giving a hasty glance around the room, he evidently decided it was orderly enough for guests.

Like she cared. She hadn't come to see his apartment, she'd come to see him.

"I hope this is a good time," she said.

"Change your mind about going out tonight?" he asked as she walked nervously into the room. She twisted her fingers together, then purposefully pulled them apart. She raised her chin and turned to face him.

"No, I didn't change my mind about going out tonight. Actually, I thought it best if I came to tell you in person that I don't want us to see each other again."

He didn't move a muscle, just stared at her as the seconds ticked by.

"Mind telling me why?" he asked at last.

She studied him a moment, hoping she'd find the right words. He looked dark and intense and more fabulous than any man had a right to. She wasn't sure she had the courage to go through with this. But for her own sake, she had to. She did not want to be paralyzed with the pain of falling in love with someone only to lose them to an early death once more.

She wasn't brave enough for that.

"We're too different," she began.

"Most men and women are," he replied calmly. Only the clenched muscles in his cheeks gave the lie to that serenity. He was just able to cloak his tension. Amber wished she had that knack.

"Okay then. The real reason is that being with you scares me."

"I scare you?" Adam asked, astonished.

"Being with you does," she clarified. "There's a difference. Of course you don't scare me. You're kind and honorable and fun to be around. That's some of what scares me."

"I don't get it."

"I could fall for you," Amber blurted out. She refused to admit she already had. She would nip that infatuation in the bud. She was fighting to keep her heart whole and safe.

For the first time since she spoke, he seemed to relax.

"Well—"

"No, don't joke about it, Adam. I'm serious. I'm not up to that. Not now, maybe not ever. I don't want to fall in love. I don't want my life to be tied to someone else's. I don't want to be a hostage to fear the rest of my life."

"It's the firefighter thing, isn't it?"

"Partly. But only partly. I don't want to get caught up with anyone. It's safer."

"Safer than what?"

"Than being crushed when a person I love dies. I felt

that way in spring, before you met me. For several weeks, I didn't know if I could even get up in the morning."

"That's a natural progress of grieving. But you did get up, you moved ahead. I know it was tough losing Jimmy, but you got past it. You have your whole life ahead of you."

"And I'm feeling safe now. The worst of the grief is gone. But not all of it. And I remember. Now I have my baby to plan for, my schooling to finish and a job as a teacher to look forward to. I feel I'm in charge of things—and I like that. I want it to continue. I do not want to be at the whim of fate and risk losing someone close to me again. So I don't want to fall for you. I don't want to tempt fate by spending time with you and trying not to fall in love. It's better if we just end it now."

She wanted to dash from the apartment. She'd said what she'd come to say, now she needed to be alone.

But Adam didn't know that. And he had his own agenda.

"You don't mean that, Amber. You can't. We have something special going here. Something unexpected that neither one of us went looking for, but it found us anyway. I don't want to call it quits. I want to spend time with you, see if these feelings can grow and strengthen and give us each other."

She shook her head. She didn't want to hear anything like this. He had to agree to end things immediately. He had to!

"Hear me out," he said, stepping closer, placing his hands on her shoulders. She tried not to notice the tingling sensations his touch caused. She was hanging on by a thread.

"I've spent my entire adult life planning to play things safe, not get involved. I vowed never to be responsible for someone else. I wanted safe, too. But you changed that. Knowing you shows me what I'm missing."

"No. You're missing nothing. This is just sexual attraction, or forbidden fruit or something like that. You don't want a serious relationship," she said.

"I do. I want one with you. I love you, Amber."

She heard the words and panic flared once more.

Wrenching herself free, she turned as if cornered, seeking a way out. Adam blocked the path to the door.

"No, I don't want to hear this."

"Maybe you need to hear this, sweetheart. It changes everything. I love you. I want you to fall in love with me, for us to get married. We'll raise your baby and have others of our own. It's corny for a firefighter to say, but you light up my life. You set it on fire."

"No!" What if she fell for his line? What if she fell all the way in love with Adam, and he died? How could she bear the pain a second time? She couldn't do it.

"No. I don't want to see you again." She took a calming breath, tried to school her voice to betray none of the agitation she felt. This had not gone at all as she wished. She'd thought, hoped, he'd agree instantly.

For a moment, she was tempted. But she was not strong enough after all. She had to watch out for herself and her baby, and risking her heart again was not an option.

"I have to go, Adam. Please, respect my wishes. Don't call me, don't come by my apartment. Let's part as friends."

"I don't want to part," he said in frustration.

"Please, don't make this any harder than it is." Could she hold out? She felt like weakening when she looked into his eyes. She saw pain there. Was it reflected in her own?

"If it's hard, why do it?" he asked.

"I have to. I just have to."

He said nothing. After a moment, he stood aside and Amber almost ran to the door. In only seconds, she was on the sidewalk, heading toward the bus line. She didn't notice the once-familiar neighborhood. She only saw the pain in his eyes, and felt the pain in her heart.

She was doing the right thing. She knew she was. But it hurt.

"Better a short hurt now than after I really got to know him, made him part of my life. This will pass quickly. To go on would have threatened everything—my very existence," she told herself, hurrying as if to outrun her thoughts.

Adam heard the door open, but refused to look at her walking away. He couldn't believe it. He'd bared his soul, told her he'd loved her, asked her to marry him. And she'd said no.

Was this how Amber had felt when she heard Jimmy died? Was this what she feared? This emptiness? Feeling stunned, unable to accept facts? He wanted to run after her and make her listen. He loved her! He had never loved another woman. Had she heard him?

Of course she had. And it had been the last thing she wanted to hear. She'd come all the way to see him in person to tell him goodbye. She didn't want him to love her. She didn't want any commitment or ties.

If the truth be known, Adam wasn't sure he wanted to love her, either. Not now. Not when she'd spurned him without giving them a chance. But feelings had nothing much to do with wants.

Only guarantees might suit Amber, and those couldn't

be given. No one knew if he'd be alive tomorrow. He didn't want to cause her pain by dying young. But what if he lived to be eighty? She had thrown away his chance at happiness because of fear. Fear of something that might never happen.

Or could happen at the next fire, a voice in his head said.

If so, all the more reason to see each other as much as they could. Life was too short to ignore what was right in front of them. How could she throw it all away?

He threw himself down on the sofa, staring off into space. Life sucked. He'd been a fool to let down his guard and fall for a pretty blonde with an engaging smile. He wanted her with a power he hadn't known before. But she didn't want him. The irony wasn't lost on him. He'd fought love for so long—even the concept. Now he'd fallen right on his face. He should have never introduced himself all those weeks ago. God, he wanted her.

The next two weeks were the hardest in Amber's life. She missed Adam with an agonizing intensity that surprised her. The situation was made worse by the knowledge he loved her and she'd ended their relationship. And by the fact she could change it back if she'd just pick up the phone.

She was tempted. At night, when she was trying to sleep, she'd remember his words of love, his offer of marriage, and be so tempted to call him and say it was all a mistake.

But then she'd remember Jimmy. The searing pain of his loss had tempered over the months since his death. But she still felt overwhelmed some days. Afraid to face the feelings that had dominated for so long.

Then she'd think about Adam and their hours together, reliving every word, every gesture, every kiss. Rolling over, she'd try to sleep, but longing rose for another kiss. Just one. Or a walk with him holding her hand. The amusement that lurked in his eyes teased her in dreams. Yet they always ended with his walking away in disgust.

Awaking in the middle of the night almost became routine. Regrets flooded, yet the certainty of her stance kept her from calling him, from trying to see him again. Better this heartache now than heartbreak later.

Jill called to invite her to a cookout. Amber declined, saying she was busy getting ready for the next school year. If Jill thought it odd she couldn't take time out for an evening of fun, she didn't say anything. She did however, say, "You know Adam's been released from disability. He's back at work. I think he's doing a stint on the rescue squad temporarily, but I know he's glad to be back in the thick of things."

"I haven't spoken with him in a while. I'm glad he's okay." Amber clung to the phone, wishing she could ask more, find out if the arm healed without a problem. Was it his choice to be on the rescue squad, or did he want to be back on the front line? Did he ever mention her to his friends?

She would never know.

"Call me sometime and we'll go to lunch," Jill suggested.

Amber was tempted, but better to make the break clean. "I'll see, once I know my schedule." She wouldn't, of course, but no need to give a reason now. Jill would catch on when Amber never called.

"Okay then. Talk to you soon."

Hanging up the phone, Amber felt as if she'd severed the last tie. She should have felt better about things. But she didn't.

She burst into tears. She missed Adam so much she ached. It was as if he'd died, almost. Except she knew he was alive and doing what he loved. She would have to make do with that, and get on with her own life. She might not have the highs being with Adam gave, but at least she wouldn't be devastated if something happened to him.

On the second Wednesday in September, Amber and Virginia went to the hospital for the new parents orientation, which Amber had rescheduled, unable to face Virginia earlier. Sara and Matt had already taken their tour, so Amber didn't know anyone else in the small group. All the women were in late stages of pregnancy. One woman looked as if she was past due. Amber eyed her throughout the tour, wondering how big she'd get herself by the end.

"I had nothing like this," Virginia whispered when they saw the labor room. It was decorated like a bedroom, with chintz curtains and a rocking chair.

"Mom said it was totally different when she had me. She feels like this is the first baby for her since nothing's done the same." She wished she could be more interested, but nothing held her interest for long these days.

When they went to the nursery, they were able to look through the viewing window at babies lying in their plastic bassinets, wrapped in blue or pink blankets as was appropriate. In the far corner a woman rocked a baby. Two rocking chairs stood empty.

"This is where the babies are on display for family and friends. We have them here for a few hours a day, the rest of the time they are with the mother. And, of course, most are only here for a day or so, then we send them on their way home."

"Most but not all?" someone asked.

"If there are complications, we may keep them a little longer." She gestured to the woman rocking the baby. "We have volunteers who help when needed. Sometimes we have multiple births, or a mother has a problem that means she can't be with the baby, so our volunteers provide that important TLC. In fact, we always need more help, so if you have some spare time, join us."

A ripple of laughter passed through the group. None of the young mothers-to-be could foresee free time.

But Amber looked at Virginia. The older woman was staring at the babies, a sweet light in her eyes.

"You should volunteer," Amber said.

"Me? I don't know much about babies. I only had Jimmy. And he grew up so fast."

"You know how to rock them, hold them. Think about it. You have time and this is a need that would be fun to fulfill."

Virginia looked thoughtful. "I'll have my hands full with my granddaughter," she said slowly.

"No, you won't. You can come to visit and she'll visit you, but Virginia, this is not your child. You need something to do in life that will give you more purpose than planning to spoil my daughter. Think about it," Amber said firmly. She was taking charge of her life with a vengeance, she thought. But she was adamant about not letting Virginia take over a major facet of her baby's life.

"Maybe I will think about it," Virginia said, looking at the babies again.

Virginia drove Amber back to her apartment when the tour was over.

"Are you still seeing that man?" she asked on the drive.

"If you mean Adam, no, I haven't seen him since the day after he kindly assembled my baby's bedroom furniture."

Virginia was silent for a moment. "I'm thinking about packing up Jimmy's room," she said slowly. "James thinks we should make it into a guest room where you and the baby can come to stay from time to time. I know we live close, but maybe you'll want us to watch the baby in the evening or something when you go out, and then just stay over rather than waken her."

"Are you sure?" Amber asked. She could hear the sadness in her voice.

"I'm not throwing things away. Some of his things we'll keep on display. But most of it has no meaning except to Jimmy and to me. I'll pack the boxes away. Maybe the baby will like to see them when she's older."

"Of course she would. And we have to make sure she knows all about her father. How good he was in sports, how much he loved to pig out on popcorn, and how much he loved all of us."

"It's so hard, Amber. I hope you die long before your baby does," Virginia said.

Amber covered the older woman's hand as it held the steering wheel. "I want to name her Jamie Marie, for Jimmy."

Virginia smiled. "A lovely name."

They drove in silence until Virginia pulled to a stop in front of Amber's apartment building. "That man was right, you know. One day you will fall in love again and marry. Just don't let Jamie Marie forget her grandparents."

"Virginia, if I ever marry again, that won't change Jamie's grandparents. She'll spend lots of time with you two, no matter what. I'm counting on that. I never knew any of my grandparents. I would never deprive my child of the opportunity to know and love hers."

"Your new husband might object to that," she said.

"Then he wouldn't be the kind of man I'd want to marry in the first place. But I have no plans to marry, so there's no need to worry."

"What about Adam?"

"We aren't seeing each other anymore," Amber said. "If I ever fall in love again, I want someone in a safe job, not to risk losing him because of what he does."

"When you're ready, I'll have James introduce you to some nice safe insurance salesmen," Virginia said.

Amber laughed. "That's a deal."

Would she ever be ready for anyone else after Adam?

"I think you're nuts," Bets said as she and Amber walked across the campus. The fall day was sunny, with a breeze from the west keeping the temperatures comfortable. The campus was full of students sauntering from building to building, checking out their schedules and arranging meetings with friends.

"You've said that every time we've talked lately," Amber said. "Your opinion is duly noted."

"But ignored," her friend said cheerfully.

"What else can I do?"

"Nothing. If you've gone three weeks and don't miss him, you were right, he's not for you."

"I miss him," she said slowly. "But it's too soon to think about getting involved with anyone. Maybe I'll feel differently in a while. But right now the fear of loss is huge. You don't get it. No one could who hasn't experienced a sudden loss like I did. I live with it every day. What if something happens to my mother? Or to Matt. He jets all over the world. What if the plane crashes?"

"Hey, flying's safer than driving. Statistically speaking, more people live to old age than die young, thought of that?"

"Not in the Army."

"Yep, even there. Or firefighters. Or cops, or wild animal trainers."

"Wild animal trainers?" Amber said.

"Well, it's another dangerous profession."

Amber laughed. "I'll keep that in mind if I ever run into one. Let's change the subject."

"To?"

"Do you think we'll like Dr. Scrubs?"

"Not a bit. A pompous ass, if you ask me. But he's the only one teaching that course this semester, so we're stuck. Gives us a good opportunity to learn to deal with problem parents. We'll practice on him. And your mother-in-law."

"She's getting better." Amber defended her.

"Impossible."

"Really, she is. She started working at the hospital as a volunteer in the newborn section and loves it. She goes there every day now to rock the babies and help the nurses however she can. It's her new hobby."

"You said she needed one."

They reached the intersection on busy 19th Avenue. Amber was heading for her bus stop across the street, while Bets would be returning to the library to look up some facts for a paper she wanted to start. For a moment Amber felt a pang she wasn't returning to the apartment she'd had— in the building with Adam's apartment. If she hadn't moved, she would have run into him by now. Even though she knew she wasn't strong enough to stand up to a committed relationship between them, she would have been able to catch a glimpse of him from time to time.

Would that have been better or worse?

Bets waited with her at the traffic light. "I'll call you later and let you know if that topic will work."

"You can make it work," Amber said. "I haven't a clue what I want to write about for my term project. Hopefully something will come to me soon."

When the light changed she said a quick goodbye.

"I'll call you," Bets said as Amber began to cross the wide street.

Out of nowhere a car sped toward the crosswalk, running the red light. Amber turned at Bets' cry, and saw the driver's horrified face, heard the screech of brakes. Events seemed to move in slow motion. Before she could react, the edge of the bumper caught her and spun her around, knocking her off her feet. Instinctively she dropped her books to cradle her baby, rolling into a ball as she fell. She felt as if she were swimming through cold molasses. The sounds vied with one another: Bets screaming her name, the sound of cars jolting to a stop, a horn blowing somewhere. Confusion reigned.

Until she cracked her head on the pavement and everything went black.

CHAPTER ELEVEN

"AMBER? Wake up. Come on, you can do it. Amber, it's Adam. Wake up."

Slowly the words began to make sense. Amber opened her eyes, shutting them tightly at the brightness which hurt her head.

"Ohhh," she moaned. Pain seemed to explode everywhere.

"That's it, open your eyes. You're going to be all right."

Adam's strong voice continued to urge her to wake up, but she didn't want to. Her head throbbed. Her hip ached.

"What happened? Where am I?" she asked.

Memory clicked. "Oh, no. Is the baby okay? Adam!" She opened her eyes and reached for his arm, clutching it tightly. "Adam, is my baby okay?"

"We're transporting you to the hospital as soon as possible. Stay with me. You're going to be fine. We're taking you in as soon as the ambulance gets here."

He put a stethoscope on and pumped up an arm cuff already wrapped around her arm, listening for her blood pressure readings. He called a number to someone to her left.

Amber looked over at another E.M.T. jotting notes on a clipboard.

"ETA for the ambulance is two minutes," he murmured, glancing at Amber and smiling. "You're in good hands, miss. Adam and I are the best."

"Modest, too," Adam murmured. "We're putting you on a backboard, to hold your head and neck immobile. Just a precaution. Where else hurts?"

"My hip. My head is killing me. What happened?"

"Car ran the red light. Clipped you on the hip. Damn driver was drunk. It's only eleven-thirty in the morning, for Pete's sake."

Amber felt fuzzy. She closed her eyes. "It's so bright. Are you sure Jamie is okay?"

"Who's Jamie?" Adam asked, glancing around. There had only been the one victim.

"She's named the baby Jamie," Bets said.

Amber opened her eyes and looked around. "Bets?"

"Right here." Her hand came out to pat Amber gently on the shoulder. "God, you scared me to death. I thought you were a goner until these guys showed up. Isn't this a kick? Adam is working the paramedic shift today and he was the first response."

"How is she?" an unfamiliar voice asked.

Amber squinted up at a uniformed police officer. Too many people, too much confusion. She closed her eyes, willing the pain to subside.

"We'll have her in the hospital for a complete workup, but I think she'll make it," Adam said. "You can check with the doctor later to arrange for questioning."

"Don't think we need to bother her. Plenty of witnesses," the policeman said, tapping his notebook. "And we have the driver."

"Am I losing you, Amber?" Adam asked.

"I'm sleepy."

"Wait a little longer."

In only a short time, Amber was strapped to a back-board, a cervical collar in place and she felt herself being lifted into the cool dimness of the ambulance. She reached out and grabbed Adam.

"Come with me," she said. She'd just been thinking about catching a glimpse of him. Now he was here. And doing his job. He hadn't once looked at her with the old friendliness, or that amusement in his eyes.

Were her injuries serious, or had he closed down because of her last declaration?

She was so glad to see him, despite the circumstances.

"We'll be right behind you," Adam said.

"Please, can't you ride with me? I'm scared." Not of the hospital, not of her injuries, though they could be serious. Amber was afraid of the gladness that swept through her being near Adam. She'd missed him so much, as if a part of her had been cut out and was now restored.

A moment's discussion and Adam climbed into the ambulance. The vehicle pulled away from the scene and gained speed.

Amber was vaguely aware of the siren, but her focus was on Adam. He sat beside her, one hand holding her wrist, his face impassive as he noted her vital stats.

"I didn't expect to see you again," she murmured, wanting some attention. The ambulance attendant sat on the other side of the stretcher, monitoring the oxygen she was getting.

"It scared me to death," Adam said, "when we got there and I saw you were the one on the ground."

"I'm really going to be all right?"

"I think so. And no problems with the baby as far as I can tell. The doctor will let you know for certain. You sheltered her as you fell. Instinctively. Mothers do that."

"It happened so fast."

"They caught the man. He rammed his car into a parked one and just sat there."

"Is he okay?"

"Drunk as a skunk. Too limber from booze to sustain serious injury," Adam said with disgust. "The police took him into custody."

"I could have been killed," Amber said slowly. "In just a heartbeat. One minute I was talking to Bets, the next I was crossing the street and that man could have killed me and my baby."

"But he didn't. Don't dwell on it. Focus on getting better as fast as you can."

Adam watched her close her eyes. There was a bruise on her forehead where she'd hit the pavement. The preliminary examination at the site hadn't indicated any broken bones, but she needed X-rays to confirm that.

There was plenty of bruising, especially on her hip at the point of impact where the car had grazed her. Serious enough; however, had she been a couple of feet farther into the crosswalk, the car would have hit her square in the middle, probably tossing her into the air, with an outcome likely far different from what they had.

He wanted to beat the hell out of that driver. How dare he endanger others with his drunken behavior? He hoped the judge threw the book at him.

He'd never forget the fear that struck when he'd climbed out of the rescue truck and recognized Amber. For a split second, he'd thought her dead. Then his training kicked in and he and Greg had got to work.

She was going to be fine, he reassured himself, willing the helplessness to fade. He'd done his job and she was going to walk out of the hospital on her own two feet. Her hand was scraped. Lightly he rubbed his thumb on the un-abraded skin next to the scrape. It was so soft. He hated to think of the trauma her body had gone through. He just hoped the baby was safe. He knew it took a lot to dislodge a healthy fetus. And Amber couldn't lose her baby after losing her husband. Adam couldn't bear the thought of that.

She might not want him in her life, but he wanted her in his. Wished things had been so different. But he respected her too much to push in where he wasn't wanted. He'd given it his best shot and she'd said no. End of discussion.

Amber had slipped back into unconsciousness by the time they reached the hospital. Adam gave the E.R. doctor a quick report, then watched as Amber was wheeled into an examination cubicle.

He went to find a phone. He looked up Matt's office phone number and called the man. Better he tell Sara than Adam.

Then he called Virginia Woodworth.

Adam was filling out the incident report when Bets hurried into the Emergency Room. "Is she okay?" she asked, coming over to him when she recognized a familiar face.

"Doctor's still with her. I've called her stepfather and mother-in-law. They're on their way here. Can you stay in case she needs someone before they come?"

"I can. You won't?" Bets asked.

"I'm on duty. As soon as I finish the accident report, I'll be back in service and may have to respond to another call. Besides, she doesn't want me here." He studied the report, pleased to note his voice had masked the pain he felt at the words.

"Don't be too sure of that. She cares for you a lot more than she wants to admit," Bets said. "Don't write her off just yet."

"She has a funny way of showing it," he commented, jotting down the final comments. For a moment he wanted to let hope in, but Amber had been brutally frank refusing his offer of marriage and spurning his declaration of love. Adam had too much pride to push in where he wasn't wanted.

"She's just scared of being hurt again," Bets said.

"There are all kinds of hurts. Did she tell you I asked her to marry me and she said no? What does she think turning me down did to me?" he asked, then could have kicked himself. He didn't need to parade the hurt Amber had inflicted. He'd get over it.

"She's not thinking, she's reacting. Give her another chance," Bets pleaded.

"If she asks, tell her I'll stop back later, when we get a dinner break. I'm on duty until tomorrow morning. But I'll check in to see how she's doing." He jotted his cell phone number on a slip of paper and gave it to Bets, asking her to call him as soon as she knew how Amber was doing. Amber never had to know he'd asked after her. If she didn't want to see him, he wouldn't intrude when he stopped back by.

He couldn't get over the clutch of fear that had grasped him when he saw her lying motionless on the pavement. Of course he'd check in. He needed to know she was really going to be fine. He wished he could stay, but duty called. Reassuring himself she was in good hands, he went back to the rescue truck, which Greg had already restocked.

"Ready to roll?" Greg asked.

"As ready as I'll ever be," Adam replied, wishing he could stay with Amber. For the first time ever, he resented his job and the need to be away when he longed to stay.

It was shortly after seven when Adam returned to the hospital and located the floor where Amber was. He was on his dinner break and had had Greg drop him off.

Bets had called several hours ago to say everything looked okay with Amber, except for bruising and a slight concussion. They were holding her overnight to monitor the baby and the concussion. By the time Bets called, both Amber's parents and the Woodworths had arrived. He felt better knowing she had her family with her, people she cared about and who loved her.

He arrived at the open door to her room, feeling awkward and uncertain. Maybe he'd just peep in and make sure she was all right. She didn't want to see him.

Amber lay in bed, propped up and talking with her mother. Sara sat beside the bed, lines of worry etched around her eyes. Matt sat beside her, rubbing her back as if in support.

"Adam!" Amber caught sight of him and her entire face lit up.

"Hey," he said.

Amber smiled. "Bets said you'd be back later. Come in."

Sara rose and went to greet Adam, giving him a hard hug. "Thank you for taking such good care of her," she said. "I was scared to death when Matt came home to get me. But I figured she was in the best hands possible until I could get here."

Matt followed, offering his hand, gripping Adam's firmly. "I want to thank you, too. She's kind of special, you know?"

Adam nodded, looking at Amber again. How very special these people would never know.

"Just doing my job," he said.

"Then thank you for taking on such a job."

Sara looked at Amber and back at Adam. "If you can stay a few minutes, I need to take a walk. We'll be back soon, sweetie," Sara said to Amber. Then she looked at her husband. In only seconds they disappeared down the hallway.

"Smooth move, Mom," Amber said, wryly.

"How are you doing?" Adam asked, going to sit on the chair Sara had vacated.

"My head is throbbing like bongo drums, but they don't want to give me any medication because of the concussion. My hip hurts if I move an inch, or if the baby kicks and stretches the skin. My hands ache, my shoulder aches and I hope I never take perfect health for granted again."

"But you're fine, other than that?"

She nodded. "I'll be various shades of purple and green for a month, I'm sure, but the doctor said I'll be fine. And the baby is fine. I'm staying overnight just as a precaution."

She held out her hand. Adam looked at it for a long moment, then reached out and gently took it in his. Her skin was warm and soft. He rubbed his thumb over the smooth texture. He'd come so close to losing her. Even if he never saw her again, he wanted her to live a long happy life.

Amber looked at him greedily, taking in the crisp uniform he wore, his dark hair, the tiredness around his eyes. She hadn't seen him in weeks. He wasn't staying long, so she had to feast her eyes on him until he left.

"Adam, I wanted to talk to you. I told my mother, that's

why she and Matt disappeared so fast. I could have been killed today."

He looked at her and shook his head. "Don't think about that. You're going to be fine."

"I know that. And I'm so grateful. But I could have been killed. If I'd been a couple of feet farther into the intersection, or if that driver had swerved more to the left, I would be dead."

"Amber—"

"No, let me finish. It made me think. Here I am, a college student. How innocuous can you get? My most dangerous thing should be if I drop a textbook on my foot. And yet I was almost killed."

"But you weren't. Don't think that way, honey. You're going to be fine." He didn't want to think another second about what might have been. For the first time he had a glimmer of understanding of Amber's position. It would hurt like hell to hear of her death. No wonder she didn't want to risk another relationship.

"This is important, Adam. I could have been killed and I don't have a dangerous job. I was just crossing the street. I've been so worried that I'd fall for a guy with a dangerous profession—but I'm the one who was almost killed. It's made me think. I've talked about this with Bets and my mother. If I had died today do you know what I would have regretted the most?"

Adam shook his head, his gaze locked with hers. He knew what he would regret.

"That I hadn't given us a chance. I've been so busy trying to protect myself, I haven't been looking at things clearly. Bets told me that. So did my mother. I'm responsible for my actions, and for the way I live my life. I don't want to become a woman afraid of shadows, afraid of things that may never happen. Jimmy didn't get to live out a full life with me. In a way, I need to be living for Jimmy as well. Doing all the things he would have loved. Making sure his daughter has the best life possible, and that the girl Jimmy loved remembers him always and lives life to the fullest as he would have done. He sure as certain would never hole up and wall off anything that would give him excitement and adventure and happiness."

"You need a chance to heal from his loss," Adam said.

"I do. And I am healing. But I'm not going to eliminate risk from my life because I might get hurt. The flipside of everything bad is everything good. What if I had died today? You would feel sad. But you'd go on. I feel sad Jimmy died, but I need to go on. He was wiser than me, he even told me to move on with life. So for Jimmy, and for me, I want the best life has to offer."

Adam nodded. He wanted the best life had to offer for her as well. He just wished he was part of it.

He squeezed her hand and stood. "I have to go." She didn't need to know that he still had plenty of time on his break. He couldn't stay here and listen to her and not take her into his arms. He wanted to demand she allow him to be a part of her life, and that she be a part of his.

"Not yet," she protested, her hand clutching his. "Stay, please. Stay in my life forever."

From the stunned look on Adam's face, Amber knew her words weren't what he'd been expecting. Maybe not even what he wanted to hear. Had he had time to reconsider? Had the words of love been foolishly said, later regretted?

"In your life as in?" he asked, as if for clarification.

"However you see me in it." She almost held her breath. Why didn't he sweep her into his arms? Was she too late? Had he changed his mind? Or had he not loved her at all.

Maybe he needed to know how she felt.

"I love you, Adam. I'm sorry I was hurtful last time we met. I was scared. I'm still scared. But now I'm more afraid of messing up the best thing in my life by being fearful of the unknown."

"A sudden change," he said. "See how you feel in a couple of days. You're emotional because of the accident."

"I know my mind. I've known it for a while, though I've tried to fight against it. How do you see me in your life, Adam?"

"I don't."

She felt as if he'd just jerked the bed out from under her.

"You don't?"

"You made it clear the other day you don't want me in yours. Today changed nothing really, did it? Wait until you recover, until the concussion heals, until you're on your feet again, then see how you feel."

"I don't need to wait, Adam. I know how I feel."

"A bump on the head changes nothing."

"No. I loved you before. I was afraid to admit it—to me or to you. And I'm still afraid, but even more so of not sharing whatever time we are allotted together. Please, Adam, don't tell me I'm too late."

He didn't say anything. Amber's heart fell.

"Please," she whispered. Had his love been so ephemeral it had already vanished?

"You asked me how I see you in my life. If I had my way, I'd see you as my wife," he said slowly. "That hasn't changed."

"Oh wow." Amber burst into tears. "You meant it before? You do love me?"

"Of course I meant it before, what did you think?" Adam said, reaching up to brush the tears from her cheeks.

"That it sounded like a proposal which I foolishly turned down," she said, sniffing. "I want a do-over. I want to accept."

He stared at her. "You'll marry me?"

She nodded, tightening the grip she had on his hand. "I love you, Adam. It's not emotions from the accident, not delusions from the concussion. It's real, and important, and strong. I've fought hard, thought I was doing the right thing. But I've been so miserable without you. I love you."

He reached out to gather her up in a gentle hug. "Oh, sweetheart, not half as much as I love you." Then he kissed her.

The blood pounding made her headache even worse, like hammers over every inch. But Amber didn't care. Adam loved her! He wanted to marry her. Together they'd share a lifetime of ups and downs and happiness. For however long their life together was to be.

Endless moments later, they pulled apart, looking into each other's eyes.

"I'm so happy I could dance," Amber said. She frowned and put her free hand to her forehead. "Except my head hurts so much I can hardly stand it."

"You should feel better by morning. How soon will you marry me?" Adam said.

"I rushed through my wedding for Jimmy. He only had a few weeks' stateside duty. I want this to be special. Not a big wedding, but not a rushed one. Is that okay?"

"Take your time, sweetheart. When it's time, we'll do it."

"Don't think I'm stalling, I just don't want to rush. But

I can't wait to become your wife. We should get married before Jamie Marie shows up, don't you think? You won't mind having a ready-made, instant family, will you?"

"Once I get used to it, I'm going to be on top of the world. But five minutes ago I thought I wouldn't see you again, and now—"

"Of course you also get my mother and Matt, and the Woodworths as well. They'll always be Jamie's grand-parents."

"No problem. I don't have any parents. They can be grandparents to all our kids if you like," Adam said, drawing her into his arms.

"All our kids?" Amber repeated.

"You didn't want to stop at one, did you?"

"I hadn't thought about it, but no, I don't want only one. Mostly I was thinking I hoped I got a chance to tell you I was wrong. Bets said she thought I was nuts. Even my mother questioned what I'd been thinking about. I'm sorry I got hurt, but maybe it is a blessing in disguise. How long would it have taken me to come to my senses if I hadn't?"

He shook his head, "I haven't a clue. Let's not think about what might have been, but about what is. Marry me and let's grow old together."

EPILOGUE

November 22

"THE line is still busy," Matt said in disgust.

Sara started to say something but the pain gripped her so tightly she could hardly breathe. She held still, holding her swollen belly, riding through the contraction.

Matt went to hold her. "Breathe, darling. Remember the Lamaze classes. Panting breaths will help you through it. We can't wait any longer. We've told the doctor we're on our way to the hospital. We'll call from there."

"She must be talking to Bets. There will still be time for her to get to the hospital for the baby's birth if we keep trying. I just wanted her there from the beginning."

"I know. Let me call Dex. He can keep trying. That way we can concentrate on getting you to the hospital and not worry about a thing."

Sara smiled. "Okay, Daddy. Let's do it."

"Try one more time," Amber said.

"We need to leave, not keep calling when they're obviously on the line or something. Every time I've called for the last half hour, the line has been busy," Adam said.

"Well, try one more time."

"Once more, then we leave. I do *not* plan to deliver our little girl. That's what they have doctors for."

"You'd do a great job," Amber said. "Oh. This hurts! I never knew it would be so painful. *Darndarndarndarndarn.*"

Adam took one of her hands and brought it to his mouth where he kissed it, squeezing hard as if trying to divert her attention from the labor pains to the ache in her hand. He hit redial on the phone.

"It's ringing."

Amber leaned back against the sofa, already gearing up for the next contraction. She should have let Adam call earlier, when the contractions first started. But she knew first babies could take a long time and there was no need for everyone to be in an uproar if the birth was hours away.

"No answer," he said when he heard the answering machine click on.

"Matt, Sara, it's Adam. Amber is in labor. We're heading for the hospital now. See you there."

He tossed the phone on the sofa. "Now, let's go."

"Maybe we should try the doctor again," Amber said.

"We left a message with his service, who guaranteed to locate him. He'll beat us there. And—"

"I know, you don't want to deliver this baby!"

The nurse met Sara and Matt at the door with a wheelchair. "Sit down, dear, you'll feel better," she said.

Sara sat down, still clinging to Matt's hand. "The contractions are coming so close together. I don't remember going this fast with Amber."

"Second babies often come quickly," the nurse said as

she pushed her smoothly along the corridor to the elevator. In only moments they were whisked to the fourth floor, labor and delivery.

"Is Dr. Anderson here yet?" Matt asked.

"He is. And a busy man, too. Another of his patients is on the way as well. Here we go. Now, here's your gown. Shall your husband help you?" the nurse asked, shaking out the shortie nightgown the hospital used for deliveries. It pulled over the head, with the back completely intact.

"Yes," Sara said, then groaned as another contraction hit.

"Timing," the nurse said, glancing at her watch.

The room was decorated as a bedroom in a private home might have been. The wallpaper was light and cheery, the furnishings of polished oak. There were frilly curtains on the windows. A comfortable chair and a rocking chair sat along the wall. Only the high hospital bed gave any indication this wasn't someone's favorite bedroom.

But Sara wasn't interested in the decor. She was fighting to stay on top of the pain.

By the time she'd gotten dressed, with Matt's help, she'd had two more contractions.

"This baby is anxious to be born," the nurse said, helping Sara into bed. "I'll pop out and let the doctor know."

Matt stepped behind her, rubbing her back, one hand on her belly.

"Hang in there, sweetheart. I'm with you every step of the way."

"Wish we could trade places," she grumbled.

"Dr. Anderson is a busy man. He has another patient already checked in," the young nurse said as she helped Amber change into a hospital issue gown.

"Sara Tucker?" Adam hazarded a guess.

"That's right, how did you know?"

He laughed. "This is one for the books. Sara is Amber's mother."

The nurse looked at Amber, then Adam. "Her mother? But she's delivering a baby."

Amber nodded, then began panting. Adam stepped up to support her. "Focus, Amber. Remember what we learned."

It wasn't often a honeymoon was spent in Lamaze classes rather than on the beach in some resort, but that's the way Adam and Amber spent their first few weeks of marriage.

None of the family had offered even a token resistance to the union after Amber's brush with death. Even Virginia Woodworth had given her blessing. Their real honeymoon would be taken later, when finals were over and Amber was recovered from the birth of Jamie Marie.

Now the birth was imminent, and she couldn't wait to hold her baby girl in her arms.

"Breathe, honey," Adam instructed.

"I am breathing. You try this for a while. Ow-ow-ow-ow, darn it, this hurts! Go find Mom and tell her I'm here."

"I can't leave you," Adam said calmly. "We'll get the nurse to let her know." He turned to the young woman and asked if she would relay a message to Sara Tucker. She assured him she would, as soon as she notified the doctor how close Amber was to delivery.

"Go find Amber. Tell her I'm here," Sara said.

"The nurse told us she knows you're here. And I'm not leaving you. Let her own husband take care of her."

Dr. Anderson came in, wearing scrubs. "So, we're about to have a baby, are we?"

"And Amber," Sara said, clinging to Matt's hand.

"And Amber. I've sent my resident to check on her. If you deliver fast enough, I can get over there for that one as well. She's two doors down." The doctor sat on a rolling stool and moved into position.

"Crowning already. You are in a hurry, Mrs. Tucker."

"Not. Getting. Any. Younger," Sara said through breaths. She gripped Matt's hand tightly and tried to smile up at him. "You better appreciate this baby," she said.

"Darling, I appreciate you and our baby." He kissed her gently, the kiss interrupted as another contraction tore through her.

"Do you know what to do?" Adam asked the resident as he checked Amber.

"If not, my husband can deliver the baby. He's an E.M.T.," Amber said, unsure as Adam about the experience of the young man at the foot of the high bed.

"I've delivered several babies in the last month alone," the resident said. "You'll be fine, I guarantee it."

Amber looked at Adam. "Stand ready to move in if I need you," she said softly.

"I heard that," the doctor said, smiling at her. "I'd say you're going to be a mother very soon."

"Two-fifteen exactly," Dr. Anderson said as he glanced at the clock once he held the baby boy in his hands. He placed him gently on Sara's stomach and prepared for the afterbirth.

"Oh, he's so darling," she cooed.

Matt studied him. "Not as big as I thought he'd be. And he needs a bath."

She giggled. "He's beautiful. And he'll grow up big and strong like his daddy."

"I love you, Sara," he said, leaning over to kiss her.

"Two-fifteen exactly," the resident said, as he handed the baby girl to Adam. "Here, Papa, hold your daughter."

Adam took the baby in the blanket the nurse gave him as the resident clipped the cord. He brought her to where Amber could see her. "Our daughter," he said proudly.

"She's so tiny. But perfect, isn't she?" Amber said, touching her gently, counting her fingers and toes.

"She's as perfect as her mother," Adam said, leaning over to kiss her. "Wouldn't her father be proud!"

"As proud as her daddy is already," Amber said. "I love you, Adam."

"And I love you, Mrs. Carruthers. Now and for always."

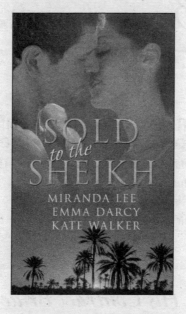